D1234500

SUNDOWN

Center Point
Large Print

Also by Susan May Warren and available from Center Point Large Print:

Sunrise
Sunburst
The Price of Valor
The Heart of a Hero
The Way of the Brave
Wait for Me
Storm Front
Troubled Waters
A Matter of Trust

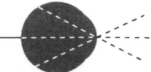

This Large Print Book carries the Seal of Approval of N.A.V.H.

SKY KING RANCH
BOOK THREE

SUNDOWN

SUSAN MAY WARREN

CENTER POINT LARGE PRINT
THORNDIKE, MAINE

SUNDOWN

ONE

Colt Kingston was in worse shape than he thought.

One good look at himself in the mirror said that he probably shouldn't be climbing at seven thousand feet, where the air became a whisper in his lungs, where his heart had to work double time, and where every movement turned his muscles into a fist.

But the view. Oh, the view from atop Avalanche Spire, just south of Denali National Park, could just about stop his heart anyway.

Colt scanned the area with his binoculars.

From the north, the massive Denali range rose, rugged and magnificent, its hulking mass thundering across the horizon. A blue-gray shadow fell upon the mountains below, sweeping down to the rich greens of a pine and fir forest, the deep blues of valley lakes set in pockets inside the rising peaks of the foothills.

Snow and ice still capped a number of low-lying peaks, glaciers running off the edge like frosting. The air smelled of the summer wildflowers, and the sunlight hung long upon the day.

"I see the plane," he said, his gaze dropping to a small white-and-red-striped crumple of metal caught in one of those glaciers, about a half mile down from the cliff where they stood. "Right where you left it, Tae."

He lowered his binoculars and shot a glance at Taylor—Tae—Price. She wore her blond hair in a singular braid, had on a pair of Gore-Tex hiking pants, a warm jacket, and a wool hat against the still-crisp Denali wind.

Her mouth tightened at the edges. "It wasn't there when I left it."

Colt's brother Dodge had walked over and now gestured for the binoculars. Colt handed them over.

"Looks like the plane slid," he said. "I can see the trail where the melt carried it."

"They must have landed in the valley above it, and the glacier carried it down the slope," Echo, Dodge's fiancée, said. She had put down her backpack and was taking a drink of water. Two golden-brown braids stuck out of her knit hat. She glanced at Tae. "I still can't believe you survived."

They stood on a ridge just above where they'd landed the Piper Super Cub that Dodge had flown, searching for the downed plane. Even the chopper wouldn't have been able to put down closer to the wreck, so taking the plane gave them more reach to confirm, well, that Tae hadn't been lying.

Not that Colt thought she was outright lying, per se, but with the position of the plane, it seemed a little far-fetched that the story went down the way she'd told it. The one that included a kidnapping, her attempts to crash the plane, surviving not only the crash that killed the pilot and her kidnapper but also a late-season blizzard.

"I can't believe I survived either," Tae said, maybe realizing that no, none of it really added up. Still, here she stood, daring him not to believe her words even as he stared at the crumpled evidence. Dodge and Echo had found her in a gully nearly ten miles away, so maybe . . .

"We need to get to the plane," Tae said. "My backpack is inside. It has my research and . . ." She looked at Colt, her pale blue eyes on him, a small glare headed his direction.

Fine. Whatever. He'd sort of thought there might be a little something between them over the past few weeks. She had, after all, sat by his bedside during those early days after his extraction from an op-gone-south in Africa. Heard his nightmares. And he'd witnessed one of her own, so . . .

But after he'd cornered her, forced her story out two weeks ago, something had changed between them. The big chill.

He should have expected that, maybe. No one liked being interrogated.

"We'll have to traverse the glacier," Dodge said, "and then ice climb down to the plane. It looks pretty precarious." He glanced at Colt. "You sure you're up for this?"

Colt didn't want to bristle at his brother's question, but still, it burned through him. "Of course."

If it hadn't been for the beating Colt had suffered while being held hostage by a group of terrorists in Nigeria, he would have been out here two weeks ago. Right after local sheriff Deke Starr had turned up with the proof that someone *was* after Tae—someone meaning some Russian mafia group.

And now he sounded crazy, even to himself.

Clearly, Colt was desperate to put a little hero back into his reflection in the mirror. The one that stared at him with reddened eyes and fading bruises. He didn't go to sleep every night without replaying that moment when the truck of jihadists pulled up in a Nigerian village and forced him and his fellow security officer to their knees. When, for the first time in years, he prayed that God hadn't completely abandoned him. Maybe, maybe not, because somehow most of them survived, including Noemi, his brother Ranger's wife, who had been a humanitarian aid worker in Nigeria.

It didn't mean that God was actually looking out for Colt. He attributed God's favor to Noemi and Selah, the other humanitarian aid worker, and maybe even the doctor Colt had been tasked to protect.

Thankfully, the doc had survived, but no thanks to Colt.

Bottom line, he'd failed.

Sometimes, before he dropped off into his sweaty nightmares, he backed all the way up to the moment they'd found the dead bodies of the villagers in the church. In that moment, he listened to his gut instincts that said, *Run*.

Or he shot first and then threw his body in front of the doctor, taking the bullet.

Instincts he'd honed during his years as a Delta Force operator. Except he wasn't that guy anymore. Wasn't even a security pro for Jones, Inc., at least not until he healed up from his broken bones and bruised insides.

Which meant he had plenty of time to focus on Tae and her crazy story about being chased by international terrorists all the way to his backyard in Alaska.

"While you were learning to fly, I was climbing and rappelling," Colt said now to Dodge. "And don't forget that one year I actually worked at the Denali Base Camp, coordinating Sky King Ranch flights."

"I remember," Dodge said as he pulled out crampons from his pack and hooked them to a carabiner. "Dad was afraid you were going to actually attach to one of the climbing crews and head up the mountain."

Colt also dug out his crampons and hooked them to the outside of his pack. The snow was soft, but it didn't mean it wasn't lethal. "I was seventeen. I wasn't allowed up."

"Since when do you follow the rules?" Dodge handed Echo the rope, one end already affixed to his harness. She clipped in.

Colt hiked up his own harness. "When it matters." He turned to Tae, who was struggling with her rig. "You could wait here . . ."

"I know how to climb. I used to climb the wall back at my gym in Seattle." She stepped away from him when he reached to help. "Besides, I want to be there when you see that I'm telling the truth."

"I never said you weren't telling the truth." He glanced at Dodge, whose eyebrows rose.

"Really?" She rounded on Colt. "When I told you my story, you stared at me so long, I thought maybe you were suffering from a hit on the head."

Yeah, well, he was, a little. "It's just . . . the whole thing sounds like something out of a Brad Thor novel. You being kidnapped off your cruise ship by your boyfriend—"

"A Russian spy!"

"Right." He held up a hand. "A Russian spy named Sergei. Who then forced you on a plane to hijack you to some secret lab in Russia."

"I never said that." Her mouth tightened. "I said that I thought he might be taking me to Russia. And that's why I freaked out. Why I opened the door to the plane—"

"Because you were *trying* to crash."

"Wouldn't you?" She was tightening her harness. "Isn't that part of your oath as a soldier? Escape, survive—or something like that?"

"But you're not military."

"My father was. And . . . well, I wasn't going to . . ."

And then she stopped. Again. Right where she always stopped—before she told him the *why* behind everything.

Secrets. Tae was full of them, and he wasn't going to let them get him, or his family, killed.

"See, you don't believe me, again."

"What?"

"It's your face." She moved her open palm in a circle before him. "You think I'm crazy." She turned to Dodge. "Do you think I'm crazy? That I dreamed all this up?"

Dodge held up his hand in surrender. "I think we're wasting time."

Probably. Because although the sun was still high, Colt's chest was really starting to ache from the lack of oxygen.

He took the rope from Echo, tied a figure eight knot and attached a carabiner to it. Turned to Tae. "It's not that I don't believe you, Tae. It's that you're not telling me everything, and I know it."

Her mouth tightened, and he had interrogated enough people to know he'd hit on truth. "Do you know how to—"

13

"Yes." She took the carabiner from him and attached it. Met his eyes. "You'll see. We'll get down to that plane and you'll see two dead bodies. And then I'll get my backpack and prove that it's all true. I'm not crazy."

"For the last time, I never called you crazy."

She hiked an eyebrow at him.

Okay, when he'd first heard her story, he might have paused for a long moment, let it sink into his head, let the what-ifs surface.

What if her story was true—that she *had* been kidnapped by the Russian mob? Why? And sure, he'd tried to pry that bit of truth from her, but she'd clammed up.

Almost as if she didn't trust *him*.

So maybe their little trek out to the bush to confirm her story had as much to do with her trusting him as it did with him trusting her.

He clipped the tail end of the rope to his harness.

"Here's how this will work," Dodge, always the boss, said. He also wore a Gore-Tex outfit and a wool hat. The fact that Dodge had agreed to come along on this crazy search . . . well, maybe things were going to be okay between him and Colt, after all. "The climb down isn't terrible, but once we reach the glacier, walk only in my steps. I'll test the snow, but this time of year, the ice can give and then—"

"You could fall a thousand feet to your death," Colt said.

Dodge gave him a look.

Well, maybe someone, and he wasn't saying who—ahem, *Tae*—should think about what she was getting into.

"If that happens," Echo said, rolling her eyes at Colt's words, "hit the ground with your ice axe, and hold on. You're the only one stopping said person from"—she gestured at Colt—"what he said."

He shot Tae a final look.

"Please. I hiked through the wilderness, alone, for five days. Survived a blizzard."

"Barely," Dodge said, probably remembering that day when he and Echo had found her, nearly frozen, in the snow near a ranger cabin.

Tae gave Dodge the same look she'd given Colt. Gone was the quiet, sweet girl who'd made them all soup.

Colt's fault, really, and for a moment he was back at the cabin two weeks ago, after he'd seen her picture taken from an assassin's phone, targeting her. He'd practically ran her down, shoved his hand over her shoulder, holding the cabin door closed so she couldn't escape, and said, his tone tight and serious, *"Spill."*

She'd morphed right in front of his eyes from quiet, hidden Florence Nightingale—his nickname for her—to Marie Curie, fierce, determined, and brave.

Even, maybe, a little bossy.

"You sure you want to know?" she'd asked.

Maybe he should have said no. Because now, as they prepared to climb down the mountain, he sort of missed Florence.

"Let's go," Colt said.

Dodge was right. The boulders created a natural stairway down the mountainside, into the valley where the glacier spilled over the side of the cliff.

Colt watched as Echo trekked in front of him. She had also grown up in Alaska and had the sure steps of a mountain goat.

But Tae handled herself just fine, holding on, checking her steps, careful.

Deliberate.

The sun still hovered high, although by Colt's guesstimation, it might be nearly six in the evening. Maybe they should have camped on the ridge after their hike from the valley floor where Dodge landed. But Colt was as eager to prove Tae right, or wrong, as she was.

He was rooting for wrong. Because the idea of some terrorist after her—and as a by-product, his family—had Colt's gut in all manner of knots.

Then again, if she'd made it up . . .

So maybe right wasn't such a bad option.

Dodge reached the edge of the glacier field. Maybe a thousand feet across, the glacier was a quietly moving river, with thousands of tributaries running through cracks in its gnarled, veiny blue surface. The frozen river fell from the top of the valley down to the edge of a cliff that dropped another thousand feet to a glacial lake below.

Working its way over the cliff, maybe ten feet from the edge, sat the mangled six-seater Beechcraft Bonanza, its wings shorn off, the fuselage twisted. When it landed, it had dragged the tail, which broke off, spinning the aircraft so that it then cartwheeled, taking off the wings.

It had ended up on its back, a fallen albatross, wheels up.

A stiff wind caught Colt's jacket, slipped down his back. He sat on a boulder and attached his crampons, then unhooked his ice axe from the pack.

"Maybe just Colt and I should go," Dodge said.

Colt nodded, brutally aware of the way his heart had started to hammer. Sheesh. He wasn't scared, but the sweat down his back and his hard breathing had him thinking that if someone went down . . . he might not be able to pull them back up.

So, if Dodge fell, they would both die.

"No," Echo said, saving him. "We go together."

Dodge's mouth made a grim line, but he nodded.

"My steps, your steps," Dodge said and started out.

Echo followed, then Tae, and finally Colt, his chest tight.

Quiet. Footsteps crunching in the snow. Dodge pressed the handle of his ice axe into the snow, testing for strength, step by step.

They edged out—ten feet, twenty, thirty.

"Stop," Dodge said, and Colt froze.

"There's a bridge here. We'll need to go around."

An ice bridge. The kind that spanned a crevasse. The kind that could disintegrate with weight and bring them all down.

Dodge backtracked while they stayed put, and rerouted. He found where the crevasse ended, and they crossed over.

The pain in Colt's chest had started to ease. See, they'd be just fine.

"It looks like the door is missing," Dodge said as they drew closer to the plane. "Is that how you got out, Tae?"

"I don't know. I woke up outside, strapped to my seat."

Dodge stepped up to the empty metal carcass, looking through the open tail.

"Any dead bodies?" Colt asked, catching up. Dodge had left about twenty feet of rope between them. Echo caught up to him, then Tae.

"I think so," Dodge said.

Tae started inside.

"Wait." Dodge held his arm up. "This plane is sitting on ice. One wrong move and this whole thing could break free, go over the cliff."

"I need my pack," Tae said.

"I'll get it." Colt shot a look at Dodge. "Anchor in?"

Dodge nodded and pressed his ice axe into the glacier. Echo wedged hers in too, and then they both unclipped their carabiners and affixed them to the axes. The rope from their anchors stretched out to first Tae, then Colt.

"I'm going with you," Tae said.

"Stay here." Colt looked at her. "I promise to get your pack."

She opened her mouth, closed it. "Please don't die."

Huh. Well, well. He gave her a smile.

She drew in a breath. "You'll see I'm not lying."

Right. He turned to the wreckage.

The back seats had been ripped from the body of the plane, one of them gone—probably Tae's, given her story. The two middle seats had fallen and lay mangled on the ceiling-now-floor. Colt eased up, through the wreckage, to the front. An odor of gas hinted the air.

Wind whistled through the cockpit window, but as he drew closer, he spotted a corpse hanging from a seat in front. The pilot.

"I have a body!" he shouted. He came closer, pulling up his scarf. The man had frozen, clearly, but with the thaw, had started to decompose.

"What about Sergei?" Tae shouted to him.

He grabbed a dangling seat belt, listing in the wind. "Where was he sitting?"

"He wasn't— He was . . ."

The hiccup in her voice made him look at her. She had turned a little wan. "He was trying to strangle me."

The quietness, the horror of her words simply ripped through him.

"I had opened the door, was trying to wreck the plane." She offered a tiny smile, a hint of Florence. But he was starting to like Marie. She *was* brave.

"Maybe he was thrown out, like you," Echo said.

Tae nodded. "Do you see my pack? It's purple and has my name on it."

He searched the front compartment. "Not here."

"I shoved it under one of the seats," Tae said and stepped inside the plane.

And that's when it started to give.

"Tae, stop moving," Colt said, climbing back toward her.

"That pack has all my research in it." She hit the floor, searching under the mangled seats.

The plane moved again, this time a bit more, as if trying to break free.

"I see it!" She lay prone, reaching out under a fallen seat. "It's wedged in here!"

He reached her, grabbed her harness. "Tae, we gotta get out of here!"

"Colt!" Dodge shouted.

And with a crack, the entire plane rocked.

"Tae!" Colt tugged at her.

"I can almost reach it!"

The plane began to slide. Slowly, but, "Tae, c'mon!"

"I'm stuck!"

The plane started to pick up speed. The rope that tethered them to Dodge's ice axe was coiling out, twenty feet of it that would stop Tae first, then Colt.

And if she didn't get unstuck . . .

He yanked on her jacket, hard. She shrieked but landed against him. They fell against the wall, and the entire plane shuddered.

He wrapped his arms around her. "Hold on!"

And then, the plane sailed over the edge into the bright blue of the Alaskan sky.

Tae should have gone right on pretending she couldn't speak, couldn't remember who she was, and quietly slipped away in the night.

Kept running.

Because then no one else would die.

She screamed as the plane dropped out around her.

"Hang on!" Colt held on to her rope, tucking her against him as they fell with the momentum of the plane.

Her rope caught them, jerking them to a stop

just below the lip of the cliff. Below them, the plane dropped, the crunch of metal echoing as it bounced. It hit the lake, some thousand plus feet below, and Tae just barely stopped herself from screaming again.

Above them, a shout lifted. Probably Dodge, trying to keep the axe from jerking free.

Then, silence. Just Colt's heavy breathing as she lay in his embrace. His arm tightened around her as he gripped the rope, his feet scrabbling for purchase against the icy wall.

"I got you," he said. "You're okay."

They hung maybe five feet below the lip of the glacier, the rope pressed into the ice, their feet dangling in air.

Her grip burned, her hands just above his. But really, her harness held her.

Colt, however, had twenty feet of slack between them.

He was a strong man. She knew that from watching him recover over the past three weeks from the kind of beating that should probably permanently disable a man. When he'd arrived home to his family's lodge in Alaska, she hadn't known the story of how he'd been captured, beaten, threatened with execution. All she'd seen was a man who refused to give up, despite the demons that he wrestled.

And he'd been funny. Sweet. Charming. Self-deprecating.

Once, she'd even found herself in his arms, holding on to him. Needing him more than she wanted to admit. Somehow, deep inside, she knew that if anyone could handle her secret . . . well, Colt Kingston might be that guy.

Probably he was, even though he didn't quite believe her. But at the moment, hanging off the cliff, his body holding hers up, he was struggling, his breaths coming fast, his arms shaking, despite his words.

"Don't let go," she said. "If you fall, they won't be able to stop the impact of you hitting the end of the rope from yanking out the axes."

"Tell me something I don't know," he grunted.

"Fine, how about this? I left my ice axe on top."

"Beautiful. Listen, truth is, I can't hold on much longer, Tae. You gotta climb up. Use my axe. It's dangling from my wrist."

But to take it off he'd have to let go with one of his hands. "No. You'll fall."

"I won't fall." But he let out a sound, deep in his chest, a struggle to hold on to both of them.

No. She wasn't going to be the cause of his death. She scrabbled her feet onto the overhang of ice, slamming the crampons in.

"Atta girl," Colt said in her ear. He brought his legs up too, his body cradling her as his feet bit into the ice around them.

"We're losing you!" Dodge shouted from above. "We can't help you climb up!"

"Hang on!" Tae shouted. Then, to Colt, "What if I hook your carabiner to my harness? That way you won't fall farther."

"Mm-hmm."

She took a breath and let go of her hold. Oops. She must have been holding more of herself than she thought because her weight settled onto Colt. He was breathing long, hard, controlled breaths.

"I can't reach your carabiner."

"Take my rope and tie a figure eight into it, near the top. Then, clip that in."

Her hands shook as she took the rope and tied the figure eight into it. She reached around behind her, trying to find the loop that held his carabiner. But she was pressed too tightly to him, gravity pulling her down.

"Take the axe, Tae. Climb up."

Tears welled in her eyes. There. She found the carabiner. "I can do this."

His arms had really started to shake.

She couldn't move the knot in without removing the other.

Which meant that, for a moment, he'd be unbelayed, and . . .

"I can't! It's too dangerous."

"I know." And then in a move that nearly made her scream again, he let go with one hand, grabbed the axe, and swung it up into the ice.

The axe bit into glacier wall, held.

"I'm getting my weight off the line. You'll be fine. You're hooked in."

Her entire body froze as he let go and swung himself onto the axe, hanging there like Spider-Man.

Except, not quite because he needed two axes to climb. Still, the heaviness on the line eased.

And then Colt unhooked his rope from his harness.

"Are you *crazy?*"

"What's going on?" Dodge shouted, an edge of fear to his voice.

"Nothing! We're fine!" Colt shouted back, clearly ignoring her.

"We're not fine! You're not tied in."

"If I fall, you don't go with me." He raised his voice. "Pull her up!"

"I'm not leaving you here!"

He grabbed the end of his rope. "When you're up and anchored, I'll hook back in."

She stared at him even as her line began to move. "Seriously. You're calling me nuts? What is *wrong* with you?"

And then, well, she could just kill him because he smiled, a little gleam in those brown eyes, and she saw something in them that she'd seen weeks ago, at his bedside.

Fight. Determination. And the reason, probably, that he just kept surviving. The man didn't have quit or helpless or even fear in him.

His voice turned quiet. Solid. "Listen, tune out everything else—me, the drop, your fear. Just focus on the next step. Climb, Tae."

Focus on the next step.

Fine. Yes.

"Don't fall," she snapped, before tears could cripple her.

"I'm not going anywhere."

Stupid, arrogant man—but she started to move, walking her feet up the ice. His rope spooled out, but as promised, he kept hold of it with one hand.

She came over the lip, dug her toes in and scrambled for her ice axe, still lying in the ice. Dodge lay on top of his axe and Echo on hers, both of them dug in with their crampons, fighting the pull of the axe from the ice.

"Come here," Dodge said, and she scrabbled to him. "Lay on this axe."

He got up, and since Colt still hadn't clipped in, no weight hung on the anchor. But she took Dodge's position while he dug in her axe next to them, then transferred some of the weight with a sling through the figure eight knots to the new anchor. He dug himself back in.

"Colt! Climb up!" Dodge shouted.

"He's not clipped in," she said.

Dodge looked at her, something of horror in his gaze.

"Climbing!" Colt yelled, and the line went taut, probably Colt testing it. Then she felt the tug as he used the rope to balance his weight, climbing up with the axe and his crampons.

She wanted to weep when his head, then body, lipped the edge. He crawled toward them, digging his axe in, as if he didn't quite want to let go of that safety.

Maybe she didn't either. Oh, she was so very tired of being brave. Of surviving. Sorry. Like she said, she wasn't in the military like her father.

Wasn't a hero. Not even close.

She put her head down in the crook of her arm, just breathing.

"Tae?"

Echo had gotten up and now came over to her. "You okay?"

Tae lifted her head, looked at Echo, nodded. But behind Echo, Tae spotted Colt, still on the ice, Dodge over him, his fingers at his brother's neck.

Tae pushed herself up. "What's going on?"

Echo turned. "I don't know."

Tae hit her knees beside Colt. Dodge rolled him over. Colt was gasping for breath.

"You okay, bro?" Dodge asked.

Tae picked up his wrist. Counted the beats. "His pulse is racing."

"I . . . just need . . . a . . . minute . . ." Colt stared up at the sky.

"Sit him up," she said. "Colt, are you having any chest pains?"

Dodge pushed him up.

He looked at her, his jaw tight.

"I'm taking that as a yes." Maybe a by-product of his still-healing organs. "Okay, breathe with me." She put her hand on his chest. "In . . . out . . ." She met his eyes. So brown. They fixed on her.

In . . . out . . . in . . . out.

He slowed his breathing, then finally leaned back and blew out a final, long breath. "Wow. That's never happened before."

"You've never scared people to death?" Tae snapped. "What was that? You could have fallen."

He lay back on the ice, his eyes closed. "At least I wouldn't have taken you with me."

She just stared at him, then at Dodge. "Seriously?"

He lifted a shoulder. "Now you know why the terrorists beat him within an inch of his life." He held out a hand to Colt. "You can stop being a show-off anytime."

Colt managed a small grin as Dodge helped him up. Then, Colt turned to her. "You all right?"

Wow, just . . . wow. "Me? You're the one who can't breathe!"

"Yeah, well, I blame my near heart attack on watching you nearly *take us all down with the plane*." His smile vanished and just like that, he was back—the guy in the cabin two weeks ago, who'd put his face in hers and practically ordered the truth out of her.

"I needed my backpack."

"Why? What was so important?"

"My journal. All my notes."

"Notes for what?"

She closed her mouth, looked away.

"Perfect." He took a step toward her. "I'm done with the games. I was nice before. Now, playtime is over. Stop lying to me and tell me what is going on." He'd lowered his voice to almost a growl, and it sent a razor under her skin.

Sure, he was a handsome man, with that dark hair, a scruff of black whiskers, those brown eyes the color of deep, rich coffee. But under all that simmered a warrior with hidden skills and the secrets to go with them.

Whoever she'd met a month ago, broken, sweet, and a little charming, had vanished.

This was the interrogator.

She took a deep breath. "You don't want to know."

His voice cut low. "I very much want to know. Just like I very much want to believe you."

"Really? You *still* don't believe me?"

"There was only one body in that plane."

"Because Sergei must have been thrown from it, like I was!" She stopped, stared at them. "He could still be alive."

"Tae. You saw that plane," Colt said. "The fact you survived is . . . well, a miracle."

It *was* a miracle. But she knew exactly what he meant, thank you, and that was just . . . *enough.*

29

She walked over to her axe and pulled it from the ice. Turned. "I'm telling you the truth. I was kidnapped, shoved onto a plane, and survived the crash. Either you believe me or you don't."

Colt's mouth tightened. He looked at Dodge. Then back at her.

And here it came. The same response she got back in Seattle when she went to her lab partner, Zoey, the same day that Faheem had died.

Hesitation. Maybe even disbelief.

Fine. She didn't care if he believed her or not. She stalked away.

"Where are you going?"

"I don't know!"

"I believe you."

She stopped. Turned to Colt. Met his eyes, hard in hers. "You do?"

"I do."

The words swept through her, hot, bold, like a rush of summer sun, and she gasped. Stupidly, tears burned her eyes. "Really?"

He nodded. "But I would really like to know why I nearly fell to my death. What was in that backpack of yours that you so desperately needed?"

She took a breath. "You're going to wish I hadn't told you."

"Try me."

Overhead, thick, dark clouds rolled in from the west. A breeze kicked up.

30

She took a breath. And then said it, the one really out-of-the-box, almost apocalyptic truth that out loud sounded all-the-way crazy.

"Because I think someone is trying to poison the world, and . . . only I can stop them."

TWO

"You do know that she sounds nuts." Dodge's voice beside Colt had cut low, which didn't help at all against the wind.

"Yeah, I know," Colt said. He had his hands shoved into his jacket, chin into the collar, fighting the snowstorm that suddenly dogged them, coming out of the northwest like the harbinger of death on the wake of Tae's words.

Poison the world?

Colt shivered, all the way to his bones, but not just from the wind that slipped down his jacket and tried to find his ears.

They'd spent the last three hours hiking back to the plane, and about thirty minutes into their walk, the clouds overhead had chased them down and started spitting sleet, then snow, heavy, wet, and brutal. The sun, which never went down, pushed shadows upon them, turning the world broody and dangerous, hiding their steps as they picked their way down the mountain.

Their plane sat in the middle of a high tundra valley, under the cover of semidarkness. Dodge had a sort of homing beacon to it that Colt appreciated. He'd stopped thinking and just kept moving his feet.

"Do you really believe her?" Dodge asked now,

falling in beside him. Echo and Tae walked out in front, with Tae hunched over against the wind.

"I want to," he said and glanced over at Dodge. Ice clung to his eyelashes. "I don't know. I just want to get back to the ranch, thaw out, and then we'll unravel her story."

"Yeah, well, I'm just hoping the storm hasn't frozen the wheels of the plane to the tundra."

Perfect. Because what Colt wanted right now, probably more than the truth, was his bed. His entire body ached, right to his cells, and he'd freaked himself out more than he wanted to admit back there on the cliffside.

He'd felt like he might be having a heart attack, the pain thick on his left side, down his arm.

He still hurt pretty good after his captivity by the Boko Haram.

Maybe Dodge was thinking the same thing, because he glanced at Colt. "What happened back there? On the ice?"

"Out of shape. No problem."

"You might need more time—"

"I'm ready to get back to work. I don't like sitting around like a pansy."

"You were nearly unresponsive for a week after we pulled you out of the camp," Dodge said. "I thought we were going to lose you."

Concern layered his voice, something Colt hadn't heard in, well, a decade. Weird. Sure, they'd made peace, Dodge forgiving him for his

33

stupid actions with Echo so long ago. But all this newfound brotherly concern had him rattled.

Colt wasn't so sure he wanted back in the family fold. He was just too prone to screwing it all up. To doing something that could get people he cared about killed.

It was easier to live without strings or attachments.

Then he couldn't take anyone with him if he went down.

"You headed back to the Jones, Inc. team?"

"Hope so." He'd been in contact with Hamilton Jones, his boss, who'd confirmed that teammate Fraser had returned to the States and was recuperating. Ham had told him to take all the time he needed before he returned.

What he needed was to do *something,* get his mind off . . . well, all of it.

Mistakes, failures, betrayals, missteps, what-ifs, and never-agains.

"You never told me why you left Delta. Or how."

"Nope, I didn't."

Silence. "Okay." Dodge blew out a breath. "I'm just glad you're safe."

There it was again, the weird thread of warmth from his big brother. Apparently, he had his own story, because Dodge had been a lot of things. Responsible, arrogant, bossy—but never warm.

"Thanks."

"I see the plane," Dodge said.

Colt looked up, spotted it sitting like a snowbird in the middle of the storm, covered in ice. Dodge picked up his pace.

Sleet and snow saturated Colt's boots, his feet nearly frozen by the time he reached the plane. Dodge had it cleaned off, but the wings were heavy with ice. And a couple pushes on the wheel struts had Dodge shaking his head.

"We're not going anywhere tonight."

Perfect. Colt wanted to howl. Instead, "I'll get the tents."

Conditions like this were why they always stowed camping gear in the back of the plane.

Two tents, four sleeping bags, two nights of MREs and rations, water, a stove, and a high beam flashlight.

Dodge and Colt pitched the tents while Echo heated up water on the tiny propane stove and Tae unpacked their gear. By the time they had the two tents up, the wind turned hard upon them, and they got into the plane to eat dinner—Spanish beans and rice and hot coffee.

"I called home. No answer," Dodge said, blowing on his coffee. "But could be that the weather is blocking our call. Dad is probably already in bed, anyway. It's late."

Colt put the hour past midnight, so probably.

"Ranger might be up though," Echo said. "He hasn't been sleeping well."

Ranger's recent eyesight loss had made him keen to every noise in the house, it seemed. Even though he and Noemi had renewed their wedding vows—this time in front of the local JP, just to make things US legal—Colt had found his younger brother asleep on the sofa downstairs.

Or more often awake, drinking coffee, listening to a podcast.

Poor guy. He'd gone from Navy SEAL sniper to the family chef and chief radio operator. But Dodge had roped him into helping out with the newly formed Sky King Rescue, as their base dispatcher.

If anyone could handle the chaos of a rescue operation, it was Ranger.

So yes, strange that he wasn't up, answering the radio. But maybe tonight, with most of them gone, he was sleeping. Or the weather was indeed blocking their signal.

"As soon as the sun comes up, it'll melt off all this ice, and we'll be back in the air," Dodge said. He looked at Tae. "In the meantime, start at the beginning and tell me everything before and including the moment you got on a plane with a Russian thug."

Tae looked back at him, eyes wide.

Huh. Well, Colt might have put it a little nicer, but yeah, what he said.

He leaned back in his seat, eating the last of his rice and beans, his gaze on Tae.

She set her MRE down. Picked up her coffee.

In the wan light that was the midnight sun, she looked defeated, almost like she might cry, and for a moment, he wanted to back up, give her room.

But today, he'd come very, *very* close to dying. Both on the cliff and afterward, when he felt like his heart was making a break for home, hammering its way out of his chest. So yes, he'd very much like to know how it came about that she held the safety of the world's population in her head.

"I'm a doctor of infectious diseases and a medical scientist," she said quietly. "I work for a private lab that helps develop treatments for some of the most terrifying diseases on the planet. Ebola. Kuru. *Naegleria fowleri*, the brain-eating amoeba."

"Yep, I'm terrified," Echo said.

A smile ticked up one side of Tae's mouth. "About three years ago, a strain of smallpox was reported in a Nepali village. Our team was brought in to investigate. No international drama, just a small group of people who took samples and brought them to our lab. Unfortunately, the entire village had died."

"Like the village in Nigeria," Colt said, his mind going back to the image of so many corpses in the village church. Maybe it was a good thing the terrorists had burned it.

"Yes. It's a rare, ancient strain of smallpox.

And I'm pretty sure that it's the same variant that killed the villagers in Nigeria, Colt. The ones you saw in the church."

He stared at her, then ran a hand across his mouth. Nodded.

"The fact that it didn't escape the village— at least, we hope it didn't—told us that it had a very quick death rate from onset. Once a patient contracts it, they don't show symptoms until very close to death. Maybe twelve hours. This is three times quicker than even hemorrhagic smallpox."

"How long is the incubation time?" Echo asked.

Colt had sort of lost his appetite, despite the bear in his stomach.

"For *Variola major*, twelve days," Tae said. "This one, we don't know. But the fact it delays symptoms is problematic. When they present, the disease is quick and lethal, and by the time people figure out they have it, it's too late."

Silence.

"Twelve days someone could have this and be infecting people and not know it?"

"Possibly." She finished her coffee. "It's an airborne pathogen, so it can be dispersed, well, in various ways."

"Now *I'm* terrified," said Dodge.

Colt was doing the math. "I could be infected right now."

"I thought of that, but it's past the incubation period."

It wasn't lost on him that if he'd been infected, he would have also infected her. And his entire family.

"The *really* terrifying part is that smallpox is very old. The earliest evidence was found in mummies in third-century Egypt. But it's mutated since then, so our more recent versions are the ones we have a vaccination for. It's the ancient viruses that are unknown, unstudied."

Outside, the wind had died, but the plane still shuddered. Their tents, staked down, rippled under the onslaught.

"The strain we found was first noted in Siberia, Russia, in the 1920s, in a gulag. It wiped out the entire prison, so they thought it had died, but we did some digging and found the story of a village near the Arctic Circle that had died of what they referred to as the *krasnaya chuma*. Red plague. The pox."

The pox. Colt leaned his head against the cold window.

"With the recent thawing of permafrost land, some think animals might have picked up the variant, maybe passed it along, although . . ." Her mouth tightened. "I think maybe it was something else."

More silence.

Then, "You think the Russians found this variant, developed it, and weaponized it," Colt said.

She lifted a shoulder. "I don't know. It might be my wild imagination, deep in the night."

Yeah, that might keep Colt awake also. Along with all his other nightmares. "The guy who had Tae's picture on his phone was Bratva, according to Deke Starr."

"So you're saying that the Russian *mob* weaponized it," Echo said. "That's deeply unsettling."

"Not just the Russian Bratva, but the *Petrovs*, one of the more dangerous offshoots, headed by General Arkady Petrov," Colt said.

"What's even more unsettling is that I dated Sergei Petrov." Tae drew up her knees, wrapping her arms around them. "I should have known that he wasn't interested in me, really. I didn't seem his type."

"What type is that?" Dodge asked.

She lifted a shoulder. "Pretty. Sweet. You know, girlfriend material."

What? Colt found her very pretty. And she'd been sweet—at least when she'd sat next to his bed, making sure he didn't die in his sleep. As for girlfriend material . . . well, if a guy were to want a girlfriend, it might be her.

If a guy had a life that had room for a girlfriend.

If, maybe, that guy had no plans to return to his job working security with Jones, Inc.

If.

Tae blew on her hands. "Sergei played me from

40

the first day he met me, at my favorite coffee shop. I have no doubt he was following me for days, maybe weeks before that, because he seemed to know all the things I like. He knew my favorite takeout place, my gym—he showed up there too—and most importantly, the fact that I worked for Project 534."

"And what do they want with you?" Dodge said. "If they're already using the smallpox virus, why does it matter if you know?"

She sighed. "Because I developed a vaccine for the strain. And if they're going to use it to threaten the world, then . . ."

Colt went cold to his bones. "Then you're the only one who can stop them."

A beat where her words earlier settled in. *"Only I can stop them."*

Right. "It makes sense," Colt said. "Why else would the Bratva assassin who kidnapped Noemi have your picture on his phone?"

"I still can't figure out why he took Noemi," Dodge said.

Silence, and Colt replayed that moment when he'd centered the Russian in his crosshairs and saved Ranger's life.

He'd hurt then, too, but he'd done his job.

See, he was going to be just fine.

"How did you end up on a plane in Alaska with a mobster?" Echo asked.

"I was working on the vaccine at the time, and

41

it had gone successfully through our first batch of trials when I got another report of a village, this time in Uganda, that had been wiped out by the same smallpox variant. I knew, then, that something wasn't right. Nepal to Uganda? No. I told my colleague Faheem about it, and he said he'd talk to our boss. That night, he was in a fatal car accident."

She wiped her fingers under her eyes. "He was a good man. Had a wife, two kids. And in my bones, I know it wasn't just an accident."

"You suspected he was murdered?"

She nodded. "But not soon enough. At the time, Sergei was insisting I take some vacation time. He booked us on an Alaskan cruise. His idea. He'd even lined up a day of aerial sightseeing"— she finger-quoted the last word—"for us over Denali from Prince William Sound. I thought it was a great idea. Maybe in the back of my head I was a little freaked out by Faheem's death though, because I brought my research with me. Just my journal and notes, but . . . I don't know. It had been a part of my life for three years. Leaving it behind felt just a little too naked. Still, I didn't suspect Sergei in the least. Sure, he was a little pushy, but I just thought I was out of the game. I didn't realize . . . anyway . . . No reason to distrust him. Not, at least, until we docked in Juneau."

Her words turned Colt sick, in the pit of his gut. A little pushy?

"What happened in Juneau?" Echo asked.

"I was approached by a man named Roy. He told me this unbelievable story about how Sergei was a Russian assassin and how my research was in jeopardy and maybe I should just hand it all over to him."

"What?" Colt said.

"My reaction too. I wasn't doing that. In fact, I was keeping it with me, wherever I went. Which was on that Beechcraft plane to tour Denali State Park. Except once we got on the plane—alone, mind you—I started to remember Roy's words. And when Sergei started speaking Russian to the pilot, everything felt . . . wrong."

She met Colt's eyes. "And that's when I realized Sergei had drugged me. I was getting woozy, nauseated, and I thought . . . well, I thought maybe Roy was right. I thought they might be taking me to Russia, and I panicked."

"You opened the door," Colt said.

"Yeah. Right in the middle of a blizzard. Sergei freaked out, jumped on me, started strangling me. The pilot was trying to keep the plane in the air, but . . . I blacked out."

Colt had stopped breathing right about the time she got to Sergei strangling her. Didn't breathe again until—

"I woke up in the snow. Alive. Strapped into my seat but alive. I needed to get someplace out of the blizzard. I'm not sure how since I was practically frozen, but I found shelter in a cave. More of an overhang, really. And then this dog came and slept with me. I'm not sure where he came from, but . . . he was like an angel."

"Goose," Echo said. She turned to Colt. "My dogs were cut from their line during a blizzard. Goose alerted us to Tae, in the snow."

"I'd seen a cabin below us, right before we went down, and thought maybe we could make it there. So I went hiking." She looked at Echo. "Goose kept me warm. Saved my life . . . at least, until you rescued me."

Echo touched her arm. "Right place, right time." She looked at Dodge.

"I know I shouldn't have pretended not to be able to talk but . . . I didn't know who to trust." She met Colt's eyes. "I guess I was a coward."

"I think you're pretty brave," he said, and ignored the way Dodge looked at him.

What? She was.

"Do you have anyone who might be looking for you?" Dodge asked.

"No. My mother is . . . well, she and I don't talk much. And my father died years ago. It's just me."

Just her.

Colt wanted to say something silly like . . . *and me*. Because hello, he'd been on the edge of desperation before. She needed an ally.

But just because a gal had sat by his bed and

nursed him back to health didn't mean he pledged her his heart.

He would, however, pledge her his protection. "Don't worry, Tae. We'll figure out what's going on."

She looked at him with such a rawness, it barreled inside and clung to him, even after they climbed out of the plane and into their different tents. Echo with Tae, him with Dodge.

He climbed fully clothed into his sleeping bag, zipped it up, and put his head inside, trying to breathe warmth into his cocoon.

"You like her."

The statement came from the other cocoon.

"What is this, a slumber party? Go to sleep."

A chuckle shook the body next to him.

"I think maybe you need to see the bigger picture here. There's a hit out on her from the Russian mob."

Yeah, that silenced his brother.

But what Dodge said next destroyed any hope of warmth—or sleep. Because they still hadn't gotten anyone on coms back at home, even when Dodge tried again before they turned in.

"Which means that Sky King Ranch is in the crosshairs."

Tae didn't know why, but finally—finally— the cold ball of fear that lived in her chest had thawed, released its grip. And sure, the eerie

June snowstorm didn't exactly help, but as she settled into her sleeping bag, watching the sun start to rise against the orange of her tent, Colt's words filtered in and settled over her.

"I think you're pretty brave."

No, she was pretty in over her head and taking him with her. What was she doing telling them her story?

Although, this time they hadn't suggested she was nuts, that she'd dreamed up a crazy conspiracy theory.

In fact, it seemed they believed her.

Had even jumped to the very possible conclusion that she was on some kind of hit list.

And what if Sergei had also survived? She hadn't wanted to suggest it aloud, but the fact that his body wasn't decomposing in the plane gave her pause. Too much pause.

Although, like Colt had said, it was a miracle she'd lived, so . . .

If she closed her eyes, she could picture herself on the doorstep of Sky King Ranch two weeks ago, Colt's arms around her, her face pressed into his flannelly chest, the smell of him, cottony and clean and solid and safe, permeating all her shattered places.

Yeah, she'd fallen hard and fast for the broken soldier who arrived home with too many secrets.

She closed her eyes. The warmth of the sleeping

bag had finally found her, burrowing into her core, along with the exhaustion from the day. In a moment, she was back at her cabin, shortly after that delicious moment on the doorstep, right after Deke had shown her the photo of herself, stored on a dead assassin's phone. Colt had charged up to her, blocked the door she tried to open, and said, *"Not a chance!"*

She'd whirled around, slammed her hand into his chest, but he'd caught her wrist, then the other, and just stared at her, his breaths hard, matching the fierceness in his eyes. And there was an edge in his voice when he said, *"Enough games, sweetheart. Spill."*

In that moment she knew the wounded man she'd nursed, who'd joked and flirted with her, charmed her with games of chess and Sorry! and called her Flo, had a side to him that was downright dangerous. Even reckless.

She'd seen it today on the cliff when he'd unhooked himself. Yes, to protect her—she got that. But it was as if he didn't care about the consequences.

Still, she didn't know what it was about him, but knew in her core that he'd never hurt her. She could still feel his arms around her when they dangled over the edge of the cliff. Still hear his voice.

"I got you. You're okay."

She was falling for this guy, and . . . and now

that her story was out, she had no choice but to leave.

"Don't worry, Tae. We'll figure out what's going on."

And get killed, like Faheem? And what about Noemi? How did she get grabbed instead of Tae?

She rolled over in her sleeping bag, tried to settle.

"You okay over there?"

Echo's voice, sleepy.

"Yeah. Just . . ." She sighed.

"He likes you," Echo said softly. "I can tell."

"No. He's just . . . well, you heard what he did in Nigeria. Distracting the guards so Noemi could get away. He's a hero. It's what he does. Besides, getting involved with me is probably a bad idea."

"Oh, trust me, Colt is . . . well, yes, he's a hero. But when he likes something, he goes after it, regardless of the cost."

She opened her eyes and Echo's were open too, her gaze on Tae.

"Really?"

"Yeah. Let's just say I have firsthand experience with that."

Tae's mouth opened. "Wait . . . you and Colt? But I thought you and Dodge were childhood sweethearts."

"We were. Always. But for a short time, we weren't exactly . . . together. And Colt sort of . . . well, he kissed me. And Dodge saw us.

48

They got into an epic fight. Dodge really hurt him, something he deeply regrets, and it sent both of them to opposite ends of the globe for about a decade. It's good to see them back again, but Colt is the guy who believes the end justifies the means. He once tracked a bear into the woods for three days to keep it from killing their cattle. Terrified his brothers to death. And their sister, Larke."

"I haven't met her."

"She lives in Florida with her Navy SEAL husband. She's expecting a baby."

Sweet. Tae didn't know why Echo's words stirred a longing inside her. After this was all over—if it would ever be all over—she was going back to her lab in Seattle, resuming her life. Alone.

No way was she ending up a grieving widow like her mother, thank you very much.

And she should probably remember that around Colt Kingston, despite his brown eyes and flannel-covered muscles.

Outside, the wind had died, sunlight shone upon the tent as the sun rose in the east. She rolled over and closed her eyes. Sunk into the warmth of her bag.

Tried to keep Colt out of her head.

Instead, she found herself in the airplane, the brutal wind tossing the plane, the scream of the engines in her ears, Sergei's hot breath on her face, his hands around her neck. The pilot shouting at him in Russian, probably to buckle up.

Then the plane started to spin, and everything turned to shadow, and—

"Tae! Wake up!"

She opened her eyes, and Echo was there, above her, hands on her shoulders. *What?*

Right. Camp.

The tent blazed orange, the sun clearly high in the sky, and her entire body had worked up a sweat.

"You were shouting," Echo said.

Tae blinked at her. "Sorry. Nightmare."

"Everything okay in there?"

Echo let Tae go, and she sat up just as the tent door unzipped. Colt crouched in front of it, fully dressed, with the sun at his back like a halo, the ground thawing behind him.

"Just a dream," Tae said.

He met her gaze. "Really?" He raised an eyebrow.

"Okay, a nightmare."

"Or a memory."

She sighed. Lifted a shoulder.

"Well, that's about enough of that."

Indeed. She nodded. Because probably Sergei was dead and she could come out of hiding and they'd be safe and . . .

And if she clicked her heels three times and

said, "There's no place like home," the nightmare would be over.

Mm-hmm. She climbed out of her sleeping bag, aware of the chill that permeated her body. But the air had warmed since last night.

"Listen," Colt said. "The sun is out, and the ice is melting. We'll be out of here as soon as breakfast is over." He reached in for her sleeping bag, probably to stuff it away.

"Did you get ahold of anyone at the ranch?" Echo asked as she climbed out, pulling her sleeping bag behind her.

Tae followed her out into the sunlight. Yes, a beautiful day, the storm clouds gone, the mountains glorious in their hulking repose, a layer of fresh snow at the peaks. Not a hint of yesterday's terror in the air.

So maybe he was right. Maybe she was safe.

"No," he said. "But it's five a.m. No reason for anyone to be up."

She turned to look at him. He wore a strange expression.

The expression of a liar. Because even she knew that Barry Kingston, his father, got up early, sometimes even before five, to pray, read his Bible, make breakfast.

Colt shoved her sleeping bag back into a stuff stack. "I think it's time we get us all home."

And despite the morning sun, warm upon her skin, the crackling fire they had built in a makeshift circle of rocks, the smell of percolating coffee, and the scent of spring in the air, she could feel it welling up inside.

The cold, hard, unrelenting ball of fear.

Ranger liked mornings the best. Mostly because in the morning, his eyes didn't hurt, which meant his migraine from the day before had vanished, and when he looked in the mirror . . . he recognized a man he knew.

The warrior who knew what he was doing, where he was going.

Why he had been put on this earth.

Yes, in that early hour, when his vision wasn't being slowly Swiss-cheesed into darkness as his macular degeneration claimed nanometers of his eyesight, he glimpsed himself.

And then . . . well, the day started.

But what Ranger was losing in his vision, he seemed to be gaining elsewhere. Like, for example, his ability to hear his beautiful wife's breathing at night, something like a song that he'd gotten way too used to, way too fast. It still surprised him, sometimes, when he woke up to see her tangled in the bedsheets next to him, the sunlight on her smooth skin, her hair in a wrap, her dark eyelashes soft on her cheek.

Wow, he loved her, and it was the one thing that kept him above water as the darkness closed in. As he dodged the realization that everything he knew of his world, his life, was slowly vanishing.

He'd gone from a decorated Navy SEAL sniper to a chef—albeit, a very good chef, if he did say so himself—and dispatcher for Sky King Air, as well as their new rescue service.

Which so far hadn't performed a rescue.

Ranger turned off the water in the sink, spitting out the toothpaste, then ran the towel over his hair one last time before he hung it on the hook in the bathroom. He hadn't shaved and still wore his pajama bottoms, but the entire house was asleep and he didn't want to wake his wife, so he'd used the hall bathroom to take a quick shower.

He opened the door quietly and headed down the stairs.

Another day to pretend he mattered in this world—well, to more than just his wife.

Noemi pretty much made him feel like he mattered all the time. But he couldn't help but sense that they all—Noemi, his father, Colt, Tae, Echo, and especially Dodge, who'd given him the dispatcher job—were pandering to him.

Giving the poor man something to do.

The sun was up, scouring the wood floor in golds and pinks. He expected to see his father sitting in the recliner near the towering two-story stone fireplace, reading his Bible, but the chair sat empty. The den door was closed, so maybe his father was doing his praying in private.

Something that Ranger had started to do.

Please, God, tell me what I'm supposed to do with the rest of my dark life. Probably not the right way to phrase the prayer, but that's where he was, so . . .

At least he was back to praying instead of feeling like God had abandoned him, or worse . . . was disappointed in him. In fact, lately, he'd been sort of feeling like an answer was close.

He did like being home, however. The familiar creak in the stairs, the faded leather furniture, the braided rug, the long, worn kitchen table where his family had dinner. The island in the kitchen where he and his brothers had waged a few recent political discussions.

He loved the way the sun heated the wooden floors and the sight of Denali and its cohorts rising out of the north, filling the back window that also overlooked their runway and the Quonset hut that housed the chopper and their two planes.

A glance at it said that Dodge and the rest hadn't come home last night, although Ranger had expected that, given the storm on the mountains.

At ten he'd tried to call, but when he got no answer, he figured they were camping at their put-down site. They had checked in when they landed, so they probably got socked in with the high-altitude storm. The weather might have also knocked out their communications.

He wouldn't worry quite yet. Dodge was a

seasoned pilot. He knew how to survive in the bush.

Ranger walked past the expansive granite island to the stove and filled the Moka pot that Noemi had convinced him to try. As she predicted, he loved the boiled, hot espresso, made Italian style.

See, a guy could change, find new ways of doing things.

He set it on the stove, then filled a teakettle with water.

Behind him, the floor creaked, and he turned, expecting his father, but the room was empty.

Strange.

He set the teakettle to boil.

Then he opened the fridge and pulled out a carton of eggs, a package of bacon. Set the ingredients on the counter.

Another creak, and this time he stilled, listened over his heartbeat. Something . . . He'd learned long ago to separate sounds, so much of his time sitting in his sniper nest, sweating in a ghillie suit, dissecting the movement of the forest or the city sounds around him.

Now, he heard a shuffle and the slightest . . . *breath?*

He whirled, shoved his arm up and just barely deflected the blade that should have hit his neck, found his jugular, and left him bleeding out on the floor.

What the—

He hit his attacker, a man about his age, dark hair, built, gold teeth, funneling all his shock into a right hook. His fist connected in a deeply satisfying punch that found his attacker's jaw and snapped his head back.

Then Ranger grabbed the man's wrist with both hands and banged his hand against the granite. The knife jerked out of the man's grip, but it earned Ranger a fist to his ear and his world tilted.

Who—

He growled, ducked his head, and grabbed the man around his middle, running him back and ramming him into the counter. Landed a couple jabs in his midsection before the attacker slammed his knee into Ranger's gut. The wind whooshed out of him.

A fist across his jaw dazed him and he tasted blood.

Why—

Ranger's hand closed on the Moka pot, now boiling, and he grabbed it up, used it as a club, and smashed it into his attacker's face.

The man shouted and Ranger followed with another shot, an uppercut that sent the man backwards. He hit the counter, fell, and in a second, Ranger was on him, his arm around his neck in a sleeper hold.

How—

The man struggled beneath him, but Ranger

hadn't completely forgotten who he was. He tightened his hold. Sleepy time, and then he'd tie up the man and dig around for the answers.

"Perestan!"

Ranger froze. Looked up.

No. Oh . . . *no!*

Another man of similar build held Noemi around the neck, a handgun pressed to her head. She still wore her pajamas and white bathrobe, her golden-brown eyes wide, fixed on Ranger.

"Stop," the man said, his word heavily accented.

Yes. Ranger let go of the man beneath him, got up, and raised his hands. It was just that simple. "Please don't hurt her."

The man on the floor fought to his feet and, with Noemi watching, hit Ranger with what felt like the force of a thousand suns. He spun, tripped, and his head slammed on the granite island. Heat exploded through him. He hit his knees.

"No, stop!" Noemi screamed, but it didn't slow down his attacker. He kicked Ranger, this time in the jaw, and he fell back, the world spinning.

Give up, give in, or give it all you've got. This part of being a SEAL, he remembered.

He rolled to his hands and knees—

"Stop."

The voice jarred him, and he froze.

Not Noemi's voice. Quieter. But in that quietness, not really a question.

More of a command.

And behind it sounded the cocking of a gun.

His father. Maybe with the Szecsei & Fuchs double-barrel big game rifle he kept in his office.

Oh, Ranger hoped.

"That's enough of that," his father said. "Leave now. I don't want to have to shoot you for trespassing."

The knife, the one Ranger had knocked from the attacker's hand, lay just ahead of him. He edged toward it and spotted his father standing in the great room.

Hoo-yah, his old man held the gun, pointed at the man threatening Noemi.

Except, *Please, Dad, don't shoot my wife.*

Because his dad had the same terrible blinding disease Ranger had.

The man holding Noemi turned to Ranger's father. "Put. It. Down."

His father turned the gun on his cohort standing behind Ranger. "You shoot her, I shoot him."

Ranger stilled.

Noemi's captor seemed to be thinking, even as the other man, the one burned and bleeding and angry, swore at him.

And then Ranger's assailant turned and looked at Ranger.

Ranger hit his feet, the knife in his grip. *Yeah, well, c'mon buddy, let's go.*

Blood dripped off the assailant's face, but he smiled. Even when he reached for a handgun from his shoulder holster.

Not so fast, pal.

"Ranger!" Noemi screamed.

Ranger let the knife fly even as he took off for the man. The blade stabbed its target in the chest seconds before Ranger tackled him.

They hit the ground to the sound of a gunshot.

No!

Noemi screamed. Ranger bounced up.

Noemi!

But she was fighting the grip of her captor, struggling, shrieking.

Instead, his father lay on the sofa, blood exploding from a wound in his chest.

"Dad!" Ranger reached him in a second.

The bullet had grazed his dad's chest, sliding under his arm, cutting across his ribs. Still, his father writhed in pain.

"Okay, okay, you're okay." Ranger picked up a pillow and pressed it to the wound. Blood puddled on the sofa, streaked his hands.

His dad nodded, held the pillow. Met Ranger's eyes. A look passed between them.

The rifle. It lay beside his father on the floor.

Ranger rounded, kicking the weapon under the sofa.

The shooter had recentered his handgun on Noemi. "Do that again and she dies."

Tears ran down Noemi's face, even as she shook her head. "Get him, Ranger."

Oh, Noemi. And the fact that here she was again, taken captive while he watched. . . . A stab of fear went right through him.

Ranger put up his hands. "Don't."

Noemi's face crumpled.

Sorry.

"On your face."

Ranger sank to his knees.

"All the way down."

He couldn't meet Noemi's eyes as he lay prone on the floor.

"Hands behind your back."

He moved his hands.

And then, the first man walked over, prying the knife from where it stuck in his chest, near his shoulder. Blood dripped down his arm, but he seemed unfazed.

He sheathed the knife, then his gun.

Then he pinned Ranger and zip-tied his hands behind him.

Rolled him over.

The man knelt before him. "Where is Taylor Price?"

Taylor? Ranger shook his head. "I have no idea who you're talking about."

Uh-oh. Wrong answer. The man stood up.

Spit. Then he kicked Ranger in the gut, possibly breaking a couple ribs, and definitely sending home the message that yes, Ranger's days as a SEAL, as a man who protected the people he loved, were over.

THREE

Call it Colt's gut, but something just didn't feel right.

And it had nothing to do with the usual nightmares, the images that found him, dogged him from the pockets where he'd tried to tuck them.

Nightmares during which one of his teammates—Elvis, or maybe Vader—came back from the dead to haunt him. But really, it could be any of his team, but especially any four of the ghosts.

No, he lived with the familiar ache, deep in his soul, was used to waking in a sweat, reliving the smells of the savanna, the tinny scent of blood, the shouts and gunfire and taste of betrayal.

This was different. A general sense of doom that had found his bones since Tae's confession last night.

And it didn't help that his brother had hit all of it home with his ominous, *"Which means that Sky King Ranch is in the crosshairs."*

Maybe. Maybe not. But those words itched at him all night—a very short night—until Colt had finally woken, staring at the bright orange of his tent, the sun already burning away the ice and snow.

And that's when he saw that Dodge had already risen. Already packed up his sleeping bag. Colt had climbed out of his bag, shoved it into his stuff sack, and opened the zipper.

Dodge crouched in front of a stone circle, stirring to life a small campfire. He looked rough. He always grew out his whiskers darker and thicker than anyone, although Colt nearly had him beat with a week or so of scruff. Still, Dodge wore a tight set to his jaw and when he glanced at Colt, gave a shake of his head.

Ah. Colt interpreted that as, *Yes, I tried to call the ranch, and no, I didn't get ahold of anyone, and by the way, put a little hurry into your let's go.*

Colt had answered with a nod. *I'm worried too.* Then went to wake the girls.

He was headed toward their tent when he heard Tae's shout. Heard Echo's attempts to wake her. His gut tightened even more. Now, at least, her nightmares made sense.

Somewhere deep inside, she was still fighting for her life in that plane. He got that, more than he wanted to admit.

Deep in his subconscious, he was still waging war with a boy soldier named Ahmed, trying to wheedle the truth from him.

Seemed like he couldn't escape people who lied to him.

Aw, he shouldn't be so hard on Tae. She'd been

63

afraid for her life. He crouched in front of the door, reaching for the zipper. Paused. "Everything okay in there?"

"Just a dream," Tae called back.

Yep. He unzipped the canvas. "Really?"

"Okay, a nightmare."

"Or a memory." Oh, Tae. "Well, that's about enough of that."

Tae looked up at him, something of hope, even relief in her eyes. He'd always thought her pretty, especially when he woke to her sitting beside his bed, her blond hair around her face, silky, those blue eyes in his.

It nudged something inside him. And he was right back to the promises of last night. *"Don't worry, Tae. We'll figure out what's going on."*

Soon they'd fixed breakfast, loaded the plane, and by the time they left, the sun had heated the wings, dissolved the ice, and Dodge eased them into the crisp blue sky without a hint of trouble.

The forecast called for clear skies, few clouds, and wind from the west. The perfect day, and indeed, Alaska was beautiful this time of year. Greening valleys filled with mountain heather and forget-me-nots, caribou running in packs, and geese lifting from crystalline-blue lakes. They passed Echo's homestead and followed the river toward the ranch.

"Everything's probably fine," Colt said through his headset to Dodge. He rode copilot. His father had taught all of them to fly, so yes, if Dodge went down, Colt could land this thing, but he would prefer not to take the yoke.

"Keep calling," Dodge said.

Colt tried again, toggling the radio. "Sky King Ranch, this is Piper N1516P, on approach."

Nothing. Dodge cast him a look, his mouth tight.

Sitting behind them, Echo and Tae wore earphones too, but said nothing.

He spotted the ranch in the distance. Nothing seemed amiss. The main house sat on a hill overlooking a private lake, three tiny cabins with shiny new red roofs gleamed in the sun. His father often took his morning coffee out on the front porch, but today it was empty.

Colt searched the road leading up to the house. Sometimes Ranger ran in the morning, part of the SEAL PT habit he refused to shake. But his brother wasn't hoofing it along the dirt road that ran across their property, along the empty hayfields and former cow pastures.

"Maybe they're still sleeping," Echo said.

"It's seven a.m.," Dodge said as he circled, then lined up for the landing.

He came in soft, despite the thick tundra wheels, like a bird on water. He throttled back, then taxied over to the hangar.

The doors were closed.

Dodge shut off the electronics and removed his headset.

Colt put his hand on his arm. "Maybe I'm overreacting, but . . . I think only we should go in."

Dodge looked at him. Drew in a breath. He turned to the girls. "Stay here."

Echo frowned, but Dodge added a "Please," so she nodded. Still, "What's going on?"

Colt glanced at him. "Maybe you should stay too. I'll go in."

"You're hurt, bro. If there's trouble—"

"I'm not that hurt." But he *had* been the one to lay on the ice, gasping like a beached salmon.

"I'm sure everything's fine," Dodge said.

Colt gave him a look.

"Fine. You girls, get in the hangar. If we're not back in five minutes, then . . . call Deke Starr, I guess."

Colt nodded. "Does Dad keep any weapons in the garage?"

"They're all locked up in his study."

"Seriously, Dodge," Echo said, "what do you think is happening in there? They're probably having breakfast—"

"They're not having breakfast!" Dodge snapped, and she recoiled. He took a breath, turned, glanced at Colt. "Let's hope we're all just overreacting, right?"

Colt nodded and opened his door.

A shot pinged off the wing behind him.

He hit the dirt, rolled, and slid behind the

tundra wheel. Which would probably slow down but never stop a bullet.

The next shot scrubbed the ground near him.

"Get the girls inside the hangar!"

Behind him, Dodge had scrambled out of the plane. "Take this!"

A .357 Taurus landed next to him. Dodge's bear gun.

Colt scooped it up. "Run!" He sent off a couple shots toward the house, near the side door where the shots had been fired.

A word tunneled through him, and he bit it back, but wow, he hated when he was right.

When he knew, deep inside, that something was going down.

And he couldn't do anything to stop it.

"What do you see?" Dodge shouted from the door of the hangar. Clearly the ladies had made it inside.

"I can't see anything!"

And then a barrage of shots peppered the plane, tearing holes through the fabric, the wing.

It popped the tire, and the plane jerked, falling.

Colt rolled away just as the plane collapsed onto its side.

Now Dodge let out a word. Colt stayed down as the shots continued to bite through the plane, the dirt beside him.

Then, suddenly, return fire from the hangar. A staccato of bullets that shattered the office window, chipped wood off the siding, and hopefully sent their shooter to the dirt.

What?

"Colt, get in here!"

More shots, and Colt looked up.

A man, not Dodge, stood at the door. He wore a brown canvas jacket, a baseball cap on backwards, and fired what looked like an AR-15 semiautomatic rifle.

From what? His father's apparently secret weapons cache?

Dodge stood behind him, gesturing hard.

Colt found his feet and launched himself at the door.

The man reached out, grabbed him, and practically flung him into the shadowed interior of the Quonset hut.

Then he backed up and slammed the door behind him.

Colt whirled and, maybe from habit, maybe from adrenaline, pointed the bear gun at him. Because hello, who was this guy?

"Pete Sutton," the man said, his hands going up as he dropped the semiautomatic to hang from the strap around his neck. "Noemi's father."

The words didn't land. And not just for Colt. Dodge, too, it seemed, just stared at the man. Blond, blue eyes, built like a tractor, and . . .

"Noemi's father is dead," Tae said. She stepped up next to Colt. "So, try again."

Colt put the man in his fifties, lines around his eyes, a bit of white to the scruff on his chin. But he had a stance about him that spoke military. In fact, if Colt remembered correctly, her father had been a SEAL.

A SEAL lost in a training accident.

"He's telling the truth."

A different voice, this time from a man who stepped out from behind their Bell 429 chopper. Lean, tall, dark brown hair, dressed in a pair of jeans and a suit jacket. He too carried a gun, but now tucked it into his side holster and raised his hands. "My name is Logan Thorne, and we're here because . . . well, it's a long story, but mostly because Pete here needs to talk to his daughter."

Colt let those words settle. And then, "Okay. If you're Pete Sutton, tell me how my brother met your daughter. Where, and when—"

"Four years ago. In Key West. I was fixing a crack in the hull of my sailboat. He nearly died in the free-diving tower."

Colt put down his gun. "Seriously. You're not dead."

"On paper . . ." He lifted a shoulder, even as he lowered his hands. Glanced toward his cohort. "She wasn't supposed to find out. Not this way, at least, but we didn't see her getting kidnapped in Nigeria either so . . ." He sighed. "You're Colt?"

He narrowed his eyes.

"I know about your capture. And I know what you did for my daughter." Pete's mouth made a line. "Thank you."

Yeah, well, Colt didn't know what to do with that. He nodded.

"What are you doing here now?" Dodge said. "And who is inside our house?"

"A couple of local hires. Russians, but they probably have ties back home," Logan said.

"Bratva?" Colt asked.

"That's our guess." Logan unsheathed his gun and checked his ammo clip. "We heard about the attempted hit on Noemi. Should have gotten here sooner. Sorry."

"Sorry? That's what you've got for us?" Dodge had paced to the door, glanced outside. The shooters had gone quiet.

"Hey!" Pete's voice sharpened. "My daughter is in there, and from what we can tell, someone has been shot."

That sent a cold shard through Colt, and maybe Dodge too because his jaw tightened. "How do you know that?"

"We found their vehicle a couple klicks down the road and got concerned about a lonely car in the middle of nowhere," Logan said. "We followed our gut and split up. Clearly we were late to the party. Pete got close enough to do a looksee through the window."

"There's a man down on the sofa, another on

the floor." Pete had also walked to the door, filling in the space that Dodge had vacated.

"We were just putting together a plan when you showed up."

A man down.

"They shot Ranger," Colt said.

"That's what I'm thinking too," Dodge said.

"We need a distraction. And a way in." Now Colt walked to the hangar door and stared at the house.

The picture window across the back would hide nothing as they tried to approach. But maybe if they were looking one direction . . .

"C'mon, guys, this is easy," Echo said from behind them. "Use the fire ladder."

A smile hitched up one side of Dodge's face. "E, you're a genius."

Yes, she was.

"Fire ladder?" Tae said.

"My dad built a ladder on the outside of our house, from our bedroom window to the ground. He always had a fear of us perishing in a house fire. Or maybe our mom did—that seems more like her. Anyway, it's been used a few times for, um, non-fire-related escapes." He shot Dodge a grin. "Mostly by me."

"So now we just need a distraction," Pete said.

"How much ammo do you have?" Colt asked Logan.

"Not enough. We need something big, like . . ."

"A fire," Tae said. She nodded to the downed

plane. "The kind of fire that creates black smoke, aka, cover."

A ripple of pain flashed across Dodge's face. But he nodded. "Yeah. Good idea, Tae. We'll get in the house, and we'll all deploy together. Do you have coms?"

Logan walked over and handed Dodge an earpiece. "Just the one."

So, Colt got the gun, Dodge got the earpiece. Sorta sounded right.

"Let's go," Dodge said. He walked over to Pete. "Gimme the gun. I'll do it."

It sort of felt like Travis shooting Old Yeller.

Pete surrendered the AR-15 and stood back as Dodge walked to the door.

Colt turned to Tae. "Stay here. Please."

She met his eyes, nodded. "But please don't die."

"You've met me," he said and winked, and yes, it felt silly, but he couldn't help himself.

Maybe after all this, they could go back to something that felt easier. Flirting. Maybe he'd even take her out on a date, see if he could talk her into a dance . . .

What*ever*. Head in the game.

Her mouth pinched. "Yeah, I've met you. Again, I say, please don't die."

Echo walked up to Dodge, took his face in her hands. "You too. Because I've waited for you too long to lose you now."

72

He wrapped an arm around her waist and leaned down.

Colt looked away, met Logan's gaze. "We have a conversation in our future, you and me," he said.

Logan nodded.

Echo stepped away.

Dodge squared his shoulders, lifted the AR-15, and fired at his beloved Piper, the one he'd purchased with his own money, his first plane, first love—

The fuel tank exploded. Flames, a burst of heat and light that had everyone stepping back.

Black smoke billowed from the body of the plane.

Dodge shoved the gun into Pete's hands, glanced at Colt.

He was already at the door. "On me!"

Then he took off. The smoke burned his eyes, blurring his vision, but he dodged the plane, then followed the smoke around the lodge as shots cracked from the house.

But not at them.

Colt dove anyway, into the tall grasses between the lodge and the lake, near the ladder built into the end wall of the house.

Dodge landed beside him, breathing hard. "Ready?"

Colt had already shoved the gun into his belt. "Let's go." He had climbed the ladder so many times he could do it with his eyes closed. "Skip the third rung."

"I know," Dodge said.

Up they went, the rungs still sturdy despite a decade of neglect. Colt reached the top, put his hand on the window, and shoved it open.

No squeak, thank you, and he tumbled into his childhood bedroom as quietly as he could.

Rolled away from the window to allow room for Dodge.

Ranger had moved out to share Larke's old room with Noemi, so Colt had moved in, now that he could climb the stairs. Dodge slept in the next room, beyond a wall their father had built to separate the large loft space.

Colt crept to his feet and eased toward the door. It was open, and from here they could look down to the great room.

Ranger sat up, his back to the wall, and he looked rough. But no worse than their father, who held a pillow to his side, in a pool of blood.

They'd shot their *father*?

Noemi sat, tied up, on the rocking chair, wearing her bathrobe and pajamas.

Colt held up one finger to Dodge, then pointed to a man standing at the front door, peering out.

Whoever he was, he wasn't a pro because he'd know that a well-trained sniper could take the guy out from five hundred yards, and there he stood, a bold target at the front door, looking into the horizon.

And Colt was a well-trained sniper.

He lifted the bear gun. The grip was smaller than he liked, and the front heavy, but it had both a rear and front sight.

Colt lay down, propped his elbow on the ground. Found his target through the gun sight. "I'll shoot. The other will come running, and we'll end this."

Dodge crept away from the door, his hand on his earpiece, relaying his words to Pete and Logan.

The man was stepping away from the door, turning—

Ranger looked up. "Colt! No!"

Colt pulled the trigger.

The bullet hit the man in a dead shot, center of his head, the mass of blood and gore hitting the front door.

Noemi screamed.

Ranger rolled toward the body.

That's when Colt saw a detonator drop out of the man's hand.

Noemi had seen her husband hurt before, but never like this.

Ranger sat against the wall in the great room, his face bloody, jaw clenched. He wouldn't look at her.

Sure, he'd been shot in Nigeria, but he'd gritted his teeth, got her to safety, pushed through, protected her, and brought her home.

In every way, he'd been the warrior she knew.

This recent pain was something deeper, pervasive, dark, something that gnawed at his soul and pushed him out of their bed to prowl the halls of his home.

She longed to soothe the darkness away, to tell him that everything would be okay, but how did you help a man recover from the loss of everything he was?

What if she hadn't gotten up, followed her brooding husband out of bed? Because she'd only made everything worse.

Someone had grabbed her from behind, smashed her lips into her teeth with a bruising hand, and put a gun to her head.

She'd heard the slamming of bodies, the grunting as the stranger dragged her down the stairs. And when she saw Ranger fighting for his life, a terrible memory sparked inside her, the one that saw her husband capable and fierce and—

"Stop." The man holding her had leveraged her against him, and Ranger . . . Ranger said the words still piercing her soul.

"Please don't hurt her."

Because of her, Ranger had been beaten, tied up, and kicked. Because of her, his father now lay on the sofa, whitened with pain.

And when her attacker put a suicide vest on her, her bathrobe over it, tied her up and sat her in a chair, she saw something inside Ranger die.

She'd spent the last few years of her life volunteering at refugee camps, trying to ease the suffering of others. But this . . . this she didn't have a clue how to fix.

Worse, this had to be her fault.

Because certainly whoever had kidnapped Noemi two weeks ago had circled back for another go-round.

She had no other explanation for the fact that she'd been assaulted for a third time in less than a month.

"Colt! No!"

Ranger's voice jerked her back to the present, and she looked at him, then up, and then—

A bullet blew out the back of her attacker's head. Blood spattered against the wall. Noemi screamed.

The man collapsed.

Ranger rolled, then leaped to his feet.

He'd gotten free. That clicked into place just as he grabbed the detonator that fell from the man's hand. "Colt! You idiot!"

It took a moment and then she realized. Ranger thought it might be a dead man's switch.

"Get down, Range!" Colt yelled, and she spotted him in the loft walkway above the great room.

And that's when a shot whizzed past Ranger's head.

The other captor. He'd come running from where he'd positioned himself in the back entryway. She'd heard shooting earlier, and now she knew why.

Ranger dove at her and threw them both onto the floor, his entire body covering hers.

She lay cocooned inside his embrace as more shots rang out.

From her vantage point, she spotted Colt, on his knees now, firing down at the other attacker.

"Stay down," Ranger said.

Sure, no problem—

He rolled away, toward the sofa, and she couldn't help but marvel as somehow in his hand a weapon materialized.

His father's two-barrel rifle.

For a second, she saw it all. Colt, on the railing, trying to get a shot at the man who crouched behind the island. And then Ranger, who had scooped up the rifle, rolled again, and rose with the gun at his shoulder, even with the counter.

He fired.

A howl sounded from behind the island, and then Ranger was on his feet, running over to grab the attacker. He dragged him, shouting and swearing, out from behind the bar, kicked the gun from his hand, and sent his fist into his face.

The man lay quiet, bleeding.

Ranger stood up. With blood on his face, his father's gun in his hands, the sun backlit behind him in the picture window, he looked like some kind of apocalyptic warrior.

And her heart just hurt.

He was born to be a SEAL.

"Is that all of them?" Colt said from the top of the stairs.

"I think so," Ranger said, and then footsteps barreled down the stairs. In a second Dodge was standing over his father, easing the bloody pillow from his wound.

Barry groaned. "Range said it just nicked my ribs, but it hurts like a son of a gun."

Meanwhile, Colt had come downstairs.

"We need a tourniquet on his leg," Ranger said, still standing over the man. "If we want him to talk, we'll need him alive."

"Use my bathrobe belt," Noemi said as she sat up.

"Honey, stay right there," Ranger said even as Colt pulled her belt out of the loops.

Colt knelt in front of the man, tied the belt around his leg, then used a wooden spoon to crank it tight. The man came to life with a shout.

"Stay down and you might live through this," he growled.

Colt got up, went to a drawer in the kitchen, and came back with an extension cord. He pushed the man over and tied his hands.

Dodge had knelt in front of Noemi, looking at the vest.

"Don't take it off yet," Ranger said. "It might be rigged to blow."

Everything inside her turned liquid at his words.

Colt finished securing the man and stood up.

"What were you thinking?" The accusation came from Ranger, and his tone had even Dodge turning to look at him.

The question was directed at Colt.

Colt's expression turned dark. "I was thinking I should probably save your sorry backside."

Ranger was taller than Colt, and for a second, Noemi actually thought Ranger might hit his brother. "Just be thankful that wasn't a dead man's switch, or we'd all be dead."

Colt glanced at Noemi, at her vest, and his mouth tightened.

Ranger shook his head as if in disgust and strode over to her.

"You okay?"

"Get this off me."

"Trying." He smelled of blood and sweat and really all she wanted was to lean into his arms. But the vest hurt, cutting into her ribs, heavy on her shoulders, and for the first time she realized that this wasn't over.

"Range?"

"I learned how to handle explosives, but . . ."

He looked at her, and something unfamiliar edged his eyes.

Fear.

Ranger was *afraid*.

The sense of it reached out, snaked through her, and turned her cold.

Colt came over to them. Crouched in front of her.

"You ever see anything like this?" Ranger said, his deft fingers running over the vest, as if helping him see it.

"Not up close. Usually, the thing is already detonated—"

"Stop talking." Dodge had gotten out his phone and was scanning the apparatus. "We've got two wires that connect to the detonators, which attach to a couple bricks of C4."

"The pockets are filled with steel balls," Colt said.

"The trigger must have a remote signal," Ranger added. "But I don't see it."

"There are wires attached to the belt buckle," Dodge said.

"If you clip them, she's dead."

The voice came from behind them. Something darkly familiar that spiraled down inside her and nudged a packed-away memory.

She stiffened. Ranger met her eyes, frowned, then turned.

Her breath caught.

What?

A man walked toward her. Dressed in khaki pants, a brown canvas jacket, short blond hair under a baseball cap, those blue eyes on her, his mouth pinched tight.

No, *no* . . .

"Master Chief Sutton?" Ranger said, and then suddenly, he turned back to Noemi, his eyes wide, and his hands went to her arms, as if to hold her up. "Breathe."

She just looked past Ranger, over his shoulder to the man. "Dad?" Oh . . . my. *"Dad?"*

"Hey kiddo," he said and knelt in front of her.

She was shaking, and now looked at Ranger who just stared at her father, wordless.

"What— Dad! What are you— You're . . . you're *dead*."

He made a face. "Let's get this off you." His fingers traced the two wires protruding from the side of the vest. "These are dummy wires. We've been seeing more of this lately. The real detonator is in the neck pouch." He put his hands to her neck, the feel of them eerily familiar, and pulled back the collar. "See, here, how it runs through the vest, hidden? You cut any of the dummy wires, and it activates this trigger. I need clippers."

Dodge got up and headed to the drawer in the kitchen.

Noemi stared at her father. Her *father?* "You

82

drowned. In a training accident. I *buried* you. Well, at least your casket."

"I know. And I'm not even supposed to be here now, but I had to know that you were safe."

Dodge handed him a pair of clippers.

Ranger put a hand on her father's arm. "You do know what you're doing, right, Master Chief?"

He looked at Ranger. Smiled. "Son, I always knew you were the right one for my daughter."

Then he clipped the wire.

No boom, no shrapnel dissecting her head from her body, obliterating everyone in the room.

Ranger closed his eyes. Breathed out.

"Let's get this off you," her father said and unsnapped the vest. She shrugged out of it, and Dodge took it and set it away from them.

Her father's eyes glistened. "I'm so sorry, Noe. I . . . I wanted to tell you. But it was too dangerous." He drew in a breath. "As it were, you nearly died because of me."

"What?" Ranger said, but she didn't care.

"Dad," she said and wrapped her arms around his neck. *"Dad."*

He held her as the whole of it swept her up, all the way from the assault in Nigeria to her fake, not-so-fake wedding to her kidnapping two weeks ago to this moment, when she'd nearly . . . well, yes, it could have ended in a nightmare for everyone. And now this.

A terrible mix of grief and joy and disbelief crested over her and she started to cry.

No, sob really. Ugly, painful sobs that racked her body.

She hadn't cried like this since her wedding night.

"Shh, honey, it's okay," her father said softly. "I'm so sorry."

Ranger ran his hand over her back, as if trying to calm her. But she didn't want to be calm.

Just for a moment, someone should take a look at their lives and, well, freak out.

"Why, Dad?" She leaned away, her body still hiccupping. "I grieved you. I stood at your grave with your teammates and . . ." The dread Noemi felt that day swept over her. The pain she went through. All for nothing. Heat ripped through her, something sharp and brutal and— "You're such a jerk!"

Then she hopped up, away from him, looked at Ranger, then back at her father. "I can't believe you did this to me."

He stood, even as Ranger came over to her, put his arm around her. "Noe, let him explain."

She rounded on Ranger. "What explanation could there be that even a little justifies making me think he was dead?"

"The one that says your father was asked, by our president, to protect America, and maybe even the world." The voice came from across the room.

She looked over and the man who stood there looked vaguely familiar, although she couldn't place him, exactly. "I know you. You . . . you were at the funeral."

"With President White, yes," he said, then walked over and held out his hand. "Logan Thorne. And if you give your father a chance, he'll explain everything."

"Not before we get Dad to medical help," Dodge said.

"I'm fine, son." Barry sat up.

"You're not fine." Colt walked over to him, crouching so they were eye level. "You need stitches at the least, and probably some tests to make sure you don't have broken ribs and internal bleeding." He grimaced as he looked at his father's wound.

Barry put a hand on Colt's shoulder. "Good shooting, son."

Ranger shook his head, his mouth in a grim line.

"Everyone okay?" Echo said, coming into the room. She walked right over to Dodge and put her arms around him. Tae came in behind them.

Stopped. Looked at Logan. "Now can you tell me what you are doing here?"

Logan turned. Colt rose, something in his expression. "Who is this, Tae?"

"This is my boss. The owner of Project 534. He's the one who brought me the virus and asked me to create the vaccine. He's the one who started this whole thing."

"Then this is his fault." Colt considered the man. Then he raised his gun. "Start talking."

She just wanted to circle back to the beginning and start over.

Tae sat on the deck of her tiny cabin that overlooked the lake on Kingston property, the mountains tracing their outline against the magnificent blue sky. The sun shone through wispy clouds, and the scent of wildflowers layered the air.

Beautiful, but oh so far from her houseboat docked in Lake Union, smack-dab in the center of Seattle, with the skyline rising over the horizon. If she closed her eyes and focused on the lapping of the lake on the shore, she might be back on her third-story deck, her boat soft on the waves, taking her morning coffee before she kayaked to her lab.

Simpler, perfect days when she could bury herself in work.

She'd been such a fool.

"You okay?"

Now she did close her eyes, because the last—very last—person she wanted to talk to was Colt. He only reminded her of the mess she'd dragged everyone into. Because she'd wanted romance. Her own happy ending.

A burn swelled her throat.

"Tae, this isn't your fault." His low tenor found its way under her skin.

She had to stop liking him. If she'd learned anything about Colt Kingston, it was that her heart couldn't be around him and survive.

She shook her head. "You heard Logan. If I hadn't run away, all of this would be contained. Now people are getting kidnapped and killed and—"

"Stop."

She turned and gone was the guy she'd seen three hours ago, the one who had a look on his face that had turned the entire room quiet.

As if he just might use the gun he'd held on Logan Thorne.

She wanted to put her hands over her ears, close out the story Logan had told her, the one that connected the pieces.

The fact that President White had put together a private spec ops team to confront what they called the Petrov problem. And she'd sort of been a part of it, without even knowing.

"Arkady Petrov is a Russian general who was behind the assassination attempt of not only one of his own generals—one of the troika in power—but also our own president. We think he's the current head of the Petrov family mob,

and is planning an attack on America, via this new virus. But now that we found you, we need you to come back and finish your work on the vaccine."

All that came out after Ranger had rounded on Colt, called him crazy, and told him to put the gun down.

She didn't really blame Colt. The last twenty-four hours had her own head spinning—from the near catapult off the cliff to the snowstorm to the siege on Sky King Ranch. And to see Barry hurt, bleeding, and in pain . . .

"This is my fault," she said. "I was played." She shook her head. "I'm such an idiot."

Colt blew out a breath as he sat next to her on the deck. "We see what we want to see, Tae. You're not the only one who's made mistakes that cost lives."

She glanced at him. He had showered since the showdown at the ranch, since Sheriff Deke Starr showed up with a coroner, took their statements, and then carted Bad Russian Guy away. They then all called a time-out to get Barry to the hospital. Dodge and Echo had left with his dad, while Ranger and Noemi holed up in the study to get the lowdown from her not-so-dead father.

Colt wore his hair longer, now slicked back and drying in curls around his face. He'd changed into jeans, a long sleeve T-shirt, and cowboy boots. The guy could grace a calendar with the dark scruff on his chin, those mesmerizing brown eyes.

He even smelled good, with a hint of flannel and pine.

But she wasn't going to be stupid again, thank you. Sure, they might have had a few sparks over the past month as he recuperated from his injuries. He'd made her laugh. Called her Flo. And sometimes she let herself linger in the memory of being in his arms.

Or daydream about being back there again.

But up close, the real Colt Kingston was dangerous. And had no intention, clearly, of slowing down. He'd been the first to volunteer to breach the house, and she didn't even want to think about the fiasco at the wrecked plane.

She couldn't—*wouldn't*—let herself fall for a man who thrived in war and danger. This was merely a time-out in his too-lethal life. And she wasn't going to be a casualty. "I highly doubt you let yourself fall for a Russian spy."

He huffed. "Not quite. But . . ." He stared out at the lake. "It's nice here. I never thought I'd be back, really."

"Why not?"

He lifted a shoulder. "Just . . . wasn't on my radar."

She frowned.

"Fine. Dodge and I had a wicked fight a few years ago, and it was bad enough that I thought I wasn't welcome back."

"What was it about?"

"Something stupid I did."

She raised an eyebrow, remembering Echo's words in the tent but not wanting to assume.

"I made a play for Echo."

He— What?

"I know. In my defense, I thought she and Dodge were just friends. I didn't realize he'd asked her to marry him. And I thought she was flirting with me, so . . ." He shook his head. "Doesn't matter now, but for years after, I wondered if she used me to force his hand. Except it backfired because he took off and joined the Air Force while I was still in the hospital."

"You ended up in the *hospital?*" Okay, when Echo said that Dodge had hurt him, she hadn't realized physically.

"You've met my brother, right?"

"I've met *you.*"

He smiled at that and glanced at her, and it was like a flash of light, right down to her gray soul.

"Please," she said, shaking it away. "I'm not saying that's a compliment. But I'm just surprised—"

"I was drunk. And I might have deserved it a little."

"So you *let* him beat you up."

"No. I just . . . well, let's just say I was glad when Ranger got between us. Could have been much worse."

"You spent ten years estranged from your family. Not sure how that can get worse."

"One of us could have died."

Oh. Maybe.

"It just feels strange to be back."

"Strange, good?"

"I've been living out of a duffel bag for a few years now, so it just feels strange to wake up every morning to the same view. But yeah, good. Good to be back with my brothers. A fresh start, maybe."

She cast her gaze to him, and he was looking at her. Smiling.

Stop. "What do you mean a duffel bag? Don't you have an apartment somewhere?"

A gaggle of Canada geese landed on the lake, their squawks loud as they rippled the water. In the distance, clouds hovered near the top of Denali, its hulk spanning the horizon in shades of blue and lavender.

"Naw. After I separated from the military, I worked for a few military contractors, doing security in Afghanistan, and then a SEAL I knew called and asked if I wanted to join up with Jones, Inc. It's a global search and rescue team out of Minneapolis, but they also do some security work on the side. I've been with them about two years."

"That's how you ended up in Nigeria."

"I was working security for a doctor who was

visiting a couple of the refugee camps. He'd heard about the Boko Haram and was a personal friend of my boss, Ham, so . . ." He made a face. "I guess I get an F on that job."

"Not without giving it your best A-plus shot," she said and nearly reached to touch the scar, still red, above his eye. "And the doc is still alive, right?"

"Yes. But we lost our Nigerian translator. A guy named Moses. Good man."

"Sorry."

"See, I get making mistakes that cost lives."

She met his eyes. He looked away.

He wasn't telling her something, and the sense of it lingered inside her. But she wasn't going to chase his ghosts. Not when she had no desire to talk about hers.

"Where's the most exotic place you and your duffel bag have been?"

He laughed, and the sound of it reached inside and again shook the hold the darkness had on her. "Me and duffel. Well, I liked Key West a lot. That was where Ranger met Noemi. But I was still Delta back then. Since then . . . I dunno. Paris is beautiful. I missed a flight trying to make a connection in Charles de Gaulle and had to spend the night there. Took a cab around the city. Froze my backside off at the top of the Eiffel Tower. The lights of the city were glorious though."

"I've never been out of the US."

"Really?"

"Actually, the cruise was the first time I've even been out of Seattle, at least since I was a kid. My mother moved west after my father died, and we never really left."

"I'm sorry to hear that. How did your father die?"

"Not sure. He was a Navy doc, and one day a chaplain and a notification officer appeared on our doorstep. He was killed in a training accident, but . . . you know. He was supposed to be on a ship. My mother spent years trying to figure out what happened. It drove her crazy. She finally decided that she couldn't talk about him anymore. She moved on, got remarried . . ."

"How old were you when he died?"

"Ten."

"That's rough. I lost my mom when I was six. Is that why you became a doctor?"

"Maybe. I don't know. My dad didn't join the Navy until after 9/11. Said he wanted to make the world a better place. I guess I wanted to also." She shook her head. "I just wanted to do it from my quiet houseboat in Seattle."

"You have a houseboat?"

"Yeah. It's docked on the east side of Lake Union. Has this beautiful view of downtown Seattle. It's gorgeous. Two stories plus a deck. Two bedrooms, chef's kitchen—"

"No wonder you're such a good cook."

She smiled at that. "Polished teak, a fireplace, a theater on the lower level, and a two-story glass wall for the view."

"Wow. That's better than a duffel."

Oh, he could make her laugh. "I never dreamed for a bigger life, not really. I kayak across the lake to work, stop off at Cool Beans, a little coffee shop near my place, on my way. I would spend all day with Faheem, or my other colleague, Zoey, working on the vaccine, and then go home and get takeout from the Thai place near my house. I'd read a book on the deck with a glass of wine, listening to Patrizio Buanne—"

"Who?"

"He's an Italian baritone."

"Right."

She shoved her hands between her knees. "I had no idea that I was responsible to save the world. And . . ." She swallowed, the truth lodging inside her like a bullet. "I'm not sure I want to be."

He leaned back on his hands. "People sleep peaceably in their beds at night only because rough men stand ready to do violence on their behalf."

She looked at him. "George Orwell wrote that."

He cocked his head at her. "Yeah. That's pretty good, Flo."

She lifted a shoulder. "I have a thing for quotes. They stick in my head."

"Well, George Orwell wrote it, but we Delta

guys used to say it. The world's peace comes at a price."

The geese suddenly lifted, flying into the blue, calling. A breeze found her, rich with the scent of wildflowers and pine.

Maybe she didn't have to leave. Maybe she could stay here.

As if he could read her mind, Colt looked at her then, something solid and fixed in his gaze, and she hadn't a hope of ignoring the sense if it— power, commitment, resolve, safety—or the way it moved inside her.

"Whatever it is, you're not doing it alone."

FOUR

Ranger was trying, really trying, to wrap his mind around what Master Chief Sutton was saying—or rather *former* Master Chief because, you know, he'd died.

They'd given him a military funeral.

Ranger had sat in the back of the church, behind the crowd, and watched Noemi sob. It had shredded his own soul.

And now he had to stand here again and witness Noemi's pain as Pete told her that his *country* was more important than telling his daughter that he was alive.

Okay, Ranger got the country over family part. Because in a way, protecting the country was protecting her, but—

"I wanted to tell you, honey," Pete was saying. "I thought you were better off, safer, if you didn't know."

They had taken refuge in Ranger's father's office, although the rest of the family had left. Dodge and Echo and his father to the medical center and Colt after Tae, who'd gone down to her cabin.

Probably to sort out just how she'd brought a couple of assassins to the Kingston family's front door.

Although that wasn't entirely her fault, given Logan Thorne's story.

"After you left, the office was bombed and your colleague went on the run."

Yeah, those words had landed with all the gentleness of a nuclear bomb. Ranger had no doubt Colt was currently doing recon on the fallout.

"How on earth would I be *better off,* even *safer,* not knowing?"

Atta girl, Noemi. She wore the same pose as Ranger—her arms folded over her chest, although Ranger leaned his shoulder against the wall.

Noemi had simply planted herself in the middle of the room, squaring off with her father.

"Because I didn't know if I'd come back. And I didn't want you worried, or even trying to find me," Pete said.

Her mouth tightened and she shook her head.

"And, if the world thought I was still alive, then you'd be in danger. They'd take you, to get to me."

"Which is what happened," Ranger said quietly. He met Pete's gaze. "That's why they didn't kill Noemi and the others in Nigeria."

Pete drew in a breath. "I don't know. We think, at first, they just grabbed them because of what they saw. But when you got away, they feared you letting the word get out. That's why they came after you in your uncle Efe's village. And then, later, here in Alaska."

"You know about Uncle Efe?" Noemi asked.

Ranger leaned away from the wall. "How?"

Pete looked away, made a face.

"How, Dad?" Noemi said, and Ranger walked behind her and put his hands on her shoulders.

"Is she chipped?" Ranger said quietly.

Pete looked back at them. "No. Of course not. I have a GPS tracker on your phone, and your passport pings, but . . ." His mouth tightened. "Mostly, you belong to a small handful of people connected to our ops group who we keep an eye on."

"You called Jones, Inc. to extract them."

"I did."

"Are the others in danger too? Selah and the doctor? Fraser?" Noemi asked.

"Maybe. They've been warned. But I had to see if you were okay myself."

"What else do you know about me?" Noemi asked.

He looked at Ranger, back to her. "I know you're married."

"You know we're married."

"I talked with your uncle in Nigeria."

She just blinked at him. "When?"

"A couple weeks ago."

"And were you going to tell me that you were alive? Or were you just going to peek in the window, watch me eating cornflakes, then leave again?"

He folded his arms. Looked at the floor.

"Perfect. That's just beautiful. Wow. How little I must mean to you." Her voice broke on the tail end. "I don't know why you bothered to cut off the vest. After all, my heart was already in tiny, shattered pieces."

He looked up, and even Ranger felt for him, a little.

"Noemi, take a breath," Ranger said, his mouth close to her ear. "He was trying to do what was best."

"No." She rounded on him. "What is best is not disappearing from your daughter's life, making her think you're dead." Her golden-brown eyes sparked. "And by the way, what's also not best is trying to take down a couple of assassins on your own."

"Hey!"

"No. You could have been killed. Your dad could have missed—he has the same eyesight as you do—and I would have watched you bleed out on the floor."

Since when was this about him?

"It's bad enough that you look like you've done all fifteen rounds with Drago!"

"Drago?"

"*Rocky IV*," said Pete. "We were big Rocky fans."

"That explains a lot—"

"No." She turned back to her father, stepping

away from Ranger. "There will be no bonding between you two."

"We're not."

"No laughing. No old SEAL stories. No buddy-buddy talk. None of it. The last thing I need is you putting ideas in Ranger's head. I get that you have a need to save the world." She looked at Ranger. "And you're certainly not good at sitting on your hands." She took another step away. "But if I find out that you're recruiting him, and he suddenly ends up missing in some training accident"—she finger-quoted the last words—"I swear I will hunt you down and you will wish you had actually gone to that big ocean in the sky."

She visibly shook and, despite her words, Ranger didn't smile.

"Honey," Pete said.

"Don't honey me. I need . . . I need just a minute here to wrap my brain around the fact that I've mourned you for years and you . . . you've been watching me like a stalker!"

"Not stalker. Worried father," Pete said.

"Stalker. And you"—she had turned to Ranger—"you swear you didn't know anything about this?"

"What? No." He held up his hands. "Noemi, seriously. I . . . no. I grieved him too. I was at the funeral."

Her mouth opened, and she turned to her father.

"President White—he was just a senator then—was at the funeral. He was *at the funeral*. And he knew you were alive."

Her father swallowed. Then, "I was at the funeral too."

"Oh, no . . ." She shook her head. "No. You watched as . . ." She blew out a breath, glanced at Ranger. Then she whirled and walked out of the room.

Slammed the door behind her.

Ranger stood in the silence, ran a hand behind his neck. "Yeah, so she's pretty mad."

"I should go after her." Pete turned.

"Nope." Ranger stepped between him and the door. "I think she needs a full minute of reprieve."

Pete took a breath. Then, finally nodded. He walked to the window, stared outside. "Beautiful place here."

"Yeah."

"Remote."

"Mm-hmm."

Pete turned. "You might need a stitch or two."

"Maybe." He met Pete's eyes. "What aren't you telling me?"

A beat. Two, and with it, Ranger's gut clenched. Then, Pete sighed.

"For the last year I've worked undercover as an agent for the Petrovs, moving weapons, gathering intel, and trying to figure out where they might be planning this attack. We know they've weaponized the smallpox. They've deployed it in a half dozen small communities over the world. It's fast, it's lethal, and it has a long incubation rate, and if we don't get a handle on where they're going to attack, this thing will be out of control before we can blink. I'm not sure if I'm blown or not, but I have to go back undercover. They might try to come after her again, so I need you to keep her safe."

"I will. With my life."

Pete considered him. "I always liked you. Don't let me down."

He looked at the man, the burled muscles, the wizened eyes, the years of battle in his countenance, and in that moment, he seemed . . . tired.

Overwhelmed.

As if the battle just might have cost him too much.

And it occurred to Ranger that maybe, given another decade with the teams, he might have worn the same look. Now, he met Pete's gaze.

"I swear it on my soul, if it depends upon me, I will keep her alive."

Problem was, Tae didn't really store anything in her brain. "This is why I wanted my journal," she said to Colt, Dodge, Pete, and Logan while she chopped onions. She didn't know why, but somehow having something to do, like cook up a big pile of spaghetti, seemed to take her mind off the swirl of what-ifs.

What if she stayed?

Barry had returned home with stitches and a wrap around his chest, but no broken ribs or internal bleeding, and he now sat in his recliner, listening to the hot debate at the island. Or sleeping. Maybe a little of both.

"Are you telling me there is nothing left of her lab?" Colt now asked.

She couldn't look at him without hearing his voice, soft yet intentional. *"Whatever it is, you're not doing it alone."*

Another reason for her to just stay. Because then Colt couldn't do what he did best—follow someone into trouble.

"No, nothing was left. They blamed it on a gas leak. Thankfully the explosion happened at night, so no one was hurt," Logan said. "But I went to check on Zoey, and she was gone."

Tae dropped the onions into the sizzling cast-iron pan, along with the venison that she'd thawed. "You sure she wasn't run over by a car?"

Silence, and she turned. "Oh please. I'm not being sarcastic. Remember Faheem?"

Logan looked at Pete, then back to her. "Yes. He was a good man."

Her eyes widened. "Did he know that the smallpox was weaponized?"

Logan nodded. "I'd met with him the night he

103

died, after he reached out to me. We think that the Petrovs were probably watching him too." His mouth made a grim line. "We're taking care of his wife and kids."

"You'd better be!" She turned back to the meat and onions, her eyes burning. "He used to bring me lunch, homemade from his wife. She made the best butter chicken . . ." She ran a finger under her eye, then reached for the Italian seasoning.

A presence beside her made her turn. "How about if I make dinner." Ranger.

Fine. She relinquished the wooden spoon and walked around to a vacated stool. Slid onto it. "Faheem took notes."

"His wife handed over everything. But they're not complete," Logan said.

"Mine are at the bottom of a glacier lake." She glanced at Colt. "Unless you'd like to go swimming."

"Can you re-create the vaccine?" Logan had slid onto a stool as well.

She sighed. "I don't know. Eventually, probably. But . . . I'd need Zoey."

"You don't know where she is?" Logan frowned.

"Did you hear my story? Cruise ship, airplane crash, hypothermia, hospital stay . . . um, no, not a clue. Why haven't you found her?"

"Zoey has vanished. We think . . ."

"Please, don't tell me she's dead."

Logan held up his hand. "Listen. I think the best thing would be for you to come with us to Atlanta. We'll set you up in a lab."

"Oh, good. A secret lab? Where I'll be chained to the floor, required to work sixteen hours a day, food fed to me through a hole in a door—"

"Hey. We're the good guys, remember?" Logan frowned. "What's going on here?"

Okay, she was being a little rough on them. Of course she'd help develop a new vaccine. But, "I can't help but feel like I've been lied to. I thought . . . I didn't know that the lab I worked for is a secret defense department facility."

"It's not. It's a private lab—really. But when we found the smallpox, we didn't know where to take it, so we brought it to Project 534. Which we knew about because White used to sit on the board."

"You don't own it?"

"No. It's owned by a private investor in Montana. I've just stepped in as the liaison to the board."

"To the president."

He nodded. "There will be no dungeons, whips, chains, or bread and water, Dr. Price."

"What's our timeline here? How close are you guys to finding the location of the attack?" she asked.

"We have a guy working undercover." Logan put his hand on Pete's shoulder. "And Pete needs to get going."

At his words, Pete looked upstairs to where Noemi was holed up.

Yeah, well, Tae might do the same if she discovered her father was still alive and keeping it from her. Talk about a betrayal.

On the stove, the water was boiling, steam rising out from the lid. Ranger seemed to know his way around the stove without looking as he grabbed a hot pad, lifted the lid, and slid in the noodles. Added oil to the water.

Ranger had already combined the sauces with the meat, and now pulled off fresh basil leaves from a plant Echo had brought over.

"Why won't the current vaccine work?" Dodge asked. "We were all vaccinated as kids."

"I doubt that. Vaccines for smallpox stopped being compulsory in the United States in 1971," Tae said. "The last endemic case occurred in Somalia in 1977." She got up, unable to stop herself, went around the island, grabbed a knife, and began to slice a loaf of French bread. "Only two laboratories have stocks of the smallpox virus. The CDC in Atlanta, Georgia, and VECTOR in Koltsovo, Russia."

Yes, just as she'd thought, her words shut everyone down. She finished slicing the bread. "VECTOR—the State Research Center for Virology and Biotechnology—said themselves, years ago, 'All you need is a sick fanatic to get to a populated place.'" She put the bread in a basket. "We are completely unprepared for the virus to reach American shores."

"We think the Russian mob wants Tae and her vaccine so that when they release the smallpox into our population, they can hold us hostage for the cure," Pete said.

"Well, I've lost my appetite," Barry said from the recliner. So, not sleeping.

"If the CDC has stockpiles, then they have vaccines too." Ranger found a serving bowl and set it on the counter next to the stove.

"Yes, they do. But what if they don't work? What if this strain is too virulent?" Logan slid off the stool and took the plates from Colt, who'd retrieved them from the cupboard.

Tae checked on the spaghetti, stirring it to loosen the strands. "Five more minutes."

She looked at Logan. "Then we start over until we get it right. Except, now we'll have to start over completely."

"Surely you backed up your research on your computer," Logan said as he set the table.

"Yes . . . to the servers in the lab."

"The ones that burned in the explosion."

She gave Logan a grim look.

"How long will it take to re-create it?" Logan returned to the counter for the glasses.

"I don't know. Without my notes, we'll be starting over." She picked up the pot to drain the water. Steam rose from the colander in the sink. "Which means that anyone can do it."

"No, Dr. Price. You're the only one who knows what's happening. If we widen the field of researchers, we risk the threat getting out."

Yeah, if the world felt like she did now . . . maybe it was better to keep it quiet. "It would help to have a strain of the actual virus instead of one we synthesize. But my guess is that also burned up in the lab."

She plated the noodles, then added butter.

"Yes, it did." Logan had returned to the counter. "Listen. We can protect you."

"Can you?" She stepped back. "Because . . ." She closed her eyes. Took a breath. It didn't matter if they could or not. *I'm going to make the world a better place.* Perfect. Her father picked now to wander into her head. She opened her eyes, turned, and was about to nod when Colt picked up her fight.

"I think that's enough, Logan. Give her some time."

"We don't have time," Logan said quietly and looked at her.

Fine. And it wasn't even a question, really. She just wanted a second or two to breathe. "Set up the lab. I'll be there when it's ready."

But Logan's ominous words sat in Tae's head throughout dinner, and even after, as Pete and Logan left.

She noticed the stiff goodbye that Noemi gave her father.

And then the house was weirdly back to seminormal. Her, washing dishes with Noemi. Echo on her way home. Ranger, Dodge, and Colt outside, trying to deal with the char of the plane on the runway. Barry listening to a book on tape, probably his Bible.

"I can't believe that this morning, we were almost blown up." She handed a plate to Noemi. "You okay?"

She took the plate, dried it. "I should be freaking out, but . . . I don't know. Despite being held captive in Nigeria, being kidnapped, and now blown up, it all pales in comparison to knowing that my father is not dead."

"Mm-hmm."

"I mean, of course I knew he could die. He was a SEAL. We lived with that possibility every day, so when it happened, I believed it. We had a funeral for him. And I grieved him and moved on with my life." She put the plate away. "I missed him, but . . ." She reached for another plate. "I just can't believe that he would lie to me. And not just any lie—a colossal lie."

"Maybe he didn't want to drag you into danger."

She put that plate away. "It sorta feels selfish."

Tae attacked the serving plate. "Or selfless. After all, he gave up knowing you too."

109

Noemi looked at her. "I guess."

Tae handed her the serving plate. "My father was in the military too. I remember thinking that it wasn't fair that he had to leave. He had a thriving practice in New York City, and after the Towers fell, he just decided to join the Navy. It killed my mother, and me. He told me to be brave, but all I did was worry about him. And then, of course, our worst nightmares came true. He died. We never found out how."

"I'm sorry. But I don't understand. Are you saying that thinking he was dead was better?"

"No. I'm saying that in his mind, he thought it was better than you worrying. He thought he was protecting you." Tae let the soapy water out of the sink.

"People do stupid things in the name of protecting others. Lying is in the category of stupid. And selfish."

Tae wiped the island. Outside, the sun hung low over the faraway mountains, turning the land a deep purple, the sky hues of light blue and deep pink.

The sun was falling, but never completely gone, just hiding behind the mountains.

She stilled.

Drew in a breath. *Zoey had vanished.* Maybe for everyone else, but Tae knew her—roomed with her in college, graduate school, and then worked with her for the past three years.

She knew where Zoey went when life swept over her.

"At least he said goodbye this time," Noemi said, still talking about her father. "So maybe he won't go dying on me again."

Tae returned to the sink. Looked at her. "Noemi, are you okay with how you left things with your father?"

Noemi's eyes filled. "It doesn't matter. I was always an afterthought to him. And now, he's already dead to me."

Tae stared at her as Noemi hung up the towel and walked away.

Wow. But she could spot hurt talking. Didn't sound all that different from her own words about her mother.

Her gaze fell on Colt standing outside, talking with his brothers. He stood with his arms folded across his chest, legs planted, nodding to something Dodge was saying as he gestured with his hands. The memory of him lying on the glacier yesterday, struggling for air, seemed so distant from the solid, brave, capable man who'd sat with her on the deck today, trying to help her sort out her life.

"Ranger says he and his brothers haven't been together for ten years." Noemi had walked back up to her. "Apparently, they had an epic fight that tore them apart."

"According to Colt, it was an actual fight. He ended up in the hospital."

111

"Yeah. I guess it was over Echo, but she says it was really about them losing their mother," Noemi said.

"They look pretty young in that family picture on the mantel without their mother."

"I think they were six. Larke was eight. So yes, pretty young. According to Ranger, Colt was with her when she died."

Oh, Colt. "Sad to grow up without a parent."

"Yes," Noemi said, also staring out the window. "You like him, don't you."

More of a statement than a question. "He's interesting. Carries a lot of secrets behind those brown eyes."

Noemi was quiet. Tae glanced at her, and she was smiling.

"What? Okay, fine, yes, I like him. But you heard my story. The last thing I want is to get into another relationship, especially one that is doomed."

"Doomed?"

She gestured to Colt. "He's not sticking around. As soon as he's healed up, he's heading back to Jones, Inc. And I'm on my way to Atlanta, apparently."

"Oh," Noemi said. "I guess that makes sense." She glanced out the window again. "It might be the last time they're all together for a while."

Colt's words rose inside her. *"Whatever it is, you're not doing it alone."*

She knew what he said. But he'd also said he was glad to be back with his brothers. To have a fresh start. And she saw it playing out as Colt now laughed, his face lighting up at something Ranger said. He too was laughing.

Only men who understood war could laugh in the face of their horrific day.

Colt needed his brothers, and apparently, they needed him.

She wasn't going to take him away from that.

Besides . . . a glance at Barry, yes, now asleep in the recliner, and the memory of Noemi's pain at saying goodbye to her father, again, even if she didn't want to admit that . . . no, Tae didn't want to put Colt in that position.

The family had just found their footing again. She wasn't going to rip it out from under them.

She'd miss this world. Miss the quiet.

Miss Colt. The thought unsettled her. But he'd been her friend. A hot, way-too-charming friend, but just a friend. Who made her feel safe. So maybe that was what she'd miss.

Time to go.

Find Zoey.

Save the world.

Without Colt.

Then no one else would get hurt.

Something didn't feel right. It wasn't the nagging tightness in his chest that just couldn't seem to release, despite the thousand times Colt told himself that he wasn't hanging over a cliff, or even taking the shot that might have killed them all.

Sure, he might attribute it to last night's conversation with the president's men, Sutton and Thorne, including Tae's words, which really should have everyone scared to their last wit.

The conversation sat in his head, his chest, his soul. *"All you need is a sick fanatic to get to a populated place. We are completely unprepared for the virus to reach American shores."*

He'd met quite a few sick fanatics over the past ten years working as the tip of the spear for his country, and off the books for Jones, Inc.

So yeah, that could account for the buzz under his skin, the way he stretched out that night behind his room-darkening drapes, staring at the slit of light in the ceiling.

It might even have been his conversation yesterday with Tae, on the deck, her story about losing her father at the age of ten, the pain that still edged her voice. And he wouldn't easily forget the way she'd looked at him when he'd told her that he was in this with her.

Had surprised himself, really, too. Because he'd seen himself heading back to Jones, Inc. and his next assignment as soon as his body stopped hurting.

Although, he'd long ago learned to live with pain, on the inside and out.

But something about watching Tae face her regrets, her failures, had tugged at something inside. And listening to Thorne berate her yesterday afternoon had only solidified the urge to protect her.

Colt punched his pillow, rolled over. His shoulders still ached a little from when he'd held both of them up over the glacier edge. And that only brought the memory of Tae tucked into his arms, so to speak.

Not the first time either. With very little effort he could conjure up the moment when, a few weeks ago, he'd found her a little rattled—right after she'd seen the pictures of the dead Nigerian villagers that Colt and Noemi had found. He got why that undid her now.

Then, he just thought the images were too vivid. He could still hear himself, *"Don't worry. Whoever was after Noemi isn't going to find us here. You're safe."*

Oh brother. He rolled back and put his arm over his eyes to shut out the light.

Bad idea, because at once, the old demons edged in. Nuggsy laughing as he cleaned his weapon, his face hidden in the darkness, just the whites of his eyes showing across the fire ring, the savanna around them alive with birds calling, the washboard rattle of insects, the occasional roar of a lion that would raise the hair on all their necks.

Or Elvis humming through the coms "Are You Lonesome Tonight?" as they lay in the bush, sweating in ghillie suits or even just dug into sniper nests watching the camp of an Abu Nidal terrorist leader.

The worst was Vader, whose deep voice still sounded in Colt's ears when he let down his guard. *"Sam, they got the drop on us!"*

Okay, now he was getting up. Colt pushed himself off his twin bed, his bare feet cool on the floor. He wore pajama bottoms but went bare chested as he walked out into the hallway, then downstairs.

The sun cascaded into the room in shades of gold and pink and blue. He could go for some of Tae's spaghetti from last night. In fact, he half expected her to be in the kitchen, making an omelet or bacon or coffee or . . .

Wow, he'd slid into the warm expectation of her in his life, in his world—albeit temporary—way too easily. Especially for a guy who had purchased a new duffel bag after leaving his in Africa.

He started to boil water and filled up the French press his father used to make coffee, then walked to the window to stare out at Denali. *"Dad was afraid you were going to actually attach to one of the climbing crews and head up the mountain."* Dodge's voice found him. Nudged him.

Maybe he always had one foot out the door, even from the beginning.

His gaze tracked to the wreckage of Dodge's beloved Piper, now pushed to the edge of the tarmac. They'd used the plow attached to the pickup and the four-wheeler to remove all the debris, working late after dinner. He hadn't realized how late until he went inside and discovered the house quiet.

Tae had stopped by on her way down to her cabin, but he'd been on the four-wheeler and lifted a hand to her. Something about her expression, the way her gaze lingered on him . . .

That was it. The thing irking him.

She wore a sad, almost regretful expression as if . . .

No. She wouldn't leave without him. Not after everything they'd been through. Everything he'd said.

But it wouldn't be the first time his instincts lied to him.

The water had started to boil, and he returned to the counter, poured the coffee into the French press and waited for it to steep.

"That smells good." His father's voice rose from the recliner.

"Have you been there all night?" Colt said, walking over to him.

"Sleep better sitting up," his old man said. "What's your excuse? It's five a.m."

"Daylight's burnin'," he said, and smiled at the

117

old phrase his father used to use to oust him from bed.

He expected a smile. Not a frown, the concern in his father's eyes. "I know about the nightmares, son."

Colt wanted to shrug off his words, to shake his head, offer a joke. But he had nothing as he stared at his old man, the fatigue lining his face, maybe even the pain.

He'd caused some of those lines, some of that pain, and . . . well, his nightmares started long before he led his team into an ambush.

"Tae—"

"Not just Tae. After you arrived, I sat by your bedside too."

"You know what I went through at the camp."

"No, actually, I don't. Noemi won't talk about it. Ranger filled me in a little. But what I know is enough to tell me that you live your life as if it doesn't matter to you."

Colt headed to the counter, to his coffee. "My life matters to me." But even to his own ears his words sounded tinny. He strained his coffee through the press, grabbed a mug, and poured it into the cup, black.

Behind him, his father went quiet.

He turned, took a sip. The caffeine hit his bones, fortified them.

Walking over to the fireplace, he stared at a picture of the family. Their mother was absent

118

in this photo, and it had always irked him a little that his dad chose this one to display.

The real last family photo was in his office, the one with their mother that last year she was with them. Colt had been five.

This photo, however, showed their family as he really remembered them. He, Ranger, and Dodge, three dark-haired boys, two with blue eyes, one with brown. Dodge stood with his hands behind his back, Ranger stood beside Larke, a smirk on his face, and then there was Colt. He wore his hat backwards, flashing two thumbs-up at the camera like an idiot.

Barry Kingston and his two amazing sons, a daughter, and one goofball.

"You've always lived your life a little on the edge of trouble, son," his father said. "Even then."

Colt turned. "It could end any moment. Why waste time thinking?" He meant it as a sort of joke, maybe, but his father gave him a solemn nod.

"I guess watching your mother die in front of you could do that to a kid."

Colt blinked at him. Then, "She didn't just die in front of me, Dad. She died *because* of me."

A beat, and then his dad opened his mouth, but Colt put up his hand. "No. I'm not a child anymore. I understand that she lived longer than we thought and that any day would be her last.

But as a six-year-old, when you ask your mom to play hide-and-seek and you jump on her off the sofa, thinking you're wrestling, and she goes down and then bleeds to death. Yeah, that sits in your head as your fault."

"Your mother wouldn't see it that way. I don't see it that way."

"It is what it is, Dad. I knew she was weak. You had taken us all aside and told us she couldn't roughhouse. But I . . . I was having fun, and I forgot myself."

"You were six. And she loved playing with you."

"I was me. I'm a troublemaker, always have been. The good part is that in combat I'm also the guy that does the stuff no one wants to."

"Like offer yourself up as tribute to distract the guards from an escape attempt."

Colt stared at his coffee. "It worked, didn't it? Ranger used Noemi's escape attempt to get into camp."

"You nearly died."

Colt looked up at him. "But it *worked*."

His father drew in a breath. "You're not less than, Colt. You're just as valuable as any of your brothers."

He didn't know why those words felt like fingers, deep in his chest. He swallowed, turned away. "Yeah, I know."

"I don't think so. I remember the fight. I

remember seeing Dodge. Seeing you. Only one of you ended up in the hospital."

Colt glanced at the picture. "That was my fault too."

"Did you even fight back?"

He raised a shoulder. "Enough."

"To make Dodge angrier."

He turned. "Listen. It's over. I apologized. He apologized. We made peace. Why are you digging this up?"

"Because I want you to stop telling yourself that you're not worth saving."

Colt's mouth opened, then closed. His jaw tightened. "You don't know what I've done."

"That's the devil talking. He accuses you to keep you from being the person you're supposed to be."

"Who am I supposed to be? Ranger? Dodge? I'm not those golden sons, okay?"

"Colt, you are just as amazing as Ranger and Dodge."

"Ah, Dad, you don't know—"

"But you *are* trapped."

He sighed. "How am I trapped?"

"You're trapped in guilt. And the devil wants you to believe you'll never be free."

"I'm free. Remember, I'm not in the military anymore." He winked, trying.

"That's not what I meant, Colt, and you know it. You're a mercenary, son."

Colt drew in a breath. "I'm not. I work security."

"You're a hired soldier, bargaining your life."

Okay, that was enough. "No. I'm not. I go into hot spots and keep people alive. Or try to." He walked over to the sink and poured his coffee out. Turned. "And sure, maybe I'm the guy who acts with his gut, but it's not because my life doesn't matter. It's that I see a way to do something—and then I do it."

"What were you thinking?" Ranger's words yesterday morning, as he stood almost right in this place, came back at him.

Colt scrubbed a hand through his hair. "I'm not saying that I don't make mistakes. Too many, actually. But it's the way I'm built. Keep moving. Don't look back."

"Don't come home?"

Colt braced his hands on the island, hung his head, closed his eyes. Took a breath. And found the truth. "I don't belong here. I haven't for years."

Silence.

He lifted his head. His father had stood up. He walked to the island. Met Colt's eyes.

"You've always belonged here. But until you forgive yourself, you're going to keep running, going to keep believing that you're trouble. Until you let God tell you how much he loves you, how much he has done for you, you'll believe you're not worth saving."

He stared at his father. Took a breath. "Maybe I'm not."

Silence stretched between them. A heartbeat. Two.

"No one is beyond God's love," his father said. Then he sighed. "It's the same thing I told Tae this morning when she asked me for the keys to the truck. But she's a lot like you, Colt. She's got it in her head that she needs to go it alone."

What? "Wait, you *gave* her the keys?"

"She'll leave the truck at the airport and the key with Sylvie at the desk."

Colt took a step back. "You know she's not coming back, right?"

"I do."

Colt stared at him. "Why did you let her go?"

"She's not a prisoner."

"She's in danger!" Colt shook his head, rounding the counter.

"You don't have to go after her, son."

Colt stopped at the stairs. "Yes, Dad. Actually, I do."

FIVE

This might have been Tae's worst decision yet. And she'd made some doozies recently. Like dating a terrorist. And probably, she shouldn't have spent a month lying to the Kingston family.

And there was the swift and brutal memory of nearly dying in a plane after insisting she grab her backpack.

But none of them compared, probably, to her escape from Alaska. Alone. Which at the time seemed like the only option that would keep Colt and his family safe.

Except it wasn't like she had a tracking beacon on her, and what if the Petrovs, or whoever, circled back around for another go at the family?

Or, better yet, maybe someone had followed her, although that might be tricky given the fact that Logan had left her with a new passport and a credit card to get her back home to Seattle.

Which she'd used because, hello, she wasn't some sort of Sydney Bristow action hero. Never wanted to be.

Her heroines were always the glasses-down-the-nose types. Okay, she had a small fantasy that someday she'd be as smart and crafty as Veronica Mars. But really, she wasn't brave or bold or even particularly tough.

Maybe, however, she'd left her stalkers in the dust—or on the tarmac as it may be—because she'd seen a plane overhead on her drive to Copper Mountain and driven straight to the airfield.

She'd hired a ride south with a pilot named Winter Starr. Caught an early flight out of Alaska and even beat the storm rolling in.

So she felt fairly smart, and was sort of banking on that as she got off the plane at the Seattle airport and caught a taxi to the Laurelhurst neighborhood.

She could almost smell the memories from her alma mater, the University of Washington, as they drove by the sprawling campus. Coffee from the Bean and Bagel, or the underground cavern where she and Zoey spent hours studying or dreaming up crazy research projects at the College Inn Pub, over cheesy bread and chili.

Yeah, they were dreamers, but in a way, she blamed Dr. Bella. The woman had put ideas in their heads.

Told them they could change the world.

Her memory of where her professor Dr. Bella George lived kicked in as soon as she drove past the Laurelhurst Park.

"Here." She pointed to a small brick house that overlooked the park, with sharp peaks, a rounded door, and lights glimmering out upon a shiny brick walk. Immaculate white roses climbed a trellis by the front stoop.

She could still picture Dr. Bella standing with her shears, clipping the roses, explaining gene splicing to Zoey and her as they weeded the garden.

Sly, that doctor. But it worked to stir in them the what-ifs.

Tae paid the driver and got out. She should have picked up a cell phone at the airport, maybe called ahead.

This was crazy. Zoey wouldn't hide here. Not if she knew it would put the professor in danger.

Then again, more often than not, even into their residency, Tae had found Zoey holed up in Dr. Bella's second-story guest room, with the slanted ceilings and old radiator heater, escaping after a two-day, nonstop shift.

After all, Dr. Bella had become like a mother to both of them.

She walked up the dark path. Okay, maybe not a mother. A quirky, outspoken aunt who spoke wisdom. Reminded Tae a little of the oracle in *The Matrix*, a movie both she and Zoey were crazy about.

Mostly Zoey, who subscribed to the conspiracy theories that suggested the world was controlled by one dark illuminati. Not Tae, but after the last month, she could admit that maybe Zoey wasn't as crazy as she sounded.

She stepped up to the door. Please let her not have brought the Russians to Dr. Bella's doorstep.

126

Okay, yes, now she sounded crazy.

She knocked.

Waited.

It had rained most of the day, and water dripped from the trees, the air still humid. She wouldn't be surprised if the sky wept again.

The door opened, light spilled out onto the stoop, and for a moment, time stopped.

Dr. Bella stood in the frame, her dark curly hair up in an orange head wrap, her brown eyes taking in Tae, head to toe, a quick assessment of her health. She wore a green shirt, black pants, and was probably just home from the university, or maybe the hospital. Tae had taken a late flight, but she guessed the hour after eight.

"Taylor, is that you?"

She nodded, offered a smile, but wrapped her arms around herself. She wore a flannel shirt, jeans, and Uggs—an acquisition from Larke's closet, donated to her by the Kingston family. She'd never been a flannel girl.

Until lately.

"I'm sorry to disturb you so late."

Dr. Bella had peeked her head out a bit, looked down the street, then practically forced her inside. Closed the door.

Then the woman turned and, just like that, pulled Tae into her arms. "Oh, girl. Girl. Where have you been?" Her voice shook, and Tae, well, she simply held on.

She hadn't realized . . . hadn't— Her chest tightened, her eyes filling. "Sorry."

Dr. Bella pushed her back, held her arms with her strong hands. "We thought you were dead."

Oh.

Dr. Bella's mouth tightened, as if she might be trying not to cry. Looked her up and down again. "You look okay." She took Tae's face in her hands, examined her eyes. "Tired though."

"I'm fine." Now. Probably she shouldn't mention the events of the past three months.

Dr. Bella dropped her hands, fixing them on her hips instead. "Where have you been? We've been out of our minds with worry."

We? "Is Zoey here?"

An indrawn breath, the dart of her eyes. Then, a quick shake of her head. "No."

Tae didn't know why that simple word finally pushed tears out, down her cheeks. "I was hoping—"

"Oh, sweetie, come with me." Dr. Bella took Tae's hand and led her through her house, past the comfy living room with the ornate oak fireplace, the clean white furniture, to the kitchen. Here, Tae had spent more hours than she could count at the granite island, listening to Dr. Bella explain tissue resident memory T-cell research or how pathogenic microorganisms cause disease, while she cooked up one of her famous omelets.

"Sit," Dr. Bella said and pushed her down onto

the bench in the kitchen nook. Then she walked over to her island and picked up the remote for the flat-screen that hung on the opposite wall and turned it on.

The television landed on some rerun of *Grey's Anatomy*, and Dr. Bella turned it up, then came over and slid onto the bench. "You two have landed in some kind of trouble, haven't you?"

This was weird, almost as if— Tae lowered her voice. "Do you think someone is listening to us?"

Dr. Bella leaned in. "Two men in suits visited me about a month ago asking if I had been in contact with either of you lately. Right after that lab you worked at burned to the ground. And right after you were both declared missing." She leaned back, raised an eyebrow. "Do you have a story to tell me, missy?"

"Yes."

"Does it involve you doing something illegal, because if it does"—she held up her hand—"I only want to know what I can do to help you get out of trouble."

"No."

"Okay. Well then, I'll make you something to eat."

"I'm not—"

"Yes, you are. I see those bags under your eyes, and you've lost weight. Honey, you are hungrier than I've ever seen you."

Huh. Maybe.

Dr. Bella got up and pulled some eggs from her refrigerator, along with ham, an onion, mushrooms, cheese, and butter.

It was like old times, almost like coming home to watch her whip up the omelet, the smells of frying ham and onions loosening what Tae hadn't realized was a tight band in her chest.

She settled her head on her arms, listening to the television drama that was in truth nothing like any hospital she'd ever worked in.

She never once had a tryst in some storage closet with a fellow intern. When would she have the time, energy, or for that matter, interest? A passing, one-time fling had never been on her bucket list. It seemed better to be alone than have her heart broken or to give herself away to a stranger.

Still, if she were to have a moment in a storage closet, it would probably be with—

Nope. They were just friends, and besides, she'd left Colt Kingston over two thousand miles away, in peace and safety.

Dr. Bella put a plate in front of her, the omelet glistening with butter, steaming, perfect, and, yes, the old professor was right.

She was ravenous.

The doctor handed her a fork, knife, and napkin, and a glass of orange juice. "Eat. Then talk."

But she couldn't really wait, so Tae started

halfway into finishing her omelet. "I developed a vaccine for an ancient strain of smallpox."

Dr. Bella leaned back, her mouth opening slightly. Then she folded her arms and smiled. "From Siberia."

"Yes, how did you—"

"There was a mention in an immunology journal a number of years back that researchers in Russia had found an ancient strain." She leaned forward. "But how did you get it?"

She had long finished her omelet before she finished the story of Sergei, the plane crash, her rescue by Dodge and Echo after a blizzard, the hypothermia, the month at Sky King Ranch, and finally her near death on the glacier and yesterday's attack at the house.

Somehow unraveling the events made her take a good look at it all. Maybe she sounded off her rocker, but the telling affirmed one thing.

She'd been right to leave Colt behind. Because all this was her job to fix. And he'd been through enough.

"I don't even know where to start asking questions," Dr. Bella said. "But here's the most important one. What will you do now?"

She sighed. "I don't know. I was hoping that Zoey would be here."

"Why?"

"Because computers can be hacked. Information stolen. But when you write it down, you remember. A wise professor taught me that."

A slow smile crept up Dr. Bella's face. "Yes. Zoey said the same thing, if I recall."

"She did. She also kept a journal. So I was hoping that maybe she still had it . . ." Tae finished off her orange juice. Set the glass back down. "But she's gone missing, so I don't know what I'll do. My old boss is setting up a lab in Atlanta, at the CDC, but without my notes—"

"After you disappeared, Zoey came to see me."

Tae stilled.

"She was afraid and she had no idea where you were. She thought maybe you'd been in on it."

"In on *what?*"

Dr. Bella lowered her voice. "You left town right after your colleague was in that car crash. Zoey thought you were in trouble. She said you came to her with some theory that your coworker had been murdered."

"She's into all sorts of conspiracy stories. I thought she'd believe me."

"She did. At least, by the time you went missing. She came here the night of the fire."

A beat.

Another.

"Is she still here?"

Dr. Bella was still considering her. "Are you alone?"

Tae nodded.

"I wish you weren't. I wish you had someone watching your back."

Oh, well . . .

"You were always so stubborn. Driven. One of my best students. But you have this fear of letting people into your life, Taylor."

"You're in my life. And Zoey—"

"I'm your professor. And yes, I know you trust Zoey, but count on your hand how many other people you can depend on."

"You met my mother."

"I did. And I understand how, at a young age, you had to fend for yourself. But this is not a good MO."

She sighed. "I know." Her admission surprised her a little, but the doctor's words had slid in, rattled free the memory of the last month.

Dinner with Colt and his father, and then his brothers when they all arrived home.

Board games late into the night, or binge-watching the *Bourne* series with Colt, as he recuperated.

"Flo, this food is delicious."

Her eyes burned. "I just don't want anyone getting hurt because of me."

"It's not your fault evil exists in the world, and you're not going to stop it by hiding. You or Zoey."

She looked at Dr. Bella. "She's alive."

A nod.

"And you know where she is."

Another nod. "And so do you. Think, Taylor." She met her eyes.

"Your—"

"Shh." Dr. Bella put a finger to her mouth. "Just in case."

"Thank you," she whispered.

"You're one of the bravest people I know." She got up and embraced Tae. "I fully expect you to save the world."

Well. "I'll try."

Dr. Bella held her at arm's length. "Okay, do you need a ride somewhere?"

Outside, the rain had started again, pattering on the window. "I'm going back to my houseboat."

"Are you sure that's safe?"

"Whoever is after me thinks I'm in Alaska. Hopefully. I need my clothes, my car, money, a shower, and a night's sleep in my own bed."

"You can hide in the back seat of my Prius, and I'll drop you near the docks, a couple blocks away."

"Are you sure? I don't want—"

"I'm already involved. Let me help you." She gave her a look.

Fine.

Ten minutes later she huddled, curled up on the back seat, while Dr. Bella blasted the heat. Lights glittered on the surface of the sunroof, and Tae imagined the route, down 4th Street to Highway 5, over the bridge, and into Portage Bay. Off the highway at Hamlin, then to East Roanoke. "Let me off at the park. I'll walk from there."

The car pulled over and in the soft light of the dash, Dr. Bella turned. "Be careful. And if you need anything—"

"I know." She grabbed her friend's hand in the darkness. "Thank you."

"Peace."

Tae opened the door and crept out, hustled over to the shadows, and hid as the car sped away.

She waited, wet and cold, as the wind caught her, then ducked her head and half ran, half stalked down the street.

The light over her dock entrance had her waging a short debate, but she stepped up, keyed in her code, and the metal gate clicked open.

She pushed through, secured it, and then headed down the row. Her home sat last at the dock, just the lake beyond for the best view. Five houseboats, two on one side, three on the other, including hers, each one a little different. She hustled past Mulroney's beautiful three-story home, larger than many on the mainland, with their masted schooner tied up at the back. And the one-level barge turned home owned by a couple of entrepreneurs who ran a local kayak shop. Past the ranch house that looked like it should be surrounded by grass, and across the dock from her moorage, all lit up like Christmas, Pip Bogart was sitting on his roof deck, probably smoking a joint by the smell that lingered in the air.

Avoiding lifting her hand in greeting, she opened the gate to the bridge to her deck, then pressed her thumb to the door lock.

Slipped inside.

Not until she heard the door click did she let out her breath.

Home. Down the hall, the sleek gray of her kitchen cabinets gleamed in the faint moonlight, and the smell of the oiled hardwood teak rose up, still rich. She toed off her boots and walked barefoot to her main room.

Despite the darkness, she knew every detail, from the quartz counters to the ice-blue hanging lights to the teal velour sofas and marbled black fireplace.

She half expected it to be tossed, some Russian thug having pawed through her belongings. Pushing her toes into her plush rug, she stared out into the lake where the lights of Seattle glittered on the water.

Calm down. She was safe. And so was Zoey. And tomorrow she'd take a drive into the mountains and restart her research.

Save the world, as Dr. Bella had said.

"Whatever it is, you're not doing it alone." Yes, Colt's voice crept into her head, and a pang of guilt—or maybe simply the strange ache of missing him—hit her chest.

But this was better, for both of them. Because despite her resolve, she had fallen way too easily for Sergei, simply because he paid her a little attention.

What would happen to her heart with the full-out protection of Colt Kingston?

Sorry, Colt.

Probably, by now, he had recovered from her non-goodbye escape and realized that he was better off without her. Free to mend in Alaska, and then get back to his dangerous life, without any complications.

She went upstairs, turned on the shower, and closed the blinds in her bedroom. Turned on the light.

Yes, also untouched. Her white comforter lay on her bed, the teal pillows perfectly arranged. The book she'd been reading on her bedside. She went to her closet—an entire room, but she lived by herself, after all—and found a pair of pajamas, her thick robe, and slippers.

Steam filled her bathroom, and she left her jeans and Larke's flannel on the bathroom floor and got in, turning her side jets on high, the waterfall fixture like a rainforest shower.

Yes, she'd missed this. Her easy, simple, uncomplicated, focused life.

One void of assassins, thugs, and global terrorist plots.

She washed her hair, shaved her legs, then got

out and pulled on her pajamas and bathrobe, put her hair up in a towel.

She was brushing her teeth when she heard a thump. Turned off the water and listened.

Nothing. So maybe it had been a wave, banging her boat against the dock, although she had pretty strong ballasts for that.

Still, all seemed quiet, so she went downstairs, brewed a cup of hot cocoa, then headed back upstairs, then outside to her deck and up the final stairs to her rooftop.

Maybe she wouldn't flip on the lights around the deck quite yet. She didn't need Pip calling out to her.

Instead, she sank down on one of her loungers, the one that overlooked the city, and curled her feet up under her bathrobe. Blew on her hot cocoa, took a sip, then set it down and pulled off her head towel. Shook out her hair to air dry.

It wasn't Alaska, but maybe she should stop comparing. Alaska was in her rearview mirror.

A shuffle, and she jerked, but a hand slipped around her mouth. "Don't scream."

What if Tae had come and gone and this time she vanished for good?

That thought had possessed most of Colt's brain the entire time he trolled Lake Union in the darkness, searching for her houseboat.

Or worse, what if she'd been taken at Sea-Tac by one of Petrov's hired thugs and—

Nope. He wouldn't go there. Wouldn't let the worry take root, find his bones. But what if—

Aw, he hadn't a hope of not imagining a dozen brutal outcomes.

And his father had actually suggested that he not go after her. But he'd made promises.

Besides, Tae . . . needed him.

Maybe this was a stupid idea. What his father said about Colt living as if his life didn't matter to him might be true. But only because some lives mattered more.

Like Tae's.

Colt didn't want to take a good look at any reasons but the obvious—she had the ability to manufacture a vaccine that the world just might need.

Please, no. But if it came to that, he would make sure she was safe to do her job.

He passed what he thought might be her houseboat twice. There weren't a lot of moorings on the east side. At least, not that fit her description of a third-story deck and a glass wall that overlooked the water. Colt had narrowed it down to three possibilities when he spotted a light flicking on in his top choice, the houseboat moored at the end of the northernmost dock.

A sliver of light through the blinds arrowed out onto the water and drew him to her dock.

Someone was lighting up a little reefer from the scent in the air. He tied up his motorboat, having cut the motor well away from the dock, letting the momentum draw him in. Then he waited in the shadows until Reefer Man went inside, turning off his deck light.

Colt sneaked aboard her boat. Security was a joke, and another good reason for him packing his duffel—not much to pack, really—and talking Dodge into flying him to Anchorage to catch the late afternoon flight. Would have gotten here earlier, but his flight had routed to Portland because of the storm. Instead of waiting for the hopper back to Seattle, he'd rented a car and driven the one hundred and seventy-five miles north.

He'd rented a boat off an app on his phone as he drove north, met the owner at a private dock, and paid extra to have it overnight. If he didn't find her by morning, he would call in his brothers. Maybe even Fraser and the guys from Jones, Inc.

Colt climbed her spiral staircase, then stepped out onto the upper deck, nearly knocking over one of many plants in huge containers that outlined the deck area.

She hadn't been kidding. Nice boat. And the view—sure, he could get used to this. If he wasn't a guy who lived out of a duffel.

Movement had him slipping into the shadows, and then Tae walked out onto the deck wearing— oh, she had to be kidding—a *bathrobe?*

It stunned him for so long that she'd sat down and pulled off her head towel before he'd realized that he was going to really scare her.

And across the way, Reefer Man had stepped back out onto his deck.

So, no cops.

Colt crouched, crept over to her, and she still hadn't turned around so—sorry, Tae—he put his hand over her mouth, pulled her against him and leaned down to her ear. "Don't scream."

It didn't work. She pulled his thumb, down and out, twisting his wrist, turning. Then she swung at him with everything inside her.

He dodged it but, "Okay, I'm impressed."

She backed away, stumbled, and fell over the lounger.

"Oh." He reached out for her. "Are you—"

"Get away from me!" She slapped at his outstretched hand.

"Tae. It's me. Colt."

Her chest rose and fell as if she might be trying to catch her breath.

"Tae—"

"I know who you are, for Pete's sake. Can't you just knock on the front door like a normal person?" She found her feet now and looked past him. Raised a hand. "Hey, Pip."

"Everything okay over there, TaeBay?"

TaeBay?

"All good." She turned to Colt. "He's stoned

most of the time. I don't know why he calls me that."

"I don't care what he calls you. Is he going to call the *police?*"

She looked at Pip. Then shook her head, walked over to Colt, palmed his cheeks, and—

Kissed him?

What?

It wasn't gentle, or particularly welcoming, but the kiss lasted long enough for him to catch up and wrap an arm around her. For his heartbeat to stop, for him to taste her, smell the freshness of her, for his hand to reach up and curl around her neck, tangle into her wet hair.

Well, *okay*—

She broke away. Pressed her hands on his shoulders. "That's good."

Yes, yes it was.

But just like that, she stepped back from him, leaving him a little reeling, his heart restarting, hard, against his chest.

What just happened?

"That should keep Pip from calling the cops."

He was still scrambling, and his voice turned a little rough. "I don't know. Do you normally kiss strange men on your deck?"

"Just shut up and come inside." She picked up her towel, waved at Pip again, then walked to her stairway.

Colt scrambled after her.

She was already to the second level, opening the door.

He stepped inside. Oh, her bedroom. Big white bed, the fragrance of a recent shower heavy in that room, the same as her scent. All soapy and lavender-smelling and—

"Keep walking, tough guy." She pointed to the door, but he turned and flipped the lock of the balcony door. "After you."

She rolled her eyes, but she walked past the second-floor sitting room, with the glass wall, then took the stairs down to the main floor.

He followed in the semidarkness, the lights of the lake and surrounding boats gleaming into the room.

She flicked on a light that hung over a plush gray rug that anchored a couple blue sofas. Orange pillows, a few blue lamps. Okay, he hadn't expected quite this much personality. But he didn't hate it.

Felt like he saw a piece of her soul.

"This is a great place, Tae."

"Research that can end global pandemics pays well." She was standing in the middle of the room, her arms around her. Now, she turned. Met his gaze, her blue eyes in his. "You scared me."

"You scared *me*." He didn't know where that came from. Maybe the thin edge of shock that remained after that kiss.

The taste of her lingered on his lips, and his

heartbeat still stuttered a little. This woman—

"We had a deal. You go, I go."

"I didn't make you that deal."

He just blinked at her. "Yeah, you did."

"You said it. I just . . . I didn't want to fight with you." Her mouth tightened. "But you shouldn't be here, Colt. I don't want you getting hurt."

"You don't want— Honey, like it or not, I'm in this with you."

"Since when?"

"Since wh— Since a couple of Russian assassins who had your picture on their phones lay siege to my house!"

His words bristled her, and she clenched her jaw. Looked away. "I'm sorry about that."

Okay, Colt, calm down. He knew better than this. Hadn't been the best interrogator on the team for his propensity to lose his cool. Mostly.

He was a doer, but he didn't lose his temper. Now, he took a breath. "I'm not . . . accusing you of anything. It's not your fault, but . . ." His hand dragged through his hair. "You can't just . . . *disappear,* Tae."

"I can." She looked back at him. "Disappearing is exactly what I should be doing."

"Not from me!"

His own tone shook him, and now her eyes widened. "Why? You don't owe me anything. I'm not your assignment."

He blinked at her. "I know."

"Then what possessed you to get on a plane and follow me down here?"

He opened his mouth. Closed it. Stared at her. Fine. "I don't know."

Her mouth tightened. She shook her head.

And in it, he saw her sitting by his bedside, worried about him or feeding him or just . . . there, when he woke from a nightmare or, worse, some deep, lingering pain.

"Maybe it's my turn."

"Your turn for what?"

"My turn to . . . listen. To care. To show up. And I happen to have—"

"A certain set of skills?" A smile tweaked her lips.

"Fine. Yes. A certain set of skills. But most of all, Tae, I know you're scared."

Her smile fell, replaced by the tight bud of her lips.

He couldn't stop himself from walking up to her. Hesitated a moment, then put his hands on her shoulders.

She met his eyes.

He blew out a breath, the rush to pull her to himself almost shaking through him.

But this was Tae. The woman who'd listened to his nightmares. The woman who'd cooked him dinner, played cards with him.

The woman that he'd called Flo because of her ability to help him claw his way out of the darkness, maybe even heal a little, inside.

He wasn't going to start something that he knew would only break both of them—well, certainly him—in the end.

So, "You can't be scared and do your job. Fear makes you focus on the past, or worry about the future, but it distracts you from what you need to do right now. Let me worry for you."

She swallowed.

He touched his forehead to hers. "I won't drop you."

Her shoulders rose and fell, and then she nodded. Stepped away. "But so help me, Colt, if you do something stupid and die—"

"I won't die. I can't guarantee I won't do something stupid."

She gave him a push, a smile, and he smiled back.

Okay. Good.

Friends.

He let the clench in his chest free. "What's next, doc?"

Maybe it was instinct, maybe he spotted something—a glimmer out on the water—maybe it was simply years of training but as she opened her mouth, every muscle tightened.

"Get down!"

He launched himself at her, pushing her down

and covering her body with his just as the glass wall shattered over them.

The glass pelleted them, but he was already scooping her up and pulling her behind the sofa with him.

Bullets chewed up her furniture, as a semi-automatic peppered the boat.

"Get behind the island!" He practically pushed her along the wood floor.

Her island, too, was taking damage. And he, without a weapon.

She had curled into a ball behind the island, but a stray bullet could find her spine, her head. He put an arm around her and pulled her hard against himself, shielding her. "Just stay down while I think!"

"We need to get off the boat!"

Yes. Given. "You got a car?"

"Yes. In the garage across the street."

"Keys?"

"In the car. The garage is locked."

"C'mon."

The shots had decimated the furniture, her walls, chipping away the island.

Sirens sounded in the background.

Way to go, Pip.

But they couldn't stay here, couldn't be taken into police protection, not without knowing how far and deep this went.

Colt hit his feet, pulled her up in front of him. "Run!"

Good girl, she took off down the hallway, toward the back of the boat. But with his sudden dark luck, someone would be waiting for them at the door, so he urged her up the stairs.

"Get to the deck!"

"What?" She scampered up the back stairs.

He hit the second story, and yes, spotted a man on the dock, stalking toward their boat.

"Only one way off this, honey," Colt said as he pushed her to the top deck. The shooting had stopped. Out in the cool, black water, the shooter lay in wait. But it was night and—

He turned and shucked off her bathrobe.

"Wait!"

He'd seen pajama bottoms and blew out a gust of quick relief at her being fully dressed. Flimsy, but at least she wasn't a beacon of white anymore.

He took her hand. "Hold on to me and don't let go."

"What?" Her eyes widened. "Colt."

"Let me worry for you." Then he took off, pulling her after him, all the way to the edge of the deck. Shots chipped at their footsteps. He lifted her over the railing. Joined her.

"Oh, Colt—"

"I got ya," he said, and then he jumped, taking her with him.

The water sucked them down, cold, shocking, but not as frigid as an Alaskan lake. He surfaced, kicking hard, still holding her hand.

"Please tell me you can swim," he said, spitting out water, pulling her toward his moored boat.

"Now you ask me," she said. She let him go, pulling hard through the water.

They reached the rental boat, and he climbed up on the ski deck. Shots hit the boat, ripped the fabric off the seats.

Aw, there went his security deposit.

"Stay down. Hold on to the deck. When I tell you, roll onto it, then slide into the boat."

"No. I'll get the lines."

He frowned, but she'd already jumped onto the back, reaching for the back mooring line.

Oh boy. But he rolled into the belly of the boat, crawled to the front, unhooked the line, then launched into the captain's seat. "C'mon, Tae!"

He reached for the ignition, cast a glance behind him.

She was scrambling over the padded back.

He turned over the motor just as he spotted a man running down the dock.

Please let this thing be fast.

He rammed down the throttle and the boat nearly leaped from the water, the momentum propelling him back against the seat.

A glance at Tae said she, too, had slammed into her seat.

"You okay?"

Shots sounded, but they vanished into the night.

She nodded, her eyes big, her hair glistening, shivering a little in her damp pajamas.

"Missed me, didn't ya?"

She shook her head. But she smiled.

No way was he letting her out of his sight.

SIX

Tac was drowning. Water filling her lungs, bursting them. Water over her head, her eyes, turning her vision black.

Water weighing her down as she flailed.

So much water, and she gasped for breath, dragging more water into her lungs.

Coughed. *Help!* Around her, the world was murky. She thought she spotted a light, far away, but even as she kicked in the water, reached out for it, the light blinked, distant, untouchable.

She was going to die.

No! She had more in her. More to give, more to live. She kicked harder, hit something, and felt herself shooting to the surface.

Kicked again.

Heard a grunt, breaking through the water, the light so much closer now.

"Tae!"

Breathe!

She gulped in a breath, broke through the surface.

"Tae!"

Hands pinned her, and she fought, breathing, kicking—

"Wake. *Up.*"

Her eyes opened.

What?

Her breaths came hard, even as her brain clicked in around her.

Not the ocean. Not drowning.

Colt stood over her, dressed in a T-shirt and jeans, his hair falling over his face, his brown eyes on her, thick with worry. "You had a nightmare."

Memory clicked in as she took in the room. Light streamed in through closed shades, over the bed and through the open door to the sitting room beyond. He'd grabbed them a suite at the Hyatt last night after outrunning—

"It was real."

"The dream?" His arms held hers, but now he released his grip, stepped back. A red welt bloomed on his face.

"Did I do that?"

"It's no biggie. You were pretty adamant about tearing your bed apart," Colt said, picking up a pillow off the floor.

She lay back, staring at the ceiling, aware now of the sweat that slicked her body. "My poor houseboat."

He made a face as he nodded.

Shooting, a jump into the lake, speeding away in the boat, mooring at another dock, the run back to her garage, slipping in to steal her own car. All while she shivered in her soggy pajamas. Now she wore a bathrobe, the one that came with the hotel room.

He had on clean pants, his wet jeans and shirt hanging on the balcony railing outside. She shook away the memory of him stripping off his shirt last night in the hotel room.

She didn't need to see any of that. Although yes, she was painfully, perfectly aware of the fine outline of his upper body. Those back muscles, a few scars and chips from warfare, the solid outline of his chest as he turned, right before she shut the door.

Nope, didn't need any of that. Because it would only scrape up all of the dangerous parts. From her kissing him on the roof—why had she done that, of all things?—to him grabbing her hand, his *"Hold on to me and don't let go"* still soft in her mind.

Not hardly.

At least last night. Today . . .

Okay, today she might still want him around.

"What was the dream?" he said, walking back from the bathroom, holding a glass of water.

She sat up and took it. "Thanks." What she really needed was coffee. But the water loosened her parched throat, still raw from her pseudo drowning. Or maybe the screaming, both real and imagined. Wow. "It's an old dream. I've had it since I was a kid, shortly after my dad left. Then in college, when I was just . . . you know, overwhelmed."

"You sounded like you were choking. Scared the spit out of me."

She took another drink. "I was, sorta. It's always the same . . . I'm drowning, and I see a light at the surface, but I can't quite get to it. Except this time." Yeah, that change connected for a moment. "I broke the surface."

He met her gaze. "Really."

She set the cup down on the side table. "Don't get excited. It's probably my subconscious agreeing with me."

"About what?" He stepped back as she threw off the covers. Glanced away, probably worried about what he'd see.

Nothing here but a big fluffy dough girl in a bathrobe. But she cinched her belt tighter, just in case, as she got up. "That I'm tired of the bad guys winning. I'm tired of running and being afraid. I'm tired of hiding."

He looked back at her, folded his arms. "Atta girl."

"I'm not brave, Colt. But . . ." She looked at him. "I'm sorry I left without you. I'm not good at depending on other people. But I know I can depend on you."

He opened his mouth, closed it. Nodded. But something she couldn't place entered his eyes. "Want some coffee?"

"With every bone in my body."

His grin lit something inside her, and she had

154

the sense, again, of breaking free to the surface. Of breathing.

"I'm grabbing a shower. And then . . . we need to go to Shelly, Washington."

"Why?" His voice lifted as he walked to the next room, probably on his way to make coffee.

"Because . . . I think that's where my colleague Zoey is hiding."

A beat, during which she drew the covers back onto the bed, picked up the pillows off the floor. A glance into the living area of the next room indicated he'd already folded his bedding, a good soldier, and put it on the end of the sofa.

Or maybe he'd never gone to bed. She wouldn't put it past Colt to sit up all night, watching for bad guys.

Probably not, since they were ten stories up, with a glorious view of Lake Washington, but still . . .

If she hadn't been so exhausted, she too might have been up all night circling the wild events of their escape.

"How do you think they found me?" She had thrown back the curtains, but stepped away from the window, a sort of reflex. Silly.

"Maybe they had your boat staked out," he said, and she turned, saw him leaning against the frame of her bedroom door, his arms folded. In the daylight, he looked every bit a tough guy, dark scruff across his chin, his hair tousled, slightly wet and finger combed at best. He'd clearly showered in the other bathroom. Those arms thick with muscle against the white T-shirt. He wore his jeans low, faded, a little loose—probably had grabbed the first available pair, who knew if they were even his—and his feet were strangely bare.

He *looked* relaxed, but she'd met him. The man hadn't relaxed even when he was in a near coma after his beating, so . . .

Still, having him here made her breathe easier.

"Let me worry for you."

"Do you think they know where we are?"

He lifted a shoulder. She stilled, her hands on a decorative pillow.

Coming over to her, he eased the pillow from her hands. Tossed it on the bed. "I'll watch our six. You just figure out the next move."

He smelled good. Fresh. The impulse to put her hands on his chest, or around his neck, and simply hold on shook through her.

And just like that, she was back on the deck of her boat, impulsively kissing him. Not a real kiss. Just a decoy to throw off Pip, but . . . wow. He'd put his arm around her neck as if to hold her there, had nudged her lips open, as if hoping to deepen the kiss, and for a second, she nearly believed it. Believed that he wanted her as much as . . .

Nope. She wasn't going to be that stupid again, thank you.

Colt was simply good at adapting, improvising, and doing what he had to in order to get the job done.

Which was why, probably, he put his hands on her arms, met her eyes. "Coffee is perking. You shower, then we'll get breakfast and head to Shelly." Letting her go, he left the room, drawing the door closed behind him.

She let out her breath, doing an inner fist pump that she hadn't jumped into his arms, and headed to the bathroom.

Except, wait.

When she opened the bedroom door, he was standing at the window, staring out at the terrace that overlooked the lake. "How about clothes? I only have pajamas."

"This will be fun," he said and winked.

"Be kind."

He laughed and left the room.

Oh boy. But an hour later, with Tae clean, dressed in a new pair of leggings, a blue T-shirt, and an oversized pink flannel cardigan that she could probably sleep in forever, they headed through a coffee shop drive-through. He'd also picked up a pair of pink Vans, which she sorta liked. More than sorta.

"Here's your bagel," he said, handing her the toasted salmon, eggs, and chive bagel and coffee. He'd opted for a breakfast burrito, his coffee black.

It felt like a road trip as they left the city on US-97, east through the mountains, Colt at the wheel. He'd asked if she wanted to drive, but really, she wasn't a great driver, and frankly, she just wanted to think. So, no. He took the keys and helmed her cute Subaru like he was born behind the wheel.

"Radio?" she asked.

He lifted a shoulder. "Talk radio. Or maybe country?"

"No classical?"

He looked at her. "Really?"

"Beethoven for Bio Chem. Mozart for Immunology. Vivaldi for Microbiology and Virology."

"What about at the gym?"

"Benny Goodman."

"He wasn't classical."

"But he can get you moving. I was in the swing dance club."

"I'll bet," he said. "Between your residency shifts."

"And volunteering at our local clinic."

"Saving lives from the start."

She didn't know if he was kidding or not. "I just . . . yeah, maybe." She looked out the window.

His hand touched hers. "Hey. I was serious. It's clearly in your DNA."

She frowned.

"Your dad. Navy doctor?"

Huh. He remembered. "Yeah. I guess. He was a

doctor before he joined the Navy, but after 9/11, after he sat at the hospital, waiting for survivors that never came . . . it changed him. He signed up a few weeks later and was deployed shortly after that."

He nodded.

"It wasn't so much that he left but that I felt somehow selfish for wanting him to stay."

"That's a normal feeling."

"I didn't want to be brave or sacrificial or even patriotic. I just wanted my dad to be home." She wrapped the cardigan around her. Despite being June, the air still nipped as they climbed into the Cascade mountains. Around them the forest began to thicken, lush green, a tangle of mystery. Or maybe protection.

"And then when he died, I felt cheated. The Navy stayed silent—and I get that. He was probably doing something, I don't know, brave. Dangerous. But we never had any closure."

"I'm sorry. That's the military for you."

"Yeah, it's just . . . I felt so helpless. I finally had to resign myself to never knowing. But . . ."

"You sometimes find yourself in the ocean, underwater."

She glanced at him. "What's your recurring nightmare?"

He drew in a breath. They were climbing a hill, her four-cylinder car fighting to the top behind a hefty Silverado. "Who says I have one?"

"Please. I was there."

He was silent, maybe thinking of the times he'd woken to his own sweaty screams.

Finally, "Mine aren't dreams. They're memories."

They'd reached the apex of the mountain, and it opened for a moment. The view of the faraway peaks, a few still snow covered, at once brutal and breathtaking. The road fell below them, winding around passes, deeper into the wild.

"About three years ago, I was a part of a rescue operation of a journalist who'd been taken by the Abu Nidal Organization, a jihadist group in Sudan. We'd gotten human and drone intel that he was there, and we managed to roll up one of their soldiers. After some nudging, he gave us the location of the journalist, and we launched a strike to retrieve him."

Colt touched the brakes to avoid running up the backside of the truck. "We walked into an ambush. Four men on our twelve-man team were killed. Two were taken and tortured."

"Oh, Colt."

"Yeah. I'd been in on the interrogation . . ." His hands whitened on the steering wheel. "I can still hear Vader in my coms, the last thing he said to me. Shouting at me that we'd been ambushed."

She drew in a breath, hating the edge in his voice. "What happened?"

"I went back and . . . I got the right intel."

She glanced at him. He didn't look at her, but his jaw had tightened. What did that mean? "Colt—"

"We had some SEAL buddies in the area, so we cobbled together a rescue team and . . . we got them back. But I was pretty messed up after losing our guys, so . . . not the best place to be making wise battlefield decisions. I separated from the military with a discharge, no honors, but I escaped a *less than*." He lifted a shoulder.

"What did you do?"

"I was a little lost. Did some odd jobs for hire. Nothing illegal, just off the books. But I was no doubt headed the wrong direction when my buddy Fraser called me. He was on the team who pulled out our guys. He'd left the SEALs and offered me a job with a guy named Hamilton Jones. Private security. Seemed like the right call at the time. Probably still is. When this is all over, I'll head back to the team."

His words panged inside her, a sort of dread. But he was here now, and that's what mattered.

"Why don't you stick around Sky King Ranch? It seems like they could use your help."

He shook his head. "Dodge is there, and now Ranger. Besides, I wasn't made to be a part of all that."

But she'd seen him with his brothers, laughing. Hmm.

"Is that why you joined the Army?"

"I joined because . . . because it seemed the right thing at the time." He gave a laugh. "I'm starting to see a pattern. But from the beginning, I knew that I was different. Made for trouble, I guess."

That broke her heart a little. But in the back of her mind, she heard again his Orwell quote about brave men doing violence to keep others safe. Yes, that sounded very much like Colt.

She glanced at him, the way he drove, calmly, with one hand—a finger, really—on the wheel, capable around the twists and turns of the highway, as if yes, he'd been built for challenge. Trouble, as he put it.

A while later, they reached the bottom of the mountain, and a small town spread out before them. She checked the map. "An hour to Shelly."

"You're sure your friend has the information we need?"

"I'm staking everything on it. We roomed together in college and then started working for the same lab. She was as meticulous with her journal as I was. I just hope they haven't found her."

She hadn't quite meant to breathe aloud those fears.

He reached over and touched her hand, then took it, squeezed. And for now, right here, she hung on and squeezed it right back.

● ● ●

Colt probably held her hand a little longer than necessary, but . . . well, he counted it as a victory that Tae hadn't pulled away. The fact that she held on told him that maybe, please, she would stop running from him.

Although it seemed he'd convinced her to trust him because she had apologized at the hotel. And had been there when he returned with her clothing purchased at the gift shop. He didn't know sizes, so he'd opted for leggings and an oversized shirt, a pair of slip-on shoes.

Wow, she was cute in pink, but he ditched that thought as soon as it hit his mind because— hello—the last thing he needed was to start thinking about . . .

Well, about how amazing she smelled after her shower, but even before, standing in the sunlight of the hotel room, her beautiful blond hair rumpled from sleep, her body swallowed in the hotel bathrobe, her eyes too blue, trusting him.

Because in that terrifying moment, he saw himself reaching out, maybe grabbing her lapel to pull her to himself and taking up where they'd left off last night.

Him, diving into a kiss that had spark and heat and all sorts of fire simmering right under the surface. And in his wildest, forbidden dreams, she responded with a soft hum of delight, maybe curling her arms around his neck, pulling him close.

And that, right there, only led to everything that could blow up their friendship, the trust he'd built. Because he wasn't sticking around—he knew that in his soul. So taking her in his arms and letting up on the brakes even for a moment could land them someplace his body might want but his heart couldn't bear.

So he hadn't reached out for her, hadn't given in to the way she looked at him, her perfect lips, the smell of her, and instead, had walked out to the balcony to get some air.

Then she'd sent him on the mission for clothing and he'd grabbed hold with a hooah that had him nearly sprinting from the room.

Somehow over the past few hours, he'd gotten his head back in the game, despite the easiness of sitting in the car with her, listening to Beethoven or Mozart or whoever this was. He couldn't believe he'd actually told her about Sudan, but . . . yeah, that felt easy too. Or maybe just not as hard as he thought it would.

And she hadn't flinched either.

"I think the turnoff is ahead," she said now, looking at his phone. He'd let her hand go a while back. His gesture was meant to assure her but felt more like he might have been assuring himself. *"I just hope they haven't found her."*

Him too.

He'd kept an eye in the rearview mirror, but his six seemed clear. They'd descended the mountains into the foothills and now the road curved around beautiful Lake Shelly, clouds playing upon the blue waters.

"I've only been here a couple times. It's Dr. Bella's cabin, but we used to come out here in the summers," Tae said.

"Dr. Bella?"

"She was one of our adjunct professors at the university. Also a doctor of medical research, so Zoey and I were sort of glued to everything she said. She became a pseudo mom, or maybe an aunt, to both of us. My mom sort of lost interest in my life after she remarried."

"Really?"

"Her new husband was a widower and had three kids, all younger than me. I think she liked being a mom, getting a do-over."

They passed tiny homes overlooking the lake, the occasional million-dollar log cabin.

"My guess is that it's hard being a single mom," he said.

"It is. Especially when you feel like your life has been stolen from you." She sat up straighter. "This is the turn."

He took it, pulling onto another paved road that led back to yet another lake. "I wonder if that's how my mom felt. Dying of cancer so young. As if her life had been stolen from her."

The landscape had thinned here, not quite as lush. More rolling hills that, as they climbed, revealed the view of Wapato Lake. They passed farmhouses and A-frames. Some with pools, a few with vineyards.

"I'd definitely feel that way." She pointed to a turn onto a dirt road. "If I was dying, I'd spend every available moment with my family."

Her words tunneled in and sat there.

"She loved playing with you." He shook his father away. "Where are we going?"

"This road Y's up here. Take the left branch."

He cut left, through forest that deepened before it opened up to a beautiful two-story timber-framed cabin with a wraparound porch and a view of the crystalline-blue lake out back.

It looked uninhabited. No cars in sight. No towels hung over the railing.

He pulled into a gravel area and stopped. Put the car in park.

"I don't like the looks of this."

She glanced at him. "It's fine." And then she was the one to pat his arm as she reached for the door handle.

His gut was firing, but he saw nothing, and by the time he turned to tell her to sit tight, she was already out of the car.

He fought past the tightness in his chest and got out. "Tae, just stay here," he said, holding out his hand. "Let me go to the house."

"Zoey!" she called out, and he wanted to slap a hand over her mouth.

"Really? Let's just shoot off a flare and tell the thugs we're here. Maybe they can put out the bread and vodka, give us a hearty welcome."

"Colt. Seriously. Look at this place." She held out her hands to the towering aspens, the smell of pine and woods and . . . safety.

Okay, so maybe he was just listening to his overactive imagination. But the last thing he wanted was to walk into another ambush, get his people—namely Tae—killed.

"Could you just . . . stay put?"

She made a face, folded her arms. "Fine. Go . . . do your soldiery thing." She waved him forward.

He rolled his eyes. And again, wished he had a handgun. But he walked up to the house, climbed up to the deck, and peered into the window, doing his soldiery thing.

Floor-to-ceiling windows faced the lake, a tall stacked stone fireplace was dry and unused. An immaculate kitchen betrayed no sign of life.

He walked on the porch around to the back of the house, to the deck facing the lake.

The place was beautiful. Secluded. The perfect hideout. A few nearby houses edged the lakeshore, with a scattering of forest between them. On the far edge of the lake, the mountains crept in to form a zigzag horizon.

A grill, fire table, and Adirondack chairs sat on the deck. He turned, listened, the breeze hushing in the trees.

Then he smelled it—the faintest scent of charcoal, or maybe fire, from a recently used grill.

He walked over to the grill on Dr. Bella's deck. Opened the lid. Dirty, the scent of burgers laced into the grate.

Someone had recently cooked and—

"Colt?"

No— He turned, sprinted for the drive, that feeling in his chest firing.

No, *no*—

Yes. He bit back a word when he spotted Tae, standing with her hands up.

In front of her was a man holding a lever-action Henry shotgun. Lean, dressed in a pair of jeans and a button-down shirt, the sleeves rolled up. Midsixties, he looked like an old-time cop, maybe, with gray hair and keen eyes fixed on Tae.

He didn't *look* like a Russian assassin. Still.

"Hey!" Colt yelled. "Don't hurt her!"

The man's gaze skittered to Colt. "Stay there, son."

Colt skidded to a stop.

Maybe a local, thinking they were trespassing.

He put out his hands. "We don't want any trouble here. We're just looking for a friend."

"What friend?" the man asked, his voice low.

"Her name is Zoey. She was my colleague back in Seattle. This place"—Tae gestured toward the cabin—"belongs to a mutual friend."

Colt took a step off the porch, and the man

turned his weapon on him. Good. "We need to find her. It's—"

"A global emergency," Tae said.

Yes, well, not to put too fine a point on it, but . . . Colt nodded, hands still out. But he was counting his steps to the old man, trying to decide how fast his reflexes might be. It looked like the man could handle himself, but—

"Tae?"

The voice came from a path behind the man, and in a moment, a woman stepped out. Petite. Pretty. Dark hair in a ponytail and dressed in an oversized University of Washington sweatshirt. "Tae!"

She broke out in a run toward Tae, who opened her arms. "Zoey!"

The man lowered his weapon.

The women locked in an embrace that had both Colt and the man looking at each other.

"Jethro Darnell," the man said. "Neighbor. Zoey's been staying with me."

Colt had lowered his hands and now walked toward the man, eye on the gun. "Colt Kingston. Tae's been, um, staying with me."

Jethro held out his hand and Colt shook it.

Jethro gestured to the women. "Zoey thought Tae was dead."

"Tae thought the same."

"They're into something bad."

"You could say that."

Jethro looked at him. "Hungry?"

"I could eat."

"I have some fresh catch over at my place."

Colt eyed the gun. "Ever used that on anyone?"

"I have a couple stories." His gaze returned to the ladies.

Tae had let go of Zoey.

Zoey ran her hands over her cheeks. "When you disappeared, I didn't know what to do. First Faheem and then . . ."

"I know." Tae put her hands on Zoey's shoulders. "You did the right thing." She glanced at Colt, then back at Zoey. "Please tell me that you have your journal."

Zoey nodded, and even Colt wanted to grab her up in an embrace.

"Let's get you back to the cabin, and then you can tell us what's going on," Jethro said. He started down the path.

Colt didn't move. Gave Tae a look.

Zoey saw it. "Who are you?"

"He's a . . . friend," Tae said.

"Mm-hmm," Zoey said, her gaze perusing him. "He's better than Sergei."

Colt raised an eyebrow.

"What?" Zoey said. "I didn't trust him from the beginning. He was . . . smarmy."

"Thanks for saying something," Tae said. "He kidnapped me, tried to kill me. I had to crash a plane to get away from him."

Zoey's eyes widened. "Wow. When you break up with a guy, you really break up."

It took a second, but then Tae cracked a smile, laughed.

"Colt's brother rescued me. I've been staying on their ranch in Alaska, trying to figure out what happened," Tae said. "My journal was lost in the crash, but I thought maybe yours had survived." Her smile dimmed. "I was worried something might have happened to you. Colt's been helping me track you down."

Colt stepped up to her, his hand out. "Glad to see you're okay."

She took his hand. "Thanks for taking care of my best girl."

Okay, Colt liked her. "My pleasure."

Zoey grinned at him, then turned to Tae. "When the lab exploded, I knew something wasn't right. I tried to get ahold of you on your cruise, but the captain said you hadn't returned to the boat and . . . I freaked out. I went to Dr. Bella, and she sent me here. I met Jethro through his daughter, Raven, who was playing covers at a local bar and grill. Jethro owns it and when we found out we were neighbors, he told me to stay with him until we got this sorted." She glanced at the trail through the woods. "You can trust him. He's ex-military, no nonsense, and . . . well, you'll like him. C'mon."

She started down the path.

Tae took Colt's hand. "It'll be okay."

But his heart still pounded, his chest burning. Something wasn't . . . right.

Still, he nodded, then followed.

SEVEN

Probably, they were safe.

Colt could notch it down to DEFCON 3. Or maybe 4.

But the falling darkness had done nothing to ease the tension from his chest.

Apparently, however, he was the only one worried. Tae sat wrapped in a blanket on an Adirondack chair across from a flickering campfire, the stars overhead cast in a glittering array of glory. She held a cup of hot cocoa, her face illuminated by the flames, and, shoot, he had to keep averting his eyes or he'd lose his focus.

Which was on the forest around him, the dock that stretched out from the shore, even the grounds of Jethro's place.

He liked it here. The cabin was small and cedar-sided. It had a wraparound porch, was set back from the water and had a firepit in the yard. Chairs around the fire, a sliding door off the deck leading inside to a modest, dated kitchen, a family room with a fireplace, a couple overstuffed leather chairs, a worn leather sofa, a coffee table.

Colt wasn't sure where they'd end up tonight. Maybe he'd stay right here, in his own chair, watching. Waiting.

When they'd arrived at the house, Tae had

disappeared with Zoey downstairs—probably to fill her in—and Colt had found a chair at the round table in the kitchen.

Jethro cooked them up trout sandwiches. The smell of the fish fillets simmering in butter had nearly made Colt weep.

"I can spot a military man when I see one." Jethro had handed him a bottle of lemonade.

"Thanks." Colt spun off the cap. "Ex-Army." No need to go into his specialty.

"Sorry about that back there. Zoey's still pretty spooked. And Bella doesn't get many visitors, so—"

Colt held up a hand. "I get it. But I smelled the grill."

"Yeah, that was a bad choice. We used it last night. My tank was empty." He raised his lemonade to Colt. "Pretty sharp there, Soldier."

"What do you know about all this?"

Jethro slid the trout fillets onto open buns on a serving platter. "Just the basics. Zoey's a medical researcher."

He didn't elaborate, so maybe he didn't know. And Colt didn't fill him in. The fewer people who knew, the better, probably.

They'd eaten dinner, the four of them. The sandwich practically melted in his mouth.

"It's the shore lunch batter," Jethro said. "I use it on my fries down at the tavern too."

After dinner Jethro had asked Colt to collect

wood for the fire ring outside. Colt didn't mind. Gave him a chance to case out the surroundings as he gathered logs from the pile. He checked out the entrance to the house—a drive semisecluded by trees. Thankfully, near the lake, the brush was cleared to an expansive lawn.

Colt found Jethro constructing the fire with the supplies Colt had gathered.

"Get what you needed?" Jethro asked as he shoved an old newspaper, wadded up, under a tent of logs.

"Think so," Colt said. "Nice place. Remote."

"We had the brush cut back a couple years ago. Better view." He reached for the box of matches, which Colt handed over.

The fire lit on the paper, licked the kindling. A crunch of tires on the gravel had Colt turning. Jethro got up. "That's Raven, coming home from work."

"Raven?"

"My daughter. She's a singer. Had a gig at the Tav this evening." Jethro looked beyond him and lifted a hand.

Colt spotted a woman with long black hair walk into view. Pretty. Large gold hoop earrings, a printed T-shirt of a girl band—the Yankee Belles—cowboy boots, and a guitar case slung over her shoulder.

She walked up to Jethro, leaned up, and kissed his cheek. "Hey, Dad. Pick up another stray?" But she smiled at Colt, her blue eyes warm. "Raven Darnell. Welcome to the hideout."

He raised an eyebrow. "Colt Kingston."

"Raven—"

She turned to her dad. "What? You know it's true." She slung the guitar off her shoulder. "Got any grub left?"

"Trout sandwiches. There's a plate in the kitchen."

"You're my favorite chef," she said. She glanced at Colt. "I'll be back for your story." Then she headed inside.

"The hideout?" Colt said after the door closed.

Jethro shook his head. "A few years ago, we had a guy stay with us who ended up being, well, sort of a spy, I think. He brought some trouble to the house and Raven's been a little wary of our houseguests ever since, so expect the third degree."

"What kind of trouble?"

"Some Russian thug. Nothing we couldn't handle."

Colt stilled.

The door opened and laughter spilled out as Tae and Zoey came out, followed by Raven, holding a plate. Tae carried blankets, and Zoey a pan of s'more fixings.

But even as they sat by the fire, burning marshmallows, Colt couldn't get the words out of his head.

A Russian thug.

Maybe they weren't as safe as he thought.

Raven had spent most of the evening grilling them on their story. He had added as little as he could—yes, military, Army, was here as a friend.

Tae had filled her in on the rest—her history with Sergei, the attack at the house, and even the recent attack on her houseboat, which had rattled Zoey.

"Do you think they followed you here?"

"I hope not," Tae said and met Colt's eyes across the fire.

I will keep you safe. He put as much as he could into his gaze without saying the words aloud.

She drew her pink flannel cardigan, along with her blanket, around her as sparks bit into the sky.

He just about got up, went over to her, and pulled her into his arms.

Instead, Jethro got up, went to the porch, and picked up his shotgun. Handed it to Colt. "I'm assuming you know how to use this."

"I can figure it out," he said. "Thanks."

"Alaska, huh?" Raven said now as she slid a golden-brown marshmallow onto a graham cracker. "Ever see any bears?"

"He killed a bear," said Tae from the other side of the fire. "When he was fourteen."

"Really?" Raven wound a string of marsh-mallow around her finger, stuck it in her mouth.

"It was bothering our cattle," he said. "My father was gone—he's a bush pilot, so he was often gone—and my brothers were busy doing something else." He couldn't remember why he'd needed to go alone, really.

Just did.

"I tracked the animal into the bush, watched him for three days, and finally set up an ambush. Back then, I could shoot a bear that was a threat to our livestock, and this one had killed a couple beef cows. I brought him home on our four-wheeler."

"His father has the hide up in the guest room where I stayed," Tae said. "He tells the story of coming home to Colt being gone and being worried out of his mind." She looked at Colt. "And then Colt shows up with the bear, like some sort of frontier warrior."

"I hardly think my father said that," Colt said.

"No. That was my interpretation. But he was proud of you, despite his fear. I heard it in his voice."

Huh.

Jethro leaned forward, threw a log on the fire. Sparks jittered into the night sky. "Fourteen is pretty young to bag a bear."

"Were you scared?"

He looked at Raven. "Probably. I don't remember. I was all about getting the bear. I got plenty scared when I got home and saw my dad

178

though." He smiled, again meeting Tae's eyes.

She smiled back.

Heat shot through him, all the way to his core.

"How about you, Tae? Did you always want to be a doctor?" Raven finished off her s'more and reached for a napkin.

"She wanted to be a scientist," Zoey said. "When we were seniors in high school, she won the science fair with a GPS ring." She held up her hand. "I have one."

Tae looked at her. "You still have it?"

"You gave it to me when I went on that hike up Mount Washington a couple years ago. I never gave it back. And after you disappeared, I don't know. I just . . . it made me feel like you weren't gone."

She took it off and handed it to Tae.

Tae slipped it on her finger, turned it with her thumb. "It connects to your phone through simple software. I updated it to sync to Google Maps a few years ago."

Colt leaned forward. "How does it work?"

"Gimme your phone."

He pulled it out and walked it over to her, used his fingerprint to unlock it, and handed it over. Then he sat down on the arm of her chair.

She held up the phone, as if searching for bars. "I'll need to download the software from the cloud." Accessing his phone's browser, she went to a site and keyed in her password. In a moment, the app had downloaded, and she turned on his Bluetooth to sync it. Pulled up the map.

"There you go." She handed the phone back.

A red dot showed on a map, putting them smack-dab in the middle-of-nowhere Washington.

"Wow."

"The cool part is that it runs on a rechargeable battery. You can put it on any phone charging pad."

She pulled down the app's menu. "The app also tracks things like your sleep time, your heart rate, and your body temperature, and it can count your steps." The page landed on a graph. She looked at Zoey. "Looks like you haven't been sleeping well."

"Yeah, well, it's hard to sleep when you know the world is about to end."

"What?" Raven leaned forward. "Is that what this is about?"

"Calm down, Raven," Jethro said.

"The world isn't about to end," Colt said. "We just— There's a threat, and Zoey and Tae have developed a way to protect us."

"From what?"

Silence.

"A biological weapon," Colt said, "that we think Russia wants to deploy."

"Seriously?" Raven turned to her father. "What is it with you that attracts international drama?"

Jethro quirked an eyebrow.

She got up. "A couple years ago, a Russian

assassin tried to kill my dad. Turns out he was part of a plot to kill President White."

Colt stared at her. Then Jethro. "What?"

"It was nothing."

"It's something." He closed the app, pocketed the phone. "We should take off."

Tae hit her feet. "Where are we going to go, Colt?"

The question pinged inside him, along with the sudden rush of his heartbeat. "Fine. But we leave first thing in the morning."

"You'll stay here," Jethro said. "I have another guest room downstairs, and, Colt, you can have the sofa."

"I won't be sleeping."

Jethro gave him a nod as he rose from his chair. Then he put his arm around Raven. "It's time for some shut-eye."

"I'll never sleep again," she said, directing a look at Colt as she let Jethro lead her inside.

"Well, I'm exhausted," Zoey said. She got up. "I do feel safer with the bear killer around." She winked as she passed by Colt.

Colt reached for another log. Stood and dropped it on the fire.

Tae stared at him. "You're not seriously going to stay out here all night."

"You should go to bed. We don't know what tomorrow will bring. In Delta we had a rule— sleep when you can."

"I'm not leaving you out here." Her blue eyes glittered against the flames.

Oh, Tae. He was right back in the hotel room this morning, wanting to pull her to himself.

He backed away, the campfire between them. "Yes, you are. Go to bed."

She pulled the blanket around her. "I like it better out here with you."

He drew in a breath. Looked away.

"Colt?"

"I'm off my game around you, Tae." He shook his head, but the truth was out.

"Off your—"

"I can't protect when I . . ." He ground his jaw and looked at her. "When I want to kiss you."

She blinked, her mouth opening. "Oh."

"Don't look at me like that. You started it."

"What are you talking about?"

"The kiss? On your boat?" He roughed a hand over his mouth.

"I . . . that wasn't . . . I mean, I was trying to make Pip—" She grimaced. "Sorry. That was for show."

Oh, what an idiot— "Yes, I know. Of course. I just . . . it's the adrenaline, maybe. You're right." Oh boy.

"But—"

"I think you need to go to bed, Tae. Please."

She was silent beside him. "I never meant to hurt you."

"I'm not hurt, Tae." He frowned. "I don't get hurt." He chased his words with a laugh. "I never— You're just hot is all, and we sorta hit it off, so . . ." He lifted a shoulder. "I clearly was headed in the wrong direction. We're all good here." Oh, he just wanted to run. But he smiled. "Really."

She just stared at him, those eyes big, so he walked over to his chair, picked up the shotgun, then sat down, the gun over his knees. "I told you that I was in this with you. But I didn't . . . well, I didn't mean in your bed. I meant . . . I've got your back. Big difference."

And now he had the sense that he was making it all worse.

She nodded. "Thank you, Colt." But her voice emerged soft. And the look in her eyes, cloudy.

"You got it, Flo." He winked at her. "And tonight, stay on land, okay? You start screaming and I'm liable to shoot someone."

She opened her mouth. Closed it. Nodded. "Good night, Colt."

His throat thickened. "Good night."

Her feet swished through the grass, onto the deck.

The door closed.

He leaned his head back against the chair, then banged it a couple times.

What. A. Jerk.

But he sighed because, well, maybe he'd needed that little slap of reality.

Because his gut told him that something was out there, in the night, gunning for them.

And he wasn't going to miss it, no matter the cost.

This was why Tae really shouldn't be in a relationship—a romantic one, at least. She had absolutely no idea what just happened.

Just that, wow, somehow, she'd really hurt Colt, and she hadn't the faintest idea how.

She headed down the stairs of the cabin to the lower level. A cozy area with deep well windows and two bedrooms—one with the door closed, clearly Zoey's, and the other hers. With the cedar-lined walls and carpeted floor, the place was snug and safe and exactly what she needed after yesterday's crazy events.

Oh, who was she kidding? The last three months had been generally off the hook, which was why, maybe, she'd been a little defensive.

"Don't look at me like that. You started it."

The conversation replayed in her head as she entered the bedroom, flicked on the light, and shut the door.

"The kiss? On your boat?"

He'd looked at her then with such—accusation? She'd dove right into the first thing that came to mind.

No big deal.

"Sorry. That was for show."

She flopped on the bed and grabbed a pillow, putting it over her head, wanting to blot out the rest of the conversation, especially, *"I clearly was headed in the wrong direction. We're all good here."*

No, they weren't. Not headed in the wrong direction, and definitely not good.

Sure, relationships weren't her strong suit, but she'd have to be blind not to see the change in body language, hear the chill in his voice.

Only moments before, he'd said he wanted to kiss her.

She should have rushed him, thrown her arms around him, held on. Because that was exactly the direction she wanted to run.

Coward.

A knock tapped on her door, and she removed the pillow—probably shouldn't self-suffocate anyway—and looked over to see Zoey pop her head into her room. "I thought you'd be by the fire."

"Yeah, well . . ." She looked at the ceiling. "Apparently we're just friends."

"The way Colt looks at you doesn't seem like just friends."

"He's just concerned. It's in his blood."

Zoey sat on the bed, legs crossed, and grabbed another pillow. "Please. The man looks at you like you might be the answer to some forbidden question."

She shook away the heat in her chest. "It's just because I nursed him back to health after he was beaten."

"He was beaten?" Zoey's eyes widened.

"Yeah. He works security for a private contractor and was taken in Nigeria by the Boko Haram. They regularly beat him, played mind games with him, and threatened to execute him." She still remembered the bruises, deep in his body, the wounds on his face. "He even goaded them into it, once, to try to help Noemi—one of his charges—to escape. He was in pretty bad shape when they finally rescued him."

"That's terrible."

"Yeah. He had nightmares, and . . . for a while, we weren't sure he was going to pull through. But he didn't want to go to a hospital, so I sat with him."

"Good thing you did that ER rotation."

"Well, I mostly fed him and kept an eye on his healing. There's a part of me that thinks he got on his feet too fast, but he's—"

"A hero."

She nodded. "And a friend. He makes me feel brave. And . . . he was the first to really believe me about the Russians wanting the vaccine."

"You like him."

"Sure. He's a great guy. Has two brothers. They're fraternal triplets, but he's the charmer.

He makes me laugh, is self-deprecating, and most of all—"

"Hot. With that long dark hair and brown eyes. Mm-hmm."

Tae laughed. "Yes. Okay. But I was thinking, determined to protect me."

"That's hot too."

Now the heat filled her, his voice again in her head. *"Hold on to me and don't let go."*

Wow, she didn't want to let go. Ever.

She shook her head.

"What?" Zoey asked.

"We kissed."

Zoey grinned. "Seriously?"

"Yeah, but . . . I was trying to get my neighbor not to think anything was weird about a strange man on my deck, so . . . yeah. At the time I just did it. I didn't think—"

"You didn't think you'd like it."

Tae drew up her knees, wrapped her arms around them. Shrugged.

"But you did."

She nodded. Made a face. "It went from this fast, sort of fake kiss to . . . yeah, I've never been kissed like that."

"Like how?"

Like the world turned quiet, and the buzzing and fear in her head stood still, and she was anchored and safe and wanted. She looked at Zoey. "Like I was the only thing in the world that mattered."

Silence. Zoey smiled. "What are you doing down here instead of outside, wrapped in a blanket with him, staring at thestars?"

Yeah, good question, but inexplicably, her eyes filled. "Because I . . . I panicked. He said he wanted to kiss me again, and I told him that the first time was a mistake." She looked at Zoey. "What is wrong with me?"

"Oh, honey. I'll tell you what's wrong. Sergei, the jerk."

Oh, right.

"So you're a little gun-shy. I mean, boyfriend number one kidnapped you and tried to take you back to his secret lair."

Tae let herself smile.

"And I'm sure Colt would get that, if you let him."

She sighed. "Probably. But maybe . . . maybe all this is for the best. I mean, I really have no idea how to be in a relationship, and . . . well, to be honest, Colt doesn't either. I mean, he's made it pretty clear that he intends to go back to his world as hired security, and I . . . I don't want to be my mother, never knowing where he is, or what happened to him."

Zoey nodded. "And it's not like you're going to follow him to the hot spots around the world."

"No. He's not the only one trying to make the world a better place. I— no, we—need to go to

Atlanta, need to re-create the vaccine, and I need to let him go."

Zoey drew in a breath. "Yes. Tomorrow. But tonight, maybe you watch the stars with a guy who makes you feel safe."

Tae started to shake her head, but Zoey touched her arm.

"Listen. I know you have this all analyzed in your head, but what if you just let go a little. You don't have to be in charge of everything. I know it's scary, and you hate feeling helpless, but instead of theorizing the end of the story, what if you just . . . let the story unravel as it should?"

"That's sounds terrifying."

"Or freeing. Not to get all Dr. Bella on you, but what if your story is better than you imagined, and by holding on, you're only creating the ending that you can see. The one you can control."

Tae considered her. Then, "Wait. This is one of your 'God loves you and has a good plan for your life' talks, isn't it?"

Zoey held up her hands. "I'm just saying that maybe there's a reason you ended up at Sky King Ranch. And it's because God has a bigger plan for you than you do yourself."

"I ended up at Sky King Ranch because I crashed a plane and hiked through a blizzard and Dodge and Echo found me by chance in a snow pile."

"By chance?"

"Okay, Echo's dog found me, and kept me alive, and then found them— Fine. I guess it's all in your perspective."

"Yes. Yes it is. And my perspective says that right now, there's a starry sky outside and a lonely man out there who is staying awake to watch for trouble because you seem to keep him breathing. And it's possible that God has ordained this exact moment."

Zoey's voice softened. "You don't have to control every moment, plan every step. Maybe you just say yes to the doors God opens."

Tae actually glanced at the open door.

"Besides, are you sure he's going back to his old life? Because I know what he said, but he doesn't look like he's all that keen on leaving you."

"Not until I'm safe."

"And that would be when?" Zoey cocked her head to one side.

Huh.

Zoey got up. "Poor guy, out in the cold all by himself—"

"Fine." Tae pulled the blanket back over her shoulders.

"I won't wait up." Zoey followed her out and headed to her own room.

"Nothing is going to happen."

"Mm-hmm."

Whatever. But really, probably, this was a

stupid idea. Still, *"I want to kiss you."* Okay, not exactly what he'd said, but that was definitely a part of his sentence.

He. Wanted to. Kiss her.

She headed upstairs. Outside, through the porch sliding door, the fire was flickering. Opening the door, she stepped out onto the deck.

Grunts. A smack. Another grunt. *What?*

And that's when her eyes adjusted to the darkness.

On the grass, Colt grappled with something. No, some*one*. Someone taller, leaner. But clearly just as tough because as she watched, the man's fist connected with Colt's jaw and spun him.

She screamed, "Colt!"

Colt bounced up, landed a kick on his way that sent the man back.

"Get inside, Tae!"

She couldn't move, watched as Colt charged the man, tackling him back onto the grass.

And then they were tangled together, hitting, kicking, beating each other.

Killing each other.

The violence broke her free.

She needed a weapon, a—

Jethro's shotgun lay on the grass near Colt's chair, which had been knocked over. The flames glistened against the metal, and she launched herself off the deck and into the cool grass. Swiped up the gun, her hands shaking.

Light splashed the area. "I got this, honey." Jethro, behind her, reached for the gun.

She nearly dropped the weapon, even as he took it, the look on his face brutal, fierce.

He turned the gun on the men. "Stop."

Colt kicked the man off him, scrambled back, giving Jethro room.

Blood streamed out of Colt's nose, but he'd gotten in his licks—the man's lip was split, his own nose bleeding, and both were breathing hard, labored breaths.

The attacker found his feet.

"Hands behind your head, pal," Jethro said.

And that's when the man turned to face Jethro in the light of the porch.

He was lean, easily six three, with short wavy dark-as-night hair and equally dark eyes.

But she knew those eyes.

A cold spear shot through her. "You."

And with her word, everyone froze.

The man wiped blood from his nose, then leaned over and spit out blood from his mouth, ignoring Jethro's command. "Sheesh. Talk about overreacting."

Colt's mouth opened. "You were *sneaking* up to the house."

"I wasn't— I just didn't want the entire neighborhood— Whatever. Tell him, Taylor."

Colt glanced at her, one eye on the man. He

apparently didn't care that blood also dripped off his chin.

"It's the guy, Colt."

He frowned.

"The guy from the cruise ship. The one who told me that I should give him the vaccine."

Colt turned back to the man, his entire body stiff.

"The name's Roy," he said now. Probably knew better than to reach out his hand to Colt. "I'm on your side."

"Really," Colt said. "Did you know that she was going to be kidnapped?"

"No. Although, we weren't surprised. I've spent the past three months looking for her." His eyes fell on Tae. "You're hard to find."

"Who is *we?*" Colt asked.

"Logan Thorne, Pete Sutton. A few others who work for President White. We call ourselves the Caleb Group. And we're here to help."

He came closer into the light. The fire had died to just coals.

Colt turned, and now ran his hand under his nose. The blood was starting to clot, it seemed.

"Pete Sutton was able to secure the information we needed. And now we need you."

Again, Colt moved closer to her, and she nearly reached out her hand to hang on to him. Just like he'd told her to.

But wow, he looked rough, bleeding, his brown

eyes fierce and dark. Watching him fight, it struck her fresh.

Colt was a warrior.

There was no way he was settling down.

"I got the information I need from Logan. I'm going to Atlanta," Tae said.

"We're going to Atlanta." Zoey's voice sounded behind her. She walked up and stood beside Tae. "We'll make your vaccine."

"Yes, but you're not going to Atlanta," Roy said.

"We're not?"

"No. You're going to Florida." He ran a hand around the back of his neck, and if possible, the look on his face was even worse than the damage to it. "We think we figured out where the Petrovs are going to hit."

"Where?" Colt asked quietly.

A beat and he made a face. "The happiest place on earth. Disney World."

Tae just stared at him, her heart thumping in her ears. "What?"

But she never got an answer because Colt leaned forward, his hands on his knees, breathing hard.

"Colt?" She knelt next to him. He was sweating. Hyperventilating. "Slow down. Can someone bring me a bag?"

But he shook his head. "No . . . that . . ." He took her hand, pressed it against his carotid artery. Met her eyes.

Fast. Too fast. His pulse hammered under her fingers. He put his hand around her wrist.

Then, just like that, Colt dropped to the ground, out cold.

EIGHT

"You could have drowned me," Colt said. He sat on the dock, the dark sky littered with stars glinting down upon him, the air brisk, laden with the scent of the dark lake.

Despite the blanket around his shoulders, Colt shivered, his body sodden through, the cold embedded deep in his bones.

"Stop being a baby. I was right there." Tae sat beside him, also wet, also wrapped in a blanket. Also shivering.

He glanced at her, and she smiled, a shadow in her beautiful eyes that betrayed the trauma earlier that night. The one where he'd fought with an intruder—although not just an intruder but some sort of secret government agent. And then he'd nearly died again, thanks to the rocketing of his heart.

"You didn't have to drown me."

"You had tachycardia, and when you passed out, you were in real danger of arrhythmia. I had to shock your system."

"So throwing me into the lake was your best idea?"

"It was either that or an ice-cold dunk into the bathtub. This was quicker."

Last thing he'd remembered before passing out

were the words *Disney World,* as in the happiest place on earth being the source of the bioattack. If that thought wasn't enough to give a guy a full-on cardiac arrest . . . But even before that, his pulse had rocketed, and not just from the fight with the attacker, but the fact that Tae *knew* said attacker.

He'd been the one who warned her about Sergei . . .

Colt had been milliseconds away from getting the guy back into a headlock.

Then everything went black, and he'd woken fiercely, painfully, abruptly, with a rush of ice and fire coursing through his body.

He sucked in a lungful of water even as he launched himself out of the lake, blinking hard into the night, coughing, spitting, gulping for breath.

Sure, Tae had been right there, up to her waist in water. And next to her, the man he'd been fighting who'd helped drown—er, save—him. But Colt's lungs still burned and he'd almost lived one of his many dark nightmares, death by drowning.

So, after he'd emptied out his lungs—and stomach—he shook himself back to the living, spotted Roy, and nearly took a swing at the guy again. Would have, except for Tae's voice.

"Colt! Calm down. You're safe. Just breathe."

Seemed like a sort of mantra for his life. He'd

whirled around and spotted her, standing under the moonlight, her blond hair glistening, her eyes big, her hand on his arm.

And then, only then, did he realize that his heartbeat had reset. Still thundering, but not racing.

Back to something at least resembling a normal pace. So he'd stood in the water and just . . . breathed.

"You okay, man?" Roy had asked, the blood from his nose now clotted.

The whole thing felt surreal.

Still felt surreal an hour later as he and Tae sat on the dock. Roy had gone inside with Zoey, Raven, and Jethro, to brief them, or maybe just to sleep.

Colt might not sleep for a week.

"Calm down. You're safe. Just breathe."

That felt a little hard to do, sitting this close to Tae, their arms touching.

She was too far into his head, despite his best attempts to keep her out. In fact, earlier, he'd nearly missed the rustle of movement, nearly let Roy creep right up to them as he fought not to think about her.

Now, it was nearly impossible to escape the fact that she'd chosen to sit out here with him in his stubborn refusal to return to the house.

"This ever happen before?" Tae said.

This? "Someone trying to drown me? Maybe."

198

She cocked her head at him. "Perfect. Exactly what I wanted to hear. No, your heart racing out of control."

He was tempted to give her another quip, something about sitting next to her, but it sounded sappy, even in his head, so, "The glacier."

In truth, the episode had him a little freaked out. He'd pushed his body to the limit more times than he could count, but never had his pulse ratcheted so high he couldn't slow it down, couldn't gain control. Until . . . "Maybe it was the stress of climbing up the ice."

"And fighting Roy."

His mouth tightened. "Nothing I haven't done before."

"Again, I don't want to know."

He looked at her. "I wasn't going to let him hurt you."

"I know. But what if . . ." Sighing. "You might have stroked out. Or suffered a full cardiac arrest. Not good, Colt. Not good."

"I'm not going to stroke out." He had stopped shivering a little. "I'm fine."

"You're *not* fine. You haven't been fine since I met you!"

He raised an eyebrow. "I remember being pretty fine when I rescued you off the houseboat."

"Oh, you are so stubborn!" She held up her hand. "Yes. Okay, tough guy, you were very heroic. No one is saying anything different. But for one second will you listen to me? Maybe you're more hurt than you realize. Maybe there is something *permanently* wrong with you."

Permanently?

Her gaze seemed to burn into him.

Fine. "Yes, maybe I've had a harder time getting back into action, feeling like myself, but—"

"You were beaten really badly."

He closed his eyes, shook his head. "I've been beaten before. It's not . . ." He opened his eyes and leveled his gaze into hers. "I'm *fine,* Tae."

"I think you should—"

"Really. Truly, cross my heart, I am fine."

She nodded. "Of course you are."

Now he frowned. "What does that mean?"

"That means that tough ex-Delta operator Colt Kingston just keeps on fighting, no matter what."

Ex. Delta operator.

He didn't know why that stung, just a little.

Colt looked out onto the lake. It was late. Or maybe early, depending on the view. The moon was falling to the backside of the night, leaving a long streak of luminescence on the water. "Yes. I do keep fighting. But it's who I am. What I do—"

"It's going to get you killed." She sighed, her words turning to a whisper. "But maybe you don't care."

Ouch. The woman was an assassin.

"I care." But even as he said it, his father's

200

words crept in, latched on. *"You live your life as if it doesn't matter to you."* No. "Really, Tae, I *do* care."

She was staring at him, hard, those blue eyes shiny. "You don't. You nearly got killed a month ago, and here you are, planning on going back into that life. And nearly getting killed along the way."

A tear slid down her cheek. What was he supposed to do with that?

He softened his voice. "Tae. What do you want from me? It's how I'm made. You heard the bear story. More than that, after my dad yelled at me, he was . . . well, all my brothers were . . . a little impressed. For a long time after that Range called me the bear hunter. And that was something because *he* wanted to be a warrior all his life. I started to realize that that's who I am too. I'm a guy who likes to step into the gap. Yeah, I joined the military to escape, but in doing so, I found brothers. And a purpose."

He turned away, stared at the moonlight fading from the lake. "The worst day of my life was walking away from my team."

Silence. A beat, and then he sighed. "Well, no, the worst day of my life was knowing I'd somehow missed something and walked us into an ambush. The *second*-worst day was signing my discharge papers."

He didn't quite know how they'd gotten here,

to that moment, but even as he spooled out, the truth settled inside. He met her eyes. "I'm not made to stand on the sidelines. Never was, never will be."

She drew the blanket around her tighter. Sighed. Looked away.

"What's going on here, Tae?"

She lifted her shoulders. Then, "I just wish that . . ."

He didn't look away, his gaze tracing the way her hair had dried, wavy under the kiss of the moon. Her profile in the night, that cute nose, the lips that always seemed to have an expression, pulling him in . . .

Oh brother. Yes, there was something wrong with him because he couldn't *not* think about her. Even if he was trouble, even if he was doomed to walk away.

She looked at him, finally. Swallowed. Took a breath and met his eyes. "Fine. I wish you weren't going back, okay?"

Really. Everything inside him stilled, the echo of her words ranging about dangerously inside until they landed, starting a smolder deep inside. He might even call it hope.

But he kept any hooah to himself and simply raised an eyebrow. "Oh?"

"Stop it. You know I didn't mean what I said earlier."

"What you said earlier?" And for the life of

him, he couldn't think of what she meant. Maybe his brain had taken a dunking in the lake too. "When?"

"Oh wow."

"Really, Tae—"

"When I said the kiss was for show!" She took a breath. "I think I'm just going to head in."

She made to stand up, but he grabbed her wrist. And that felt desperate, but so did his soft, "Stay."

And probably he was going to hate himself later, but he tugged her down onto the dock, in front of him. Not quite in his lap, but within reach.

Her eyes widened. "What are you doing?"

"What I should have done a couple hours ago," he said as his hand slid around the back of her neck.

More sirens, but he moved in anyway until—

"No." Her hand pressed his chest.

He stopped, a full-out screech that turned him cold. "Oh, Tae. I'm sorry. I totally—" Wow, he read that wrong.

"It's not you." She looked away. "I . . . want to kiss you, Colt. I do. But in my head, there are voices calling me foolish and how can I want to kiss you after . . ." She swallowed. "After . . ."

Oh, Tae. Because right then he got it, and the realization burned through him, made him want to hit someone. "Sergei."

She still wasn't looking at him, but she nodded.

He blew out a breath. Wanted to ease away, but at the same time, he didn't want her to feel somehow sodden or ashamed or whatever might be going through her head at the moment. "I'm not Sergei."

"I know that."

He reached out and touched her face. Moved her gaze to his. "Listen. What I mean is that not only would I never kidnap you or strangle you or even try to use you—of course not. But I also would never lie to you, scare you, make you feel helpless or trap you into something you don't want." The very thought of that knotted his gut. He blew out a breath, then softened his voice. "I'm not going to hurt you, Tae."

She looked at him, those beautiful eyes searching his. "But you're going to leave me."

He drew in a breath. "I'm not going anywhere. At least, not right now."

A muscle pulled in her jaw.

"Listen, yes, someday I'm probably going back to Jones, Inc. But we have a lot of miles between now and then and . . . who's to say what will happen? All I know is that . . ." He swallowed. Oh well, what did it hurt? "You're just about the most amazing woman I've met, Tae. Brave and pretty and . . ."

"You're just impressed that I saved your life."

A beat. And in it his heart just about exploded all over again.

This woman . . .

"Yes. Yes, I am." Then he tucked a drying curl of hair behind her ear. "You keep saving my life, Flo, and I'll keep saving yours, because, like I said, we're in this together. But"—he held his hand up—"I'll follow your lead. If we're just friends, then . . . I'm cool with that. I can just be here to protect you."

Her smile came slowly, lit with something in her eyes that he didn't want to guess.

Okay, he wanted to, but he shouldn't. "Tae?"

"I thought you said you couldn't protect me when you wanted to kiss me."

"I'm willing to give it my best shot."

She laughed. "There's the tough guy I know."

He looked out at the water, just starting to streak with light. "I think we're safe, for now."

"Are we? Good."

And then, just as he looked back at her, she leaned in and kissed him.

Her lips were cool, soft, and she wound her hand around his neck to hold him there, and—

Maybe he'd already died, long ago, in that water, because just like before, the world dropped away. The pain and fear of the fight, the dunking in the lake, the what-ifs before them, the chill in his body. Just the perfect sense of the night stirring around them and Tae in his arms, surrendering to his nudge to deepen their kiss. Her other hand touched his chest, as if testing his heart—okay, yes, still alive, honey—as he drew his arm around her and pulled her close.

Very, very much alive. In fact, as she kissed him, something woke, deep inside.

That part of him that said . . . what if?

Tae smelled of the piney night air, the scent of water on her skin. She tasted right and perfect and when she sighed, and relaxed, something akin to the slow, simmering burn of a sunset spread through him.

She just might be perfect. Smart, sexy, funny, tough . . .

Oh boy, he was in trouble. Because suddenly the last thing he wanted right now was to leave.

Especially when she leaned away, smiled at him, then took his face in her hands and kissed him again, this time with some urgency, some oomph in her touch.

Mm-hmm. Maybe he'd just stop thinking about tomorrow and listen to his words sounding deep in his heart. *"I'm not going anywhere. At least, not right now."*

In fact, if his heart had a say, maybe never.

And when she made a noise deep in the back of her throat, as the wind stirred around them, the morning drawing out of slumber, he felt his heart slow, his breath thicken in his chest, and all the fight inside quieted.

Everything just . . . stopped hurting.

Stopped whirring in his head.

And for the first time since he could remember, he tasted it . . .

Peace.

She had stopped shivering, and so did he as he pulled his blanket around both of them, then rolled them over, his arm under her head, her beautiful eyes fixed on him.

Nope, he wasn't going anywhere.

Then he lowered his head and kissed her again. And finally stopped thinking all together.

Ranger's side of the bed was empty, again. Noemi rolled over and ran her hand over his side of the sheets.

Cold.

Which meant he'd been up for a while, falling prey to the lure of the sunlight that streaked past the room-darkening shades, into their cozy loft bedroom.

Or maybe he'd just been driven from his bed by whatever nightmares had plagued him—probably his most current one, of a bomb detonating in his living room, killing everyone he loved.

Yeah, that would get her up in the middle of a sunlit night too.

She rolled over, threw an arm over her eyes, tried to settle back into sleep, but now her brain was rolling over the terrifying events of only a few days ago. It landed, however, on the moment her father appeared from beyond the grave. Her thoughts trekked past his flimsy explanations all the way to the moment she said goodbye to him after dinner.

It wasn't a goodbye, more of a standoff, really, with the cool folding of her arms across her chest, the set of her jaw—mostly to keep from crying, but he wouldn't know that—to him shaking Ranger's hand. Her father had met her husband's eyes with a look, as if confirming a promise, and again, she'd felt cut out.

Now, the look sat in her brain like a spear, a fresh wound of betrayal bleeding through her thoughts, her morning.

Her father had a stronger connection with Ranger than he did her. Swell.

"Noemi, are you okay with how you left things with your father?"

Tae's words. And behind them, Noemi again heard her response. *"It doesn't matter. I was always an afterthought to him. And now, he's already dead to me."*

Clearly not, because she'd spent the past two days what-iffing and . . .

So much for sleep, because now she was imagining her father tied up and beaten by a couple of Russian thugs, his cover blown . . .

Nope. She wasn't going to lie here and conjure up terrible endings . . . especially the one where she ended up burying him, again. Grieving him, again.

Noemi threw back the covers, pulled on a sweatshirt over her pajamas, tied her hair back in a handkerchief, and headed to the bathroom.

Then she washed her face, brushed her teeth, and stared in the mirror, trying to figure out what it was that caused people she loved to lie to her.

No more. If Ranger was keeping a secret from her, she was going to ferret it out.

She headed downstairs, expecting to find him in the kitchen, maybe talking to his father over a cup of coffee. Nope. Barry's recliner was empty and the kitchen void of anything that smelled like morning brew.

The view called to her—the golden spray of light on the mountains turning them a deep blue. She walked over to the window and stared out across the southern hills, across the fields covered in purple fireweed and yellow madwort. Such beauty fighting for life in an unforgiving land.

Just before she turned away, she spotted Ranger. Dressed in a pair of running shorts and a jacket, he ran along the dirt driveway, his gait strong, his steps sure. He wore a light stocking cap, his dark hair curling out the back, and now put his head down, as if fighting for the last few yards.

No, gearing up for a sprint, because he shot off in a dash toward the house. She lost him as he came around the end, toward the entryway, and expected to hear him coming in.

Nothing, so after a moment, she walked to the

back window and spotted him heading into the hangar.

Huh.

She went to the cupboard, grabbed a water bottle, filled it with water and ice, then shoved her feet into a pair of old sneakers she found by the door and headed outside.

The air held the fragrance of summer—the scent of wildflowers, pine, and the slightest chill scraped from the towering mountains that shed magenta upon the valley. She liked it here—so different from the humidity of Africa, or even the mugginess of Florida, but really, anywhere Ranger was, she wanted to be.

The look that passed between Ranger and her father stirred up in her mind again, and suddenly the wound raked open.

Oh, he'd better not be planning on doing something . . . crazy. Like join up with her father. The thought burrowed into her chest as she walked into the shadowed hangar.

In her worst nightmares, she'd lose him. No, both of them. Ranger and her father.

And this time it would be for good.

Dodge had spent the past two days disposing of his burned plane, and Ranger had helped him clean the hangar all while waiting to hear from Colt, who had taken off two days ago in search of Tae.

Now *there* was a woman dogged by demons.

Even when Noemi had bunked with her down at the guest cabin, Tae had fought her way through the night. Noemi didn't know what had passed between Tae and Colt, but the fact that he'd taken off, chasing her down to the Lower 48, felt very much like something a Kingston brother would do.

They just didn't know how to quit.

Which was why she wasn't surprised to see Ranger at a pull-up bar in a workout area that he and Dodge had clearly built over the past forty-eight hours. A weight set, a mirror, a bench. They had crafted their own version of Gold's Gym.

Now, Ranger hung from the bar, his legs crossed, grunting as he worked his upper body.

He'd taken off his jacket and T-shirt and thrown them on the bench.

Oh. My. Goodness. Now this was worth trekking down to the hangar.

Her man had form. Barely an inch of fat on his entire body. The way he hung from the bar, his muscles taut, showed off every delicious ripple in his back, his shoulders, those amazing sinewy arms.

Mm-hmm. And she didn't harbor a millisecond of guilt for freely admiring him. After all, that was the privilege of being his wife.

Yes, she was a rabid fan of workouts.

He dropped to the ground, breathing hard, not seeing her apparently, because he walked over to the weight set, and from the AirPods she spotted, he didn't hear her either.

Picking up two weights, he stepped back, then did a slow lunge, his back to her. Deliberate. His jaw set.

As if he were thinking about something in particular.

She walked over to the bench and sat down. The hangar collected the cool morning air, despite the sunlight that streamed in through a window.

For a guy who had recently been beat up, Ranger had bounced back well. Fast.

As if pushing through to gear up for something.

The thought wound a fist into her stomach.

He finished his lunges, then bent and did some rows, his back muscles clenching. Sweat dripped down his spine.

She, however, shivered.

He finished the rows, put the weights back, and then turned, sitting on the mat, as if getting ready for sit-ups.

His jacket lay on the bench, and she reached for it.

Something fell out of his pocket, onto the mat. What?

She glanced at Ranger just as he looked up. Blinked at her. His mouth fell open, and he looked at the phone that had bounced on the floor.

He pulled an AirPod out. "Noemi—"

His tone should have warned her, but she was

busy ignoring it, trying not to take a flying leap into conclusions. "What is that?" She stood and picked up the phone, a tiny Nokia.

He'd gotten up. "It's a phone."

"Really? Wow, I thought it was a bunny. Of course it's a phone." She opened it. No code, so she went to the outgoing calls. Nothing. "No, amend that. It's a *burner* phone."

He reached for it, but she yanked it out of his reach and stepped away.

"Noemi—"

She opened the contacts.

One number.

One. Number.

She rounded on him, and he'd already taken a breath, ran a towel around his neck. And wore an expression like she'd just caught him spilling state secrets.

"Whose number is this?"

"I can explain."

"Perfect. Start now."

"Please, give me the phone." He held out his hand.

"Are you kidding me?" She took another step away from him. "You got this from my dad, didn't you?"

Ranger's intake of breath was another spear, and it hit all the open wounds at once.

"You . . . jerk."

"What?"

"You and my dad are up to something, aren't you? That's why you're doing all this training." She shook her head. "What, are you going to join him and his super-off-the-books special presidential black ops team?"

He blinked at her, and then his mouth tightened to a tiny bud. "No."

"Really." Her eyes smarted. "Please, do not lie to me, Ranger. Not after everything we've been through."

His jaw tightened. "I don't know what you're thinking, Noemi, but how exactly am I going to do *nothing* but sit here and watch—or not watch, as the case may be—as the world implodes around me?"

Oh, Ranger.

His eyes lit, burned through her, his voice roughening. "Do you have *any* idea what it felt like to watch those guys tie you up and strap a *bomb* to your body?"

"That had everything to do with you being outnumbered, not your blindness." She kept her voice calm, because she could see the frustration roiling in his eyes. "And yes, I think I understand a little about watching someone I love being *hurt*. Tied up. Bleeding. And thinking that maybe he's going to get himself killed. And that's not the only memory I have of you risking your life to save me or others, so save it, Jack. You don't have the corner on worry."

214

"Yeah, well, I'm not going to let it happen again. Not if I can stop it."

A beat. And in that moment, she ached for him, for the struggle that raged through him. He was so not helpless, not for a second.

But a huge part of him was fighting hard to believe it. To get back up.

And she didn't know if giving him a hand might mean losing him, for good. Her voice lowered. "What I want to know is why my dad gave you this phone. Is he recruiting you?"

He looked at her, then sighed. "It's in case something happens to you. Or in case he gets blown and needs to alert me."

She had nothing, his words streaking a chill through her. Her hand shook a little as she held up the phone. "So this is the emergency bat phone, alerting you should he somehow put me in danger?"

"Something like that."

She shook her head.

"This is why he didn't want you to know he was alive. Because he didn't want you to worry."

"I'm more than worried. I'm angry. Since when do you and my dad get to keep me in the dark about my own safety? I'm a big girl—"

"Who has been kidnapped, twice, and generally gets herself into trouble." He took a step toward her and put his hand around the phone.

She didn't release it. "Gets herself into trouble?"

His mouth tightened, but he didn't take the words back.

"Wow, so now I'm a liability."

"I didn't say that."

"I can take care of myself."

He had the infuriating audacity to raise an eyebrow. And for a second, the words were right there, words that could sting, take him apart— *probably better than a man who is going blind.*

But no, she would never say that. Because the thought stung her too.

She hadn't quite realized just how much she depended on him to be . . . well, super. A super SEAL.

Ranger was smarter, stronger, faster, and had more skills blind and with his hands tied behind his back—literally—than she ever had. Or would.

And he was fighting to stay that way. In his eyes.

Maybe even hers.

Her throat thickened. "Fine. But I'm not a child to be protected."

"No," he said softly. "You're the woman I love."

What was she supposed to do with that? Her eyes burned even as she released the phone. She looked away, but he put his hand to her cheek, turned her face back to his.

"If anything happened to you, I . . ." His jaw tightened. He swallowed. His blue eyes turned rich with emotion. "Maybe this phone is for me. So I have a way to make sure I can protect the most important person in my life, to the best of my abilities."

"Range—"

"No, listen to me, Noemi. Your dad is into some dark, dangerous stuff. And I don't want it coming home to us. But if it does, I want to be ready."

"Hence the turbo workout."

"Hence me getting back to my regular PT."

And then he smiled.

She saw it then—the man she'd met in Florida so many years ago, that solid sense of tomorrow in his eyes. The guy who seemed almost invincible.

"I get it, Range. I do. My dad always said once a SEAL, always a SEAL. But . . . I guess I thought things would be different now. Because . . ."

He drew in a breath. "I know. I just, I just can't be the guy who stays home and cooks or answers the phone. I . . . I'm not that guy."

"Always a SEAL."

He lifted a shoulder. "Whatever. Right now, I'm your husband, the guy who is trying to keep you safe." And now he wore so much vulnerability, even worry, in his expression, how was she supposed to stay angry?

"Fine. As long as my father doesn't drag you into his dark world," she said and stepped up to him, her hand on his chest, over his beating heart.

He pocketed the phone, then cupped her face in his hands. "Yours is the only world I want to be in. We're in this together, I promise." He leaned down and kissed her.

She'd come to know him over the past few weeks of being married, to know the differences in how he kissed her, held her. Sometimes he was lost in a place of hunger, sometimes gentle and sweet, loving her out of that tender pocket reserved for her. Sometimes his touch was even fierce, almost resolute in his determination to prove to her that they belonged together.

This . . . this kiss was different. Not hungry, not desperate, not even tender. But something seemed so right, so perfect, she didn't know where he started and she ended.

He deepened his kiss, wrapped his arms around her, molding her to himself. She didn't mind the scent of hard work or the heat of his body. She just lost herself in the way he enveloped her into his world. His heart.

Wow, she loved this man. Her husband. Her future.

She pushed away, a smile tugging at her mouth. "Your workout about finished?"

He met her smile. "Not quite."

Oh. Boy. She laced her hand into his.

Garbled sounds came from the phone in his pocket.

She stilled and Ranger let her go and reached

into his pocket for the phone. Looked at it and answered, turning it to speaker.

Then he held up a hand to keep her from speaking.

Muffled voices. She leaned in and looked at Ranger, frowning.

"Is that—"

He put his finger over his mouth.

Russian?

"*Shot eta*, *Peyotr*? *Kakoi*—"

Grunts, a shout, then the call cut off.

Her eyes fixed on his. "Did we . . . did we just *pocket dial* him?"

"And blow his cover? I dunno." But the yes was in his expression.

No— No, she was *not* going to be the cause of her father's death.

Noemi turned and sprinted for the house.

"Noemi!" Ranger took after her, and of course, beat her to the door. Which he slammed his hand on before she could open it.

"Range!"

"Stop. Just . . . breathe."

She rounded on him and couldn't help the tears that burned her eyes. "Breathe? He could be fighting for his life *right now*. Because of me."

"Us. And we don't know what is going down." Ranger grabbed her by the shoulders. "Let's call Logan. See if he's checked in."

"Yes. Fine. But if he's in trouble, then I'm going

to find him." She put her hands on Ranger's arms and pulled his grip off her. "There's no way that he's dying. Again. Not when I can do something about it."

"*We,*" he said. "And not when, but *if* we can do something about it. Agreed? We're not going to blow in without some surveillance, a plan. We do things my way, and you obey everything I say, got it?"

"We're back to that?"

"We never left it."

Her mouth pinched. "Fine. But what you know, I know. And no more sneaking away in the middle of the night, got it?"

He considered her a moment. Then, "I swore to your father I'd keep you alive. Please don't make me break my promise."

She touched his face. "Deal. Now, please help me keep my stupid father alive."

He kissed her palm. Held it to his heart. "As you wish."

"This feels so surreal." Tae drew up one leg and locked her arms around it and leaned against the oval window of President Isaac White's personal task force team jet.

"Yeah. This beats any official transport I've ever taken," Colt said, sitting beside her in a creamy-white bucket seat. "Ham, my boss, has a private plane he uses for our team, but it's not a Gulfstream." He ran his hands over the padded arms. He'd pushed the seat back, like a recliner, and had spent the last couple hours snoozing.

The guy was clearly exhausted. She didn't know when Colt had last slept, really, because every time she'd woken the last couple days—at the hotel, on the dock—he'd been awake and watching for trouble.

Or watching her, a look in his eyes that had found its way inside, set up camp.

Oh boy, she was in trouble. And his words to Roy this morning, when the super spy was arranging transportation to Florida, which included a drive back to Seattle and waiting for President White's private jet to arrive, didn't help either. *You'd better count me in, pal, because where she goes, I go.*

She'd almost broken out in tears.

Clearly, he'd meant what he said back on the porch in Alaska a few days ago, because here he was, even reaching out and lacing his strong fingers through hers. "It's going to be okay."

Which part?

The part where there were Russian mobsters trying to kill her? Or, even better, plotting to unleash a bioweapon on American soil? Maybe the part where she had to figure out how to synthesize a vaccine from tidbits of genes and incomplete gene splicing?

Maybe best was the part of her heart she was losing—and fast—to a guy who wasn't going to stick around. Yes, that was her favorite version of "It's going to be okay."

Hardly.

Still, she produced a smile and nodded. "Yeah. I know. I just . . ." She shook her head, her gaze landing on Zoey across the aisle, asleep, and beside her, Roy, who had commandeered this flight.

"I feel like I've lost all control of my life."

"Welcome to the service of Uncle Sam," Colt said. He wore a pair of clean jeans and a dark brown T-shirt, his Oakley sunglasses backward on his head, which pushed his long dark hair behind his ears. A dark stubble layered his chin.

Yeah, that helped her heart say no. "I just . . . I had a good life. A simple life. I went to work. I came home. I read a good book. I—"

"Internet dated." He raised an eyebrow.

She sighed. "Okay. Maybe I *did* want more. But more only got me into trouble."

He smiled, something flirtatious in it. "You seemed to like trouble last night, or maybe I should say this morning."

"Stop. And by now it's yesterday. We passed midnight long ago."

His gaze dropped to her lips, and a burn pressed her face. "Colt."

He grinned. "I just think that you only *tell*

yourself that you want a safe, simple life, a life without complications, because that keeps you from needing anyone. Which means no one can ever reject you or leave you . . . or hurt you."

She swallowed.

Yeah, she'd lost control all right, because she'd spent the last four hours, as they'd traveled through the night on the red-eye from Seattle to Florida, reliving yesterday's early morning kissing on the dock as the sun rose into a glorious amber and blue sky.

He'd been sweet, clearly meaning his words about never making her feel helpless or trapped or pushing her into something she didn't want.

She'd definitely wanted to find herself in Colt's arms, to taste on him the night—and his strength and the way that, when he kissed her, her world felt at once both exciting and yet safe.

Because that was Colt.

In fact, he'd been the one to slow them down, pressing his forehead to hers. *"I need a breath here, Flo."* And then he'd rolled over, pulling her with him to settle her into his arms as they watched the sun rise.

She'd fallen asleep right there, warm, despite her soiled clothing, and so very exhausted, and it wasn't until Jethro came out and announced breakfast that she woke.

Colt had smiled at her, already awake, the sun in his eyes, and all she could hear was, *"We have a lot of miles between now and then and . . . who's to say what will happen?"*

She knew *exactly* what was going to happen. Because the more she leaned in, the deeper the wound would be.

But he was still here, like he'd said—not going anywhere—leaning his head against the leather pillow on the luxury seats, his gaze on her, a half smile on his face as if trying to read her mind.

"What if you just . . . let the story unravel as it should?"

Well, thanks for that, Zoey.

"Where are we?" Colt asked now, his eyes darting to the window.

"Nearly to Florida, I think. We're still pretty high, but according to the flight tracker, we should be setting down in Orlando in less than an hour. Do you know where we're headed after we land?"

"Roy says they have a lab near Patrick Space Force Base. That's about an hour east of Orlando."

"On the ocean." She looked out the window. "I've only been to Florida once. When I was seven, we went to Disney World." She turned back to him. "It was amazing. My dad was just finishing his residency and he somehow got time off to take us. We did all the parks, and I even dressed up like one of the princesses for a day."

His mouth quirked up. "Which princess?"

"Mulan."

"I should have guessed that."

"Why?"

"Because Mulan is clever. And brave. And isn't afraid to do the hard things."

She put her leg down. Shook her head. "That's not me. I'm not a soldier like you are."

"It's *totally* you." He sat up and took her hand. "Tae, take a good look at your life. Even before you survived a plane crash and a blizzard and an attack on your houseboat and—well, all the things—you dealt with deadly viruses on a daily basis. That alone is enough to keep anyone awake at night. And you act like it's no big deal."

"It's . . . not, really. I train and take precautions and . . . I know what I'm doing."

He was nodding. "And then you tell yourself to pay attention and go do your job."

"Yes."

"It's no different from what I do. Bravery isn't the absence of fear. It's doing what you must do, despite the fear. Flo, you're one of the bravest people I know."

"I've never felt brave."

"Just because you didn't want your dad to go to war doesn't make you a coward. It makes you a child who loved her dad."

Her eyes burned. "I did love him." She looked at Colt's hand in hers. "He was gone all the time, even then, and the fact that he dropped everything to take me to Disney— It felt magical. Safe. As if I mattered."

"You matter, Tae."

She lifted a shoulder, looked away. He reached up and nudged her gaze back to him. "You matter. It's why your dad went to war—to make the world safer for you."

"Was it worth it?" She hadn't meant to ask it aloud, and it came out as a murmur, almost a breath, but Colt stiffened as if it had hit him.

"Worth what?"

"Going to war. Giving up his life. Sacrificing . . ." She swallowed.

"Sacrificing you."

She nodded. "It doesn't feel like it." Her throat tightened. She'd thought she was over this grief, but sometimes it just appeared, like a rogue wave, washing over her, taking out her feet, slamming her to the ocean floor, bruising.

She couldn't breathe.

Colt met her eyes. In his gaze a thousand words roamed, and he searched her face as if trying to find the right ones.

Wow, he had beautiful eyes. So brown, with flecks of gold at the center, as if there might be a treasure buried deep inside.

A treasure she very much wanted to uncover. In fact, the more time she spent with Colt, the more she found herself wanting more. Yes, more of his arms around her, more of his laughter, more of his bossy charm. Because being with Colt was simply . . . addicting.

In fact, he was everything she hadn't realized was missing from her life.

"Yes," he said finally, softly. "It was worth it. Because my guess was that it wasn't as easy to leave you as you think it was. The man who brought you to Disney World, the man who enlisted after 9/11 to make the world a safer place, had one reason in mind . . . his daughter."

His gaze met hers again, and she saw in his eyes his words *"People sleep peaceably in their beds at night only because rough men stand ready to do violence on their behalf."*

And for a moment, she was back at Jethro's, watching Colt fight for his life. No, *her* life.

She slipped her hand over his arm. "You're a good man, Colt."

He frowned. "No. I'm not, actually, Tae. I'm— I've done a lot of things that a good man shouldn't do. But I've done them for a good reason, and that's what keeps me sleeping at night. But let's not get me confused with the actual good people in the world like your dad, and . . . well, you."

She just blinked at him. *What?*

He offered her a smile. "But around you, I do feel like I'm a halfway decent guy." He winked.

The pilot came over the loudspeaker and told them that they were starting their descent, and he turned away.

No. No, that wasn't right.

Except it made sense, didn't it? *"From the beginning, I knew that I was different. Made for trouble, I guess."*

Oh, Colt.

But maybe it was the kind of trouble that she needed. The kind that would keep her alive.

And without a doubt, he was exactly the man she needed right now, when her life felt like it was skidding off the rails.

She just wouldn't think about the end of the story.

The sprawling city of Orlando came into view as she stared out the window, Roy's words in her ears. *"We think we figured out where the Petrovs are going to hit."*

It couldn't be Disney World—not only because of the unthinkable chaos and destruction wrought by unleashing a bioweapon on hundreds of thousands of children and families, but even, technically, the fact that Disney World was under a no-fly zone, with some of the most advanced security in the world.

It seemed impossible, all ways around.

"Why a vaccine and not an antiviral?" Colt said as the landing gear went down.

His question came out of the blue, but not so far from her thoughts either. Uncanny how he could almost read her mind.

"Because, for smallpox, the vaccine acts as

228

an antiviral. The body produces antibodies that allow it to fight the virus."

"Won't that make the person sicker?"

Across the aisle, Zoey was leaning over Roy, looking out the window.

"We don't actually inject smallpox into the body. We use another virus that is similar to the smallpox virus called vaccinia, which is also a poxvirus but less harmful. In the past, we used cowpox. We'd draw fluid from the pustules of an infected cow, separate the virus from the fluids, then use the cowpox virus as our base vaccination. The cowpox is similar enough that when it invades the body, the body attacks it and creates memory cells that will attack any substance similar to it, like smallpox."

"So why doesn't the current vaccine work?"

"The common thought was that cowpox, the vaccinia virus, and the variola virus, which is the causative agent of modern-day smallpox, were all derived from the same ancient smallpox virus. But the Russian sample is just different enough that the cowpox and vaccinia aren't a match. We tried the monkeypox virus, but that didn't work, and then we discovered a horsepox from a breed of Mongolian horses with the right genome sequencing that was 99.7 percent similar to the ancient pox. Unfortunately, the horsepox we need is quite rare and we ran out of samples. We found a supplier of the more common form of horsepox and were able to synthesize a replica using a fragment strand, genome sequencing, and a DNA synthesizer. We then ran trials and discovered that it did create the right T cells and the memory B cells that can fight Smallpox R. R, for Russia. We call the virus S-poxR."

"I'd call it Ivan. Or maybe Igor."

"Are you kidding?"

He lifted a shoulder. "Maybe." He smiled, a cute dimple forming on his cheek.

"Our problem now is that our only sample of S-poxR was destroyed in the fire. The CDC has smallpox in small quantities, but that is newer smallpox, samples that were taken from the 1940s to 1977, when the last case occurred. We need an ancient sample."

"How are you going to get it?"

"The world got lucky. Zoey is actually a molecular anthropologist and has colleagues at the Mütter Museum of the College of Physicians of Philadelphia. They found in their Civil War collection what amounted to vaccination kits—old, person-to-person kits that doctors used to vaccinate soldiers against smallpox."

"Person to person?"

"Crazy, I know, but the process was to take the fluid from smallpox pustules from one person and scrape it into the arm of the next person—just enough that they'd create antibodies. They also developed pustules and the procedure would continue."

"That's chilling. And gross."

"Desperate times."

"Right."

"The CDC doesn't have the right equipment to sequence these ancient DNAs, so the smallpox samples got shipped to the McMaster Ancient DNA Center in Canada, where they mapped the DNA. McMaster was working with small sections, maybe fifty base pairs long. But they were able to create an approximation to the ancient smallpox. And it was close enough that when it was injected into a subject vaccinated with the horsepox-based vaccinia, it was appropriately repelled."

"Subjects?"

"Mice, monkeys, dogs."

"Not humans?"

"That's the next phase of trials, but because of the similarity to the current vaccinia, we have strong indicators that it will be effective, if necessary."

Tae paused as the plane touched down. "Honestly, before we got our sample from Russia, I'd never really studied smallpox. Now, it scares me to death with the mortality rate and how easily it can be synthesized."

"And you can re-create this Mongolian horsepox?"

"With about 30kb of the horsepox genome, yes. But we need to obtain it from a commercial provider—which is highly regulated, as you can imagine, with layers of paperwork. And we'll need a strand of the ancient pox from McMaster to test it against."

"Can they get it?"

"I'm sure the president has some pull."

"And you can re-create the vaccine?"

"Yes. Now that I have access to Zoey's notes. With the right equipment, we can resynthesize the horsepox, and thus, create the vaccine. Hopefully."

"How long will it take?"

The plane slowed to a stop.

"Depends. Normally, years, to make sure the vaccine is safe for human trials, but we've done all the hard work. Now we just need to re-create it, and . . . well, test it."

Colt unbuckled. Stood up. Held out his hand to her, maybe to help her out of her seat. "Let's hope we won't need it."

She took his hand and found herself tucked up next to him in the narrow aisle. He let go, but then perched his hand on her shoulder to keep her from falling back into her seat. With his other hand, he grabbed his duffel bag from the overhead compartment.

The temptation to lean her head down on his chest, to put her arms around his waist, to close her eyes and hold on, hoping the world might just stop, swept over her.

Loving him now was worth it, even if she had to let him go later.

She sighed. Yes, love. Because she hadn't a hope of putting the brakes on her heart. Especially when, as he put the strap over his head, wearing his bag cross-body, he also leaned in and kissed her forehead.

Then he met her eyes, taking hold of her heart with his smile.

"Ready to save the world?"

"Yes," she said and took his hand again.

NINE

If Colt ever worked for the government again, it would definitely be as part of the Caleb Group, with their Gulfstreams and Escalades and beach safe houses slash mansions by the shore.

"*Hel-lo,* taxpayer money," he said as he got out of the SUV and stood in the paved driveway of the three-story, um, small resort on the barrier island off Melbourne, Florida.

The L-shaped, all-white house sat back from the road, via a thin corridor edged with thick palm tree growth and tangled moss that was probably riddled with trained alligators that defended it from passersby. Across the highway was a never-ending stretch of beautiful, nearly white sand beach. The property faced the Indian River, but with the acreage around it, not to mention the tall cement fencing, it screamed, *Stay away.* And the high-security lights only added a "really, don't even think about it, no—and I mean you—trespassing" vibe.

In every corner, every nook, and even mounted on tall light poles that lined the driveway and popped up in obscure places of the yard—cameras. Which meant that no one got onto this property without being seen. Colt imagined a cadre of security guys shut up in some room nearby, watching him gape at the house.

He closed his mouth, smiled for the cameras.

So, exactly the place to hole up for a bit while hunting bad terrorists and a killer virus.

Really, the hideaway was comprised of two houses. The main house that faced the river and another house, connected to the first by a breezeway, with a garage space on the lower floor, living space above it.

Grass surrounded the houses, and through the windows on the main floor in the main house, Colt spotted a gorgeous pool facing the river. A long dock jutted out into the water, and at that was docked a suh-*weeet* cigarette boat.

"Did we confiscate this house from some Colombian drug lord?" Colt asked as Roy got out.

They weren't exactly pals quite yet.

Roy glanced at him, still a little miffed, apparently, at their throw down the other night. He sported a crack over his nose and a puffy eye, but enough of a look that Colt knew he'd earned Roy's respect.

Which was why, yesterday, when they'd nearly had their *second* throwdown in Jethro's kitchen at just who might be going along for the next leg of the journey—and Colt had offered an ultimatum, something cool and even, but ready if he had to put some say-so into his words—well, Roy had considered him a moment, then simply nodded.

Bam. A win for Colt.

Now, Roy shut the driver's door and came around the side. He'd picked up their ride in a long-term parking lot outside Orlando International Airport. "It's not ours. It's owned by a donor of the Caleb Group."

"Right. Named President Isaac White?" Colt said.

"Not White. It's owned by a big-name movie star," Roy said. "Winchester Marshall." He gestured to the grounds. "All the security is to keep away the paparazzi."

He thought he recognized the name, some action star. Tough gig then, pretending to get shot at while guys like Colt . . .

Aw, it wasn't worth it.

More, given the heat on his skin, the sun coming up, the salt that ladened the air, and the sound of waves on the endless beach across the road, this might be the slickest protection detail he'd ever scored.

Even if he'd probably spend most of it locked away underground, watching Tae stare into a microscope. Still, it was better than returning to Alaska and sitting around watching his brothers move forward with their lives while his ribs healed.

And his heart stopped hurting.

Physically or otherwise.

Colt rounded the back and pulled his duffel out

of the SUV, put it over his shoulder. Tae came up beside him, her gaze on the house. "Wow."

"I know."

Roy strode up behind them and grabbed Zoey's bag. Colt wasn't so thickheaded that he couldn't see the way Tae's friend looked at the guy, her eyes sorta glazing over at his big muscles.

Okay, rein it in, Colt. It was just that some guys got it all—looks, height. Clearly Roy didn't make his living sitting in the back of a Humvee, eating dust, and trying to keep some rich humanitarian doctor alive in the darkest reaches of Africa.

Roy certainly wasn't Brad Pitt or anything, but fine, he could probably be called good-looking. Dark hair. Built. He could certainly handle himself. But Zoey should probably notch it down a little because Roy put off a "here today, gone tomorrow" James Bond vibe that should send any woman running.

Then again, here was Tae, holding on to Colt's hand. And he certainly wasn't a home and hearth guy either.

Or maybe he was.

"Was it worth it?" Her question had settled inside, tugged at him.

To keep her safe? Yes. Anything. Absolutely.

To leave her behind? He was starting to doubt the answer.

"Is that a pool?" Tae asked as they headed up

the marble steps to the double teak doors. "I need to go shopping, pronto."

"That can be arranged," Roy said, glancing over his shoulder.

She stiffened, her eyes widening.

"I'll go with you," Colt said quietly and tightened his hand as they walked into the house. Clearly Roy still gave her the willies.

He still gave Colt, well, if not the willies, then at least he put him on edge.

He had secrets. A past. And way too much clandestine knowledge in his head to be trusted fully.

Laughter echoed off the polished marble floors and nudged something familiar.

Wait—

The hall opened up into a great room with a soaring two-story ceiling, grand windows that allowed light to pour into the space. Teal walls, a stone bar with stools lined up against one wall, a huge gray sectional facing an impressive flat-screen on the other. And seated on the chairs and the sofa were a cadre of men, most of them dressed in cargo shorts and T-shirts.

"You brought in Jones, Inc.?" Colt said to Roy, but his gaze went to Hamilton Jones, the former SEAL and current owner of the SAR/security team. He wore his blond hair short, had on a pair of shorts and a black collared T-shirt, the word UNDAUNTED written on the breast pocket. He stood up from his stool, his hand outstretched. "Colt. You're a sight for sore eyes."

He pulled Colt in and thumped him on the back, and again, Colt was aware of how much space Ham took up in a room.

Standing behind Ham was North, another former SEAL who'd helped rescue Colt in Nigeria. Also blond, but built like a lumberjack, North greeted him. And then Colt turned to Jake Silver, again, a former SEAL who Colt met during their scuba training a year ago when Jake had joined the team. Ham had brought them all to Minnesota for a meetup and some diving in the lake that bordered his property. Colt had spent a couple evenings on Jake's Hobie Cat, catching the wind on said lake.

"Hey, you're here."

The voice issued from the stairway that overlooked the great room. Colt turned, his heart thumping. "Fraser?"

His buddy Fraser Marshall stood, healthy and whole, grinning from the second story. Last time he saw Fraser, the man had been his wingman in captivity with the Boko Haram, trying to stay alive and figure out how to escape, even with his broken wrist.

"Hey, buddy," Fraser said. "I knew you were too stubborn to die."

Tae's hand tightened in his.

He glanced at her. She knew the shape he'd

been in when they'd pulled him out. But so did Fraser. Colt nodded. "Always. How's that wrist?"

Fraser threw down a towel from the second story. Colt caught it. "Better every day," Fraser said. "Get changed. We're taking the boat out."

"You guys on vacation here?" Colt turned to Ham.

"It's a sweet setup, but no. We're here for the same reason you are. There's a national threat and President White asked us to help. We'll brief you later tonight. For now, we're just doing a training evolution. I'm dropping you all off out in the ocean. You get to swim back," Ham said.

"Right now?"

"It's not luck, dude," Jake said. He headed up the stairs, as if to go change.

Right. One of the SEAL sayings. *It's not luck, but hard work.* Colt turned to Ham. "I forgot how many former SEALs you have on the team."

"There's plenty of room for Delta," Ham said. "I'll loan you a shorty if you want to join us."

A shorty—as in a short wet suit.

And weirdly, suddenly, his chest tightened. As if somehow the thought of diving into the ocean and swimming five klicks back to shore might sink him.

Not even a little. "Gimme ten to get us settled."

Tae looked at him. She wore a *be careful* look in her eyes. But then swallowed and hiked up a smile.

Huh. Still, it raked up the memory of his weirdly temperamental heart. That, and the fear Tae wore in her eyes that night on the dock. So maybe he didn't have anything to prove to anyone. At least anyone outside himself.

So this favor, he could do for Tae. For now. "Actually, I think I'll sit this one out. I need to keep tabs on this one." He nodded toward Tae.

She exhaled, a visible sign of relief.

"Okay. But join us at PT tomorrow morning. Beach run."

"Aye, aye. Where are we?"

"I have you upstairs with your brother. Tae, you and Zoey are in a room together."

But Colt had stopped on— "Brother?"

Fraser had come down the stairs. "Actually, brothers, plural. Dodge and Ranger, along with Noemi, arrived a couple hours ago."

"Noemi is here?" Colt asked, meeting Fraser's gaze. "Why?"

Fraser blew out a breath, looked at Ham. "I think you need to talk to your brothers."

Colt headed toward the stairs, Tae behind him.

"End of the hall on the right," Fraser said.

He reached the top of the stairs and turned, but Tae pulled him to a stop. "Colt."

"What?"

"I think . . . I don't think PT is a good idea."

"Tae—"

241

"You had tachycardia, Colt. You could have had a stroke."

He put his hands on her arms, met her eyes, so blue in the glittering light. Softening his voice, he said, "I'm fine, Tae. I know you're worried. It's nothing. I had a fight, and the adrenaline made my heart beat a little fast is all."

Her expression said she didn't believe him. So he pulled her to himself and kissed her. Nothing fancy, just a sweet, perfect kiss. Something to assure her.

Instead, the calm swept over *him,* through him. So maybe he was assuring himself.

He put her hand to his chest. "See? My heart is just fine. I'm not going to have a stroke."

Her hand stayed there, warming him, almost as if she hated to let go. "Okay. I just . . ."

"I'm fine, Flo. Please, don't worry." He took her hand, and they walked down the hall, past a couple bedrooms, and at the end of the hall, he found the double doors closed.

He didn't bother to knock.

The large room, with seafoam green walls, a king bed, and two bunks built into the wall, was empty. Sheer white curtains blew over a pair of open doors to a balcony. Conversation drifted in, and Colt headed toward it.

Ranger and Dodge stood on the balcony, overlooking the river, watching motorboats skim the water. Noemi sat in a wicker chair, her feet up, her hair back in an orange scarf, wearing shorts, a T-shirt, and flip-flops.

"Hey," Dodge said, turning. "How are— Whoa, dude, what happened to you?"

Right. He'd forgotten he still looked banged up.

"He got into a fistfight," Tae said from behind him.

Colt looked at her. "Really?"

"Please. They're not remotely surprised."

A smile tweaked Ranger's face.

"For your information, some goon tried to kill her on her houseboat, so yeah, I might have been just a little jumpy when Roy the Spy sneaked up on us a couple nights ago."

Dodge raised an eyebrow. "Who's Roy?"

"Ham's contact. Works for the Caleb Group," Ranger said, then turned to Colt. "He got the jump on you?"

"Not even a little. I heard him coming. He was lucky I didn't shoot him. Although, yeah, he nearly tricked me with a little throw-the-stick-in-the-brush decoy and— Anyway, I still had him."

Ranger looked at Tae, as if in confirmation.

"He did. But he's still hurting."

He stared at her. "Please tell them *all* my secrets."

"We already know them, bro," Ranger said and put a hand on his shoulder.

Last time he'd seen Ranger, the man had appeared undone, his world in pieces.

This Ranger, only a few days older, had a sense of purpose. Even, well, he looked a lot like the SEAL Colt had known years ago, back at Key West, trying to pass his free-diving certification.

"What are you guys doing here?"

Ranger removed his hand. "Noemi's father is undercover, you know, with the Petrov Bratva."

"Yeah. Our new friend Roy said that he'd gotten us the information we needed. Said the Petrovs are holed up somewhere around here?"

"Downriver a few klicks. Ham has all the details," Ranger said. "But that's not why we're here." He ran a hand behind his neck. "Before he left, Pete gave me a burner phone. Just in case something happened to him—or, to us. He wanted to stay in touch—"

"We pocket dialed him." Noemi had stood up and leaned against the railing, her back to the river. She wore a stripped expression.

"You *what?*"

"It was in my pocket, and we were . . ." His gaze went to Noemi, and he cleared his throat. "Anyway, somehow the phone was dialed. And when we realized, it was clear that—"

"We think we burned him," Noemi interrupted again. She glanced at Ranger, back to Colt. "We called Logan, and he confirmed that he hadn't checked in . . ."

"You think he's dead?"

"Colt, c'mon," Ranger said and glanced at Noemi.

Colt held up his hands. "I'm asking the question. Because what I hear you saying is that you want to *rescue* Pete. And before we all decide to risk our lives—which, calm down, of course I'm in—we should at least confirm that the man is still alive, right?"

Dodge nodded. "Yes. We should. So we have a plan." He folded his arms, a slight grin on his face. "How do you feel about going for a swim?"

"You too?" Colt shrugged. Apparently he was getting wet. "Fine. Sure."

"There might be some running," Dodge said.

"It'll be just like old times," Ranger added.

"Since when did our old times include sneaking into a Russian mobster compound, avoiding what I suspect will be killer Dobermans, and sneaking around trying not to alert the Draco thugs to our presence? Unless . . . wait. Why do I feel like this plan just might get only me hurt?"

"You always were the tough guy," Dodge said.

"Aww . . ."

"C'mon, Colt," Ranger said. "It's time to go on a bear hunt."

Ranger had forgotten how much he loved to dive.

Or maybe not forgotten, just lodged it back in his brain so that the memory of former glory days wouldn't surface to cut off his breathing.

But yes, right now, he was in his quiet, perfect happy place. Twenty or so feet above him, the world had turned black, the sky moonless, the stars out, and they had dappled the platinum water of the Indian River with pinpricks of light as Colt and Dodge had driven their boat down the river toward Stingray Point, where the Petrovs had quietly set up their compound, some fifteen klicks away from the Marshall mansion.

A house he could sort of get used to. His bedroom—the one he shared with Noemi—looked out over a pool, and beyond that, the river. They'd spent much of yesterday doing recon, then taking a ride down the shore for a look-see at the compound. He'd spotted manatees in the shallows, and earlier tonight, as they'd been finalizing their sneak and peek, a pod of dolphins swam by.

Friends in the water.

Normally he'd have his team with him, working with hand signals as they approached their target, the mission goals, step-by-step, entrenched in their minds.

Now, it was just him, a lobster run—solo dive—twenty feet down, sneaking through the brackish waters to the Petrov compound, his night vision mask attachment turning the water an eerie green as he scraped along the bottom.

At least he wouldn't alert any of Petrov's people who might be patrolling the compound to his presence with a dive light. He had to admit Jones, Inc. had some stellar gear.

In fact, he liked all the Jones, Inc. guys. Ham in particular. He knew the former SEAL from Team 5 by reputation, his snafu in Afghanistan being something the fellow frogmen talked about in quiet tones. The betrayals, the casualties, the fallout.

But Ham had landed on his feet and brought some friends with him. Ranger knew Fraser Marshall, too, had connected with him on some training ops in early days. Apparently Fraser had a cousin with some money who let them use the house, not to mention his high-speed cigarette boat.

Ranger liked a ride with muscle.

Although gliding along in silence, just the hiss of his own breath into the rebreather gave him a moment to think, to prepare, to focus.

Yes, he missed this.

"I'm in position." Dodge's voice came through his earpiece, and although Ranger couldn't respond, he appreciated knowing just what might be going on above surface.

Ranger ran the map, and the mission, through his mind as he kicked quietly into the canal that edged the southern point.

The Russian compound sat on twenty acres of secluded property—at least secluded from the road, where tall coconut palms intermingled with the crooked live sand oaks, and shorter-needle palms amid a tangle of undergrowth. Good cover for clandestine insertion, but not so great for the quick sneak and possible grab of tonight's mission.

Better insertion point was the grounds to the west that led to the water. Light shone on a pool area, but cover could be found in clumps of dwarf bottle palm trees, date palms, jasmine, and firethorn bush—enough landscaping that under the cover of darkness a guy could pick his way inside.

Especially with a distraction. *C'mon, Colt.*

Probably they should stop using Colt as the sacrificial lamb, but the guy so easily embraced it. He always wore a sort of glint in his eye that screamed, *Bring it.* Which was probably why he got into so many scuffles. His brother was the toughest guy he knew.

Even so, Tae's words hung in Ranger's head as he drew closer to the shoreline, thick with mangroves. *"Something's not right with Colt."*

The words raked up Dodge's description of Colt lying on the glacier, fighting for breath.

The guy was probably out of shape and definitely still healing. *"We promise to keep him safe,"* he'd told Tae. *"He's just a decoy."*

Unless, of course, Colt made it more. Something his brother had been known to do. All Colt had to do was drive the boat a little too close to shore on the south side, where the dock jutted out, and rile up any security. Yes, it might entail him getting stuck, even hauled off the boat, but the point was to keep the Russians occupied while Range crept out of the water like a primordial beast and entered the house.

Or rather, *fortress*. At first glance, it might look like a resort, but given the lighting, the U-shape of the courtyard, the second-story balconies that no doubt contained watchful eyes, getting in wouldn't be a walk in the park.

But Ranger had devised a plan for that too, after doing a couple flybys over the house last night with a high-altitude drone.

Armed with intel, he'd spent most of the night and some of today laying out the plan with Colt and Dodge and Ham's team. Although for expedience, the Jones, Inc. guys decided to wait upriver. No reason to bring an entire assault team to what was basically a reconnaissance mission. He and Dodge and Colt could handle it.

In many ways, this was a trial run training exercise for any possible assault on the compound, except it included real bullets. And everything that came with that.

But they all wore vests, coms, and were armed with a quick exfil—Ham's guys waiting in a rented speedboat, a quick assault force if they needed it.

It wouldn't come to that. They'd get in, slip out, mission executed.

Ranger edged around the mangroves—no getting through there—and toward a break in the shoreline. *C'mon, Colt!*

As if reading his mind, Dodge piped into his ears. "Colt's on target. Making a ruckus now."

Dodge was positioned just south of Colt on Bee Gum Point, nestled into the shoreline, tracking Colt's movements via the NOD scope attachment on his rifle.

Yeah, Ranger missed that too. Sitting for hours—days, even—in a nest, watching, devising plan B or C or even D scenarios should things turn south. Rooting out vulnerabilities in their plan, even advising his team lead on options, given his position.

He just missed being actually *useful*.

Movement in his periphery made him turn and for a second, his mask loosened, the NOD array on the front nearly dislodging it with his movements. He clamped down on his mask, focusing on the scuttle of dust rising from the riverbed.

Somehow, despite the green hue, down here his vision didn't seem so compromised. Maybe because everything was a little hazy, shadowed. But, he could see just fine, thank you, the alligator that sat, buried in the tangle of mangroves, some ten feet away. A long snout, big eyes, and an eight-foot tail, at the least. Creepy in the murky water.

Hey there, buddy, nothing to see here.

Still, Ranger reached for his dive knife, just in case the animal decided to shift.

The creature watched as Ranger floated by, probably sizing him up. He probably looked like a manatee.

Twenty feet past the nest, Ranger found the infil point, possibly a dog trail to the water, no more than two feet wide, but enough for him to climb to shore, remove his NOD apparatus, his fins, the rebreather, and tuck them all away, along with the second rebreather and mask he carried in a waterproof bag.

Just in case Pete was still alive.

Please, God, let Pete be alive. He couldn't bear to see what his second death—real this time—might do to Noemi. She wasn't as okay with letting her dad go as she let on.

In fact, she wasn't really excited about Ranger getting back in the water either, but she said nothing as he'd gotten ready today. Kissed her goodbye. "See you later," he said.

"You'd better," she replied and blinked back tears.

Yeah, she was tough. But maybe not tough enough to let him back into this life. Even if he was in operating shape.

Tonight, however, he never felt better. In just his booties and his wet suit, he crouched on the trail, his eyes adjusting. "I'm in position," he said softly, his ear coms now working under the hood of his wet suit.

"Colt's got most of the security team on the dock now. They're yelling at him, but the boat is tangled in the mangroves. You're clear."

"Good copy, Dodge." How Ranger wished he had his P226 tucked into his belt, but the last thing they needed was a slew of casualties, the appearance of the local law, and any hope of procuring the bioweapon destroyed.

No, he'd go in armed with his combat knife, and really, if he did this right, no one would get hurt.

He slipped out of cover over to a dwarf palm, crouched, scoured the area, and headed toward the house.

Motion detector lights would flicker on if they picked up anything larger than a raccoon, but he'd already located the lights, so he ran a path in his mind, through the landscaping, finally hitting his knees as he scrabbled toward the outer wall of the house.

Shouting lifted and hung in the air from the north. He glanced around the edge of the wall, across the deep aqua pool and the dark-green grass to the far docks.

Colt stood on the seat of his boat, yelling at a handful of heavily armed thugs.

"Don't make them too angry, bro," Ranger said softly into the coms. Last thing he wanted was to go diving for Colt's body. Or even to have to abort his search for Pete and divert to getting Colt out of an unmatched brawl.

Although the thought of a good fight also steamed his blood.

"Too late," Dodge said. "Hurry up."

Roger. Ranger crept along the edge of the house, tried a door, found it locked, then darted across a trellised patio and found a sliding glass door, the room inside dark.

He eased it open and slipped inside, too aware, suddenly, of the slick floor under his wet boots. Unzipping them, he yanked them off and stuck them into a pocket of his vest.

They'd identified movement last night with the drone, had pinpointed where lights had gone on in the house. Noemi had thought she'd seen her father outlined in one of the windows, but she couldn't be sure. Still, Ranger had obtained some old online photos of the place when it was up for sale a year ago and mapped out the location in his head.

Now, he kept low and walked the length of the great room, stopping just before he hit the stairway.

"Colt's still tangled up in the mangroves," Dodge said, "but it looks like someone is headed to the house. Get a move on."

Ranger headed up the stairs, his feet quiet on the landing. Got his bearings at the top.

Third door down, right side. The balcony overlooked the northern bay.

He gripped the doorknob with his left hand, the right holding his knife. Quieted his heartbeat. Then he eased the door open.

A hand caught him around the throat, slammed him against the wall.

Ranger's arm jerked up, breaking the hold free even as his left swung hard.

He connected with cheekbone, and the man stumbled back, hit the bedframe. Bounced off it, lit.

Ranger blocked the right hook. "Pete. It's me. Range." He gave him a push, nothing too hard, but enough for Pete to step back.

He stood, breathing hard, his eyes widening on Ranger. "What the— What are you *doing* here?"

And for a split second, Ranger heard him, the old man, years ago when he'd told Ranger to stay away from his daughter. *"The last thing she needs is a broken heart over a man who might not come home."*

Yeah, well, this was not that day.

"You haven't checked in. Logan is worried." Ranger's mouth pinched. "Noemi is worried."

Pete looked a little worse for wear, shadows under his eyes, a red mark on his cheek where Ranger had clocked him. Oops.

"Is she okay?" Pete wiped a hand across his face. "I had to destroy the burner phone, but—"

"She's okay. Are *you* okay?"

"Yeah. After the call, I had some explaining to do. Said it was for a shipping contact. But they're watching me. I haven't been able to leave."

"Do you know where they're keeping the virus?"

"Yes. It's in the pool house, in a number of small containers. They had it motored up the river a week ago."

"Do you know when the attack is?"

Pete shook his head. "But it's soon. They're expecting someone—I think it might be one of the Petrovs—to arrive any day. He's in charge of the deployment."

Outside, voices lifted, shouting.

"Dodge, what's going on?" Ranger said into his coms.

"Colt has the boat off the mangroves, but he's run into the dock. I think he's pretending he's drunk. A few more guys have peeled off to the house. You need to exfil."

Footsteps sounded on the stairwell, carried through the house.

"You gotta go," said Pete.

"Noemi will kill me if anything happens to you."

More footsteps.

"Listen, if I leave, we won't have inside intel."

"And if you stay, you'll get made. Noemi can't take you dying again."

Something ticked in Pete's expression. "I'm sorry."

Pounding sounded at the door.

Ranger headed for the closet and tucked himself inside just as Pete opened the door.

Keeping the door open just enough to see through the sliver of light, Ranger ducked back out of the stream as one of the men thundered into the room.

Wow, he wished he knew Russian.

Pete had his hands up, rattling off fast Russian, but from the expression on the man's face, the look in his eye, it wasn't working.

Yikes. Ranger had seen those looks before, something dark and unhinged and—

The man held cuffs up toward Pete.

Shoot. Yes, Pete could have taken him, could have hit the floor, taken out the man's legs on his way down, and brought the fight to the ground.

Instead, the old SEAL held up his hands in surrender.

A heartbeat. Two. *C'mon, Pete.*

Whatever hand Pete was playing wasn't panning out because the guy pushed Pete to the wall and shoved the business end of the gun to his head. Nice, now Ranger got a front-row seat to his father-in-law's execution.

Nope. Pete wasn't dying on his watch.

It took two steps—he could do it with his eyes closed, really, the way he'd worked it out in his head—and the man was on the floor, Ranger's knife slicing his carotid artery.

Pete stilled, his gaze on the man. He let out a word.

"It's done," Ranger said. "Let's go."

Pete just blinked at him. Then in three steps he was across the room. He grabbed his cell phone and handed it to Ranger. "Put it in your waterproof pouch."

Ranger slid it into the pouch inside his wet suit.

Pete pulled his P226 Sig out from a side table. "They're in the hallway. We'll need to go over the balcony."

He flicked off the light before he pulled open the French doors. Heat slicked into the room like a furnace. Ranger stepped out into it, after Pete.

Darkness bathed this side of the house, and it took a second for Ranger's eyes to adjust. "We're on the balcony, north side. Make some noise, Colt."

Seconds later, Colt's engine revved. Shouting followed, and in his mind's eye, he could see Colt spinning in circles, or maybe he'd plowed right into the dock. Whatever. Ranger just needed enough time to get back in the water with Pete.

Pete had thrown a leg over the balcony railing, shimmied down, and now dropped to the ground. Ranger followed, dropping softly.

Motion lights flicked on in the distance, and Ranger grabbed Pete's shirt and pulled him into the balcony shadow. He pointed to the path where he'd come in, and Pete nodded.

Ranger went first, his memorized route kicking in. Along the balcony edge, to the front side of the house, leapfrogging landscape bunkers all the way to the mangroves' edge.

Above them, shouting came from the room where Ranger had dropped Pete's attacker.

"Ready?" Ranger asked.

"Go," Pete answered.

Ranger ran along the wall, then fell to his knees and crawled through the dark grass to a spray of dwarf palms.

Seconds later Pete edged in beside him. "Keep moving."

Ranger scampered to the next tree, Pete on his tail, and finally the last bunch of palm and jasmine.

The shouting grew as their posse streamed out of the house, the yard lighting up with the movement.

Perfect. Now they'd have to run to the mangroves under the football lights.

"See the break in the mangroves? That's our exfil."

"Roger."

Ranger took off, no need to crawl anymore, running hard for the break. Shots sounded behind him, and a bullet seared the air close to his ear.

Behind him, Pete had fired off a shot, then another.

Ranger launched into the cover of the mangrove trail, crouched, and kept running. Dragging out his bag on the way to the water, he dove in.

Pete wasn't behind him.

He turned and spotted the man on shore, crawling. Ranger bit back a word when Pete collapsed, hard, rolled into a ball.

Ranger scrambled back out and dove for him, grabbing his collar. "Where're ya hit?"

"My leg. Just get me out of here."

In the wan light, Ranger made out the dark wash of blood streaming from his upper leg. A quick look said it wasn't the femoral artery, so they had time.

Ranger fitted on his fins, the rebreather and mask, and pulled Pete into the water even as he shoved the rebreather into his mouth. Pete clamped onto the mouthpiece and fitted on the mask.

Nodded.

Ranger took Pete down, just as a man broke through the path to the shore.

He fired a shot into the darkness.

But they were already in the grasses, Ranger's NOD attachment lighting the way. Blood from Pete's leg clouded the water. Perfect.

He kicked hard away from the mangroves, and the neighborhood nesting gator, and towed Pete farther out and down. And there, parked at the bottom, in the wan green light, Ranger ripped apart Pete's pants leg.

Not the femoral, but a through and through in the lower part of his thigh. He signaled Pete to hang on to him, and then, with Noemi's father gripping his vest, Ranger towed the man through the water, into the open river.

Six minutes later, he surfaced some three hundred yards from shore, at a buoy designated for pickup. Pete had lost a lot of blood, and Ranger held him aloft around the chest, kicking hard.

A motor sounded in the distance. In the starlight, Ranger made out Colt standing at the helm, his hair blowing back. Dodge sat on the bow, searching the water with his night vision scope. Ranger waved, and the boat slowed, then the motor cut and it drifted toward them.

Ranger swam over, his arm around Pete. "Get him up. He's been shot."

Colt and Dodge leaned over and pulled Pete from the water. Ranger threw his gear in, then grabbed his brothers' hands and let them haul him into the boat.

He sat on the deck, breathing hard, as Dodge wrapped Pete's leg in a tourniquet. Colt retook the helm, turned on the lights, and hit it.

The boat leaped to life, almost immediately planing out over the chop of the water.

Dodge sat down next to him. "He's going to be okay. The bleeding is already slowing."

Ranger leaned his head back, stared at the blinking stars, and smiled.

Hoo-yah.

She hated every single minute of this waiting game.

Tae stood by the pool, her arms folded over her body, staring out into the darkness. Next to her, Noemi's gaze was also pinned on the dark night, in the direction that Ranger, Colt, and Dodge had gone in the high-powered cigarette boat of their host.

Tae had her answer.

It *wasn't* worth it.

Not by the look on Noemi's face.

And probably not by her face either, if she took a good look because . . .

Because she just couldn't lose him.

And that fact was exactly why she shouldn't let herself fall for Colt—something she knew, but what was a girl to do? Colt Kingston was a hard man to resist.

Especially today, when he went with her to the lab that Logan had set up twenty minutes away, on Patrick Space Force base. The way Colt had asked her about the machinery, the process of making a vaccine, as if her world, her life, mattered very much to him.

He made her feel smart, important. Desired.

And then brave. Because when they'd returned

to the house, before he disappeared with the guys for one last briefing of their secret op tonight, he'd taken her out on a Jet Ski. Like they were on some kind of vacation.

She'd left all the craziness behind as she held on to Colt, the wind in her hair. He smelled of the sun, of coconut oil, his hair tied back, looking every inch like some beachcombing bum.

One look at his body, however, said something else. Sure, he had war wounds—still a few fading bruises, a thick scar on his shoulder, another along his back, something he'd gotten in basic training, apparently—but he was a solid, muscled package of get it done. Truth was, she probably had nothing to worry about tonight.

Colt knew how to handle himself.

Really.

So she could probably unwind her arms, unleash her breath, and let go of the knot in her chest.

Except what about—

Nope. He'd said it—multiple times. He was fine. Just. Fine.

Still, "They're going to be okay, right?"

At her question, Noemi looked over. She wore her hair down around her face, a pair of white shorts, a coral top, her feet bare. She looked clearly at home in the heat, less oppressive now that the sun had gone down. At home in the heat, and in the world of her former-SEAL husband because she'd spent the day with Ranger, going over the plans for tonight.

"Please tell me they know what they're doing," Tae said.

Noemi got up. "Yes. Ranger is a SEAL. I don't want to admit it, really, but he lives for missions like this, and Colt—well, you know him well enough to know that he always comes through. They're going to be fine." But she swallowed at the end of her words, a cue that despite her expression, those golden-brown eyes holding Tae's, she too might be a little worried.

"You're worried about your dad."

Noemi's mouth pinched. "Yes. I know he can take care of himself too, but . . ." She shook her head. "It never gets easier, I guess. Even when you expect this life. It's probably a good thing they never actually talk about their missions, or I would lie awake at night imagining all sorts of dark scenarios that probably aren't true."

"I don't know how you grew up like this."

"I didn't. I grew up in boarding schools. I think my parents sent me away specifically so I didn't have to worry, but . . . well, yes, it was always in the back of my mind. But my mother made sure that when we were together, it mattered. They'd pick me up for summer break and we'd spend it camping, or at a theme park, or at a beach. Later, after my mom died, my dad took me camping at a ranch in Montana. Taught me how to survive. His own mini SERE school."

"SERE?"

"Survive. Evade. Resist. Escape, Pete Sutton style."

"No wonder you lived through captivity."

"Well, I had help. Namely, Colt. And Fraser."

"The blond guy whose cousin owns this place?"

"Yeah. They were both there, protection detail. I've never met tougher men. Except Range, of course." Noemi smiled. "He downplayed how hurt he was to get me to safety."

"That sounds like a Kingston brother." Tae turned back to the dark water. Across the river, the red, green, and white lights of Palm Bay twinkled against the night. "I think Colt is more hurt than he lets on."

"He'll be okay," Noemi said. "But will *you* be okay?"

Tae frowned at her.

"When he goes back to Jones, Inc."

Oh. "Yes, right."

"Because I see the way that you look at him. Girl, you're a goner. And he looks at you like he wants to gobble you up."

Tae smiled. "He does, doesn't he?"

"And I'll bet he's a great kisser." Noemi winked.

Tae laughed. Then, "Do you hear that?"

A hum sounded up the river, and she and

Noemi walked out to the edge of the grass, near the water.

A light parted the darkness, another behind it, farther down, and Tae couldn't stop herself from running out to the end of the dock.

The boat came into view, Colt at the helm. He raised a hand to her, gave her a nod.

Tears bit her eyes, and her knees wanted to buckle.

Calm down. The last thing he needed was to see her worry.

Good try. Because as Colt cut the power and brought the boat to a gentle glide up to the dock, she was wrapping her arms around herself, trying not to cry.

Get ahold of yourself!

See, not even a little brave.

Dodge threw a line to Noemi, who tied up the boat at the bow.

Colt glanced at Tae, frowning, but turned toward Ranger and a man in the back of the boat.

Pete. He was sopping wet, his blond hair invisible against his pale skin, and wore a grimace. His hands clutched a wound on his leg, tied tight with a tourniquet but still seeping blood.

She wiped her cheeks, grabbed the boat, and climbed in. "What happened?"

Ranger crouched next to him, moving his arm around his body. "Shot."

He hauled Pete up, who groaned.

"Dad!" Noemi had jumped in too. Tae wanted to get a look at that leg, but she stepped back to let Noemi closer. "What happened?"

"It's a long story," Ranger said.

"Is he going to be okay?" Noemi asked her father and Dodge as they climbed out of the boat.

"Let's get him to a hospital," Tae said. See, she was fine. She'd already stopped shaking.

"No," Pete said. "It's a gunshot wound. There'll be questions." He looked at her. "Can you stitch me up?"

Oh boy. "We'll see. I can try."

Ranger and Dodge carried him down the dock, Noemi close behind, but when Tae turned to follow, Colt caught her around the arm. "Hey!"

She turned back and he met her eyes, his gleaming in the night. His man bun had come untangled in the wind, but he wore a solemn, almost piercing look about him. "You okay?"

And then, shoot, the tears caught her up and she shook her head. No, no—

"Flo?"

She couldn't stop herself. She threw her arms around him and held on.

"Oh," he said, and then he closed his arms around her.

She buried her head in his shoulder, hating herself.

He just held her tight, in the swaying boat,

rocked by the waves of the other boat, the bigger one that held the Jones, Inc. crew, just coming to the dock on the other side.

"Something we're missing?" said a voice—she didn't know whose.

"It's all good," Colt said. "Nothing to see here."

He released her, met her eyes. Ran a thumb across her cheek.

She held his face. And couldn't stop her crazy words. "Promise me you'll always come back."

He blinked. "Tae."

"Promise me. Because . . ." Tears blurred her eyes again. "I just can't love a man who is going to . . ." She closed her eyes, looked away.

"Tae . . . I can't—"

She was wrecking everything.

And, apparently, panicking, because all thought left her but her first impulse.

She kissed him. And maybe she didn't mean to kiss him with such force, but she just couldn't hear the truth.

He wasn't the kind of guy not to go full throttle into a fight. Which meant he also wasn't the guy to make silly promises.

What he could do, however, was kiss her.

Colt wrapped his hand around the back of her neck and held her tight, kissing her back.

A few whistles sounded from the boat on the other side of the dock, as the crew unloaded, but it seemed Colt didn't care. His kiss was thorough

267

and sincere, and he met her eyes when she pulled away.

"Tae?"

"Nope. That's all I want. Just . . . don't say anything else, okay?"

His eyes widened. He nodded.

She forced a smile. Took his hand as he helped her out of the boat.

But really, her heart wanted to scream.

Because that wasn't all that she wanted. Not even close.

TEN

Tae's words kept ringing through Colt's head as they went to the kitchen, where Pete lay on the table. Colt stayed back, quiet with the rest of the guys, as Tae opened Pete's jeans farther, took a look at the wound.

"I just can't love a man who is going to . . ."

Oh boy.

So maybe she hadn't actually told him that she *loved* him. Just that, in the remote chance that she ever did . . .

And then there were the tears. Wow. She'd *really* been crying, and seeing that up close rattled him more than he wanted to admit. So much that he'd just about made a stupid promise that he couldn't keep.

Sure, yes, if it was within his power, he would prefer living, thank you. But most likely, he'd also be the guy who ran in, powered by his impulses, and jumped on the grenade. Which meant that any promise he made he was likely to break.

"It didn't hit anything major," Tae said, all work and focus. "But he needs an ER."

A small argument ensued, again, in which Ham sided with Pete, and finally she agreed to stitch Pete up. But it would require Novocain.

About a half hour later, Logan Thorne showed

up with the right supplies, like a doctor making house calls.

By then, most of the guys had peeled off. Jake and North headed to bed, Ham and Pete going over what he knew about the compound and the Petrovs' plans.

Pete and Noemi hadn't exactly talked yet, but by the way Noemi kept pressing her hand to her mouth, turning away, shaking her head, yes, there was a conversation coming.

Probably one between Colt and Tae too, but . . . yeah, he'd sort of like to dodge that.

"I just can't love a man who is going to . . ."

He wanted to hit something because, yes, he knew this was coming.

Just wasn't ready, quite so soon, to break her heart.

To be the bad guy.

Tae had gotten the supplies, shot Pete with enough Novocain to put down a horse, and then gone to work stitching up the layers of his leg like she might be a plastics resident.

Colt sat on a stool next to Ham, drinking a Powerade, watching her work. Her face masked, her hair tied back, her hands gloved. Pete laid with one arm over his eyes, exposing a couple thick scars on his forearm.

Clearly this wasn't his first go-round with a needle and thread, probably not even away from an ER.

Tae closed the entry wound, then turned him over. Pete tucked his head into his arms.

The exit wound was uglier. "This is going to take some time," she said.

"Let's talk," Ham said to Colt and gestured outside.

He still—hopefully—worked for the man, so Colt nodded and followed his boss.

The air had cooled with the deepening of the night. It was late—well into the wee hours. Ham walked over to one of the deck chairs that edged the deep aqua blue of the pool. To Colt's surprise, Fraser was already camped out in a lounger.

"Hey," Ham said as he sat down.

Colt took another chair. The sound of the sliding door made him glance behind him. Dodge had joined them. His brother's cool voice in his ear today had done something to Colt, grounded him, maybe.

Like old times, Ranger had said earlier. Not really, but . . . yeah, he liked working with his brothers. Felt almost right. Normal.

"With Ranger's actions tonight, pulling Pete out, we might have ignited the timeline for the bioweapon deployment," Ham said.

"Sounds like Range had no choice," Dodge said.

Ham held up his hand. "I'm not pointing any fingers. Just saying that we need to get into the compound as soon as we can and get hold of the

271

canisters. Pete can give us a thorough lay of the land, but we need a plan."

"I can help with that." Ranger had come outside too. He'd changed out of his wet suit into a pair of shorts and a T-shirt, and now held a power drink as he walked up to them.

The man seemed on top of his game, even with tonight's semifiasco. Although saving Noemi's father certainly wasn't a fail.

They *had* gotten eyes on the compound and the Petrovs' force of strength.

Ranger sat down on a chair. Leaned forward. "I have a photographic memory. I can trace the entire compound, with the lights and the patterns. I have no doubt we can figure out a way to get us in there, grab the bioweapons, and exfil without casualties." He took a drink. "Especially if we're armed with more than my utility knife."

"We will be," Fraser said.

Ham crossed his arms over his chest. He turned to Colt. "How many guards did you see?"

"I had seven on the dock with me. Another on shore, and my guess is that there might have been a couple watching me in the shadows. Had a funny feeling in my gut."

"That was just your dinner," Ranger said.

Colt chucked his empty bottle at him.

Ranger caught it. Tossed it in a nearby trash can with a flick of his wrist. Clearly there was nothing wrong with his eyesight tonight.

"How are they outfitted?" Ranger asked.

"Standard stuff—AR-15s, probably picked up locally," Colt said.

"We'll need eyes on them 24/7 until we deploy so we know they haven't moved the weapon," Ham said. He turned to Ranger. "You and I will work up the op."

Ranger raised an eyebrow. "Okay." He took a drink.

"Colt, since you and Tae are already friendly, you tag along, see what you can do to help her and Zoey get that vaccine ready. I'd like us all inoculated before we go in. If I understand this virus right, it might be airborne, which means a stray bullet into one of those canisters kills us all."

Colt sighed but nodded.

"You okay with that?" Ham asked.

"Yeah. Sure."

Ham gave him a long look. Then, finally, "Let's get some shut-eye. Beach run, 0600." Then, "You good to join us, Colt?"

What was it with these people? "Try and keep up, squid."

"You get to say that once."

"Okay, old man," Colt said.

"He likes trouble," Dodge said, rising. "Can't stop running his mouth."

"This mouth kept Ranger alive today, buddy."

Dodge rolled his eyes but grinned.

273

Overhead the stars sparkled. Ranger had gotten up too. "I'm going to check on Noemi. She's completely freaking out about her dad."

"Speaking of Dad, how is he?" Colt asked.

"Echo is staying with him." Dodge walked up to his brother. Put a hand on his shoulder. "Good work tonight, Sam."

Colt looked at him, the old nickname sliding through him, latching deep inside.

"Sam?" Ham asked.

"My dad used to say that Colt went in, guns blazing," Dodge said, "and then it sort of evolved to calling him Sam, after Samuel Colt."

Colt had never really liked it. Not until his Delta buddies also caught on to the same very uncreative nickname. But hearing it now, out of Dodge's mouth . . . he didn't mind so much. "Thanks, bro."

Dodge headed inside with Range.

Fraser got up. "Thanks for not destroying Win's boat tonight."

"Win?"

"Winchester Marshall, my cousin."

"The actor. He's your cousin, huh?"

"Second cousin, actually, on my dad's side," Fraser said. "He's from here, so he bought a place even though he's not around much. There's a few more Marshalls floating around here somewhere." He headed inside. "Meet you all on the beach."

Colt should go to bed too, but sitting out here, in the tempered heat of the night, his chest had stopped hurting, and somehow he could breathe easier too.

Maybe it was because around these guys, he didn't feel like such a villain. Didn't feel like a jerk for doing things in the night he couldn't talk about.

And liking it.

He shook his head.

"There it is again. That look," Ham said.

A beat, then, *Fine*. Ham might get it. "I think Tae has feelings for me."

Ham raised an eyebrow.

"I'm not being arrogant. She said so on the boat."

"No, I was thinking maybe you have a thing for her too. I saw the way you kissed her tonight."

He held up his hand. "Just, hold on. Yes. We've kissed. And there's something . . . sweet about her. And maybe even a little, well, she just sort of calms all the buzzing in my head, you know? She's smart and pretty and—"

"I'm not reading the wall here, Colt. What's the problem?"

Sometimes Ham said the strangest things. But, "I'm not sticking around. I'm not made for long-term relationships, and she knows that, but I feel like maybe that hasn't sunk in. I'm only going to hurt her."

Ham drew in a breath. Deep inside, Colt sort of wanted to be like Ham someday. Past forty, Ham still bore the frame of an operator. Wizened blue eyes, his short dark blond hair wind worked, a haze of whiskers on his chin. Still, Ham could outrun, outfight, outthink most of them.

But recently—and Colt hadn't gotten the entire story—Ham had settled down, gotten married, acquired a daughter, and generally made room in his life for people he could come home to.

"Why aren't you sticking around?"

He looked at Ham. "Seriously?"

"Yeah. Listen. You're one of the best security guys I have. And I'm ready to deploy you as soon as you're ready, but, Colt, that doesn't mean you don't need someone solid in your life. Someone to come home to."

"No, you don't get it. Her dad was military. And he died—some classified op—and she's still wrecked over it. I can't do that to her."

Ham nodded, his eyes on him. "That sort of sounds like her decision."

Maybe, but Colt had seen her tonight when he'd pulled up to the dock. Racked with worry. And then there it was again, *I just can't love a man who is going to . . ."*

"She's brave, but she was completely unraveled tonight, and it sort of . . . honestly, it freaked me out. I never thought—"

"That someone could love you that much?"

Ham's words landed like a punch to his chest. Colt nearly put his hand over the wound, looking for blood. "No, um . . ." Sheesh, his entire body hurt. "She doesn't *really* love me. It's just, you know, adrenaline."

"Women don't fall in love like men. They don't need the thrill, not as much. They see the potential, the future in a way we can't."

"That's the problem. There's no future here."

"But you kissed her."

The way Ham put it tightened his breath. "Yeah?"

"You might need to put the kibosh on that if you're not planning on making this anything serious."

Right. And yep, Colt knew that, at least deep inside. The part that he tried not to listen to.

"Unless you think you might love her back."

And just like that, Ham's words wrapped around his chest and squeezed.

No. No . . . *shoot.*

What was he *doing?*

"No. That's not happening. You're right, this is a bad idea. I need to do right by her and shut this thing down."

"Colt—"

"Listen, any woman who loves me is going to get hurt, because, yeah, I'm that guy who kicks the door down. And not because I have a death wish, but because that's just how I'm built. And I'm never going to change."

He didn't mean for his voice to rise.

Ham just considered him. Finally, "And having someone love you means you'd have to care what happens to you."

"Now you sound like my father."

"I'm not saying that you're reckless. We all need the guy who isn't afraid to lead. But what if she *does* love you? How is that so terrible?"

His chest hurt again. "I gotta get some shut-eye." He stood up.

Ham also rose. "This isn't about her loving you, is it? It's about *you* loving her. And that's what has you freaked out."

Colt glanced toward the kitchen, to the light streaming out into the black. "Like I said, no girl in her right mind should love me. Because at the end of the day, I'm only going to break her heart."

"Or she'll break yours. And that's what has you running."

He stared at Ham, a beat, a breath, and finally, "I'll see you on the beach in the morning."

He left Ham standing there and headed inside.

Pete and Noemi were in the kitchen, talking in low tones. Tae stood with her back to him, at the kitchen sink, putting away the supplies. For a moment the shape of her, the feel of her hair in his hands, the sense of wanting to reach out and just pull her to himself and hold on, swept over him.

Then he sighed and headed up the stairs.

"It's not a match."

The dire words came from Zoey, sitting on a stool in their lab, dressed in her Tyvek jumpsuit, wearing her dead air hood, her gloves, booties, mask, and goggles. Tae, similarly dressed, might not have even heard her, but she was sitting in silence, staring at her own slide of genome-sequenced cells, thinking exactly the same thing.

Three days into their research and they were failing. What was worse was that every day she and Zoey got a negative read from the Cryo-electron microscope, every day their synthesized horsepox sequence failed to replicate close enough to the ancient strain of S-poxR, was a day the world—namely Colt and the guys planning a recovery of the bioweapon—went unvaxxed.

Naked, into the world of pathogens.

Tae stepped back from the microscope and stretched. She probably should be sweating inside her Stay Puft Marshmallow Man suit, but the positive pressure air filtration system kept the lab at a cool 68 degrees.

Logan had also outfitted the lab with every-thing they needed, with vials and test tubes and stainless steel surfaces and equipment, including computers and DNA sequencers and the giant

Cyro-electron microscope, which sat on a vibration pad, surrounded by walls filled with water to keep the temperature even.

The entire lab, located in a secluded area of Patrick Space Force Base, was sleek, up-to-date, and contained three layers of protection, including a UV light bath that sterilized their suits before they exited into a clean room, where they discarded the suits, then stepped into another UV bath.

She'd never been so clean.

Temperature-controlled glass walls surrounded the lab, and Logan or Roy would stop in and ask for updates via the coms system connected to the lab.

Always, however, Colt waited on the other side of the glass, their own personal bodyguard.

"Are you sure the McMaster lab sent us the right samples?" Zoey asked. "Because these still look too much like the vaccinia for our current-day smallpox."

All she could see of Zoey's face were her hazel-green eyes.

"Without an original sample, we can't be one hundred percent sure it works." Tae blew out a breath, which only fogged her glasses. She waited while the air in her suit cleared it and turned to look through the glass. "But we have to come up with something. We're running out of time."

Colt was standing, arms folded, watching. He

had a sort of dark fierceness in his expression, and despite his gaze, she guessed he was far away. Maybe back in Sudan. Or any of the other dangerous places he'd been that he didn't talk about.

Places he was someday going back to.

"I'm going to tweak the sequence, do another computation," Zoey said.

They'd spent their first day in the lab just sequencing the ancient virus they'd gotten from McMaster, using targeted enrichment and synthetic molecules that matched the S-poxR genome. Then they'd resequenced them into a 200,000-genome DNA strand that approximated the Russian pox.

They'd spent the last two days trying to approximate the horsepox sample to the Russian pox.

"I don't understand why our notes aren't accurate. Did Faheem change something and not document it?"

"Maybe we just don't have the right sequence for the ancient virus. I'd give just about anything for the original . . ." Zoey sat down at her computer.

"By the time we get our hands on that, it could be too late," Tae said.

Colt rapped on the window, pointed at his watch. She glanced at the clock through the window. No wonder her stomach growled. "It's nearly seven p.m."

"What?" Zoey looked up. Sighed. "I am hungry."

"You think? It's too much work to stop and eat—"

Colt rapped on the window again.

"What's his deal?" Zoey said as she finished her update on the computer.

"He's been here for twelve hours. My guess is that he's a little grumpy."

Actually, he'd been grumpy for three days, if she were accurate.

Right after she'd told him that she'd . . . yes, she'd sort of dropped the L-word on him. What. An. Idiot.

She wouldn't label his grumpy behavior a full-out sprint from their relationship, but after she'd stitched up Pete, she'd half expected—okay, hoped—that Colt might be waiting up for her. Yes, it had been late, so she wasn't completely surprised that he'd retired, but . . .

With everything inside her, she wanted to return to their conversation, maybe roll it back.

She *didn't* love him. Didn't . . . but yes, she'd been a mess just thinking about him, well, doing what he did.

It didn't help that in the back of her mind, she heard her mother's scream when the Navy came to the door. But that was different. Her mother hadn't known her father was doing something special ops-y.

Tae had her eyes wide open when it came to Colt.

So maybe his cold shoulder was the best, for both of them. Because any more time in his arms, around his magnetic, self-deprecating charm just might push her right over the edge and . . .

Well, *this* was her real world. Sterile. Machinery and labs and quiet work that saved lives. A world with many, many layers of protection, despite the risks.

Zoey had set her machine to run her computations. "Let's go. I'm dying for some Mexican food."

"Maybe we should come back later. See what your computations spit out."

Zoey stood at the door, ready to open it and step into the UV room. "I know we're up against a deadline, but you can't do anything hungry and tired."

Colt had leaned into the microphone that connected their rooms. "Ham called. I need to get back."

And that didn't bode well at all.

"We're close," Zoey said. She pushed the button and they stepped into the chamber, let the UV lights turn their suits purple as they disinfected them from any pathogens.

"Even if we do match the horsepox to the ancient virus from McMaster enough to produce antibodies, we still don't know if it's a match for the S-poxR, and, well, if it works on humans."

The light clicked off and the outer door buzzed open.

They entered another chamber and shed their Tyvek suits, hoods, gloves, booties, glasses, and hung them on hooks where they'd be stored in another UV chamber.

Then they stepped into a second compartment, slid on a pair of dark glasses, and repeated the bath.

"We won't have time to test it before the guys have to deploy."

"You know," Zoey said, "we talked about this, but I'm rounding back to it. Maybe you stop dreaming up worst-case scenarios and just . . . do what you can. Let God take care of the rest."

Just like before, the light in the chamber clicked off and the door opened.

Colt stood in the opening. He wore a pair of dress pants, a button-down shirt, and his hair pulled into a man bun, his brown eyes on her. "You okay?"

"Yeah," she said, following Zoey into the room.

"Any luck?" He unlocked their lab to the outer hallway.

"We're close," Zoey said, just as Tae answered, "No."

Colt raised an eyebrow, then he slipped on his sunglasses and opened the outer door.

The heat always washed over Tae like a sauna,

sucking out her breath, prickling sweat along her skin. The last hour of the day sent fiery light into the parking lot. Colt unlocked the Escalade and she slipped inside, the leather seats burning.

Zoey climbed into the back. "Why can't we have a government-issued convertible?"

Colt smiled, and it had the effect of cool sweet air upon Tae's parched spirit. "How's this?" He opened the sunroof even as he turned on the air conditioning, full blast.

She leaned back against the seat. Closed her eyes.

Driving toward the base exit, he flicked on the radio.

She didn't recognize the song, but Colt started to hum as he tapped his hand on the steering wheel.

"I got scars to prove I don't need you but the heart knows that I always do . . ."

He waved at the guard at the security gate, then pulled out into the highway and headed south. The sun hung over the Indian River to the west, bleeding out upon the water and along the horizon.

Zoey leaned toward the front seat. "Any chance we can pick up a burrito from that shop along the strip?"

"Robburritos?" Colt asked.

"Yeah. I love their pulled pork burrito."

"No problem. You want something?"

285

Oh. He was talking to her. She looked at him. Wow, he was a handsome man. The setting sun pulling out the strands of amber in his dark hair, and although he'd started shaving every morning, he wore a thick, devastating layer of shadow on his chin.

He'd rolled his shirtsleeves up, exposing his strong forearms, and he drove with his fingertips on the wheel, his head bobbing a little to the next song.

Like he might not have a care in the world.

The man was an enigma. Faced danger without blinking. Then ran from her when she hung on too tight.

But maybe this was on her. She'd practically dove at him, practically told him that she'd fall apart if . . .

"No. I'm not hungry."

He considered her a moment, then nodded.

Okay. Fine. She was starved, but at the moment, eating felt . . . well, it wouldn't remotely cover her hunger.

He pulled up to the hole-in-the-wall burrito stand. "Be right back."

The hickory and barbecue scent of the smoked meat seasoned the air.

Zoey toed off her shoes. "You sure you're okay?"

"Yeah."

"It's a nice night for a beach walk."

Tae glanced back at her.

Zoey was waggling her eyebrows. "I was thinking I might get Roy to take a walk with me. He's . . . interesting."

"He's trouble is what he is. He's a spy, Zoe. And probably an assassin and completely terrifying and—"

"I like him. He's intriguing. And hot."

"Oh wow."

"What? You have your own hot soldier, why not me?"

"I do not have . . . a hot . . . soldier."

"Excuse me, um, Colt is all sizzle."

Tae rolled her eyes, but she couldn't deny a smile. "Yes, he is very . . . smoldery. But the fact is, he's not mine. And . . ." Her smile fell. "I blew it. Again."

"What?"

"I totally freaked out when he went on that mission a few days ago. I was practically crying by the time he rolled into port, and then I did something really stupid. I asked him to promise me that he'd always come home."

"No you didn't."

"Yeah, I know. And you should have seen his face. Like, I dunno, I'd asked him to walk through Disney World in his underwear or something. I tried to get out of it."

"How?"

"I kissed him."

Zoey's mouth opened slightly, and she held up her fist for a bump. "You go, girl."

"Nooo—it was pitiful. And afterwards, he completely dodged me and now . . . well, he can barely look at me. So . . . well done, Taylor. At least he didn't kidnap and try to kill me."

"If that's your bar for success, I think maybe you're setting it a little low."

"I'm not— No, I mean, what's my problem? I'm a researcher. I spend years searching for the right genome sequence and about thirty-five seconds falling for the wrong guy."

"I'm not sure you even need that long when you find the right guy. Which may or may not be Colt, but I guarantee that you never looked at Sergei the way you look at Colt."

No, she hadn't. She'd just been lonely. And maybe desperate for escape.

But she never, not once, wanted to follow Sergei as he drove out into the night.

Shoot.

Zoey leaned forward between the front bucket seats. "Truth is, Tae, falling in love isn't safe. And loving a guy like Colt . . . yeah, I get why you might put on your brakes. But at the end of the day, you need to gather up all the evidence and decide whether your hypothesis is right or wrong. Is it worth it to love this guy, despite his crazy life, or not?"

Hmm.

Colt came out of the shop carrying a couple bags. He glanced at her through the windshield and smiled.

A thousand volts hit her and heated her down to her core.

Oh boy.

"You might consider, in that equation, that it's not as much about the worry when he's gone, but the way he makes you feel when you're together." Zoey glanced at Colt when he opened the door. "Hey there, handsome. What do you have for me?"

"Pork burrito." He handed her a bag, then held another out to Tae. "And chicken for you. You need your strength."

She took it. "Thanks."

Because, yes, she did, if she wanted to survive loving Colt Kingston.

"You're getting ready to deploy, aren't you?"

Noemi knew it was a dumb question, really, because Ranger stood in their room, gearing up, doing some sort of mental dance with his equipment, closing his eyes, running his hands over every placement of weaponry.

As if readying himself for battle.

And seeing him stand there, doing this prebattle warm-up, just . . . just . . .

She left the room so she didn't say anything stupid.

Noemi wanted to strangle her father, the man with nine lives.

Because unlike him, Ranger just had the one. And it belonged to her.

Which was why she then followed her father out to the edge of the dock where he stood, watching the last shimmer of gold along the horizon, a finger of light scraping across the platinum water.

"If he dies because of what you dragged us into, I'll . . . I'll—"

"Never forgive me?" He glanced at her, his voice soft. "North saw the Petrov boss arrive today. They could deploy any day. We need to move. With or without the vaccine, we're rolling out at midnight."

Her jaw tightened at his words, then— "You did this."

He looked at her, and yes, she meant her tone.

"You brought this fight to our doorstep, and if you'd just . . . stayed dead, then my husband wouldn't be prepping to siege a Russian mobster's compound—and you do know that he's going blind, right? Or does that not factor into your thinking?"

Oh, she was lit, and she ground her jaw, trying not to . . . well, to go back inside and beg Ranger to stay.

Because she desperately wanted to believe the words she'd said to Tae the other night. *"Ranger*

*is a SEAL . . . He lives for missions like this,
and . . . They're going to be fine."*

As if reading her mind, her father said quietly,
"Ranger knows what he's doing."

He turned back to the sunset and now stood
with his hands in the pockets of his cargo shorts,
wearing a T-shirt, his bandaged leg the only
evidence of the terror-slash-operation three days
ago.

She'd stood there in the kitchen that night,
watching her father get stitched up, all sorts of
scenarios playing through her mind.

He could have been shot in the chest.

Ranger could have been shot in the chest.

They *both* could have been shot in the chest.

She could have been an orphan and a widow in
one night.

Yeah, it was that thought that had kept her staring
at the ceiling the past few nights, alone in her bed
as Ranger and Ham worked scenarios, drawing
out the compound from Ranger's recollection and
sorting out the details of their op.

"You remember that sunset in Key West? The
one where you met Ranger?"

She looked at her father. He was tan, evidence
of his time here in Florida, and the sun in his
blond hair turned it burnished to match the
whiskers on his face. He was every bit as built as
a SEAL twenty years younger, and it still struck
her anew that he was *alive.*

Not dead.

And tougher than she thought, and that went for Ranger too, maybe. Lately he had seemed . . . well, more alive. More himself. Strong. Confident. Undaunted.

The man she'd met in Key West.

She sighed. Turned away. "Yes. I was taking pictures—"

"And he walked up to you, thinking you'd taken pictures of him."

She glanced at him. "How do you know that?"

"Noemi, you are not as far from my thoughts as you think." He turned. "We were staying at the same hotel. I was on the balcony, watching the same sunset. I knew Ranger was a SEAL the moment he walked up to you. I thought maybe you two would have a little, I don't know, vacation romance, maybe, and he'd walk away."

"He did."

"No. He wouldn't have if I hadn't panicked. I told him to stay away."

"I know. He told me."

He nodded then, his jaw tight. "I was wrong."

"Yeah, you were." She had just started to come around to forgiving her father for the derailing of her life—after all, she couldn't hold a grudge against a dead man—when he'd decided to resurrect. She was currently trying to re-find her footing in forgiveness.

"I'm just glad you two found your way back to each other."

She blew out a breath. "He saved my life, you know. In Nigeria."

"I know. And you saved his back, according to him. Reminded him that God wasn't finished with him yet. Gave him purpose."

"No, I think you did that." She shoved her hands in her pockets. "He's pretty amped up about this op."

He nodded. Then, "Honey, you have to remember that he's a SEAL, even if he's no longer active duty."

"I . . . I'm just . . ." She looked away from him. "Scared, I guess. I know what it feels like to lose someone you love, especially on a dangerous op."

Out in the river, fins cut through the water—dolphins, on their way out to the ocean.

"You know," her dad said quietly, "it wasn't easy leaving you."

No, she didn't know that. Tears pricked her eyes.

"I already told you my reasons why, but it didn't make it easier. I told myself that God would watch over you, but when you were taken by the Boko Haram, I panicked. I called Ham. And because of Fraser and Colt, he called Ranger. I had no idea he'd be circled into the op, and I know I should have backed away, trusting

God. But I just, I had to know you were okay." He scuffed a hand over his mouth. "So I came to Alaska. And then I handed Ranger that stupid phone and . . ." He sighed, turned, his blue eyes on her. "I get the struggle. You have to let him go, without strings, so he can focus on the job."

"I don't have the first idea how to do that."

"You do that by realizing the relentless love that God has for Ranger. That he is perfectly and wholly in his hands, regardless of what happens."

"Dad, that doesn't mean he'll survive."

"No. But it does mean that God's grace, his love, will be enough, whatever happens. For both of you. You just can't imagine it right now because you haven't needed it yet."

She gave him a look.

"Okay, maybe you have."

"I nearly came apart when you died."

"But you didn't. You kept going. You're stronger than you think, and when you've come to the end of your strength, God is there."

"I don't think— I'm not as strong as you think."

He put his hands on her shoulders. "Your mother was the strongest person I knew. She left her family to pursue her education. She fought the language barrier, the cultural barrier, and she married a man who dragged her around the world. She was strong enough to stick around so I had someone to come home to. I might have been the tip of the spear, but she was my home base."

Noemi looked away, her eyes burning.

"With everything in me, I believe God brought you and Ranger together. You need him. And he needs you. His encroaching blindness has shaken him to his core. But at that core is a fighter, a man who knows what he's doing. I saw it out there when he made a decision to save my life, and then toughed it out to drag me to safety. Ranger is a born SEAL. He's born to run into danger. And you, honey, are born to be his wife. To give him a safe place to land. It's not a job for every woman. But it is a job for you. Because, Noemi, you're just like your mother."

She stared at him, her jaw tight. Don't cry. Don't— "Daddy . . . just . . ." Aw. "Just don't die on me again. I don't want to lose you . . . I can't— I'm sorry I was so angry."

"Aw, honey. I don't get off the hook that easily." But he smiled and pulled her to himself.

As he held her, those strong arms around her, the embrace was so terribly familiar, an ache that at once burst to life, then soothed as healing crested over her.

"You might think that when Ranger deploys, you're left here alone, but you're not. God is with you. Keep clinging to him and pray your husband home. Your fear is an opportunity to draw nearer to God. And when he's home, make it worth it. You do that, and you'll be doing your part to save the world."

"She giving you any trouble, Master Chief?" a voice said from behind them.

Her father let her go, grinned down at her, then over her shoulder. "Always."

She laughed, then turned, swiping her cheeks.

Oh, Ranger. He'd shaved, dressed in a collared, short-sleeve shirt, a clean pair of cargo shorts, a pair of flip-flops—reminded her completely of the man she'd met once upon a sunset. His arms were tucked behind his back.

"Please. Take her off my hands." Her dad stepped back. "But don't get home too late."

Her dad winked at her, patted Ranger's shoulder, then headed into the house.

Ranger smiled at her. "Put on a pretty dress. I'm taking you out."

"A pretty—"

He held out a bag. "Got ya something."

She reached in and pulled out a dress, creamy white, sleeveless, filmy. "Trying to relive a memory?"

He leaned down, put his arm around her waist and pulled her to himself. "Or make new ones," he said into her ear.

Then he kissed her. He was the night, sensuous, surprising, sweet. He tasted of danger and when he trailed a kiss down her neck, then caught her face in his hand, she raised an eyebrow. "Are we going to make it to dinner?"

"Go upstairs and change," he said, his blue eyes

on hers. "But better hurry—you take too long, and the answer will be no."

She laughed as he let her go.

And then she headed upstairs.

It might take her quite a while.

After all, it took time to save the world.

ELEVEN

Colt just needed some air.

Not that he didn't have enough fresh air out by the pool at the Marshall mansion, but somehow walking along the beach, his feet bare in the sand, the surf curling around his ankles, soapy and cool, the moon hanging like a smile in the darkness . . . It allowed him to slow his heartbeat, spool out his thoughts.

Get some distance between his idiot self and the guy who needed to get his head in the game.

Tonight. They would roll out tonight, and sure, it seemed like an op that he'd done a thousand times before, but this time . . .

This time his brothers were involved.

Maybe that's why Colt's chest hurt, why he'd felt a little out of breath tonight when he sat with Ham and the guys and mapped out the mission.

He had never felt this stirred up over a mission since . . .

Yeah, okay, maybe he'd been a little more amped when he'd rescued his brothers in South Sudan. But still, this mission, despite Ranger's strategy, the workup, the contingency plans— frankly, Ranger had thought of everything—had Colt's chest in a knot.

Or was it Tae? The fact that he knew he'd hurt

her. Of *course* he'd hurt her. He hadn't gone looking for her in the evenings, after bringing her home from the lab, despite watching her from his balcony as she sat by the pool with Zoey.

And that made his chest ache even more, because her laughter trickled up to him, wound through him, and all he could think of was the way she'd kissed him on the boat.

As if he meant something to her, and it tossed him right back to her words—*"I just can't love a man who is going to . . ."*

A crab scurried near his foot, and he watched it rebury itself in the soft sand. Yeah, he'd done the same thing. About a month ago, he'd woken up into a world where Tae—or Flo, as he'd called her then—was his sunshine and light. And then the minute it got real . . .

Crab in the sand.

Wow, he was a jerk.

He should talk to her before he left. The thought had hung around in his brain all day as he watched her work in her lab. She was so precise, so smart. She shouldn't be with him. She needed someone who was . . . like Fraser Marshall, maybe. The guy was quiet and thoughtful and didn't say stupid things.

And probably if a woman said she loved him— or could—he loved her right back.

Because Fraser wasn't reckless or impulsive. Fraser hadn't been the guy offering himself up as tribute back in Nigeria every time Abu wanted to make a point. Not even once had Fraser been forced to sit on his knees, a machete to his neck, waiting . . . waiting . . .

A wave came in, crashed to Colt's knees, then fell away.

Fine. Yes, Colt might want to love Tae more than he wanted to admit.

But then what? He made stupid promises that he ended up breaking, and then he'd really hurt her.

And he'd be right back to not being able to look at himself in the mirror.

He stopped, stared out at the ocean, his hands in his pockets as he watched the dark horizon. A pelican rode the waves, probably shopping for dinner in the fading light.

Breathe.

Truth was, guys like him often got the girl, but they didn't get the happy ending.

And something inside him didn't want the girl without it.

"Colt?"

He stilled.

"The guys said you were out here," Tae said.

He closed his eyes. Sighed.

"Colt?"

"Yeah." He turned, dredged up a smile.

Wow, she was pretty. Her blond hair shone in the moonlight, and she wore a pair of shorts, a sleeveless button-down shirt that she'd tied in a knot at her waist. She smelled good, too, some kind of flower, maybe. And she was barefoot, her sandals hanging from her fingers.

"Hey," she said, and smiled, and everything inside him turned to liquid. "I . . . I hear you guys are deploying later tonight."

"Mm-hmm."

Her smile fell. "Am I interrupting some sort of . . . pregame ritual?"

Aw. "No." He ran a hand around his neck. "I just . . . wanted to clear my head."

"I should leave you."

His stupid hand just reached out and grabbed hers. "No. Stay."

She smiled, something slow, and wove her fingers through his.

And just like that, everything whirring inside him—his chest, his head—slowed.

"You feeling okay? Your heart beating normally?"

Not in the least, but, "Tip-top." The last thing he was going to do was mention the strange tightness in his chest, and the bout of nausea a few days ago.

Or last night, when he'd taken a night run with Fraser and had to take an ice-cold shower to slow down his heart.

It had occurred to him that maybe he wasn't ready for a full-out op. But maybe it was just,

"I've never been out in the field with my brothers. Not like this."

"Your brothers seem pretty capable. Ranger seems to have worked everything out."

"Along with Ham, yes. There will always be contingencies, but . . ." He'd never forgive himself if they died on his watch.

"Colt. Your brothers know what they're doing. They *did* get you out of Nigeria."

"Yeah." He gave her a smirk. "But Ranger had to get married to do it."

"I don't think he minds."

Probably not. He'd seen Ranger go upstairs in search of his wife before Colt had left for the beach.

"Still. This feels different than our fun and games a couple days ago. I keep wondering if we should just hand the op over to the FBI, but Roy and Logan are keen on keeping this in-house with the Caleb Group. Says if the FBI knows, then Congress knows, and then suddenly the general population finds out and we have a worldwide panic."

"I can see that. He brought in a couple more guys tonight."

"Yeah, that's Skeet. He's on protection detail with us. And Orion, a former pararescue jumper who works on the SAR side."

"And who's the girl?"

"Oh, she's his coms person, Scarlett. She'll run

a drone over the compound. It'll keep us alerted to their movements."

"Which means you'll know what you're getting into."

"It's not satellite coverage, but it'll work. And Orion and Dodge will be sitting overwatch to the north and south of the island. Ham and Fraser will run point on two different teams. Ham, North, Skeet, and I are going in through the road entrance, via the forest, while Fraser, Jake, and Logan are going in by boat."

Probably he shouldn't give her all the details, but she could have overheard anything during their briefings the last few days.

"We'll give them a two-front war. And in the meantime, Ranger and Roy will retrieve the package."

"Do you know where the bioweapon is being kept?"

"Pete says the pool house, but Ranger worked out a couple other places they might have put it. If not, I guess we'll get one of the guys and start asking questions."

His gut tightened a little on those words, but he shook it away. This wasn't Sudan. They weren't walking into an ambush.

Hopefully.

"Sounds like you have it all buttoned up," she said. "What has you out here pacing?"

The water had risen as they stood on shore,

the tide coming in. The ocean pooled in rhythm around their ankles.

You. Us. The wrong goodbye.

"What are *you* doing here?" Coward, but the real words clogged inside him.

She dug her foot into the sand, the wind catching her hair. "I was thinking that maybe . . . well, I just wanted you to know that I'm glad you followed me to Seattle and to thank you for being here. I feel safer with you . . . locked in the box with me."

He smiled then. "It is a box, isn't it?"

"Tiny. And the walls are closing in because I haven't figured out the vaccine yet. So, please, don't get near the virus."

"That might be hard, since that's the mission objective."

"You know what I mean. We're not sure the virus is airborne. That would be a mutation of the pathogen, but it could be. And . . ." She looked away, out into the darkness.

He couldn't stop the words pulsing inside him. "I promise."

She looked back at him, her eyes big. "What?"

"If it depends on me, Tae, I'll come back. I won't do anything impulsive or . . ." He shook his head. "I'll come back."

Her mouth opened, a quick intake of air. "I know I shouldn't have asked . . ."

"No," he said as he dropped his flip-flops and

reached up with his free hand, curling it around her neck. "You have a right to ask. Because . . . well, because of this." He pulled her to himself.

He kissed her with all the hunger that had been building for the past three days, the thirst of needing her in his arms, in his dreams, his life, the hope that he hadn't wanted to admit.

A future that just might be his, if he did this right.

And maybe he *did* do it right, because she dropped her sandals and wound her arms around his neck. Then, with a hum deep inside her, she stepped close, molded her body next to his and deepened the kiss.

Oh . . . yes. She tasted sweet, her lips soft, and he had the sense that around him, she too became less buttoned up, let her brain stop calculating genome sequences or whatever she thought about deep into the night.

It was just her, letting go, letting him catch her.

And she caught him right back.

He circled his arms around her and dove in, and he could practically feel his heart loosen—but it didn't hurt, not right now at least—and vanish somewhere in the beautiful twilight, in the heat between them and the sweet release of everything he feared.

Maybe he wouldn't hurt her.

Maybe they would complete their mission

without casualties and he would come back, and yeah . . . maybe they had a future.

He could let himself love her.

And then he could finally go home. Stay.

And maybe a guy like him could live happily ever after.

Maybe.

Ranger could run the op with his eyes closed, he'd gone over it so many times in his head. And that was probably a good thing because tonight, for some reason, he was hyperaware of the dark spots in his eyesight.

This might be his last op, so he'd make it the best. No casualties. One hundred percent mission success.

Now, he hung out under the long dock that stretched out on the south side of the island, his rebreather rendering him silent in the dark water as he listened to Ham and Fraser check in as they set their teams in place. Overhead, the moon had rounded midnight, over to the wee hours of the morning.

Ranger would wait until the teams cleared out the traffic, drawing attention to both sides of the camp, and then he and Roy would run a play up the middle, right to the pool house. Secure the canisters and then call in the big dogs, once the smoke died down, to transport them into government custody.

Felt like old times.

Beside him, Roy was a ghost in the water. He emanated a dangerous quiet, even when he wasn't in stealth mode, but his eyes were embedded with a story that said he could keep up with their assault team just fine, thank you, and still slip unseen into the night.

"In position." Jake's voice came through the coms.

Ranger had gotten some of Roy's story from Ham during their strategy sessions.

Roy, along with Logan, had been on Ham's SEAL team, had been one of the guys separated from the team during an ambush deep in the Afghani mountains. Logan had been captured by the Taliban, along with Roy. Ranger didn't want the details of what the terrorists had done to them. But they'd been rescued by an unsanctioned op put together by Ham and a guy named McCord— ironically the father of his brother-in-law, Riley, Larke's husband.

McCord and Ham had rescued Logan and Roy.

And then things went south.

According to Ham, the CIA made the reported-as-dead SEALs an offer they couldn't refuse, then secured their yes by casting blame for a Pakistani general's assassination on them.

Logan refused to play ball and disappeared for the better part of three years before he resurfaced in Alaska. Ham didn't know the details of how

Logan ended up on President White's private task force.

Roy had joined up with the spook squad and spent three years in Europe, doing wet work and gathering intel and generally being the guy who kept everyone safe and sleeping in their beds.

Now he, too, was on White's private payroll, along with another retired spook—a female—and a black ops guy who'd worked in Russia, along with Pete.

And probably more, if Ranger were to guess.

"Dual entry on my call," Ham said softly.

Ranger glanced at Roy, who nodded.

Fraser also found out that Roy—real name, Royal Benjamin—and Orion Starr went way back to a day when Orion had been one of the pararescue troopers on that fateful day in Afghanistan. So it was a good ole boys reunion when Orion showed up to join the rest of Ham's team.

Ranger had been sorta—just a little—jealous of the camaraderie of Jones, Inc. The inside jokes, the ribbing, the pregame routines as they checked their gear and talked through the mission.

Which was why he'd bought his pretty wife a dress and planned a date that had sorta gone down differently but exactly as he'd hoped. With a firm reminder in his head that this life wasn't his.

Not after today.

But right now, with the voice of Scarlett Hathaway, Ham's coms person, in his ear giving them drone awareness updates, with Ranger ticking down the seconds to when he'd emerge from the waters like some swamp creature, with Ham and Jake indicating they were in position . . .

He was dialed in, the point man for operation Red Redemption, Ham's name, but Ranger liked it.

"Three, two, one . . . execute," Ham said.

Shots went off, quick and quiet from the east side of the compound. Ham's team, with Colt attached. They'd had to work through the tangle of forest, no small feat given the thick brush of southern Florida.

Ranger would much rather take the way of the water, where he felt like a seal, slick, fast, unstoppable. Even with his current eyesight challenges.

"Two down," Jake said. "We have three more engaged."

"Heat sources are outside the building, Range," said Scarlett, probably reading her drone's stats. "To the west and east. One remaining, near the garage on the northeast side."

Interesting, but he'd make his way to the pool house first.

He met Roy's eyes in the darkness, nodded. Execute.

Then he dropped the rebreather, set the

watertight bag for his M4 on the dock, shed his fins, and pulled himself up. Unzipping the case, he retrieved his weapon and scanned the area.

All clear.

Roy did the same behind him.

Ranger shed his scuba kit, hid his equipment by the dock, and in a moment had cleared the space, then ducked down into the thick foliage beside the dock, on land.

Roy landed on the other side, also buried in the shadows.

Ranger indicated their next stop, a clump of towering pine trees, and Roy nodded. In a moment they were there. More popping sounded from the west side of the compound. Shouting, most of it in Russian.

The lights had flickered on with all the movement, illuminating the compound, and Ranger spotted a couple thugs running his direction.

Before he could move, Roy had stopped one of them.

The other ducked behind a tall palm.

"Cover me," Ranger said, and Roy nodded.

Shots from Roy's M4A1 peppered the tree and Ranger took off, running for the edge of the house. He ducked under the eaves, sighted, then took out one of the high beam lights that bathed the grounds.

It shattered and blessed darkness dropped over them.

Then he rained down cover for Roy, who followed him. Roy shot out a light over the patio area, and Ranger scooted in, toward the pool house.

More shots to the west, and it started to sound like a real gun battle. "I'm at the pool house," he said as he reached the door.

Roy had darkened the lights around the perimeter of the pool, then another light, farther away to the west.

Ranger pulled on the mask dangling around his neck and secured it over his nose and mouth. "Breaching Primary."

He glanced at Roy, who'd also pulled on his respirator, just in case. He'd set up near the door, nodded, and Ranger kicked it open.

Flashed his light over the room. "No joy," he said, and tried not to let that shut him down. "Moving to Secondary target."

Pete had figured that the Russians wouldn't keep the material too close to the house, but still under guard, and— "Where is that other heat source, Base?"

"Twenty feet south of the garage," Scarlett said.

Roy gestured with his head, and Ranger fell in behind him as they crossed the pool area, back out into the shadows. Roy decimated another light.

"Two more tangos down," Jake said. "Ham?"

"We're pinned down," Ham answered. "Colt is

311

headed around the back. Going to flank them."

Colt, improvising as usual.

Except, his brother had changed since coming to Florida, had a seriousness about him, something in his eyes that suggested that maybe some of his last few months had impacted him.

Made him taste his own mortality.

Ranger knew the feeling. He sidled up to the edge of a huge three-car garage outbuilding, right behind Roy.

He spotted the target that Scarlett had seen, a man hunkered down at the edge of the house, scanning the driveway.

From here, Ranger could also make out the four men in crouched positions near the house, shooting into the blackness at Ham and his team.

A couple SUVs and a van were parked in the driveway.

Roy pointed to himself, and Ranger nodded as the man rolled out, then hit the door with his foot, breaching. He disappeared inside.

The guard turned at the sound, and Ranger pulled the trigger.

Then he moved into the garage behind Roy.

No lights, but Roy was shining his beam over the contents—a couple trucks, a four-wheeler, some lawn supplies.

No containers of an ultratoxic, smallpox bio-hazard virus.

How Ranger hoped they hadn't moved them off property.

"Hey, Ham, the van's moving. Tango inside." Colt's voice via coms.

A couple shots, and Colt's voice came back. "Clear. I'm taking a look inside."

"Hang tight, Colt. We're on our way," Ranger said.

He headed for the exit.

Bullets pinged the door. Roy yanked Ranger back, his hand gripping his vest, and they pressed against the wall. "We're pinned down," Roy said. "Anybody got eyes on our shooter?"

"I see him," Ham said. "Stay put."

"Tango down. I'm in the van. Yep, these are the canisters," Colt said, and Ranger met eyes with Roy.

Colt didn't have biohazard gear. "Get out of there, Colt," Ranger said, trying not to growl.

Silence, and Ranger glanced at the door. Shots peppered the exit. "Ham?"

"Sit tight."

Two pops.

"You're clear."

Ranger stepped out, rolled around the end of the building, Roy behind him.

A quiet had descended over the compound, the remaining lights eerie between shadowed plains. Ranger tasted his heartbeat, the swish of adrenaline in his veins.

"I need a path to that van," Ranger said into the coms.

"Copy," Ham said. "We have three tangos between us, but Colt's in the van. He's taking it out of the—"

Ham cut off the transmission as shots sounded.

Even through the haze of light, Ranger spotted the van starting to move.

"Colt, don't let any of those bullets pierce—"

And then his blood turned cold as he spotted one of the tangos rise, an RPG banked into his shoulder. Aw . . .

"Ham?"

"I see it. I'm moving."

But Ham was still hunkered down behind an array of palm trees, the bark being shredded by the targets protecting their shooter.

Ranger had the better shot. Especially if he tucked himself in along the eaves of the house. He pointed to his sniper nest, and Roy nodded.

Then Ranger took off, through the shadows, head down, the steps ground into his brain. He shut out the pops, the shouting, and rolled into the nest even as he lifted his M4 to his shoulder. *Please.* A quick sight, more instinct and muscle memory than precision—

He pulled the trigger.

A hit. The shooter jerked forward.

Not soon enough.

The RPG fired, streaked toward the van.

Ranger wanted to close his eyes. "Colt, hit it!"

The van surged ahead, the missile flying past the tail end, missing and slamming into a grove of palm trees.

The ancillary explosion hit the van, and it surged up, over—

It landed on its side and skidded into another set of trees.

Roy materialized beside him and neutralized one of the other shooters while Ranger found the man pinning Ham down.

And then Range was on his feet, running toward the van.

"Finish it, Jake," Ham said, rising. "We need you here."

"Copy," Jake said as Ranger reached the van and flashed his light inside.

Colt was trapped in the driver's seat by an airbag. He raised a hand. "I'm good."

"No, he's not," said Roy, his light shining into the back windows. "The canisters are out of their cases and one looks damaged."

"We need to get him out of there," Ranger said. "The longer he's inside, the greater chance he's infected."

The distant gunfire had died, and Jake was confirming, heading their direction, but Ham talked over him.

"Any way to secure the area to get Colt out of there?"

"Nope," Ranger said. "Get everybody back. Roy and I will get him."

Ham peeled out with Skeet, and Ranger heard him stop Jake and his crew at the edge of the driveway.

"Let's get in there," Ranger said. He climbed up on the side of the van. "I'll get Colt. You secure the canisters."

"Copy," Roy said. "I'll get the waterproof containers." He radioed to Jake's team to bring the containers while Ranger stood over the window.

"Cover your face, Colt," he said.

Colt looked at him, face covered in camo paint, and held up an arm, tucked his head under it.

Ranger masked up, then broke the glass to the window with the butt of his weapon. Then he cleared the glass, lay prone, and reached in. With his dive knife, he popped the airbag.

Held out his hand to his brother. "C'mon."

Colt clamped his hand around his brother's and let Ranger lever him free.

Meanwhile, Roy put on his mask, opened the back end of the van, and rolled the damaged canister into a black waterproof case that Ham had delivered.

Then, just like that, it was over. Colt, a little dinged up but alive, and Roy securing the other canisters in another container. They dragged the booty away from the van.

Then Ranger picked up the RPG, reloaded it, and turned the van into a fireball to burn off any remaining residue. The fire would neutralize the virus before it could disseminate into the night.

In the glow of the fire Ranger glanced at Colt.

He was grinning, although standing away from them. He raised a fist to Ham, who raised one back from where he stood, six feet away.

No, he hadn't changed one single bit.

Ranger walked closer. Stopped.

Colt's eyes shone against the firelight. "That's how you bag a bear."

Ranger just looked at him, shook his head. "You should have waited. Now, you're probably infected."

"I'm fine." Colt lowered his hand. "I took out the driver. They almost made off with the canisters."

"We would have stopped them." Ranger's voice sounded calm, but he felt the fraying at the end of it.

"At what cost? What if they'd gotten away from us? Or maybe crashed at a shopping mall?"

Colt stood, facing the flames, fierce, a trickle of blood down his face from a cut in his forehead, and for a second Ranger was a kid, watching his brother drag in a bear carcass, filthy, smelly, bloody, and triumphant.

And Ranger felt it anew. Someday his brother was going to come home in a body bag.

But maybe he was right. Mission accomplished. And no casualties.

Not yet, at least.

Bam. Ranger held up his fist.

Colt grinned, then, again. "Not bad for your last gig, huh?"

His last gig. Ranger was trying not to think about that.

"Hey Colt," Roy said and walked over to him. "I think this is for you." He handed him his mask.

Colt's grin vanished. He made a face, then grabbed the mask and put it on. "Thanks."

Roy gave him a nod, his mouth tight.

North had picked up one end of a container, Skeet on the other, and ran behind Jake and Ham, who had the other containers. Fraser, Colt, and Ranger spread out to protect them from any snipers left on the grounds as they ran toward the dock. Logan and Roy were waiting for the FBI to arrive to secure the Russians.

Orion pulled up in the big boat that Ham had procured for the team.

Ranger grabbed up his gear from the hiding place, then piled into the cigarette boat that Dodge drove.

Colt jumped in with him. He banged Dodge on the shoulder before going to sit a few feet away from them.

Dodge glanced at Ranger. "Don't tell me."

"Yep," Ranger said.

"Let's go home," Colt said, his voice a little muffled. "I'm hungry."

Dodge shook his head as he pulled away, in front of Ham's boat.

Ranger sat on the edge, in the back, and pulled off his hood, his face to the morning. Okay, fine.

Not bad for his last gig.

And over the horizon to the east, dawn lit the water with a bloody trail of light.

At least she wasn't crying.

Tae sat in one of the patio loungers, the heat rising with the sun, now simmering fire red across the horizon, staring south.

Waiting.

They'd been gone six hours. She knew because she'd joined Noemi on the patio deck as they'd watched them leave. No teary goodbyes, not even a kiss. Ham had asked them to stay inside until after the crew left. Something about keeping them focused.

Yeah, maybe he was right. Because last night, as Colt had kissed her, he'd seemed anything but focused on his mission.

Although maybe that's why he'd kissed her with such urgency, such hunger.

Then again, everything about Colt was urgency and hunger. He'd pulled them back into the sand, and by the time they'd come up for air, she'd found herself cocooned in his arms, the tide nipping at their toes.

He'd finally slowed them down, same thing he'd done at the dock, pressing his forehead against hers, again. "We need to stop," he'd said quietly. "Before I get in over my head."

Too late. She was in way over her head. And hanging too hard on his silly promise, the one she knew he could never keep. *"I'll come back."*

Now, she drew up her knees, her arms around them, holding on to that stupid promise with everything she had.

A blanket fell over her shoulders, and she looked up to see Noemi walk past her. "I know it's not exactly cold out, but sometimes having something to wrap yourself in helps," she said as she sat on another lounger.

"Any updates?"

Noemi wore a white dress, a beacon in the night, her hair back in a multicolored scarf. "Scarlett and Dad are on coms in the kitchen. I waited until they were heading home, but I just had to get outside. Breathe. All that shooting . . . I didn't realize how intense these ops are. I don't know how Scarlett keeps her cool."

Tae either. She blew out a breath.

"They'll be fine. At least that's what I keep telling myself. But they do know what they're doing. Most of them are SEALs, and Colt was Delta Force. Really, they've been in much more harrowing situations than a shootout with some Russian mercenaries."

"It only takes one stray bullet."

Noemi raised an eyebrow.

"Sorry. Not helping, I know."

"Well, they're not bulletproof, but the Kevlar helps."

"I don't know how you stay so calm."

Noemi wrapped herself in a blanket. "I'm not. I'm just trying to remind myself that God is watching over them, and all I can do is pray."

Huh. Tae hadn't exactly prayed since . . . well, long before her father had been killed. Besides, "You think God is going to protect them when they go in, armed to the teeth, ready to kill?"

"I absolutely do. In the Bible, God is repeatedly with his people when they're fighting evil. I think there *is* such a thing as a righteous battle, and when we are on the side of saving lives . . . well, God is about life and truth, so I think that puts us on his side. At least that's what Ranger says, and I'm really starting to believe."

Well then. "Pray for Colt, too, okay?"

Noemi smiled. "Done. But you know, I've discovered you can pray yourself."

Tae shook her head. "Nah. God and I . . . we . . . I think maybe I'm on my own here."

Noemi frowned.

The golden dawn cut through the palm trees, fractured light bleeding through the thick fronds.

Fine. "I did a lot of praying when my dad left for war. I was ten, and I thought maybe if I was a very good girl, my dad would come back. I prayed every night before I went to sleep, and I obeyed my mother, and I did all the things, and still the Navy chaplain landed on our doorstep. God clearly didn't care."

"I used to think that way. That if God didn't answer me, or not in the way I wanted, that he didn't care or even like me. But that's not true. I've started to see God at work all over my life. Now and in the past. He wasn't ignoring me. I just didn't see his work until I wanted to."

"I felt pretty ignored. I mean, I don't even know how my dad died. Just one day, gone." Tae looked out on the water. "At least today, I know what's going down."

"And that's better?" Pete had come out of the house and now walked into the sunlight.

She looked at Noemi's father. He had a sort of determination, a sturdiness in his gaze that made Tae want to trust him.

"There's a reason the military doesn't disclose details to family. Before or after missions."

"It's cruel, if you ask me," Tae said. "My mother spent years trying to figure out what happened to my dad. We never even got his final letter. Just a flag and a gold star pin."

Pete wore a sorry expression. "That's a good sign that his death is classified."

"That's what we thought." She glanced up the river. "At least, if something happens to Colt, I'll know how. And why."

"He's going to be okay," Pete said. "The op is over. They're on their way home. No casualties."

Tears bit her eyes, and she gritted her jaw against them. Silly. Stupid. "Did they get the canisters?"

"Yes."

She wiped her cheeks. "I don't know how you guys do this. One mission after another, saving the world from disaster."

Pete looked at Noemi. "It's not without costs." Then he walked away, toward the dock, hands in his pockets, limping still from his injury.

"He's talking about the fact he played dead, right?"

"Maybe. Probably. But my kidnapping scared him to death. That's why he came to the ranch."

"I still can't believe you got away. You're every bit as tough as a SEAL."

She laughed. "Hardly. I broke my zip ties and ran through the woods. Not exactly tough guy behavior."

"You broke through your zip ties? How?"

"Oh, that's easy. The key is to get them really tight so you can leverage more force when you bring your hands down. Like this." She put her hands up, together, and then brought them down, hard against her belly. "You pull out even as you force your hands down. It's not hard once you get the hang of it."

"This happen a lot?"

"When your dad is Pete Sutton, it does."

Tae laughed. Oh wow, her entire chest released, the darkness in it scattering. Especially when she heard the motor of the boat echoing from downriver.

She got up, dropped the blanket and headed toward the dock.

The river had turned to fire under the dawning light, and against the sun, she spotted the cigarette boat behind Ham's larger charter boat.

The charter bumped up to the dock first. Pete came up the dock and helped them tie off the boat, and the men jumped off. Heavily armored, solemn.

She backed up to let them pass, then stepped to the side as a few of the guys—Jake, Skeet, North, and Fraser—carried two large containers up the dock. They walked past her with a nod.

Warriors, just doing their job.

"Put them in the garage for now," Pete said. "We'll need to get them to a secure facility pronto."

The men seemed strangely subdued, and it struck her as— "Is everything okay?"

Ham nodded. He wore black pants, black shirt, black vest, black hat, black war paint. The look gave her a cold shiver. But not as much as the stir of something she couldn't name in his eyes.

Dodge brought the cigarette boat to the dock, and Ranger hopped out to secure the line.

Colt sat in the back of the boat, dressed like Ham. He looked up when he saw her. Blood trickled down his face.

And he wore a mask over his mouth and nose.

Oh . . . no . . . no. Everything inside her seized.

"Colt!" She took off toward him.

The arm that snaked around her belly just about took her out as Ham caught her, pulled her against his armor, swung her around. "Sorry, Tae. Not so fast."

"Let me go!" She pushed at his arms, but he wasn't budging. Instead, he dragged her down the dock, away from Colt, who now got out.

He stood away from her.

Ham brought her to the grass. Colt trailed behind Ranger and Dodge a good six feet.

Tae tried to untangle herself from Ham, everything inside her shredding. "What *happened?*"

Ranger had unzipped his wet suit, pulled the top down, and tied the arms around his waist to keep them from dangling.

Noemi ran into his arms. Ranger picked her up, holding her tight against him. Kissed her.

Tae turned back to Colt, her heart pounding, fighting not to do the same.

Colt had come off the dock, but Ham still had his arm around her.

"Let me go, Ham."

"Just calm down, Tae. He's fine—"

"He's bleeding! And why the mask?" But she knew the answer. She looked at Colt, shook her head. "You got exposed to the virus."

He stayed away from the group, away from her. "There was an accident."

She stared at him, feeling punched. Then she wrenched Ham's arm off her. "How long were you exposed?"

"I don't know. Three minutes? It might be nothing but—"

"How?"

"I was in a van that crashed. The container was punctured. I'm probably fine, Tae. I just . . . we need to—"

"Stop. Okay, listen. Keep the mask on. Somebody get a hose, and let's wash him down. Then, strip out of everything, go inside, and take a shower. As hot as you can stand. And, with bleach. Do we have bleach?"

"I saw some in the laundry room," Noemi said.

"Every inch of you, bleached. And then rinse well. Ten minutes under the hot water. Someone get him clean clothes. As for what you're wearing, that can be washed—hot cycle, also bleached—and that goes for everyone. I want everyone hosed down and bleached."

She didn't care that she'd gotten bossy. She rounded, looked at Ham. "Everyone. Even me.

The last thing we need is to somehow carry the S-poxR out into the world."

Then she turned back to Colt. "You stay in your room. Alone. No visitors until I come back."

"Where are you going?" Colt said.

She turned and her gaze caught on Zoey, who'd come out of the house.

"We're going to the lab to create a vaccine that will hopefully save your life."

TWELVE

Colt was going to be just fine.

Really.

Please.

Tae looped the stethoscope around her neck and stepped back. Colt sat on the bed of his now-sterile, very secure, somewhat prison-like room at the Cape Canaveral Hospital, where Logan had pulled a netful of strings to create the quarantine pod three days ago.

Poor man was watched day and night by Logan, as well as a friend he'd flown in—Lucas Maguire, who'd been a trauma doc in the Navy. Apparently he was some ad hoc member of Jones, Inc. also.

Lucas seemed more like a *soldier* for Jones, Inc. than a doctor, but Tae didn't want to ask too many questions. He was a handsome man—early forties, brown hair, thick beard, built. She didn't know why, but having him around made her feel a little like she might be under scrutiny.

Still, Colt was *her* patient, her subject, and she'd made him promises when she'd visited shortly after his arrival at the hospital, just to check on his vitals. And to confirm that he was still alive and not spiking a 104 fever.

So far, so good. He'd even been grumpy and

dressed in a pair of scrub pants—he refused the standard gown—and had spent most of his time glowering at Lucas, telling him he felt fine.

Good. Grumpy and healthy were better than a raging fever, pustules, and bleeding from his eyes. Which she mentioned.

He told her he felt like a leper.

Well, that's what he got for pulling his save-the-world stunt. Angry seemed the best place for her to land with her emotions. It certainly had fueled the first forty-eight hours as she holed up in her lab.

Occasionally, he'd text Zoey silly memes about getting infected with a terrible disease, which Tae didn't appreciate as she and Zoey worked to synthesize the vaccine.

She guessed it might just be his way of dealing with the looming what-ifs.

Tae had wanted to weep when Zoey read the results of the analysis from the Cryo-electron microscope some twenty-four hours into their research.

"It's a match." Zoey looked just as tired as Tae felt. Every bone in her body ached, and her eyes burned, but once Roy and Logan secured the containers, they'd been able to extract the virus code from the living S-poxR. And using the genome sequence, they knitted it into the horsepox. And then, the vaccinia.

Just one dose. They'd been able to synthesize

just one dose, but if it worked on Colt—thank you, live subject—they'd make more.

And then they'd inoculate everyone. The world.

"Are you sure this will work?" Ranger asked the question yesterday, when she'd emerged from Colt's room, then the UV bath, and finally the third chamber where she garbed up.

"No. But there's a good chance. We were able to inoculate him within the forty-eight-hour window. He can develop antibodies based on the horsepox, and they should fight off any infection."

So, they'd watched. Waited.

And the only way she got near him was dressed in head-to-toe Tyvek booties, gloves, mask, and vented helmet.

So that was pretty.

Now, a day after his inoculation, she took off the bandage on his arm.

The man was shirtless as she examined him. And yes, she noticed the lean body, the scars he wore on it. His three-day beard and wry smile only made her more aware of the closeness of him. He was barefoot, still in scrubs, his hair a disaster, and, shoot, all she wanted to do was pull off her mask and kiss him.

Or wring his stupid, reckless neck.

But he *had* saved the world—or at least Disney World—so what was a girl supposed to do with that?

"So far, no vesicles or any redness in the vaccination area," she said into a microphone she was wearing that both recorded her assessment and informed Lucas and Logan where they stood outside the plastic walls.

But it had only been twenty-four hours.

"Any itching?" She replaced the bandage on his arm. A rather impressive arm, as it were. In fact, it stirred up memories of being in said arms at the beach. When he'd made her promises he had no intention of keeping.

Now, he was a landmine to her heart, the way he grinned at her. "Just the itch to get out of here," he said.

"Not quite yet."

"C'mon, doc. I'm tired of eating hospital food. I'm not contagious. I read up on the smallpox vaccination, and as long as I keep it covered, then I'm fine. You all are freaking out—"

"Freaking out?" She stepped back from him. "You could potentially be carrying the one virus that could wipe out the world, and you call us freaking out."

He sighed. Scrubbed his hands down his face. "I feel fine." He met her eyes with his, so brown, so pleading . . . aw, she couldn't focus around him.

"Tae. Think about it."

"I'll draw some blood. As long as I don't see any markers, then . . . yes, okay, you can go. But you'll have to cover up the injection site and . . . don't sneeze on anyone."

He smiled, and then reached out and put his arm around her. Pressed his forehead to her plastic visor. "Does that include kissing?"

Oh, he was trouble.

Especially when, three hours later, she walked in with the news of no viral markers.

"Told you that I was fine," he said as he headed for a shower.

She was waiting for him in the hallway when he emerged ten minutes later, wearing a pair of new jeans and a collared black dress shirt, a pair of flip-flops. He smelled good. As they exited the hospital, the night dropped around them, the salty air thick on her skin.

They drove back to the safe house in the Escalade and arrived in time for pizza.

"Colt!" Dodge got up, and Colt bumped his fist as he came into the house.

"Hey."

Ham and Fraser also got up, greeted him, others raising their hands, or pizza slices as it were.

They all sat in the great room, or at the bar, and in the background, music played from a Bluetooth speaker. Someone's eighties playlist.

"I'm walking on sunshine . . ."

Colt grabbed a chair, turned it around backwards. Straddled it. Sat and set his folded arms on the back. He looked every inch a triumphant warrior.

She'd freaked out for nothing, maybe. Still, the drug was experimental . . .

Breathe. He was fine. Laughing. Eating a piece of pizza.

"I'm headed upstairs to take my own shower," she said. She felt gritty, unkempt, and downright itchy herself.

Colt glanced at her, those brown eyes saying something. *Meet you on the beach later.*

And she met them. *Definitely.*

She just needed all this to be over, for him to be okay, and maybe for them to figure out what happened next.

Ham had ordered everyone to stay put after the mission—just in case Colt was infected and they all needed shots. Which, in her mind, wasn't a terrible idea. Especially since it seemed Colt had no side effects from the vaccination.

Maybe they'd done it—created the S-poxR vaccine.

They'd have to start trials, but second stage could be with an allotted group of volunteers, the Jones, Inc. guys, maybe. And then they'd progress to a larger sample and—

"You ready to come back to Jones, Inc.?"

The question floated up after her, as she ascended the stairs, and she didn't want to hear the answer.

Especially didn't want to hear him laugh, and slap hands with someone.

"We'll see."

We'll see?

It wasn't a yes, and even as she stood there, looking down, he looked up at her.

Winked.

Her entire body lit on fire. *What?*

She attributed her thickening throat to the last three days. She was just tired.

And maybe he was simply rattled. Sitting in isolation so long had probably gone to his head. Because he *was* rejoining the team.

But her words to Pete as she'd waited for Colt to come home ran through her as she got into the shower. *"I don't know how you guys do this. One mission after another, saving the world from disaster."*

No. She wasn't a girl who could live like this.

If only Colt wasn't so . . . so *good* at his job.

"People sleep peaceably in their beds . . ."

A half hour later, the great room was empty as she walked out of her bedroom. She wore a T-shirt and yoga pants, her wet hair braided. Tired. Ready to sit under the stars.

She walked out to the pool area where Dodge, Jake, Skeet, and North played basketball in the water. Lucas had joined them and was talking with Ham. Ranger and Noemi were missing, as was Pete. And Zoey and Roy, so that was interesting.

"Anyone seen Colt?" she asked as she stepped back from a spray of water.

"Beach," Ham said, and grinned as he gestured with his head back to the house and the ocean beyond.

Beach.

She was turning to leave when Lucas's voice lifted over the shouts of the pool.

"Did you guys track down that last canister?"

Last canister? She slowed, even as she walked to the door.

"No. Whoever took it is in the wind." This, from Ham. "It's not enough to threaten any of the theme parks in the area, but Roy is tracking it."

Last canister.

Even a small amount, in the wrong environment, could be disastrous.

She took another step. And then . . . nope, she couldn't let it sit. She turned and walked over to Ham. "You think there's a canister missing?"

He was on a lounger, dressed in a muscle tee and a pair of board shorts, as if he'd intended to get in the pool. Lucas, beside him, wore a polo shirt and Bermudas. Both men bore the physique of the military, and for a second, she felt like she'd walked in on a clandestine planning meeting.

Then Ham nodded, gave her a grim look. "The canisters were in padded boxes. The one that was damaged had been opened, and after we gathered up all the canisters, we discovered one space empty. Either it never had a canister—doubtful. Or it went missing—more likely. Also, Roy and Logan have secured all the Russians that were at the compound. Only one casualty. The rest are hospitalized or in interrogation. No one has given up the contact Pete mentioned arriving, but we think he might have left earlier, with one of the canisters."

"Why?"

He looked at Lucas. "Maybe to run a test."

Cold snaked through her. "A test?"

"Yes," Lucas said. "At some nearby event or facility. But all the camera footage was stored off-site on a digital system, and our hacker hasn't figured out where yet."

"You have a hacker?" Tae asked.

"Logan does," Lucas said. "And, ironically, she's Russian."

"We need to be ready to spin up when she nails that location," Ham said. His gaze roamed back to her. "We need that vaccine, as soon as you're ready to roll it out."

"Depends on Colt. But so far, he seems to be handling it well, and if he was exposed, he's showing no signs of illness. We'll keep him monitored, but I think we could petition it for use under the emergency use authorization."

"I'll talk to the president," Lucas said.

Just like that. Talk to the president. Who *were* these guys?

"Zoey and I will get to work on creating more doses in the morning. It'll be small-scale stuff until we're given official authorization—"

"Tae!"

She turned and spotted Noemi running around the end of the house, breathing hard. "Colt's having a heart attack!"

Time stopped as Noemi's words cut through her brain. What—wait—*what?*

"Where?" Ham was on his feet.

Noemi bent over, catching her knees. "We were at the beach, and he came down and was talking to Range—"

Ham didn't wait for the rest. Just took off around the house, Lucas on his tail.

No—*no*— "Call 9-1-1!" Tae shouted and took off after them.

The house was situated across the two-laned road from the beach, and she hadn't put on shoes, but she didn't care as she ran after Lucas and Ham. She was passed by Dodge, Orion, then Fraser. They held up a car and she sped over the pavement, then caught up fast when she hit the beach.

Colt was on the sand, Lucas over him, giving him mouth-to-mouth. Orion dropped to do compressions.

Colt's entire body jerked with the force of them.

Please don't crack his ribs. But Orion had

been a pararescue trooper. He knew how to keep people alive.

In the distance, a siren whined.

A hand slipped into hers. Held. Noemi.

Tae stood there, wordless, as the guys started shouting at Colt.

"C'mon, bro." Dodge stood over him. "Breathe!"

Ranger had walked away and stared at the dark wall of night that pressed in from the ocean.

"C'mon, Colt." Ham hit his knees, grabbed his wrist, feeling for a pulse. "Not this way."

"Not this way."

Oh . . . no . . .

"Not this way."

Noemi squeezed her hand.

Shouts and flashing lights—the EMTs had arrived.

Lucas and Orion kept working.

Don't give up!

Tae stood there dumbly as two EMTs got out, as they handed Lucas a mechanism to administer bagged air. Then they patched Colt.

"Clear," said the one, and Orion leaned away.

They sent a shock into Colt's chest.

Nothing on the monitor.

She pressed a hand to her mouth.

"Again."

Her eyes filmed as his body jerked.

"We have a v-tach rhythm."

She thought the voice might belong to Lucas.

338

"Resume CPR," said one of the EMTs, and Orion again began to pump as Lucas continued to squeeze the oxygen bag.

They got Colt onto a board, and then all the guys carried him up the sand, Orion still doing his work. They put him in the back of the ambulance. Closed the door.

And then she just stood there as the ambulance left her and his team in the parking lot, listening to Pete's sad truth in her heart. *It's not without costs.*

The darkness folded in around him.

Colt tasted the sweat running down his face, felt the terrible beat of his heart, and deep inside, he knew that he should wake up. *Could* wake up, if he wanted.

But the memory took him deep, swallowed him whole, and suddenly he was tucked into the grimy knot of a savanna woodland, overlooking the jihadist camp.

And it was happening all over again.

Around him, insects buzzed, the scent of a dung fire stank the air, and under his black BDUs, camo grease, and body armor, everything itched. He had burrowed under a tall Borassus tree, dug in, and waited for the go from his team lead. He was probably alerting every animal lying in wait by his smell, including a lion he'd heard roar in the darkness.

Still, the adrenaline, the buzz of these moments reminded him of stalking the bear, so long ago. The heat in his veins before the battle.

Thirty yards away, in a pocket surrounded by hills, acacia, and Borassus palms, captured in a circle of trampled grasses, sat a small compound of terrorists. The Abu Nidal jihadist group. And imprisoned in a dirt building without windows at the south end was their target, journalist Rowen White.

Only *not* a journalist, but a member of the CIA and a senator's younger brother, which was the problem.

Too many secrets in Rowen's head for him not to be rescued. Or executed, which *wasn't* an option, at least not for Colt's team leader, Ace. Which was why they'd hunted Abu Nidal soldiers for a week, in and around local villages. Why they'd snatched one, dragged him into their safe house, and employed some pressure. The young man had spit out the location of the nest almost too easily.

That thought sat in Colt's gut even as he listened to Elvis humming through the coms. *"Are you lonesome tonight . . ."*

"Cut the serenade," Ace said, tucked into the darkness on the other side of camp. He led the assault team, with Elvis, Nuggsy, Batman, Irish, Leroy, Rags, and Nelson. "Sam, you ready?"

"Ready." Colt found his feet. Vader nudged in

behind him. The green of his NVG illuminated his path over to the prisoners' hut.

"Marsh, you got eyes on the target?" Ace asked one of their overwatch snipers, tucked somewhere in the hills behind them. Across the camp, watching the west end, was Nuggsy, a youngster who'd only recently joined the team.

"They just brought White out to relieve himself. He's back in the nest now," Marsh said.

From the intel of Ahmed, the young man they'd nabbed, they'd learned the strength and rhythm of the camp.

And that they were running out of time. White was due to be sold any day.

Then the fun and games would really start.

"On my word, we go," Ace said.

It should have been easy. According to Ahmed, only a handful of soldiers remained in camp. But even as Ace's command hissed into the coms— *Execute!*—as Colt ran forward, toward the edge of the camp, he felt it in his gut—no, his *chest*.

Something wasn't right.

Gunfire burst from a location on the east side of the camp, Ace's team, keeping them occupied.

Colt and Vader scurried along the edge of the handful of huts, staying low, headed for the building that held White.

The compound came alive with soldiers, now swarming out of their huts. The acrid bite of propellant, shouts, the peppering of gunfire smoked the air. In the chaos, he and Vader edged toward the prisoner.

"Entering Primary," Colt said as he confirmed—no guard—and kicked in the flimsy door.

Vader peeled into the opening, gun out. Colt stepped in behind him, even as Vader yelled. "Sam—ambush!"

A shot, and everything inside Colt seized as Vader dropped, a shot to his head.

Instinct. Colt pointed and pulled the trigger. No thought, just a tap to his chest, to his head, and the so-called journalist lay in a puddle.

But even before Colt pulled the trigger, he knew—*not* the journalist. Not even an American, but a man dressed in White's clothing.

"It's a trap!" Colt snarled into the coms.

"Get out of there!" Ace shouted.

But Colt was trapped, bullets obliterating the door. He pressed his back to the wall, glanced around the edge.

A shot nearly shaved off his nose.

"I'm pinned down."

"Copy," Ace said. "Hang tight."

Colt waited, not looking at Vader, his heart a fist, slamming against his chest.

And then the compound blew. A thousand projectiles pinging against the hut, men, supplies, shrapnel. Colt ducked, ears ringing, then grabbed Vader, hoisted him up over his shoulder, and fled.

He dove behind a hut, trying to catch his breath. Vader hit the dirt, his body a rag.

Colt ground his jaw, tried not to let his gorge rise. His ears still rang, but he could hear Ace shouting at him.

"Back to rally point!"

Right.

He grabbed Vader again, hoisted him, and then, with a grunt, ran.

And ran.

Ace caught up to him, four hundred yards from camp. A shot had ripped through his arm.

But most importantly, only Irish was with him. They each carried a body. Leroy. Batman.

Which left Nelson, Rags, Elvis, and Nuggsy back in the savanna for their corpses to be brutalized. Or worse, if they weren't dead, to be tortured.

No! Colt stumbled, dropped Vader, and vomited, his hands bracing himself.

Irish too. Batman was still alive, a shot to his leg losing too much blood. Someone had tied off a tourniquet and tranq'd him, but he lay in the grass, moaning.

Marsh had shown up, and now stepped away, calling for exfil.

Ace stood, pacing, watching their backs. Nuggsy arrived, out of breath.

They hadn't been chased. Just expected. Just *ambushed.*

The Black Hawk arrived within minutes, and they loaded Batman and Leroy onto the deck along with Vader, and then Irish and Colt piled in with them.

Ace and Marsh climbed in last, their feet on the skids as the chopper arced away.

Colt wanted to empty his gut, again, at leaving his men behind.

Ahmed had lied to them.

Of *course* the punk had lied to them.

But even as they sped through the darkness, back to their camp, a hot ball formed in Colt's chest.

Ahmed had lied . . . and his brothers were paying the price.

Colt was practically out of the chopper before it landed. Thankfully Batman was still alive, so the medics rushed to help him.

But Colt headed straight for the makeshift prison of their patrol base, more of a hideout with a few key personnel.

He probably looked like he felt—bloodied, destroyed, soulless. Maybe someone had tried to stop him. It seemed, however, that he'd had a hole right to Ahmed's cell.

He could still hear the echo of the door, slamming against the wall, the roar of his own voice.

And then, Ahmed's screams.

Piercing, burrowing through him, shredding him—

"C'mon, Colt. Don't give up on us!"

His chest exploded with bright light and pain—

"C'mon!"

He opened his eyes.

Lights. A doc, garbed, masked, standing over him with hands up. Another holding paddles.

What?

He gasped, and beside him, a monitor beeped.

"He's back," the doctor said and handed off the paddles.

Oh wow—he'd been shocked. No wonder flames consumed his body. Oxygen poured through a mask over his mouth and as he blinked, he realized—

Hospital.

He bit back a shout even as he reached up to take off the oxygen mask.

A doctor grabbed his arm.

Then a voice. "Calm down, you're okay."

He knew that voice. Searched for it.

Dodge.

His brother stood back from the bed, his arms folded across his chest. He was wearing an expression that Colt hadn't seen before.

Or maybe he had. Once. When he'd been in the hospital, so long ago, after their epic brawl.

When Dodge had re-sorted his insides.

He'd woken in the hospital. His father had been at his bedside, praying maybe, and in the reflection of the window, Colt had spotted Dodge at the door wearing exactly the same—worried? tormented?—expression.

"Please stop dying on us." This from one of the doctors. Lucas Maguire.

"Sorry?" he said, his voice muffled.

Dodge sighed, roughed a hand across his mouth, looked away.

"If you're trying to get away from us again, bro, this is not the way." Ranger. He stood at the end of the bed, and now came up, put his hand on Colt's leg.

"Why does this keep happening?" Dodge asked.

"We did a chest X-ray and echocardiogram. He's got myopericarditis," Lucas said, stepping away from him. "My guess is that after his event in Nigeria—"

"Event?" Ranger said. "They beat him within an inch of his life."

"Yes. And probably damaged his heart. It's not uncommon for the sac around your heart to become inflamed after a trauma like that, which probably accounts for some of the breathing issues he had, like the one on the glacier."

Colt glanced at Dodge. He cocked a head at him. "Lucas was trying to save your life. We told him everything we could about your condition. It might have been easier if you'd been honest with us from the beginning."

Honest about what? So he'd been a little winded . . .

346

"But that's not the only problem. The pericarditis—or inflammation—caused a cardiac tamponade, which is fluid built up in the pericardium. Which led to his arrhythmia. And then cardiogenic shock."

"Perfect." Ranger shook his head.

"And then he got exposed to the S-poxR, and the vaccine caused myocarditis, or the inflammation of the actual heart muscle. Colt here has cascading issues that have led to myopericarditis, and we're going to need to figure out how to reverse the damage."

"Clearly he needs a new heart," Dodge said.

"I know you're kidding, but if we can't get this under control . . . yes, he might need a transplant."

Colt just stared at him. "Seriously?"

The other doctor stepped in. Bearded, wise eyes, a big man that Colt wanted to trust. His baritone voice threaded through him, stopped the strange roil of panic he'd been trying to ignore. "I'm Major Elroy Austin, the cardiothoracic specialist here at the Cape." He unslung his stethoscope from around his neck, placed it over Colt's heart, leaned in, and had a listen.

Big hands, and he reminded Colt of Ace, his team leader. Weirdly, it helped him relax.

The major leaned up. "First, we're going to do a pericardial tap and drain the fluid around your heart. If that doesn't work, we'll have to take you into surgery and do a pericardiectomy, or the removal of part or most of the pericardium."

"Wait," Dodge said, "that sounds dangerous."

Thank you. What *he* said.

The major crossed his arms over his chest. "Survival rates are high. About eighty percent five years out from the surgery—"

"Stop." Colt moved the oxygen mask aside. "Just . . . listen. I'm fine. I'm just a little banged up. We don't need to start removing pieces of my heart."

Yes, *mea culpa, mea culpa*, he should have mentioned something to someone, maybe. The fact that for the past two weeks he had felt out of breath, as if a hand were squeezing his heart. But no need to go overboard here. He lay back. "Let's do the tap. And then . . . just wait. I can beat this."

"You can't *will* your heart to be fixed, Colt," Lucas said.

He stared at the doc. "My heart was broken long before Nigeria," he said softly. "I don't expect it to get fixed. But I don't want to surrender it quite yet."

Lucas patted him on the shoulder. Looked at the major. Nodded.

They walked out, and Dodge and Ranger came up, each on one side of the bed. Ranger's lips were pursed. Dodge ground his jaw, his arms still folded over his chest.

"What?" Colt asked.

"You should have told us before the assault on the Russian compound that you weren't okay."

"I *was* okay! I just felt a little . . . off." His chest still burned where they'd shocked him, and fatigue pressed him into the bed, but . . .

Fine. He sighed. "Truth is, I should have been dead a long time ago."

Ranger glanced at Dodge. Back to Colt. "Are you talking about Nigeria?"

"No. Yes." He sighed, stared at the ceiling. And then, what did it matter? "I wasn't just discharged from the military. I requested a separation."

Ranger frowned.

"Why?" Dodge asked.

"Because . . ." Yes, it was getting harder to breathe. "I lost it. I killed someone."

"We've all killed people," Ranger said quietly. "In action. It's part of our job."

"No." Colt looked at him, but saw an image of Ahmed's face, bloodied, beaten, crying, before he blinked it away. His throat tightened. "I killed a prisoner. A person who'd set my team up to walk into an ambush."

Ranger shook his head. "I don't think—"

"He was a kid, Range. He was a seventeen-year-old kid who I . . . who died after I interrogated him."

Silence.

He closed his eyes, but couldn't take the image in the darkness, so he reopened them. "I killed that kid. Not intentionally, but . . . it doesn't matter. I had murder in my heart." Colt winced, looked at Dodge.

He was wearing a strange look.

"Clearly, my heart isn't in great shape. But I'm definitely not the kind of guy who deserves a transplant, so, if my heart goes . . . that's what I deserve. I've probably cheated death long enough. It's time for my sins to catch up with me."

Then he closed his eyes again. And listened to his heart struggle to beat on.

THIRTEEN

She'd killed him.

No, Colt wasn't dead yet, but Tae couldn't pry the accusation out of her head as Lucas came out to where she waited with the other nonfamily members—Ham, Jake, North, Pete, and Noemi, although technically, she was family.

They gathered in a private section of the waiting room, Ham standing, his arms folded, feet set as if assessing the situation for battle. Noemi sat with her father, who leaned forward, his head in his hands.

Jake and North were milling around, holding coffee. Roy and Zoey hadn't returned from wherever they'd gone, but Logan had shown up at the hospital to help get Colt admitted.

He, too, had disappeared, however. Because that's what the government did—stepped into your life, wrecked it, and vanished, leaving you with the shattered pieces.

Only Dodge and Ranger had been allowed into the ICU with Colt, and even the extra brother was pushing it.

Somehow Lucas got him in, but really, it wasn't like Tae could look Colt in his beautiful brown eyes and face the truth.

This was her fault.

If she hadn't given him the untested vaccine—

The team now circled around Lucas, who wore a visiting staff badge around his neck.

"He's stable, and we did some tests." Lucas gave a rundown of what they'd discovered, explaining the cascading layers of trouble. Tae could hardly hear it, but her medical mind was tracking every step.

Yes. No wonder the vaccine had caused the heart attack.

She wanted to strangle Colt herself, if he survived the procedure.

"Major Austin will be doing a pericardio-centesis," Lucas said. "It's under a local anesthetic. They'll insert a large bore catheter at an angle into the chest, guided by an ultrasound. An electrocardiogram, or ECG, will be recording, and if there are complications, we'll move him into surgery and perform a pericardi-ectomy."

"What is that, exactly?" Noemi asked.

Tae could have told her. It was dangerous. And meant that he'd never be cleared for spec op duty again.

And that thought only pressed a thumb into her guilt.

Even if Colt lived, she'd wrecked his life. His future.

Although, Tae's mind traveled, for a moment, to his *"We'll see"* statement.

Huh. But really, he was probably just saying that to keep her calm.

He'd never intended to walk away from his spec ops life, and she knew it, deep inside.

Even if he made it, he'd never forgive her. She might be ill.

"It involves removing the damaged pericardium," Lucas said in answer to Noemi's question.

"They'd have to crack his chest," Tae said to Ham. She wondered if he was figuring it out. Colt, off his team.

"What is the mortality rate of a pericardiectomy?" Ham asked.

"Between five and fifteen percent," Lucas said.

"How did this happen?" Noemi asked.

"Probably left over from his trauma in Nigeria," Ham said.

Tae nodded, looking away.

Outside, rain spat on the windows.

"That accounts for the heart attacks?" Ham asked.

Of which, Colt had suffered three more since arriving. Three times he'd gone down, three times they'd brought him back.

"And the pericardial tamponade he had in Seattle," Tae said. "The heart attacks are from myocarditis, which is a known but rare side effect of the smallpox vaccine."

All eyes turned to her.

She looked at Lucas. "Right?"

"Yes," he said grimly.

"Which means what?" Ham asked.

"It usually means his heart is beyond repair," she said, and now she really wanted to throw up. "He needs a heart transplant." Even as she said it, the world swayed. She sank into a chair.

"You're way down the road there, Tae," Lucas said. "We have other options. ACE inhibitors we can try to get his blood pressure down. And beta blockers. If we have to, we can even implant an ICD."

Silence.

"It's like a pacemaker," Tae said softly. "Implantable cardioverter defibrillator. It restarts his heart when it stops. Over and over."

"I'll let you know how the pericardiocentesis goes," Lucas said quietly.

She closed her eyes, her face in her hands.

"You don't look so good, Tae." When she opened her eyes, she saw that Ham had crouched in front of her. "Can someone get her some water?"

She sat up. "I'm fine. I'm not the one whose heart is exploding because of something I gave him—"

"Hey. Calm down. It's not your fault."

She stared at him. "Then whose fault is it? I'm the one who created the vaccine. I'm the one who decided to stick it into Colt's body." Her voice shook, and she looked away before she burst into tears.

Wow, she was tired.

"You had no choice." Ham reached for a bottle of water that Jake handed him. Opened it and handed it to her.

She took a drink. Sat back. Met Ham's blue eyes. He wore worry in them.

"It never ends," she said.

"What never ends?" He slid onto the chair next to her.

"The evil. It's like on the beach. We stomp out one terrible virus or terrorist group and a second later, something else washes in to fill it. It's useless."

She glanced down the hall, to the ICU room. "And people like Colt or my dad pay the ultimate price. It's not worth it."

"Who says it's not worth it?" Noemi said. She had gotten up and walked over to Tae, sat beside her. "Colt got hurt because he was trying to keep us alive. Over and over. To me, to Selah, it was worth it. He saved our lives."

"I know. It's just . . . what about the people he leaves behind? Dodge, Ranger, his sister. His dad." Silence. And yes, these guys would deem it worth it—they were all heroes. She looked at them. "What about the people who love you?"

"It's never an easy choice," Pete said quietly from his seat across the waiting room. "But we have to believe that we're making a difference." He looked up at her. "You're making a difference, Tae."

She shook her head, her eyes burning. "I don't know. I just feel like whatever I do, it's one bad choice after another. Everywhere I turn I feel . . . helpless."

"No surprise there. Do you really think that you will be able to save the world?" Ham said.

She frowned. "Um—"

"Saving the world is not your responsibility. That doesn't belong to any of us. Our job is just to do our part. Show up, with the talents God has given us, and say yes to the mission he's given us. That's it. You're going to feel helpless if you think it's up to you."

"It feels overwhelming."

"Only because you're looking at the big picture. And . . . the ending that you want."

"Why else am I doing all this?"

"To make the world a better place. One battle at a time."

Pete had gotten up. He limped over to her. "The role of a soldier isn't to ask why, or even determine the course of the fight. Our job is to just say yes." He sat in the chair across from her. "We fight for the people we love. For the people next to us, and the people we left behind." He gave her a sad smile. "Like your dad did."

The words sluiced through her. "What?"

"I did some asking, and . . ." He looked at Ham. "I realized that I knew your dad."

She stared at him, words escaping her.

"Have you ever heard of the battle of Tora Bora?"

"No."

"It was the first battle in the war in Afghanistan," Pete said. "A CIA spec op group, along with Delta and some selected Tier One operators, went after Osama bin Laden. We were trying to root him out of a series of caves in eastern Afghanistan, near Khyber Pass. Mostly it was the CIA and Delta, but we were working with some tribal groups as well as the British SAS and German KSK, so it was a huge joint operation. It was our first real hunting mission. We knew there would be casualties, and since it was early in the war on terror, the government went to extra lengths to keep casualties low. Your dad was flown in as emergency medical personnel on-site."

"He was a top trauma doc at NewYork-Presbyterian Hospital, so . . ."

"Yes, well, we needed him. There were bunkers hidden everywhere, and just when we thought we cleared an area, a group of al-Qaeda or Taliban operatives would pop up and ambush us. It was chaos, scattered, and should have given us insights into how the war would be for the next twenty years. Bin Laden escaped to Pakistan, but the part I remember was the day we happened upon a cave that we thought had cleared. We were searching it, and suddenly a fighter came out of nowhere with a Kalashnikov and opened fire. I took three bullets, one to my leg, one to my arm, and one here." He pointed to a faded, thick scar on his neck. She hadn't really noticed it before.

"I was bleeding out, and they were afraid to move me, so your dad choppered into the site to save my life. He stitched me up right there, then stabilized my leg and arm, and . . . he saved my life, for sure."

His expression turned grim. "Your father died a few days later, in an IED attack. Again, he'd gone into the site, and this time, a group of Taliban killed him and everyone in the bunker."

Twenty years ago, but the news punched her again.

"The thing is," he continued, "I remember him trying to keep me alive as they carried me out of the mountains to the chopper. We talked about our kids. He showed me a pic that he kept in his helmet. He very much thought about you, Tae. He wanted to come home to you, just like I wanted to come home to my daughter."

Her throat closed.

"I never saw him again, to thank him. But you need to know that his sacrifice was very much worth it to the people he saved. To the loved ones they left behind." His gaze went to Noemi. "And to the people who went on to save others' lives. Like me saving Ranger's life when he nearly drowned in Key West. And Ranger saving Colt's life in Nigeria. It's all knitted together in God's timing and purpose. But we can't possibly see the big picture. And from our vantage point, yes, it seems like evil is winning."

She stared down the hall. They were taking a long time.

"The fact is, if you try to depend on yourself and all your amazing talents and abilities to fight this war, you will run dry. The more you try to control, the more you find slipping out of your hands. You must trust in God, in his victory. And in his goodness, even in the face of defeat. In fact, it is God's goodness in us that even desires to fight evil. Without him, we *would* be helpless."

She didn't want to hear it. "Pete. God abandoned me long ago. I spent years asking God for answers to my father's death. My mom nearly went crazy with it. And he never answered."

"Until now."

She blinked at him.

"Now, when you most need to know that God hears you. When you are run dry. Now, when that truth can save you from what the enemy wants most . . . despair."

Silence.

"You are not alone," Ham said.

Funny, that's what Colt had said.

And for a moment, her mind tracked back, to the past three months. To the moment Echo and

Dodge had found her in the snow. To Colt's words, after they'd found the plane. *"The fact you survived is . . . well, a miracle."*

Huh.

Footsteps made her look up. Dodge came down the hall, Ranger beside him.

She braced herself.

Dodge walked right up to her. "The procedure went well, and he's breathing better. Now, we just wait." He glanced at Ham. "And pray."

"There's a chapel somewhere in this building. Do you want to join me?" Ham stood up and held out his hand to Tae.

She glanced at Pete. He met her gaze with a smile. Nodded.

She rose and took Ham's hand.

He was still alive.

So that was good, right?

Colt opened his eyes to the morning sun slanting through the second-story window of the hospital, the skies blue, tufted with clouds. The room smelled of cotton and antiseptic. The only sounds, the hiss of the oxygen machine and the steady beep of the ECG machine attached to his chest with pads.

He needed a drink, his mouth parched, but his hand was taped up with IV lines, and he hadn't a clue where the nurse's call button was.

He was a little sickened by his own weakness, the thrumming ache in his chest, the fact that he'd caused such a ruckus.

The worst part was that he'd *known* something wasn't right. He wasn't so stupid as to not notice his struggled breathing, the ever-present tightness in his chest. But he'd thought he could push through, work it away.

Ignore it and get the job done.

This wasn't him—sure, he'd been wounded before and had spent a good amount of time recuperating from his wounds in Nigeria, but . . . no, he didn't go down without a fight. He just wanted to tear out the IVs, get out of this flimsy hospital gown, and go back to work.

"You ready to come back to Jones, Inc.?"

The question floated in his brain. Yes. With a fist pump. Except that's not what he said to Ham, and maybe even then he'd known something wasn't right. Because it was the only thing that accounted for his answer. *"We'll see."*

It hadn't been a play for Tae, although she'd looked at him from the top of the stairs with so much yearning in her eyes, he couldn't help but want to reach out to her.

Had been planning a sweet rendezvous on the beach, something that had been roaming his brain for three days.

And then his heart had to betray him.

A knock came at the door and a nurse came in.

"Good morning, Mr. Kingston. I'm just here to take your vitals."

"Still alive," he said, and offered her a smile.

She smiled back, moved him to a sitting position, and then promptly stuck a sheathed thermometer in his mouth. Her hands closed around his wrist for a pulse, and even that movement hurt.

Yep, he was pitiful.

The nurse removed the thermometer. "Your temp is normal. And pulse is good." She looked at the ECG reading. Smiled at him, as if he'd passed an exam. "Anything I can get you?"

"Freedom?"

"Not quite yet. How about some breakfast?"

"I'd be happy with some water."

"That we can do, Master Sergeant."

He raised an eyebrow. Apparently, Logan had used his former rank when admitting him. No wonder he landed a private room. Colt didn't bother to correct her.

Maybe he needed that rank, just a little.

She patted his shoulder, then left.

No, more than a little. The military had been his entire life. Given him purpose.

Brothers.

And then came Jones, Inc.

Yeah, he needed to get out of this bed and back to work if he wanted to live with himself.

Another knock on the door, and he expected

to see the nurse. Instead, Dodge backed into the room holding two cups of coffee. He was grinning, although unshaven and wearing yesterday's clothing.

"I sneaked in some diesel fuel," he said and handed Colt a cup. "Although yours is decaffeinated."

"Aw, c'mon. I'm not a pansy."

"Sorry, we don't need anything exciting that ticker of yours." Dodge pulled over a chair and lowered himself into it.

"You didn't go home last night."

"Someone needed to stick around and sign the donor papers if you decided to kick off."

The coffee went to Colt's bones and, caffeinated or not, fortified.

"I'm not giving up my parts yet, bro."

Dodge raised his cup. "Congratulations on living through the night."

"Thank you. Now get me out of here."

Dodge leaned back, sighed, and propped his ankle on his knee. "Sorry, but I've got some bad news."

Colt drew in a breath. "Please, don't—"

"Doc says your operating days are over."

Wow. Talk about a punch to the sternum. But no. Nope. Nada. He shook his head. Turned back to Dodge. "Doc doesn't know me."

"Your ticker isn't . . . it's not a go, Colt."

His jaw tightened. "That's not going to work

for me. I . . ." He shook his head. "It's who I am. It's . . . it's all I have."

"That's not true."

"It is true!" He didn't mean to snap, but, "C'mon, Dodge. What's your earliest memory of me? Probably jumping off the sofa to take you or Ranger down. Let's be honest here. I'm not a pilot. I'm not a sniper. I'm the guy who gets it done."

Dodge hadn't moved, didn't raise his voice, still unflappable. "Yes. You are. And now you're just going to have to figure out how to get it done without . . . well, so much excitement."

Colt blinked at him. Then stared at the ceiling.

"I was wounded. In Afghanistan. My chopper was shot down."

He looked at Dodge. "What?"

Dodge nodded. "I was retrieving a SEAL team who had been pinned down, and during the rescue, the Taliban got a shot off. I woke up in Germany, went to Walter Reed. For a while I thought I'd never walk again. The Air Force gave me a medical discharge."

"I didn't know."

"Just like I didn't realize you'd left Delta. But I felt the same way, that my life was over. And I really didn't want to go back to the ranch. Not after . . . well, the way I left things with Echo."

"But you two worked it out."

"Not easily. I was angry at Dad for siding with you—"

"He didn't side with me."

Dodge raised an eyebrow. "He did. He sat by your bedside the entire time you were in the hospital. While I sat in jail, by the way."

"I didn't know that." Colt remembered waking up, seeing his father praying. And, of course, Dodge. However, "I didn't know you were in jail."

"For a week. He didn't press charges against me—said you declined, but really, it felt like I was in prison for ten years. Because I refused to forgive—you, Dad. Echo. And that's its own sort of prison." He made a face, then stared at his joe. "We make our prisons, Colt. Hand down our own sentences. And we don't have to do that." He looked up at him. "*You* don't have to do that. There's a life beyond what you see . . . you just have to let go of the one you're hanging onto."

Colt stared at him. His brother did seem different. Less angry. Less bossy. Less . . . judgmental. Colt's throat tightened, his voice thinning. "I don't know how to do that."

A pause. Then, "I was thinking about what you said last night. About your defective heart."

"I was on drugs, let's not forget that."

Dodge managed a slight smile. "The problem is that you *do* need a new heart, bro. And you have for a long time. Before the event in Sudan, even before our fight. Because your heart was broken the day Mom died. You heard the lie that you caused it, or that you were trouble, or darkness, or whatever, but like a virus, it got inside you and infected your entire body. Your vision. Your life. Told you that you weren't worth saving—and then you went out and lived that lie. But you *are* worth saving, Colt."

"No—"

"Just listen. You need . . . for lack of a better word, a vaccine. Something to awaken your system. Give you some defense. You need truth, buddy. And here it is, so pay attention."

Really?

"You can't fix your heart on your own, no matter how much you try to redeem yourself. And you can't just patch up the old, broken heart, either. You need a fresh start. But to get that, you have to surrender your old, faulty heart to God and let him put in you a heart of faith. A heart that belongs to him. And that changes everything because suddenly you don't have to worry about proving yourself, fixing yourself, redeeming yourself. You are already redeemed. And now you're a different kind of warrior. No longer a mercenary, but a soldier for the Lord. At his command."

Colt blinked at him.

"Just think about it. Your whole life you've done things your way. What if you started doing things God's way? You might be surprised at what he has waiting for you."

He took a sip of his coffee. Stared at it. "Mom loved you." He met Colt's gaze. "It was fitting you got to be with her when she died, because, Colt, you were so much like her. She was her own person. An artist. A fighter. And in the end, she died on her own terms."

"She died because I was wrestling with her."

"She died because she lived her very last moment doing what she wanted to do. Being our mom."

Colt looked away, his eyes burning. Aw, now he was really a softy.

"She would be proud of you, Colt. Very proud. I know I am."

He might need more oxygen. But even as he turned back and looked at Dodge, something swept through him.

Forgiveness. Peace.

Wholeness.

"I don't want to be broken anymore," he said quietly. "I don't want to be trouble."

"Maybe just the right kind of trouble," Dodge said. He nodded toward the door. "There's someone waiting outside who'd really like to see you. But brace yourself, she's pretty angry, so I'd start with an apology."

Dodge got up. "And then, if you promise to behave yourself, I'll see how soon you can get out of here." He went to the door. Stopped. "For the record, I'd really like to see you come home."

The words settled inside Colt like a breath.

Home. *"Until you let God tell you how much he loves you, how much he has done for you, you'll believe you're not worth saving."*

And then, Tae walked through the door. The reminder of how much God had done for him. She wore a pair of Bermuda shorts, a white T-shirt, her hair back in a messy bun. She closed the door and just stood there and, shoot, if his stupid heart did exactly what it wasn't supposed to—started banging its way through his chest.

When she didn't move, he offered a smile. "Hey."

"Don't hey me," she said. "I'm keeping my distance so I don't walk over there and strangle you."

"You missed me."

"You are the biggest . . . *jerk.*"

Oh.

"You nearly died because . . . because of me. Because I gave you that stupid vaccine—"

"Stop." He used his Delta tone. "This is not your fault. This is my fault, through and through, from the van to even jumping into a mission when I wasn't a hundred percent. I could have cost lives, and I know better." He met her eyes. "It won't happen again."

She blinked. Swallowed. Opened her mouth, then closed it. "I thought you'd put up more of a fight."

"I'm done fighting, Tae."

She looked away, wiped her hand across her cheek. "You can't operate anymore. And that's my fault."

"C'mere."

"No." She stayed where she was. Folded her arms, her jaw clenched.

"What—why?"

"Because . . . I know if I walk over there, you'll do something charming and then suddenly I'll be crying or even crazily kissing you and . . . and . . . that's not going to happen."

"I promise to behave myself."

"Now you're just lying."

He grinned. "C'mon. Don't be mad."

"I'm furious. And worried. And . . ." She sighed. "Sad. You scare the wits out of me! I can't help but think this is all my fault."

"Give me a little more credit than that. Haven't you met me? I can't stay away from trouble."

"Yes, I have met you. And that's the problem. Yes, you are trouble. One second you're kissing me on the beach, and the next you're having a heart attack."

"It wasn't quite in that order."

"It felt like it!" She held up a hand. "I think we just need to admit the truth here."

If she wasn't going to come to him, he was going to her. He pushed his bed button to sit up more. "What truth is that?"

"The truth that we're too differ— *What are you doing?*"

He'd taken off the ECG pads, and when the machine started beeping, turned it off. "We're not that different, Tae. In fact, we're very much alike." He pushed to his feet. "We're both driven by our hope to matter. To save lives."

"Colt, sit down."

He grabbed the IV stand. "Since the day I met you, you've been my Florence Nightingale. Just looking at you makes me feel better. Healed." He walked toward her, dressed in his silly hospital jammies. "Whole."

"Says the guy with a defective heart."

"Swollen, honey. It's just . . . a little bigger than normal. Like the Grinch."

It earned him a tiny smile. "Stop."

Not on his life. "Don't you see, Tae, that you're a crusader. And you need someone to watch your back. And that's me." He reached her and now put his arm over her shoulder, bracing himself against the wall, trapping her.

"And that's you, huh?" She put her hand on his chest. "Even with your broken heart?"

He leaned in, kissed her neck. "It's not broken anymore." He looked at her. "Because you make it worth saving."

She gaped at him, then rolled her eyes. "See, I knew this would happen."

"What?"

She kissed him. Nothing crazy, just a gentle whisper on his lips. But in his head, he was sweeping her up into his arms, pulling her against him, deepening his kiss, drinking in the taste of her. Tae. Yeah, she very much healed him.

And maybe, just maybe, Dodge was right. Maybe Colt would let God show him what might be on the other side. Because, frankly, it just sorta hurt to get in God's way.

She leaned back. "Now get back into bed. Before I call the nurses on you."

"They like me. Think I'm a hero or something."

"That's because you are, tough guy."

He turned around, pulling his jammies shut behind him. "No peeking."

She laughed, and he climbed back into bed. She helped hook him back up to the ECG machine just about the time his nurse came back in.

"You turned it off?" She shook her head, checked the machine. "Don't tell me you're going to give us trouble, Master Sergeant."

"Brace yourself," Tae said, her eyes shining.

"No ma'am," Colt said. He took Tae's hand. "My trouble days are over."

Tae rolled her eyes again.

He laughed, but yes. At least, as much as it was up to him.

Please, God, give me a new heart.

Tae sat down in the chair beside Colt's bed as the nurse left the room. "Your latest blood work shows that you have developed antibodies against the horsepox virus, which means it's working."

"Don't lab rats get some sort of reward for surviving?"

She cocked her head.

"Too soon?"

"Depends on what kind of reward you want."

"I have some ideas."

"They'll need to be tame ones." She raised an eyebrow. "No excitement."

"Like a walk on the beach."

"Not a walk on the beach. I don't know how you do it, but even that is way too exciting." But she smiled.

"Fine. How about a date. Disney World."

"You're kidding, right?"

"Sorta."

"You know there is still one canister out there."

"They didn't find it yet?"

She shook her head. "But Logan says that Jones, Inc., and that means you, can stand down. He and Roy are after it."

He stared at her hand, still gripped in his. "I don't like it."

"I know. But you can only do what you're asked to do. You have to let God do the rest."

He looked at her, raised an eyebrow. "Really?"

She shrugged. "Something I'm working on."

"I like it."

"Me too. So, yeah, I'll go on a date with you. And then . . ."

"Then?"

"Then, we'll see."

He could live with *we'll see*.

For now.

"I don't like walking away from this."

Ranger couldn't agree more with Ham's words. Only problem was that Ham meant the hunt for the last S-poxR canister.

Ranger meant Jones, Inc. The sense of being the tip of the spear. He still hadn't quite shrugged off the adrenaline of the assault, almost five days ago now. Still remembered how it felt to take down the shooter who'd nearly killed Colt.

And now Ranger got to go back to Alaska where he made soup—albeit good soup, yes—and answered the radio.

Hoo-yah.

He and Ham sat at a picnic table just off the beach near the mansion, next to a small Mexican place that Colt couldn't stop raving about. Noemi left to get another drink, inside the small hole-in-the-wall café.

He picked up a chip. Dipped it in the queso. "What can we do?"

Overhead, the sky was a perfect blue, not a hint of storm. They sat under an umbrella, the sounds of the ocean waves soft against the shore.

Ham set down the overflowing pork burrito he was eating and grabbed a napkin for the juice that ran down his wrist. Sopped it up. He wore a T-shirt, the sleeves tight against his biceps, shorts, a pair of sunglasses. The man always looked like some SEAL poster child, despite being away from the Teams for a number of years now. But like Noemi said, once a SEAL, always a SEAL, and probably that was the problem.

In his bones, Ranger would also always be a SEAL.

"We do nothing until Roy and Logan track it down. But I can't escape the idea that whoever has it is still planning to use it, somewhere," Ham said.

"Not Disney."

"No. Probably at none of the Disney resorts, or even the surrounding big parks. The Disney complex area is one big no-fly zone. The only place you can fly inside the perimeter is a former airstrip that was once used for private planes, and Mr. Disney himself."

"Really." Ranger took a drink of his bubbly water.

"They're actually having an air show this weekend. Small planes, acrobats, bombers—the usual. But the security will probably be crazy, even there."

Ranger capped his drink. "And now, we just sit on our hands and wait."

"And hope we find the canister before the S-poxR is deployed," Ham said.

"It's always hurry up and wait."

Ham picked up the burrito again, rearranged the wrapper. "It took ten years to get bin Laden. But it happened." He held up his fist.

Ranger bumped it. They hadn't been on the DevGroup team who took the terrorist leader out, but it was a win for all SEALs.

Ham took a bite of the burrito. Set it down and wiped his mouth. "I know what you can do while you're waiting."

Ranger reached for another chip. "Hmm?"

"Join Jones, Inc."

Everything inside Ranger stilled. "What?"

Ham wiped his fingers. "I need a guy like you on my team. You think on your feet. Adapt. See the big picture. You're not afraid to do the hard things. And your attack strategy worked."

"Only because my brother intercepted the getaway."

"And you didn't hesitate to keep that from being a disaster either."

"Doing my job."

"I'd like it to be full time. For us."

Ranger drew in a breath. Past them, at the beach, the sun baked the sand, the water rolled in frothy rhythm, and a windsurfer rode the waves, farther out, letting the gusts take him airborne. It looked freeing. Easy.

Like he'd been born to do it.

"I'm going blind, Ham."

Ham still wore his sunglasses, so Ranger couldn't read his eyes, but his mouth tightened to a grim line, a nod.

Here it came. The apology, the pity, the backpedaling—

"I know."

Ranger had nothing.

"Pete told me when I floated the idea, although he was two thumbs-up."

"Noemi will kill him."

"Probably. But Pete sees what I see. Maybe you're not in the field, but you see things, Ranger. You strategize in your head, you see the scenarios . . ."

"I don't need your pity, Ham."

He paused. "If you think that is what this is, then you haven't been paying attention. I'm not in the business of handouts. You work for me, you *work* for me."

"I'm no good to you if I can't roll out with you."

Ham stared at him. Then took off his glasses. "Who told you that?"

"I'm just being practical."

"You're seeing the world through your feelings. Not through truth. Not through God's eyes. If he's called you to something, Range, he'll equip you, even if you don't know how."

"I need to see to shoot."

"Who says you have to shoot?"

"I'm a sniper."

"Exactly what makes you good at strategy, what-ifs, and contingency plans." Ham put his glasses back on. "God's promises don't depend on your feelings. They depend on his Word. Stop relying on yourself and let God use you how he wants."

Ranger stared at him, the taste of his offer gathering inside. Yes. He could be a point man. Out on the field, they had to utilize all their senses . . . for years he'd anticipated, imagined, plotted . . .

Wait. "I can't do that to Noemi, Ham. She's been through so much. Her dad's death and sort of resurrection. The kidnapping in Nigeria and Alaska . . . the siege on the house. I just . . . I just can't do that to her."

Ham took another bite of his burrito. Set it down. Again wiped his mouth. "Noemi is a SEAL's kid. Has it occurred to you that maybe God has especially designed her to be in this with you?"

Ranger pushed away his basket of chips. "She's the bravest woman I know, smart, capable, and, yes, she's all in for the adventure, but . . ." He shook his head. "No."

"Range—"

"I'm trying to be real here. Yeah, I'd love to

join Jones, Inc. But then what? I love her, and Noemi deserves more than me part time. She deserves better."

"And you think you'll be your better self hanging around Sky King Ranch, making soup?"

What, could the guy read his mind?

He picked up his drink. "I can't follow my gut on this one, Ham. Thanks for the offer, but no." The water soothed his burning throat.

"I get it," Ham said. "I have a wife and a daughter too. But I also know who I am."

Ranger looked at him. "I guess I'm still trying to figure that out."

"I hope you saved me some chips." Noemi's voice fell over his shoulder. She swung a leg over the seat and slid in next to him. "I'm starving."

He pushed the basket to her. He'd lost his appetite anyway.

FOURTEEN

Just calm down. It wasn't forever, but it *was* a beautiful day.

A date. With Colt. And that's all.

Tae wasn't going to get too far ahead of herself.

Ever since kneeling with Ham in the chapel six days ago, something had shifted inside Tae. She wasn't all the way to *let it go, let it go,* but she had shades of *trying* to let go. Trying to not need an order and a plan and a look too far ahead. Like today, agreeing to hanging out at an air show, enjoying herself with Colt while a terrorist was on the lam.

"Here you go." Colt passed a basket of fries to her as he sat down next to her.

Breathe.

Three days out of the hospital, six days from his near-death experience, and the man had bounced back, gotten some sun, and looked the picture of health.

Even if he moved slowly.

But yes, proving how resilient he was, swollen heart and all, Colt had transformed from wounded warrior to tourist, with his dark Oakleys on his head, his hair pulled back, not quite clean-shaven, but just enough scruff for him to look like he might be having a time-out from life. He

379

wore a pair of cargo shorts, flip-flops, and a blue T-shirt that barely concealed the bandage he still wore on his puncture site. But the shirt somehow brought out the deep brown hues in his eyes as he'd come downstairs today, a string backpack over his shoulder, carrying an umbrella and sunscreen.

"Ready for fun?" He'd smiled at her, and it simply felt surreal.

Like she hadn't just spent the last three months running—literally—from Russian gangsters.

But if they all wanted to escape into the Never-Never Land of pretend-the-world-isn't-imploding, then she would too.

"I expect cotton candy," she said. *"It's not a date without cotton candy."*

"I'll remember that." He had winked and slid on those glasses, and the Russians mostly dropped out of her brain.

Leaving only the feel of Colt's hand in hers. Holding on.

They'd piled into the Escalade with Dodge, Ranger, Zoey, and Noemi.

Ham, Fraser, and the Jones, Inc. drone operator, Scarlett, who was waiting for her fiancé, Ford, to come home from deployment, were hanging out for the weekend at the house while the rest of the Jones, Inc. guys had jumped on a plane last night and headed back to Minnesota.

Pete, Logan, and Roy were still using the safe

house as a general HQ, but had gone out for the day.

Which meant that Tae probably had to figure out what happened next between her and Colt.

Alaska?

Florida?

Whoops. Nope. She just needed to lean into the glorious day, munching on the salty fries Colt had fetched for her, sharing his soda.

Dodge had been the one with the air show idea and had made them tour the grounds, forcing his brothers to listen as he quizzed a guy with a new standard D-25 biplane, which "had a wingspan of forty-five feet and a top speed of one hundred miles per hour," according to its owner, an elderly gentleman who sported a leather jacket and goggles.

"My grandfather used her for rum-running back in the Prohibition era. With the big high-lift wings and wide landing gear, she can just about land anywhere."

And that's when Dodge began talking about his now-destroyed Piper Cub with the tundra wheels, and Colt had steered her away to watch the remote-controlled planes take to the sky. Not toys, but larger planes that took some finesse to operate. The pilots took them through loops and dives that mimicked the show to come.

"The day is supposed to end with a drone light

show," Zoey said. She planned to stay on at the lab, continue to work on the virus.

The invitation was open to Tae.

Maybe.

Nope. Not thinking about it today.

She did wonder, however, what went down between Zoey and Roy, because he'd left last night, and hadn't come around today. But she hadn't gotten Zoey alone for days for a catch-up.

Hopefully Roy didn't do something stupid and break her heart.

Zoey seemed fine, however, as they all toured a massive Lockheed C-5 Galaxy, a B-17 Flying Fortress, and an F/A-18 Super Hornet. Dodge joined them for the Chinook tour, then showed them the Black Hawk, which he'd flown.

They finally climbed into the stands, joining some five thousand other watchers, children, teenagers, couples, and families, as biplanes and even wing walkers soared overhead.

A glorious day, the highs in the upper eighties, but it had already rained today, which had tempered the air. Tae couldn't help but think that they'd certainly escaped disaster because an event like this, with so many children and teenagers running around to bring home the virus to their friends, would have been the perfect target.

Especially if the virus had deployed during a rainstorm. There was no real proof that it could be carried by the mist in the air, but it attached to human fluids, and the disease was more prevalent in tropical areas, so . . .

Just the thought had her holding her breath.

"You okay?" Colt reached for a fry.

She forced a smile. "Yeah."

"Stop thinking about it."

"What?"

"Please. I know you. You're thinking about infection rates."

Her eyes widened.

He grinned, then put his arm around her and kissed her temple. "Calm down. Me too. Let's shrug it off."

Right. Because now it sat like a burr under her skin.

"My dad used to tell this story about 9/11 and how he was on his way to work—he was teaching at Columbia part-time—and he walked through some of Central Park on the way. The day was gorgeous. Blue skies, autumn in the air. I'd just started fourth grade, and we were planning a trip to the Bronx Zoo. Then the world just—erupted. The first plane hit the tower, and it sort of boomed all across the island. He could only see smoke, so he ran the rest of the way to the school. He was watching on television when the second plane hit. He left work and headed to the hospital. It was a Level 1 trauma center, but the longer they waited for survivors, and didn't get any, the more he realized that he couldn't just wait. So he went down to the site. But by that time, the towers were down and there was chaos and . . . he couldn't do anything. He enlisted five days later."

Colt threaded his fingers through hers.

"I guess, now that I hear myself tell it, I might have done the same thing."

"Hard to understand when you're ten years old though," Colt said. "People running toward danger, not away."

She looked at him. Heard his words in the hospital. *We're both driven by our hope to matter. To save lives.*

Maybe they did belong together.

Stop. Enjoy.

Overhead, the sky rumbled and suddenly six vintage World War II Navy planes blasted by them, maneuvering together. "They're fighter jets," Dodge said from the seat below them.

He was eating popcorn, a kid at the circus.

Noemi and Ranger sat next to him. Something had gone down between them because Noemi was all tight smiles today.

The jets simulated a couple bombing runs, complete with pyrotechnics, which had the crowd cheering. Then a plane flew overhead and dropped out a team of paratroopers.

"Someday I'll tell you about the time my chute didn't open," Colt whispered into her ear.

She looked at him. "No. No you won't."

He grinned. "I lived. I had a buddy who—"

"Nope." She held up her hand. "I'm starting to agree with Pete. The less I know about the danger—past, present, or future—the better."

"I wanna hear it," Ranger said. "My favorite are night jumps. All that darkness, a thousand tiny lights below. The quiet, despite the roar in your ears. It's truly flying."

"Yeah, those are fun." Colt held out a fist.

Ranger met it. "We did a mission where we jumped out over the Gulf of Aden, near Yemen. Hit the water, deployed a Zodiac, motored close to shore, deflated the Z, swam the rest of the way with tanks, got out"—he took a breath—"infiltrated, took out our target, swam back out, reinflated the Zodiac, and hooked up with a submarine all in one night."

"Just the one mission?" Colt asked.

"Nope." Ranger grinned.

"You guys are crazy," Tae said.

And they even looked alike as they shot each other wild grins.

"No. They're brothers," Noemi said. "Couldn't keep them out of trouble if we wanted to."

Funny, she looked at Ranger with almost a hint of accusation.

"Please keep your wild stories to yourself," Tae said to Colt. "You're freaking me out."

"Really."

"Yes. I'm just going to . . . trust that God loves you as much as I do."

He stilled next to her.

Whoops. She'd done it again.

She glanced at him. He'd gotten very quiet, looking up at the parachutists.

Aw. Why did she always have to take control of everything?

Because yes, while he might have said that they belonged together, it didn't mean he was going to use the L-word.

Nice, Tae.

She stood up. "I . . . I'm going to use the restroom."

"You need me to go with you?" Colt got up to let her out.

"I think I've got this, but thanks, champ."

Really, she just needed to splash some water on her face, tell herself to calm down.

See, this was exactly how she ended up on a plane with a Russian gangster. Put her heart out there too fast without thinking it through.

She walked past a hamburger stand, a concession stand with merch, and a giant A-10 Thunderbolt with teeth painted around the gun on the front, parked in front of a small hangar.

Just let it go. Let it go . . .

She was passing by a truck with a logo of a drone, the words AERIAL MEDIA written on the side, when she spotted him. Lean, strong gait, dark hair, the set of his jaw . . .

Her steps stumbled, as she watched him pass her.

No, that *couldn't* be—

She was simply seeing things, the thought of her epic mistakes with Sergei conjuring up facsimiles of the man. Besides, this guy wore a uniform from the drone company. And he walked right by her without even looking up.

So not arrogant Sergei in the least.

Talk about jumpy.

Tae entered the bathroom—mostly empty—and as she washed her hands, she stared at herself in the mirror. She *didn't* love Colt. How could she? Love meant commitment and long-term plans and . . .

And Colt was anything but commitment and long-term plans. But his promise kept running around her head. *"I'll come back."*

Then again, he'd also promised not to do anything impulsive. Or reckless. Like hijacking a van filled with a hemorrhagic virus. But . . . he *had* come back.

And had certainly fought to live.

Aw . . . of course she loved Colt. Loved the way he just knew that, yes, she'd jump off the edge of her houseboat with him. Or climb up the side of a glacier, or even keep him alive with a vaccine she'd conjured up.

He believed in her. In them, given his words in the hospital.

She met her gaze in the mirror. *Let it go, Tae. Let God finish the story.*

Outside, the crowd roared, so something exciting was happening. The sun had sunk into the horizon.

Tae walked out of the bathroom, heading back toward the stands. Overhead, red smoke drifted down, dragged out of the tail of jumpers, creating ribbons in the sky. She stopped, cupped her hand over her eyes to shade them, watching.

She simply wouldn't think about Colt—

A burly hand clamped over her mouth.

What?

She got her hands up but was yanked against a body that viced an arm around her neck. A man.

And then she was dragged behind the toothy Thunderbolt.

She kicked back, but the arm around her neck was squeezing off her breath. Her air cut out, black dotting her vision.

How could no one see her? She wanted to scream, but the grip muffled her voice.

No!

She clawed at the hand, fighting, peeled off a finger—two—but couldn't get air past the hand. Managed to inhale through her nose but by this time, the man had dragged her back, toward the hangar. She shot out an elbow, but it only skimmed his ribs.

"Perestan!"

She froze, even as he jerked her right arm and

wrenched it up behind her back. She knew that voice.

No.

Then he kicked open the door and pulled her into the shadowed, hot-as-a-sauna hangar.

"No!" She spun right and found herself face-to-face with the man she'd left in the plane.

Sergei?

How—

He gripped her throat and shoved her up against the wall. Her grip clamped on his wrist, fighting to pry his hold free, even as he moved close, the stink of sweat and unwashed breath casting over her. Then, quietly against the roar of her heartbeat, "You didn't think I died, did you?"

She spit on him.

He roared, and she was right back in the plane, the moment he'd tried to strangle her, as the pilot fought to keep the plane aloft over the pull of the open door.

"This time you will," she gasped.

And then he laughed, something sharp and piercing, and shook his head. "You think you're brave? You're nothing."

He grabbed her by her hair and half dragged, half led her into the rear of the hangar. Threw her against the wall, and even as she fought him, he grabbed her hands and zip-tied them.

"Now," he said as he stepped away, breathing a little hard. "The fun begins."

• • •

Noemi didn't know what was worse—sitting here listening to Ranger talk about the epic life he'd lived, knowing that he'd never have it again. Or knowing that he *could* have it and had walked away, because of her.

Overhead, the parachutists tied knots in the sky with red ribbon, doing acrobatics as they joined hands or rolled away from each other.

It looked like flying, and a glance at Ranger said he was reliving every glorious moment, a smile on his face that could just about do her in.

She'd meant her comment to Tae about not being able to keep the boys out of trouble. Because over the past few weeks, the truth had drilled home . . .

Ranger would never be happy hanging around the ranch, fielding phone calls, tending the kitchen, and just . . .

Well, fading into the shadows.

Sure, he was a team player—it was the hallmark of the SEAL teams. But he was his best at the front of the action, as part of the solution.

Ham had offered him that. Noemi had heard the conversation on her way back to the picnic table, had even slipped into the shadows to hear the whole thing.

Her heart just about shattered when Ranger had given his answer. *"I'd love to join Jones, Inc. But then what? I love her, and Noemi deserves more than me part time. She deserves better.*"

What was wrong with her that his answer only made her angry? She'd tried to push it away, to be grateful, to embrace his sacrifice . . .

It only dug a hole inside her.

"You want something else to eat?" Ranger said. He'd finished off the popcorn earlier and their soda was empty.

She wasn't in the least hungry. In fact, the sight of food almost made her ill. But she couldn't sit here a moment longer, her entire body buzzing with frustration, so—

"Sure. I'll get us a couple of hot dogs."

She got up and headed out of the row, past Dodge who also got up to let her by. He held out a fiver.

"Can you get me one too?"

She took the bill. "The works?"

"Yep, plus relish."

Gross. "Sure."

She worked her way out and went down the stairs.

She'd just gotten way too used to having Ranger around. Sheesh, she'd lived for years as a SEAL's daughter. And then on her own. It wasn't like her life would change terribly if he joined Jones, Inc. So what was her problem?

She headed toward the hot dog stand.

A hand grabbed her arm, and she turned, stiffening.

"I was calling your name. Didn't you hear me?" Ranger had caught up to her.

"Sorry." She folded the fiver, put it in her pocket. In the stands, the crowd cheered as the divers hit the tarmac. Around them, the smells of the air show—fried foods and gas from the planes—mixed with the heat and soured the air. "I just need a drink."

"Are you sure that's all?" he said and stepped into a line. "You've been . . . quiet. For the last day or so, and . . . is there anything wrong?"

Everything. Nothing. Oh— She tightened her jaw as she stood by him, this amazing man who had saved her life, twice, who had broken her heart so many years ago, only to piece it back together. He wore a pair of cargo shorts, flip-flops, and a short-sleeve shirt, his sunglasses propped behind his head, a picture of a guy comfortable in his own skin.

The events of the past week—or more likely, Ham and the team—had done that for him.

Ham's voice dug around inside her as the line moved. *"And you think you'll be your better self hanging around Sky King Ranch, making soup?"*

No, no he wouldn't. She knew it in her soul.

"But I also know who I am."

"I guess I'm still trying to figure that out."

No, he wasn't. Her husband knew *exactly* who he was.

He just didn't want to admit it—or rather, didn't want to admit it to *her*.

And that—*that* was what made her angry.

"Are you sure you're okay? Because I can practically feel the heat burning off you," he said, glancing down at her.

She stared at him.

He raised an eyebrow.

"Okay, fine, you want to know?"

He stilled. "Now I'm not sure."

"Too late." She hooked his elbow and pulled him out of line, past the concessions area, into a shadowy space between the bleachers and the food stands.

She rounded on him but kept her voice low. "You're just like my father."

"How?"

"In all the ways, hello." She shook her head. "I don't know what is worse, my father pretending to die to keep me safe or you living your worst life because you don't want me to worry."

He just stared at her, frowning.

"I know you're falling on your sword, Range."

"I— What?"

"Really?" She put her hands on her hips. "I heard Ham. I know he offered you a job."

"Noemi—"

"Stop. I am not going to be the bad guy again."

"You're not the bad guy."

"I will be if you spend the rest of your life hating it. I thought my worst nightmare was losing you again. But I think my worst nightmare is losing *you*." She patted his chest. "The guy you were made to be."

He caught her hand on his heart. "What are you saying?"

She sighed. "Listen. I spent my entire life watching my dad vanish—"

"And I don't want to do that to you again."

"So don't. Keep me in the loop. Don't vanish."

He stared at her. "I don't—"

"And don't do anything stupid."

His mouth closed. "I don't do stupid things. Especially out in the field. I'm not Colt."

"No. But you are . . . you are in a more challenging position than you were."

He drew in a breath.

"You might not have noticed, Range, but you're a Kingston. You are just as stubborn as your brothers."

His lips pursed and he looked away.

"You don't want to admit when you're in over your head. When you've gone too far and you've found yourself in trouble. I'm afraid that you're going to get people killed. Yourself killed."

He looked at her, his blue eyes fixed in hers.

She matched his hard gaze with her own. Finally, "I'm angry that you didn't give me the choice to say yes. To be as brave and willing as you to do the hard things. Do you not know me at all? You're not the only warrior here."

His mouth slowly hitched up. "I know that, princess."

Her eyes narrowed. "Then promise me that you'll stay wide-eyed and won't let your ego make promises that your eyesight, and body, can't keep."

He took a step closer. "My body can keep a lot of promises."

She put her hands on his chest. "I know it can. But you're still not invincible. And"—she drew in a breath—"I can handle letting you go if I know you're not out there trying to prove something." She lifted her face to his. "Because you don't have to do that, not anymore."

He nodded, slowly.

"Being an operator and being my husband aren't mutually exclusive. And I get that now. And I want you to get it also." She wound her arms around his neck. "You're going to join Jones, Inc. Because once a SEAL, always a SEAL, right?"

He smiled. "Mm-hmm." Then he kissed her. And in it she tasted all his promises, all his I dos and all the happy reunions ahead.

Because he was also stubborn enough to keep his word.

• • •

So Tae said she loved him.

So *what?*

So . . . Colt swallowed, watching the final load of sky bums as they spun out of the sky, their red ribbons of smoke intersecting as they fell.

"I'm just going to . . . trust that God loves you as much as I do."

He'd just been knocked off guard is all. So much to take apart.

Trust. God. Loving him. Her, loving him.

Yep, a lot.

The problem was, maybe he didn't know what love looked like. Felt like.

But maybe that was okay. First in the door meant he wasn't afraid to see what waited on the other side.

In fact, the thought of it didn't even freak him out. Not anymore.

All day, as they'd walked around the grounds, the air thick with the smell of popcorn and cheese curds and hamburgers, and as kids marveled at the planes—not unlike Dodge, really—the normalcy of it all had lodged inside Colt.

This could be his life. His tame, not-out-of-control, no-trouble life. He hadn't given much thought to the idea of actually walking away from Jones, Inc. because, sorry, Dodge wasn't right.

He wasn't done operating.

396

But maybe . . . maybe it looked a little different. *"What if you started doing things God's way? You might be surprised at what he has waiting for you."*

For sure he needed a time-out. A chance for his body to heal. Mostly, he was tired of doing things Colt's way. Tired of never getting it right.

Tired of acting like his heart, his life didn't matter.

Tired of being a mercenary.

Not when he had someone to live for. He checked his watch.

Tae had been gone for twenty minutes. Weird. Maybe she was getting something to eat.

Still, it itched at him. He got up. "Watch my stuff," he said to Dodge, who nodded.

Then he slid out of the row.

He walked past the burger joint, and then a cotton candy stand—shoot, he'd forgotten—and a pretty cool A-10 Thunderbolt with fangs. He made it all the way to the door of the closest ladies' room without seeing Tae.

Huh.

A woman came out and he made himself stop her, ask if she'd seen a beautiful blond in a pair of shorts and an orange shirt in the bathroom.

Nope. Worse, it was empty.

Huh.

And that's when his chest began to hurt. Not a lot, just a *tharrump* that he knew had nothing to do with a sudden swelling, or even a heart attack, but . . .

Something wasn't right.

It was the same thump he'd felt the second before Vader kicked open that door.

Calm. Down.

She'd probably already returned to the stands, and he'd just missed her.

But just in case, he searched the area—a quick scan of the concession stands, the Lockheed C-5 Galaxy, and even the other set of stands, in case she'd gotten lost.

Nothing, and by the time he got back to his row—no Tae—his chest really burned.

"Tae's missing," he said to the group as he slid back into his seat and picked up his backpack.

"What do you mean, missing?" Noemi said.

"She's been gone for thirty minutes," he said. "Which is weird, right? For a bathroom run? And, according to someone I practically accosted, she's not in the bathroom."

"Did you go to the right bathroom?" Noemi said, getting up. "Because there are at least three here."

"I'll check too," Zoey said and followed her. "You take the one by the entrance. I'll go to the back."

Maybe he was overreacting. Just listening to the buzz of worry in his head.

He sat down and picked up his phone. Why hadn't they taken the time to buy her a phone?

They'd been so consumed with the vaccine, and then, of course, he'd been in the hospital—

Wait.

Her GPS ring. He pulled out his phone, then swept open the GPS app. Was she wearing the ring? He couldn't remember. Maybe, although she'd taken it off while she worked in the lab— he did recall her dropping it into a box before she stepped into the UV chamber.

The app loaded, and then, like the shiny nose of Rudolph on a dark night, the red button lit up.

"Never mind, guys," he said to his brothers. "I found her." He got up and pushed down the aisle, then down the steps.

Overhead, the night was closing in, and the show broke for intermission. The crowd surged out around him as he exited the stands.

He paused, watching her stats. Her heart rate had climbed, over a hundred now, was still rising. And rising along with that, her body temperature.

He threaded through the crowd, toward the beeping red dot. Past the burger stand, past the Thunderbird.

He stopped, trying to unravel the location.

The hangar? It could easily fit a couple small planes, wing to wing. A large steel door rolled down over the entrance.

He turned, headed toward the building, right up to a smaller security door beside the larger hangar door.

Locked.

He peered inside, his hand to the window.

Stilled. Along the floor of the hangar, a hundred tiny blue, red, and white lights were flashing on. Drones for the upcoming show.

He spotted a dim light at the back of the building, and just barely, made out two bodies—

One of them was Tae!

And she was *fighting* a man, kicking at him, her hands clearly tied in front of her.

What? His hand went to the handle, trying it again.

Colt's head just about exploded when the man slapped her. "Tae!"

She spun, hit the wall, and crumpled.

Now he would have his heart attack.

He stepped back, breathing hard.

Stop. Think. Don't just bash the door down. Because there were a lot of steps between the door and Tae, and who knew if her attacker had a weapon.

Still. Colt wasn't going to just stand out here and . . . wait.

He pulled out his phone. Ranger answered on the first ring.

"I found her," he said. "Some goon took her, just slapped the snot out of her. She's tied up in the hangar by the Thunderbird."

"Tied up? What— Never mind. We're on our way."

"Hurry." He hung up. The sky was darkening, the shadows thickening. He moved again to the door and peered back in the window.

Tae still lay on her side. The man who'd hit her sat at a bench, in front of a laptop, the light illuminating his face. He was clean-shaven and wore what looked like a uniform. Dark hair, dark eyes, lean face. . .

Wait. The man looked *Russian*.

The missing Petrov.

And then it clicked.

Drones. Aerosolized S-poxR.

And the forecast called for more rain.

Aw— Colt crouched near the entrance, thinking. No weapon, just his bare hands, but that was enough. She was all the way in the back of the hangar, and a glance inside said Tae *still* wasn't moving.

He stalked out to the Thunderbird, his pulse hammering.

Ranger and Dodge burst out of the darkness, breathing hard.

"What's going on?" Ranger said.

As if in answer, the large door to the hangar opened.

The men stepped back into the shadows of the plane.

Night had fallen, a blanket of heat and darkness, the lights in the stadium not enough to breach the outer areas. But enough for Colt to again make out the hundred or so drones the size of oversize shoeboxes that sat on the floor of the hangar like so many buzzing insects, ready to deploy, their lights blinking patriotic colors.

"What are those?" Dodge whispered.

"Drones," Colt said. "For the light show."

"I don't get it."

"It's the S-poxR," Ranger said, because clearly he'd figured it out. "The last canister. I'll bet those drones are armed with the virus."

"If they deploy the pox, it will infect everyone watching."

"Disney World." Dodge's gaze lifted to the park, some half mile away. "Even if the pox disperses, the rain could carry it over."

"And if not, what are the odds that at least some of these families are headed to any one of the Disney resorts in the area? They get infected and it's all over. You saw the contagion rate," Ranger said.

So much for the happiest place on earth.

"Pete was right," Ranger continued.

The lights in the hangar flicked on.

"What's Tae doing in there?" Dodge asked.

"I don't know. Maybe she figured it out," Colt said. "He hit her."

Ranger shot him a look. "Put it aside, Colt. Focus." He turned back to the building. "We need to get those overhead lights out and shut down this show."

"Agreed," Colt said. "They're fluorescent. One shot takes an entire fixture down."

"What, you going to pull out your slingshot, David?" Dodge gave him a look.

"Or we find an *electrical box* to the building." Ranger turned to Colt. "Is there another way in?"

"Maybe there's another door around the back?"

"Go," Ranger said to Dodge. "And if you see an electrical box—"

"On it." Dodge slipped away into the darkness.

Colt crept closer to the hangar, Ranger behind him.

"There have to be some security people here," Ranger said.

"That's a great idea," Colt said. "Maybe we can have a standoff with a couple of the peashooters they carry. If we're lucky, he'll only shoot Tae in the head."

"Did you *see* a gun?"

"I saw him *hit* her, he doesn't need a gun. Maybe just a shot in the head with a wrench."

Ranger put his hand on his shoulder. "Colt, you're in no condition—"

He shrugged him off. "Sorry, Range, I'm not made like you. I can't just sit on my hands."

"I hardly— Wait."

His word made Colt turn. Tae was up. On her feet. Her arms free.

403

Run! Colt nearly shouted it.

But instead of heading toward the door, she ran toward the back.

"What is she doing?" Ranger said.

On the hangar floor, the drones hummed to life, their propellers whirring.

The door started rolling down.

And then, just like that, the lights cut off.

No—*no!*

Ranger might have shouted, but Colt had nothing but instinct.

He dove and rolled inside the hangar just as the doors came down.

They barely missed him.

Night collapsed around him.

Pitch-dark, no NVGs, no weapon, and a hundred drones between himself and Tae.

I'm coming, honey.

Because yeah, he got it.

Love said *I got you*. Love said *whatever it takes*. Love said *you're worth it*.

And wow, did he love Tae.

He scrambled to his hands and knees, crawled along the floor, mapping out what he remembered.

"I will find you, Taylor."

Colt stilled as the voice echoed through the hangar, angry, sharp, and Russian.

Stay quiet, Tae.

A shot sounded. Tae screamed.

It reverberated through the hangar and echoed right into the chambers of Colt's heart.

And everything inside Colt simply stopped hurting.

Hang on, Tae. I'm coming.

FIFTEEN

Now what?

Tae wasn't sure just how she had ended up crouched in the darkness, huddled next to a workbench, becoming as small as she could, her hands over her ears as the world exploded around her.

No, wait, she knew exactly how . . .

Colt had been in her head just minutes ago when she had lain on the floor, tied up, helpless, panic causing her gorge to rise.

Focus.

Just because pain seemed to encase her entire face, her jaw out of whack, didn't mean she had to unravel.

"Just tune out everything else . . ."

Those words. Spoken to her as she'd hung over a cliff, staring at the impossible.

"Focus on the next step."

Colt's voice in her ear had jerked her back to herself as she lay, crumpled. Overwhelmed.

Terrified.

Helpless.

No, *not* helpless. Because she wasn't the same woman who'd been duped and fallen for a man who only wanted to hurt her. Only wanted to use her.

406

She knew what real love looked like, even if Colt couldn't say it. Commitment. Protection. Kindness. Helping her be the person she longed to be.

"Flo, you're one of the bravest people I know."

Hardly, but she knew that she refused to let Sergei win. Because it wasn't hard to do the math. She was pretty smart, and she knew exactly what was in those drones.

The air show was full of families and military and was the perfect place to release the smallpox. Most of the tourists would head to Disney World, and really, with an incubation and contagion period of twelve days, and a twelve-hour window of death once the symptoms started, it was every epidemiologist's nightmare.

Every terrorist's dream.

She refused to look too far ahead.

Focus.

Because if Tae didn't stop Sergei, no one could.

And that's when Noemi entered her head with her story about the zip ties. *"You pull out even as you force your hands down. It's not hard once you get the hang of it."*

Tae had kept her eyes closed, playing it out in her mind. Planning. No, not planning—stirring up her courage.

Sergei had stepped away from her, possibly believing that he'd knocked her out. A quick peek and she spotted him at a bench, with a computer.

Getting ready to deploy the drones, now lit up and humming.

Her gaze tracked to the door opener, near the back door.

He shifted, and she closed her eyes. Counted her heartbeats.

Now.

She exploded. Rolled to her feet, brought her hands down, hard, and apparently God was generous in handing out the miracles, because the ties snapped.

Around her, the drones started whirring.

No!

She took off for the door opener.

Sergei looked up, but she was focused. Fast. She hit the wall and slammed her hand on the door opener.

The door began to close.

"Stop!" Sergei's voice, behind her. She put up her hands to protect her face just as his fist came at her.

The lights blinked out.

The doors collapsed.

Darkness, but not so dark that Sergei's fist didn't find home. Pain exploded in her ear.

She grunted and fell.

But on her knees, despite the world spinning, she moved. Her reflexes saved her from a kick that glanced off her and mostly hit the wall.

She scooted away, clamping down on her

scream, her breaths. Past him, along the wall, she kept her head down.

The drones had spun to life, gone airborne, the room alive with the buzz of flying spiders.

"I will find you, Taylor."

The gunshot stopped her. It pinged against the wall, hitting one of the workbenches, echoing through the building.

She screamed.

Keep moving!

She crawled to a workbench, found a pocket, and wedged herself in, drawing up her knees.

Now, she held her breath. Only Sergei's computer hummed, light splashing out into the swarthy darkness.

"You can't hide from me, Taylor. You should know that by now."

In the blinking light, she spotted him trying to get the door open, but some genius had cut off the electricity. *Yes!* She hoped she knew who that genius might be.

Please, Colt, be looking for me. But maybe she shouldn't wish it. After all . . .

Aw, forget it. With everything inside her she longed for Colt to be the guy to break down the door and find her. To yes, rush right into trouble to sweep her up and save her and—and maybe that's exactly why the world needed guys like Colt. For moments when there was no choice. When the worst had to be done.

When trouble was the only answer.

But even trouble needed someone to love him. To stand her ground and believe in him, and pray for him, and be there when he came home.

So yes, she got it. *Please, God, if you're listening . . . send Colt.*

And maybe it was selfish, but she sorta thought that maybe that was exactly the prayer Colt might want her to pray.

Around her, the drones crashed into the walls, each other, screeching, rebounding. An airborne minefield. Releasing the S-poxR virus as they fell to the cement.

The place was a toxic war zone.

Sergei had returned to his computer, was maybe trying to shut down the drones, but one flew by and clipped him, and he too dropped to the floor.

Vanishing into the darkness.

She had to get out of here.

Focus.

"Bravery isn't the absence of fear. It's doing what you must do, despite the fear."

She closed her eyes to Colt's voice. Solid. Unwavering, and tried to clamp down on her trembling.

And just like that, she was ten years old. Standing at the door as her father crouched in front of her, dressed in his uniform, as she sobbed. And as if it were yesterday, she felt his hands on her shoulders, heard his low, solid voice.

"God is with me, Tae. And with you. And nothing can separate us from his love. Not evil. Not war. Not sickness. Not even death. I'm in good hands. And so are you, Tae-bear."

Oh, not now. But the words welled up inside her, pushed out tears.

Fine. She opened her eyes to a hundred tiny lights flashing through the hangar. Flickering upon the floor, the walls.

The far door.

Okay, so if Colt wasn't going to show up, she'd try something else. *Please, God, rescue me.*

She shot a glance toward the computer's glowing hue.

Reaching up on the bench, her hand closed around a tool. A screwdriver. She tucked it close.

That could work.

As if she'd use it, but she *had* kicked out the door of her airplane, so maybe.

She edged out and ducked as a drone buzzed just over her head. It hit the wall above her and shattered, the blades still spinning as they crashed over her, plastic and metal raining down.

She bit down on a scream, and hunched over, scuttling away, along the edge of the room. Caught herself again before she cried out when another drone zipped close, hovering just over her head.

"You're mine, *dorogaya*," Sergei said, his voice singsong, something deeply sinister as it mixed with the buzz of the drones. "I know you miss me."

He didn't sound close, but his words sent fire through her, ignited her entire body.

Move!

She hunkered down, combat style, and shimmied along the floor, through the darkness, away from the flickering lights.

Around her, more drones collided, exploded. She put a hand over her head, the other gripped the screwdriver. Kept her breath tight.

The lights were blinking out, one drone after another propelled into the wall, the ceiling, another drone. *Just stay along the perimeter and—*

A hand reached out and grabbed her jacket.

No! She rolled onto her back and with everything inside her, stabbed at her attacker with the screwdriver. He slapped her wrist away, then grabbed it, holding. "Stop!"

The voice seized her. She froze. Made out his face in the erratic light.

Colt!

He pulled her up, into his arms.

Oh. *Oh*—she couldn't breathe, her heart too fast, her face dug into his neck. He smelled of the night, of safety and protection and everything she needed him to be. *Thank you, God!* His arms tightened around her, as if trying to hold her in place against his heart.

"How are you here?" She tried to keep her voice low into his neck, his ear.

He pushed her away, his forehead to hers. "Are you okay? I saw him hit you." He made a little sound at the end of that, a growl that lit something inside her.

"I'm okay. But the drones have deployed, Colt. The S-poxR."

"We'll keep it contained. I think Dodge took out the lights, which means he also took out the electrical to the building. The door isn't going to open."

Dodge. Of course, the Kingston brothers to the rescue.

"You shouldn't have come in here."

"Seriously?" He pulled her tight against him, his voice now against her ear. "Where you are, I am. Haven't you figured that out yet?"

She closed her eyes, hung on, her hands clutching his shirt. Oh, she wanted to stay here. Right here. Secure in his embrace.

"You need to get out of here," he said.

No.

He held her away, his brown eyes hard in hers. "Go for the door. Ranger is outside."

"Not without you."

"Yes. Without me. I need to shut this guy down."

"It's Sergei."

A beat, then, "What?"

"Sergei, the guy who—"

"Yeah. I know who you're talking about." His jaw tightened. "Get out of here, Tae. Now."

As if in emphasis, shots pinged near them, over them.

In a second, Colt had her on the floor, his body over hers. Oh, this couldn't be good for his heart. Or hers.

Especially when he leaned in and kissed her cheek, his lips near her ear. "I love you, Tae."

Then he rolled away and melded into the darkness.

Colt!

She felt naked on the floor without him, all the heat of his body vanished.

No. *Please.*

The lights had diminished by half, but still the drones buzzed, whirring through the air, bouncing off the walls. Hitting the windows, cracking them.

Tiny bombs of toxin and danger as they exploded.

Run. The word pulsed inside her.

No.

She was done with running. Running, hiding, cowering . . . *done.*

Through the blink of the patriotic lights, she spotted Colt moving across the floor. Or maybe it was Sergei . . .

But what was she going to do—jump in and save Colt?

She'd seen him fight.

Swollen heart or not, she had no doubt that Sergei wasn't walking out of here a free man.

She sat up.

What if the drones got free? They could break a window, escape into the night.

She had to shut them down. And not just because of the pox but because of the light they emitted. One lucky shot, illuminated by the drones and—

Nope.

Colt wasn't the only brave one here.

Wasn't the only one who was ready to do violence to keep people safe.

She hit her knees, kept her head down, turned, and headed back the way she came.

For a second, after Colt left, Ranger simply stood there, feeling punched.

Because, just like at the compound raid, he couldn't help but think one of these days Colt was going to end up in a body bag.

But not today.

Ranger could feel the vibrations from inside the hangar, hear the whir of the propellers, the hum of the motors. The banging as the drones slammed against the walls.

Colt, you idiot!

He should have lunged at him, grabbed him back, but his brother was too big, too fast—too *Colt*—to be stopped.

And now, if their theory was right, his brother was in there, with his fragile heart, getting infected all over again.

Then again, maybe he was the only person who *should* be in there, with all that toxic biohazard. A guy whose body would repel it.

Still. Colt was in there. With at least one bioterrorist, maybe more.

Ranger stood outside the building, trying to take it all apart.

Breathe. Settle down. Focus. Words he would have told himself while sitting in a sniper nest, seeing things go south.

Now, think. He turned to take in the situation. Crowds milled outside the hangar to the front, waiting for the drone light show. Local security—a handful of guys, mostly retired cops, or even ex-military soldiers who weren't in the least prepared to be infected—milled around, looking for kids smoking cigarettes, the occasional pickpocket.

Colt was right. The last thing they needed was a hostage situation. Or a shootout.

And until Tae's vaccine went through trials . . .

Colt's heart issue might have been a factor in the negative outcome, but they couldn't be completely sure.

Which left him and Dodge against who knew how many inside.

First, they needed eyes on the place. Ranger

416

approached the door and looked inside. Dark, so the likelihood that a shooter might spot him was low. Still, he only took a quick look.

Inside, blue, red, and white lights flickered on and off as the drones bounced off each other, crashed against walls, or tangled together.

Like creepy flying spiders.

He leaned back, closing his eyes, imprinting the layout into his head.

Then he leaned in again and focused on the floor. Despite the shadows in his vision, he spied a couple of bodies—made out Colt's form—bulky, moving deliberately against the far wall. Another form on his tail.

Tae?

Ranger tried the door handle, but it was still locked.

Again, he veered away, closed his eyes. Locked the layout of the room into his brain.

A final look, and this time he spotted movement against the back wall. A shadow. Hopefully not Dodge.

A shot sounded, and a muzzle flared against the veil of darkness.

Gotcha.

He closed his eyes and jerked back, hating the flare that now burned in his vision. But he had the room. And behind the guy, had spotted a door.

Their entry.

Ranger rounded the hangar, about to sprint for the back, and nearly plowed down Dodge.

His brother caught him, moved him away, and they spun in the grass.

"What—"

"I took out the electrical panel," Dodge said, breathing hard. "But I couldn't get in. Door's locked."

Ranger blinked at him. "Have you never breached a door?"

Dodge frowned at him. "Um, *pilot*. If you want, I can hijack a plane and we can drive it into the hangar. But I'm not a SEAL. I don't breach things or blow things up or—"

"Fine. Whatever." Ranger roughed a hand over his mouth. "As far as I can tell, there's only one shooter, but there may be more. Tae is still in there, and so is Colt, and there's about a hundred or more drones flying around like bees. My guess is that they're deploying toxins as they crash into the walls. Or maybe even as they're flying—who knows. Bottom line, it's lethal in there but we still need to get in and shut this down."

"With what?" Dodge asked. "A tank? A bulldozer?"

"That would release the virus." He scratched his head. "A lockpick would work."

"You can pick a lock?" Dodge asked.

"Um, SEAL. We don't just kick in doors. But

I left my kit at home, so . . . what do you know about the door? Inward, outward?"

"Inward."

Could be a kick, or two. But if it was a steel door, he'd need something with more heft. And once inside . . . "We need masks. And yes, a weapon would be stellar, but not necessary."

"I'd like to not go in there blind and barehanded."

Ranger looked at him. "Sometimes this is all we get, bro. We go in blind. Use our instinct. Trust each other. God."

"I know. Don't get me wrong, I'm in. I just need a second to dial in here."

"Let's find something to breach with, something heavy—"

"What are you breaching, sailor?"

He stilled and Noemi practically materialized in front of him, only her yellow shirt a beacon, along with her beautiful smile.

He didn't know why, but he pulled her against him, hard. A one-armed hug. Kissed the top of her head. "You're safe."

"Of course I'm safe. What's— Wait. Did you find Tae?" She pushed away from him. "I had a weird hunch when I didn't find you back in the stands, so I grabbed a security guard."

Oh no.

But the man who stepped up behind her out of the dark could have been Noemi's very well-built big brother. Pete Sutton shoulders, solid, and a set to his chin that seemed like he wasn't afraid to do some damage.

"Abe Marshall," the man said and held out his hand.

Ranger shook his meaty grip. "We need something to breach the door of the hangar."

"Why?"

"We need to get inside."

He cocked his head.

"Listen," Ranger said, "our friend—a woman— went missing, and we know a guy took her in there."

Dodge looked at him, and Ranger sent him back an *ix-nay on the errorist-tay*.

Abe gave him a look. "How about keys?"

"You have keys to the hangar?" Dodge asked.

"I do," he said in a low baritone. "I can open the door for you."

"No." Ranger pressed a hand to the big man's chest.

Abe looked at the hand, and Ranger removed it.

"Okay, it's not just a domestic scuffle . . . there's reason to believe—"

"The guy has a bioweapon, and we think he's going to deploy it here," Dodge said.

Ranger turned to him. "Really?"

"Yes." Dodge faced Abe. "Our brother is in there, as well as some drones that we think are armed with a deadly virus. And if they get out into the open—"

Abe held out the keys. Dodge took them.

"Can I borrow your weapon?" Ranger asked. Not exactly a peashooter. The man wore a blocky 9mm Ruger P on his hip.

"Are you kidding me?"

Ranger got it. "Listen. I know this sounds flimsy, but I promise we're the good guys. And if we don't stop this—"

"Let me make a call—"

"We don't have time!" Dodge said.

Wow. Ranger glanced at him, brow up.

"Listen. I'm former Air Force. Ranger is a former SEAL. And the guy in there, our brother, he's Delta Force. We've been tracking this virus for a while. It's lethal, and if we don't stop whatever is going down, it's going to get worse. Much worse. You're going to have to trust us."

Abe considered them for a moment. Then, "Fine. But I'm calling for backup."

"Good. But keep them back." Dodge headed for the door.

Abe pressed the gun into Ranger's hand, then stepped back, pulling out his flashlight. This he also handed to Ranger.

"Thanks," Ranger said. "Stay clear of the building." He turned to follow Dodge.

Noemi grabbed Ranger's arm.

He rounded back to her. "Babe, I—"

"I know you have to go. I just wanted to say I love you."

He grabbed her around the back of the neck and kissed her. Quick. Solid. Forever. "You're my girl."

She met his eyes, hers so dark and beautiful. "Yeah, I am. So come back to me."

"Has it occurred to you that maybe God has especially designed her to be in this with you?"

Yeah, she was.

"Good copy." He took off for the building.

Dodge was already by the door, trying the keys. "You open it, let me go in."

"*We* go in."

"No. Only me." He met Dodge's eyes. "Because you're a pilot."

Dodge stood up. "No. I was on the mission with you in Nigeria. I can shoot."

"We have one gun, bro. And I'm used to shooting in the darkness. You close this door behind me and don't open it again until I come out."

Dodge didn't move. "No. We have one gun. And I'm the one who can see."

The words hit Ranger like a punch.

"You miss, you shoot Colt. Or Tae or . . . I don't know."

Ranger drew in a breath. He'd hit his target just fine at the compound.

"You are just as stubborn as your brothers. You don't want to admit when you're in over

your head. When you've gone too far, and you've found yourself in trouble."

He slapped the gun into Dodge's hand. "Listen up. You go in the door, there's a workbench to your right and a wall to the left. The shooter is against the wall. And probably Colt by now, so look alive. The drones are popping lights in and out, so keep your eyes down so you don't get flashes across your vision. And don't hesitate. You see the guy, you shoot the guy. I'm right behind you."

Dodge took the gun, turned off the safety.

"In the words of the immortal Benjamin Martin, aim small, miss small."

"Aw, those were Dad's words." Dodge put his back against the wall.

"Still good. Listen, you better live through this."

"It's Colt you have to worry about." He bumped his fist, then reached for the door handle, his hand on the key.

Ranger met Dodge's eyes.

Dodge nodded.

Ranger opened the door, and Dodge swung into the lethal, swarming darkness.

Run, Tae.

Please.

Colt hunkered down, his eyes on the drone lights, searching the hangar for Sergei.

Shoot at me again, jerk. Because then he might track the sound, get a fix on the man.

Maybe even see the muzzle flash, and *bingo*.

He was going down. And not just for what he'd done to Tae, but to him, and generally the rest of the world.

For all humankind, Colt would take down Sergei Petrov.

But *especially* for Tae.

Colt's entire body buzzed, the adrenaline hot inside him, his pulse in his ears. He took a breath. Another.

Focus.

The lights flashed, on and off, the computer still running the drone show program, a shower of red, blue, and white erratic lights. Colt had found cover behind a couple of huge tires, and now settled his gaze along the wall, searching for a shadow. An outline of gray.

Or maybe a face.

Movement caught his eye, and he jerked his attention toward it.

There—near a workbench, just outside the glow of the computer, a man. In a blink, Colt memorized him. Lean build, dark hair, wearing a black collared shirt, an emblem on the breast.

Who had he killed to get the uniform?

The question burned inside Colt, lit, and for a second, he saw Tae being slapped.

His entire body turned into an inferno.

He wanted his hands around the man's throat.

Wanted his fists in his face. Wanted him on the floor so he could—

And just like that, he was back in the cell with Ahmed. Crouching in front of him, his hand around his neck. Pressing Ahmed to the wall.

"You knew it was an ambush!"

Maybe it wouldn't have gone so south if Ahmed hadn't spit on him, the moisture joining with the blood that streaked Colt's clothing, his hands, his face.

"You deserved it!"

He'd hit him for the first time then.

Ahmed was tough—had the sass of a boy soldier, someone armed too young in his life. He'd fought back.

It only made Colt angrier.

He'd come back to himself about the time the kid wrestled his hands over his face and started screaming.

The guards rushed in. Colt's fists burned with open cuts, bruises.

The boy was still screaming, swearing, kicking, spitting, and a couple guards pushed Colt away, one in his face, yelling.

Colt pushed him off, charged back in. *"Tell me where White is!"*

And when another guard tried to intervene, Colt leveled him too.

It worked. He'd cracked the kid, and he blubbered out a location—not far from the one they'd attacked.

"Scum like you shouldn't be allowed to live."

The words still resounded through Colt, even after he'd rescued Nelson and Rags, the bodies of Elvis and Nuggsy. Even after Ace hauled him into HQ after the op and told him that Ahmed had died of a heart attack, a rare condition possibly exacerbated by Colt's actions. All the way until they told him the kid had only been seventeen.

Colt had gotten up, walked out of HQ, and lost it.

And then went back in and asked to be released from duty.

Now, as Colt stared at Sergei, who also searched the darkness for the woman Colt loved, he heard the words again . . . *"Scum like you shouldn't be allowed to live."* And again, tasted the fury, the desperate hunger for justice.

The urge to hurt the people who had hurt those he loved.

It all boiled up inside him. But this time, it wasn't a kid but a man who had terrorized the woman he loved.

Colt waited until the drones moved away from him, then ran along the edge of the building, scooting in behind a rolling toolbox. Closer.

Sergei had gotten to his feet, was crouching. Smiled. *"Gdye toodah?"*

Where are you? See, he could figure out Russian.

Sergei's shot pinged off the ceiling, rebounded into the room.

Gotcha—

And then Tae screamed.

What was she still doing in the building?

This needed to be over.

Colt launched himself at Sergei—ten steps, but by the time the man saw him, he was close enough to kick the gun from his hand.

The crash to the cement floor cost him, jerked out his breath, just for a second. Then, Sergei landed on him and sent a punch into his chest that nearly swept the wind out of him again.

But Colt wasn't done that easily. He rolled and swept up his leg. Sergei slammed into the concrete. Colt followed with an elbow to the man's chest.

Then he lurched up and landed a fist, right in the sternum.

Sergei sucked wind like a fish, and Colt scrambled to his feet.

But he was slow—slower than normal—and by the time he turned, Sergei had found his knees and was lunging for the gun.

Colt leaped toward the weapon, but Sergei grabbed his foot and tripped him.

He crashed onto the floor, pain spiking up his knee. Then Sergei landed a kick to his ribs.

Oh—

Something broke inside of Colt. Wounds opened, his heart slammed against his ribs.

Everything hurt.

He lay, breathing hard, pain shredding him. *"Scum like you shouldn't be allowed to live."*

The memory razed through him, and with a shudder he realized . . .

Maybe, all these years, he'd been talking about *himself.*

"Until you forgive yourself . . ."

Sergei scrambled for the gun, and Colt flipped over, groaning, breathing through burning ribs, and grabbed his leg. Tripped him. Then he yanked the man back.

"Oh no you don't—"

He swung his fist into Sergei's face.

The man swore, blood exploding from his nose.

Colt fought to his knees and leaped again for the gun.

Sergei landed on top of him. They crashed into the cement. Colt let out a howl and didn't care. But his fingers latched around the barrel.

Sergei grabbed the handle, his finger reaching for the trigger.

An elbow bashing into Sergei's face had him sliding off, wrenching the gun around.

Colt deflected the barrel as a round went off near his ear. It rang, the flash blinding.

Sergei hit him, a fist in his jaw, and heat

exploded through him. But Colt pried the gun away and it went spinning across the floor.

And then it was just Colt and Sergei.

He didn't care how tough the guy was, Colt was tougher.

Colt rounded with a fist that knocked the man off him, then rolled and landed on him. Dodged the hit to his face and landed another blow.

Sergei got an arm up, his hand around Colt's neck, but Colt tore it away and pounded his fist into his side. Bones crunched.

Colt didn't know where it came from, but suddenly heat scraped up the side of his body. He gasped, the pain shearing through him, his entire body lighting on fire.

Sergei lifted a shard of plastic, blood dripping from it.

One of the destroyed drone pieces.

"Time to die—" Sergei ended with a word Colt barely heard because Sergei kneed him in his open wound.

The pain could split him.

He fell off the man with a deep grunt, gritting his teeth. Gasping.

Get up— *Get—*

Sergei rose. Walked past him, swept up the gun. Dropped the plastic shard. Pointed the gun at Colt. "Everybody has a right to be stupid, but some people abuse the privilege. You will die. And she will belong to me."

Colt kicked out. It grazed Sergei's knee.

He stumbled back, then righted himself. Laughed. "C'mon, you can do better than that."

"C'mon, Colt. You can do better than that."

He stilled, another memory raking through him.

His mother's voice. Her face, smiling down, as she tickled him, wrestling with him. He squealed, squirming. Laughing.

"C'mon, you scamp."

She wasn't trying hard, he knew that, but still he wrestled himself away from her. Bounced back, laughing.

And she sat on the floor, too, grinning at him. *"There you go. My tough little Colt. See, you're stronger than you think. Now, it's your turn . . . I'll hide, and you find me."*

His vision cleared, the pain dropping away. *"Colt, you were so much like her. She was her own person. An artist. A fighter."*

Maybe he had found her, buried within himself.

"People sleep peaceably in their beds at night only because rough men stand ready to do violence on their behalf." Yeah, that. Because maybe he wasn't the villain, but the hero.

Somewhere above, a crash sounded. One of the drones, maybe, finding open space. But it made Sergei glance up.

That's all Colt needed. "Don't think so, Petrov."

He found his feet, and as the drones fell around him, propelled himself at Sergei.

A shot went off, resounding in his ears as his body collided with Sergei's.

Then they both hit the floor.

SIXTEEN

Sergei was going to kill Colt.

But Tae couldn't watch the fight. Ever since Colt had launched himself at Sergei, she had focused on one thing.

Get to the computer.

She'd scooted around the edge of the room, nearly on her stomach, going from workbench to tires to table to finally getting on her feet and ducking behind a toolbox.

Right about then, she'd heard Colt howl, and deep inside she knew—just *knew*—he was having a heart attack. Or bleeding out. Or maybe Sergei would just shoot him and—

Stop! She was what-iffing herself right into a panic attack. Writing the end of the story with a dire conclusion.

Focus. Get to the computer.

The sound of the grunts and gasps and smacks that could only mean crunching bones from the fight could crumple her, but she searched for the computer and spied it on the workbench where Sergei left it.

If she shut down the program, the drones would land, stop deploying the toxin, and then, at least, they could contain it before one broke through a window.

And leeched the virus out into the world.

Because that's why she was here. She couldn't fight men like Colt could, but she *could* fight the evil they created.

She tuned out another terrible growl of pain from Colt and scrabbled over to the computer. Opened it.

The program was still running, twelve minutes left.

The drones would escape long before then.

As if confirming her fears, another drone hit a window, cracking it. The drone bounced off, however, toward the ceiling, slamming hard and dropping.

It shattered onto the floor.

She reached up to grab the computer, pulled it down to her lap, but a drone swung down, near her head. She screamed, ducked, and the computer fell on the floor.

No! Scooping it up, she crawled with it under a table, the drones buzzing like wasps around her.

She opened the computer.

The screen had locked.

Of course it had locked. Because just when she thought—

"Saving the world is not your responsibility. That doesn't belong to any of us. Our job is just to do our part."

Okay, yes. *Think, Tae.* She bit back a sound of frustration and typed in Sergei's name.

Nothing.

Tried *her* name.

Nothing.

Think. She closed her eyes.

Tuned out the whir of the drones, the fighting, the sound of her pulse whooshing in her ears.

Focus.

She saw Sergei, on the cruise, working on his computer. She'd sat down beside him in his stateroom with a set of binoculars, on loan from the ship, to watch whales. He'd closed his computer to sit next to her, asked her about something—she couldn't remember. Maybe her family, friends.

She'd been *so* stupid. It was a miracle her mother hadn't been caught in the cross fire. As it were, Zoey's entire life had been upended.

Focus.

Sergei had kissed her, tried to pry her attention away from the whales. She'd let him, then pushed him away.

He'd been a little angry. Oh, how she should have paid attention.

Focus, Tae.

He'd gone back to his computer. Sat down at the table.

She'd felt guilty. Had gotten up to apologize. She remembered his fingers moving on his keyboard—no, his number pad—to unlock his screen.

A number. No, a date. Something that stuck in her head as odd.

"Time to die."

The curse word at the end tore her gaze from the computer, and she looked up just as Sergei kneed Colt in the body.

He fell away, rolling, grunting. Oh—he was really hurt—

Stop. Because what was she going to do? Tackle him?

"Show up, with the talents God has given us, and say yes to the mission he's given us."

Her heart stopped when Sergei reached down and picked up a gun. It glinted bloodred in the light. He pointed it at Colt.

"Everybody has a right to be stupid, but some people abuse the privilege. You will die. And she will belong to mc."

No. She never would—

The words moved in her head.

She *knew* that quote.

Stalin.

And the memory, the numbers, the *date* clicked into place. March 5, 1953. The death of Stalin.

She typed in the numbers—03051953.

Nothing.

Colt kicked Sergei in the knee and for a second, she thought he might go down. Instead, he stumbled, then laughed. "C'mon, you can do better than that."

C'mon, Colt. You're stronger than you think!
Focus.

But all she could think was *"The death of one man is tragic, but the death of thousands is a statistic."* Dr. Bella, about the sacrifice of their jobs.

Wait, in Russia, they did their dates backwards—or forwards, depending on the perspective. Day, month, year.

05031953. Please—

The screen unlocked.

A timer ran in the middle of the screen, counting down the minutes remaining. Ten minutes, thirteen seconds. She spotted a cancel option at the bottom of the box.

She looked up to see Sergei pointing a gun at Colt's head.

She bit back her scream, because . . . because the last thing he needed was her, falling apart.

Please, God!

A crash sounded above her, and she looked up to see open sky.

Cancel!

"Don't think so, Petrov." Colt's voice rang through the building.

She clicked the button, and just like that, all the drones dropped from the air.

And for a second, a breath of relief filled her lungs.

They did it!

A shot sounded, and she looked up to see Colt and Sergei land on the floor.

They lay still, neither of them moving.

She stared at the huddle of their bodies in the darkness, everything inside her frozen.

"Colt?"

He didn't move.

What— *No!*

She pushed the computer away. Not like this— "Colt!" She scrambled to her feet, scooped up the screwdriver, and ran toward Colt. But with the drones dying, the room was turning pitch-dark, so dark now she could barely see shadows.

"Colt!"

A hand caught her arm, and she whirled around.

A high beam hit her eyes and she blinked, then struck.

Her attacker dodged, then yanked the weapon right out of her hand. Grabbed the light from his mouth. "What are you doing?"

Ranger. She'd nearly taken out his eye. "Ranger?"

She didn't have time to unwrap it. Wrenching free, she turned to Colt, now illuminated in Ranger's light.

And advancing toward them, holding a handgun, was Dodge.

A pool of blood leeched out from under Sergei's and Colt's bodies.

"He's bleeding!"

Ranger caught her around the waist. "Hold up— Just stay back."

"What?" But she froze as Dodge pulled Colt off Sergei.

Blood soaked his shirt, and he moaned, then sat up.

In the glow of Ranger's light, Sergei lay dead, a shot through his head.

She looked away from the gore.

"Colt!" She ran over to him.

He was trying not to make any noise, but his hand pressed his chest, and deep rumbles emerged from inside his body.

"Um . . . so . . . you still alive, bro?" Dodge asked.

"Yep," Colt said, his voice tight. "But I think I'm headed back to the hospital."

"Are you having a heart attack?" She reached for his shirt, and he caught her wrist.

"No— Just—"

"Lay back." She practically pushed him to the floor, kicking away a dead drone, then lifted his shirt.

A wound on his side oozed blood. "You've been stabbed!"

"I'm fine," he said.

"You are not fine." She glanced at Sergei. Back at Colt.

He smiled, one half of his mouth tweaking up. "Had you worried."

What a jerk.

But oh, she loved this stupid, aggravating, stubborn—

She kissed him. Hard, because if he was going to pretend not to be hurt, she would too. Besides, what was she going to do? Not kiss him with everything inside her? Not pour out her hope and relief and love and reach for the end of their story?

After all, they did just save the world.

Colt eased her away. "Okay, okay, I give. I might be a little broken." But he touched her face with his hand. "I think I'm just going to lay here and let you guys figure out what happens next."

Tae got up and found a rag in a pile on a nearby bench as Colt worked himself to a sitting position.

Colt's gaze cast between Ranger and Dodge. "That your handiwork?" he said, nodding to Sergei and his mess.

"What are brothers for?" Dodge said. He smiled.

Colt met it with his own smile, and she almost felt the healing between them.

"I thought you were just a pilot."

"I can shoot. You're not the only one who joined the military."

"Yeah, but Ranger and I are actual—"

"Stop talking, before Dodge decides to shoot you too." Tae knelt next to him and pressed the rag to his wound. He grunted but reached up and held it in place as he grinned.

"Now what?" Tae said. "You're all infected."

"I guess we're your next test subjects," Dodge said. "Good thing I don't have a broken heart."

"Not broken. Just big. Big heart."

"Oh, for Pete's sake." Dodge shook his head, then looked at Tae. "What about you?"

"I was vaccinated long ago, in the first round."

"I thought you said it wasn't tested on humans."

"Aw, I sorta don't count myself."

"Wow. You and Colt belong together," Ranger said.

Colt gave her a grin. "Yep."

And she had nothing for that. Oh, he was trouble.

Delicious, perfect trouble.

"Okay, well, as long as Colt doesn't need to be life-flighted out of here, we'll figure out a way to detox this place and go home." Ranger pulled out his phone.

Colt looked at Tae. "Go home."

"I heard him."

He laced his fingers through hers. "Here's the deal. Remember, I live out of a duffel bag. And where you go, I go. So . . . home is wherever you want it to be. As long as we're together."

"Where do you think I'm going to go where you won't find me, anyway?" She leaned in. "You're a very hard man to escape."

"Finally, she gets it," he said winking at his brothers, and then he kissed her.

"Is it stupid for me to suggest a little rest?" Major Austin stepped back from where he had finished stitching Colt's latest wound. He'd already shared the X-ray results of his chest. Two bruised ribs, but nothing Colt couldn't handle.

As long as he kept things on the down low.

"Not stupid at all. I'm ready for some beach time. A little R & R, for as long as it takes."

Really. Truly. He meant it. In fact, he'd even told Ham that he was out, for the foreseeable future, during their conversation at the airfield last night, when Ham drove over to join Logan and Roy as they oversaw the retrieval of the drones and final S-poxR canister.

Unfortunately, that foreseeable future included Colt spending the night in the hospital, *again.* For observation.

He could have been observed just fine back at the mansion, hello. Next to a pool and in some sunshine.

But maybe Tae was right—after his second exposure to the S-poxR, some time in isolation while they all underwent testing probably wasn't a terrible idea.

So he'd spent a very long night in a plastic room, next to Tae, next to Dodge, and even Ranger.

Dodge and Ranger had received doses of Tae's experimental vaccine and so far, not a hint of any complications. And after what felt like Colt had opened a vein for Zoey to test his blood, not a hint of the disease was found in his system either.

Yay for white blood cells, and memory B cells, or whatever it was that kept his body in working order.

Or maybe he should be thanking God, because it seemed very much that he'd been given a second chance. A new heart, as it were.

One that suddenly felt very much alive. Hopeful.

Ready for a different future.

He just wasn't sure what that looked like.

He reached for his shirt as he slid off the table. Winced as he tried to pull it over his head.

But Tae was right there to help, still with the slightest hue of worry in her eyes.

Dodge and Ranger, along with Noemi, were waiting outside his room when he finally emerged.

"Ham texted. Said he wanted to talk to us," Ranger said.

Apparently Ranger was now on the payroll of Jones, Inc., news he'd dropped on Colt last night while his youngest brother paced his cell slash hospital pod.

Dodge had spent much of his quarantine time on the phone with Echo, assuring her that, no, he wasn't going to develop pustules and bleed from the eyes. He hoped.

Today he was grouchy and clearly itching to get back to Alaska. He led them out of the hospital.

Logan was waiting for them in the Escalade. He wore a suit, was clean-shaven and all business, as he met them on the curb.

He eyed their appearance, then shrugged and got in the driver's seat.

Whatever that meant.

Tae got in beside Colt in the back. "Zoey called. She's going to be staying on here in the Florida lab. I told her we'd probably be going back to Alaska."

He looked at her. "Sure."

Except she frowned and turned away. Huh?

He took her hand. "Babe, I meant what I said. We're in this together."

There was the smile he wanted. He kissed her, then leaned back against the seat.

But what was he going to do in Alaska? He wasn't a pilot. And the last thing Dodge needed was another bossy brother around.

Rest. Right. He took her hand and stared at the palm trees, the ocean as it combed the beach. He didn't hate it here.

Dodge's words roamed through his head as they drove into the driveway, bordered thickly with palms. *"And now you're a different kind of warrior. No longer a mercenary, but a soldier for the Lord. At his command."*

Right.

Lord, what do you want me to do?

Logan pulled up behind a small army of black SUVs in the drive.

"What's going on?" Ranger asked as Logan put the car in park.

"You'll see," Logan said.

Colt followed Ranger out of the car, turned and helped Tae out, and then followed Logan and Dodge into the house.

They walked past a gauntlet of security guys, dressed in suits, wearing coms and shoulder holsters. Colt wished for his uniform, or at least long pants.

Especially when he emerged to the main room and spotted Ham standing in a suit, dress shirt, and tie.

"Where's the funeral?" Ranger said.

Ham nodded toward the patio.

Colt followed his gesture and spotted Pete Sutton, also dressed in a suit, his jacket unbuttoned, his tie caught in the wind, his hands in his pockets, nodding to a man with his back to them. That man also wore a suit.

A fist was starting to form in his chest.

"You're needed outside," Ham said.

"All of us?" Dodge asked.

"Just Colt and Taylor. For now."

Hmm. Okay.

"Maybe I should, uh, change first?" Colt said, looking at his attire. Grimy shirt, cargo shorts. He might even smell a little. Or a lot.

"Now," Ham said.

Colt took Tae's hand and they headed outside.

Pete looked up as Colt closed the sliding glass door. A beautiful day soared overhead, the sky brushed with wispy clouds, the heat tempered by last night's storm.

More men in suits were stationed around the yard.

Colt walked out slowly. "Hey Pete, what's up?"

And then the man talking to Pete turned. Good-looking, dark hair with gray on the sides, a disarming smile. The presidential pin on his suit lapel. "Sergeant Major Kingston?"

What?

President Isaac White had always reminded Colt of George Clooney in a way, and he couldn't get that comparison out of his mind as he straightened to attention, letting go of Tae's hand. "Sir."

"I hear you're to thank for stopping a terrorist attack on our soil." He held out his hand.

Colt met it. "It wasn't all me, sir." He glanced at Tae.

Her eyes had widened.

"I talked to Ham and Pete and they told me about your role. The country owes you a debt of gratitude."

"Right place, right time."

President White's deep blue eyes fixed on him. "Right man."

The words swept in, settled.

"In fact, before we get started, I wanted to ask if you'd do me a favor."

Before they got started with what? "Anything, sir."

"I'd like you to join my Caleb Group. It's a small, covert team, on special assignment to track down the Petrovs' activities around the globe, as well as other threats. But you'd be working with Pete and Roy and Logan and a few others."

Colt had nothing. He glanced at Tae again. She gave him a wan smile.

He sighed. "Sir, I'd be honored. But I'm not sure I'm the right fit."

"You're exactly the man we need, Colt."

"Thank you. But . . . you see, I've got some healing to do."

President White chuckled. "Don't we all?"

"Actually, sir, I think I need to—"

"Rest. I know. And that's why I'd like your first assignment to be here, in Florida." He turned to Tae. "Helping Tae set up and run her lab."

"My lab?" she asked.

He nodded. "With all the possible biological threats out there, I can't think of anyone I'd more depend on to protect us. It would be under the Caleb Group, so you'd report directly to me,

Taylor, but you'd be in charge. Run it how you want."

Colt raised an eyebrow.

"And you, Colt, would be our liaison, and—"

"Chief babysitter?"

The president laughed. "Let's say head of security. Pete says you're pretty good at keeping people alive."

Huh. "Yes, sir."

"Good. Because I just went to all the effort to tow Taylor's houseboat into the nearby marina, and I was hoping I didn't make a huge mistake."

"You towed my houseboat here?" Tae said.

"Shipped it, actually," Pete said. "We did our best to repair it, and since the lab in Seattle was destroyed, we hope you'll stay on here. If not, we can ship it back—"

"No. This is . . . amazing. Thank you."

"No, thank you, Tae. Your father would be very proud of you."

She blinked. Frowned. "What?"

"Pete and I served together, and he filled me in. I knew your father, Taylor. Dr. Aaron Price. Good guy. A real hero. Made the world a better place."

She nodded. "Yes, he did."

"Like father, like daughter," White said.

Tae looked away, but Colt had spotted tears filming her eyes.

White turned back to Colt. "Okay, ready to get started?"

"With what?"

"With the ceremony," said a voice, and he turned to see Logan walking out of the house.

But more, behind him walked—

"Dad?"

"So, this is where you escaped to," his father said. He looked better, still walking slowly, but not as stiff. He too wore a suit, a tie, and was minus his usual gimme cap.

"What are you doing here?"

"When the president calls me and asks me to get on a plane, I say yes."

And now Colt had nothing.

Then the sliding door opened, and Ranger and Noemi walked out. His brother had put on a clean shirt and pants, Noemi in a white sundress. And behind her— "Larke?"

His beautiful sister, with her rounded belly, her long dark-blond hair now tied up in a bun, wore a dress, a pair of sandals, and walked hand in hand with a ruddy-looking Navy sailor, dressed in his whites.

"Riley, I'm guessing." Colt held out his hand. He'd never actually met his sister's husband, another active-duty SEAL.

"Good to meet you." Riley grinned. "Glad I was home for this."

For this?

And then Dodge came out of the house, also

448

wearing a change of clothes and holding hands with Echo.

In a *dress*.

Yes, this was weird. "What is going on? What ceremony?"

"The private one where your country thanks you for your service," Logan said. Only then did Colt notice that he carried three boxes.

White cleared his throat, then addressed them all. "For your valorous acts at the airfield, and in other ways, I'd like to give you three the Medal of Valor."

And he was in his grimy shorts and a sweaty, bloody shirt.

As if reading his mind, the president asked, "Do you want to change before we start, Colt?"

He looked at his clothing, at Tae, and something about the fact that he was receiving an award in his soiled clothing, trouble in the middle of his put-together brothers, felt almost right.

So, he stood at attention, in the middle, between Dodge and Ranger as one by one, they received their awards. The Air Force branch for Dodge, the Navy branch for Ranger, and the Army branch for Colt.

The medal hung from his neck, heavy, solid, warm in the sunlight.

"Thank you for your service, men," the president said.

And because none of them had really shaken the military out of them, they saluted.

449

Their father smiled, his eyes shining.

Well then.

Hours later, Colt followed Tae down the dock to her permanent slip inside the Melbourne Marina. Her houseboat sat gleaming and undaunted under the sunlight, the bow facing the private gate, the massive picture window—now repaired— reflecting the skyline of the mainland. He carried groceries, some staples to get Tae started.

For now, he'd stay at the mansion, but he fully intended on moving in, soon.

If Tae would have him, forever.

She unlocked her gate and stepped aboard, then unlocked her door and went inside.

"Wow, they fixed everything." She wandered down the hall to the kitchen.

Colt set the bag of groceries on the counter. Indeed.

Tae ran her hands over the quartz kitchen counter, the new appliances, the gleaming teak floor. Colt's gaze went to the new flat-screen. But then beyond, to a turtle swimming in the harbor, its head just above the surface.

He walked to the sliding door, then stepped out and climbed the stairs to the third-story deck.

The view was spectacular. It looked out past the harbor to the Indian River, to the handful of sailboats skimming the waves, the shades of twilight tipping the water.

He drew in a breath.

"What are you doing?" Tae came up behind him and put her arms around his waist, her cheek to his back.

"Believing."

"In what?"

He turned and put his arm around her. "In a fresh tomorrow. In happy endings."

"Me too," she said quietly.

"C'mere." He pulled her to a deck chair. Positioned it to face west, then sat and brought her down to sit with him. He settled his arms around her waist.

"What are we doing?"

"Flo, we are sitting here and watching our first of many sundowns."

"You sure you shouldn't go lay down or something?"

He kissed the back of her neck. "I've never felt better in my life."

Then he tucked her back against him, his gaze on the deep amber sun spilling out among the buildings.

And decided that he would probably learn to surf.

EPILOGUE

One Month Later

She would have loved to see this.

Barry, dressed in a suit, a tie, his cowboy boots, stood up from where he knelt in the grass and stared out at his rolling land, covered in purple fireweed and tiny green scrub pine.

"Yes, Cee, you would be happy."

A spray of daisies from the garden planted so long ago near the house, lay on the ground next to the stone marker.

CAROLINE KINGSTON. WIFE. MOTHER. DAUGHTER. WATCHING FROM HEAVEN.

He knew it in his heart. Because that was the promise of salvation.

He'd gotten up early, spent time in his recliner, and the Lord had given him Psalm 100. *Shout for joy to the LORD, all the earth. Worship the LORD with gladness.*

Indeed.

"They came home, if you haven't already noticed. All of them, one by one, a miracle really."

The wind carried from the faraway mountains, their purple shadows casting down into the valley. The days were starting to get shorter now.

In another month, darkness would descend upon them, blanketing them into the long winter.

But in the endless night, he could see the aurora borealis, and it made him feel closer to heaven, reminded him of the divine. So much beauty, seen best in the deepest night.

"It's Dodge's big day. He's marrying Echo. Which I always knew he would. I told you about it, remember? Back when he was seventeen. Echo's just like you, really. Brave and smart, and she loves Alaska."

The wind caught the daisies, rustled them.

"He and Colt made peace. I don't know how, but Colt seems at peace with losing you too. He missed you the most, I think, but, of course, all of them did. He's come back to us, whole, and I think he's finally forgiven himself." Barry drew in a breath.

In the distance, an eagle soared, aloft on the winds.

"Colt met a girl too. I think he's waiting to propose, not wanting to interfere with Dodge's big day. That's a good sign. Apparently he can be taught." He laughed. "I guess he got that stubborn piece from me, but I think you might have had something to do with that too."

He looked out toward the house. The boys had cleared out the hangar and set up chairs and tables on the inside for the reception. The ceremony would take place on the tarmac.

Echo had insisted her dogs attend, so they each had a place, hooked onto a gangline near the altar, an arch made from the props of Dodge's sacrificial plane.

But he'd bounced back, tuning up the Beaver. He'd even gone out on a couple late-season rescues for his new Sky King Rescue service.

Movement on the porch caught Barry's eye.

Larke, coming out to check on him maybe. The wind pressed her dress against her bulging middle. Probably she shouldn't be here so close to her due date, but he couldn't keep her away. Especially with Riley on deployment. Maybe being at home was the wisest thing.

Dodge had picked her up in his plane and made the many hops from Florida to Alaska over a four-day stint.

Barry turned back to the marker. "Ranger got my eye issues, Cee. But the docs caught it sooner, and he's being treated at Mayo, in Minnesota. He's going to be okay. He's already married— sweet girl that you'd love. She's exactly who he needs."

He bent on one knee again. Put his hand on the marker. "I nearly joined you a month or so back. But not quite yet, honey. See, I'm going to be a grandpa—"

"Dad!"

He stood up. "I wish you were here, and not just looking down on us. I miss you, Cee."

He ran a finger under his eye, found a smile, and turned. "Larke. You shouldn't be hiking all the way out here in your condition."

She wore her hair long, a blond braid down her back, lace woven through the folds of her hair. She had on a white dress and cowboy boots.

"Woof. Maybe you're right." She put a hand on his shoulder, the other on her belly. "The boys want to see you."

He put his arm around her. "What now?"

"I'll let them tell you."

He raised an eyebrow and then walked with her to the house.

Inside, the smell of roasted venison filled the great room, and on the island was a spread of baked potatoes rolled in foil, rolls, and a heap of pasta salad.

It wasn't a large crowd for the wedding—Echo and Dodge wanted it small. But the Starr family was coming, and the Remington boys from the mine, the Bowie brothers, and probably even Dodge's hockey pal Moose Mulligan.

And, of course, Echo's parents would be there. They had renewed their vows just a month ago, in a ceremony over at their homestead.

Barry walked upstairs, knocked on the door of the boys' bedroom, then opened the door.

His boys. Home, finally, and reconciled. They wore similar black suits, white shirts. Dodge's hair had always been curlier than the others, and he wore it just long enough for it to spill out under the hat he usually wore, only not today.

Ranger, however, wore his hair military short on the sides, a little longer on top, but always tip-top.

Colt let his grow, although he'd cut it recently, and now tucked it behind his ears.

Handsome, strong men. Warriors.

Barry wanted to burst with the pride that welled inside. "Okay, so what's the problem?"

"I'm going to have to kill Colt," Dodge said.

Colt shook his head. "Listen, I'm telling you—"

"He says that he shouldn't be my best man."

Colt just held up his hands. "I'm just sayin' that probably, given everything that went down, I'm not the right choice."

"But you're second born," Dodge said.

"Why does it always have to be so . . . logical with you? I mean, it's not like I *don't* want to be your best man, but really, don't you think it will be a little weird for Echo, given the fact that she had a hot crush on me?"

Oh no.

Colt grinned.

"She never loved you, man. Get over it," Dodge said.

Ranger had been standing by the mirror. "I'll do it."

"See? He says he'll step in."

"Why don't you want to do it? What, are you

afraid of screwing up? All you have to do is hold the ring."

Colt's smile dimmed, his tone turning serious. "I just . . . this wedding should have happened ten years ago. And if it hadn't been for me, it would have." He shoved his hands into his pockets. "Sorry. I wish I could get past it, but it keeps coming back to me."

"Aw, Colt," Barry said. He walked over to his son. "Listen. It's hard to live with regrets. I know . . . I have a few of my own. But regrets are the devil's tool. He uses them to accuse us. To tell us that we'll never escape the past. But that's a lie. The moment we're forgiven, the past is done. The only thing we should remember from them is our salvation. God's intervention. Our memory of the past should remind us that we have a God who saves."

Barry met his middle son's eyes, then gave a look to Dodge and Ranger. Back to Colt. "Let the sun go down on the past. It's a new day. Let's walk into it with grace."

He clamped a hand on Colt's shoulder. "If Dodge says you're the best man, then you're the best man."

Dodge grinned. "What Dad said."

Colt lifted a shoulder. But nodded at Dodge.

"Ready?" Ranger said, taking another look in the mirror.

"Let's roll," said Dodge.

Outside, the crowd had already gathered, some of them taking chairs, others milling around. Barry left the boys and greeted Sheldon Starr and his wife, along with Ace and Moose Mulligan. Peyton Samson and Nash Remington came in together, holding hands, and he spotted a few of the Starr kids, Winter and Shasta. Then there was Dodge's buddy Malachi, along with Goodwin and Levi, chatting up Ranger and Colt.

Noemi emerged from the house dressed in an orange skirt, a white blouse, her hair wrapped. She wore the bright coral beads that Ranger had given her on their wedding day.

How Barry wished he could have seen that day—to see Ranger dancing up the aisle the way Noemi told it. Now, Noemi fairly glowed, and if he wasn't imagining things, he suspected that maybe Larke wouldn't be the only one giving him a grandbaby soon.

Larke and Tae came down the aisle and sat on the groom's side, next to Noemi.

The music started—Goodwin was running the sound via his iPod—and the guests took their seats.

Barry stepped up to the front, under the arch, with his Bible. Because Dodge had asked him to.

He met Dodge's eyes and nodded.

His son strode up the aisle, followed by Colt, then Ranger. They stood beside their brother.

Oh, the man was beaming. Even ran his thumb along his cheek, wiping away a little wetness.

Yeah, Barry got that.

Down the aisle came Dr. Effie Yazzie, the former head of OB-GYN of a hospital in Anchorage. She now worked out of her own office in town. She took her place in the front row.

Peyton and Winter followed. They wore their own dresses—no one was getting too fancy here—and stood opposite the boys.

Goodwin switched up the music, and the sounds of "A Thousand Years" drifted into the air as Echo came out of the house on her father's arm.

She wore her golden-brown hair down, flowing, a wreath of wildflowers around her head, and had on a simple white gown that looked out of the 1970s. Maybe it had been her mother's.

Her gaze fixed on Dodge, and Barry looked up.

Thank you, Lord.

Yes, a glorious day, and somehow, he didn't stumble over his words. Somehow he asked the right questions, gave the right pronouncement, and finally, Dodge kissed his bride.

Even took his time to the applause of the crowd.

Barry introduced the couple, and they headed down the aisle and the entire thing was downright perfect.

All the way up to the moment when, two hours

later, on the dance floor, Larke's water broke.

But that was okay too, because Dodge and Effie simply packed her up in his Beaver, along with Colt and Tae, Noemi and Ranger, Barry, and Echo. They spent the night in the hospital, pacing, waiting for the arrival of Riley and baby Aurora Caroline.

It wasn't until the next morning, as Barry held his granddaughter—the second-generation Cee— as he stared down at her tiny fingers and hands, those blue eyes that couldn't quite open, that tuft of dark hair, that he realized . . .

The dreams he'd mourned had no place in this moment of joy. That yes, his yesterdays—*all* of their yesterdays—held broken, irreversible grief and lost moments that would never return. But with every sundown came a new morning. Redemption. Hope.

And as he looked out onto the day, the faraway horizon, with the sun casting down from the snow-tipped mountains, through the greening valleys, all the way to the deep blue of Cook Inlet . . .

The view was glorious.

ACKNOWLEDGMENTS

What a fun series to write! I hope you have enjoyed reading the story of the homecoming and redemption of the handsome Kingston brothers.

When I envisioned this series, I knew the boys were wounded, but I had no idea the journey they'd take to healing, and I'm so grateful to the Lord for the people he put in my path to help construct this trilogy. I'm especially thankful for my sweet daughter-in-law Precious, for her help on *Sunburst*, and my amazing husband, Andrew, for all his airplane and mechanical expertise.

I need to give a shout-out to the spark for this series, the amazing Dwayne King, an Alaskan pilot and missionary we served with in Russia, who today lives in Alaska, training bush pilots and missionaries. Wise and kind, he was definitely the prototype for Barry.

Thank you to Revell for partnering with me on this series. I'm so grateful to Andrea Doering and Robin Turici, as well as the talented Barbara Curtis who has such an amazing memory of my previous books. And a big high-five goes to the Revell marketing department, especially Michele Misiak and Karen Steele. Thank you for your hard work.

And finally, to my amazing readers. Thank

you for reading my books! I hope, in this series, you've been reminded of the incredible grace and second chances that the Lord offers. You are never without hope, without redemption, without the day when you can embrace forgiveness, put the past behind you, and start new.

Live in freedom. Live in hope. Live in joy.

The view is glorious.

In his grace,
Susie May

Susan May Warren is the *USA Today* bestselling author of more than 85 novels with more than 1 million books sold, including the Global Search and Rescue and the Montana Rescue series, as well as *Sunrise* and *Sunburst*. Winner of a RITA Award and multiple Christy and Carol Awards, as well as the HOLT Medallion and numerous Readers' Choice Awards, Susan makes her home in Minnesota. Find her online at www.susanmaywarren.com, on Facebook @SusanMayWarrenFiction, and on Twitter @SusanMayWarren.

Center Point Large Print
600 Brooks Road / PO Box 1
Thorndike, ME 04986-0001 USA

(207) 568-3717

US & Canada:
1 800 929-9108
www.centerpointlargeprint.com